ACCLAIM FOR L

"A historical mystery and sweet modern-day story entwine to offer a message of healing, hope, and second chances set in charming Cornwall."
—Rachel Linden, author of *Becoming the Talbot Sisters* and *Ascension of Larks*, on *The Secrets of Paper and Ink*

"In a delightful weaving of past and present, Lindsay Harrel creates authentic characters around a moving story that both inspires and encourages. *The Secrets of Paper and Ink* is about broken people, second chances, hope, and—my personal favorite—the incredible power of story."
—Heidi Chiavaroli, Carol award-winning author of *Freedom's Ring* and *The Hidden Side*

"In *The Secrets of Paper and Ink*, Lindsay Harrel explores the power of love—and how it influences us to make choices that bless others, as well as ourselves. Or sometimes, we can do just the opposite and make choices that harm us and others—all the while calling it love. Harrel pens an honest, true-to-life novel that's woven through with the Truth that offers hope when our decisions—or the decisions of the ones we love—wreck our dreams for happily ever after."
—Beth K. Vogt, Christy-award winning author

"A bucket list from the diary of an organ donor sparks a healing journey for two sisters in this poignant tale from Harrel . . . [*The Heart Between Us*], with many descriptions of delicious foods and famous landmarks from around the globe, will please readers of travel fiction looking for an inspirational story."
—*Publishers Weekly*

"Narration by both Meg and Crystal, full of emotion and soul-searching, will resonate with anyone who has struggled to see another point of view. Both characters are drawn as independent and persistent, occasionally to their detriment, but not too stubborn to get past stumbling blocks. Harrel's

(*One More Song to Sing*, 2016) second novel is a charmingly gentle read that will please those who enjoy faith-based, hopeful fiction with a delightfully positive tone."

—*Booklist* on *The Heart Between Us*

"Harrel's second book is a well-crafted, compelling story about love, hope, relationships, family importance, and God's trustworthiness."

—*CBA Market* on *The Heart Between Us*

"Lindsay Harrel has penned a charming story that is sure to touch the hearts of her readers. Through the stories of Megan and her sister Crystal, readers get a glimpse of adventure, restoration, conquered fears, and realized dreams. Lindsay will no doubt win readers with this heartfelt story."

—Lauren K. Denton, *USA TODAY* bestselling author of *The Hideaway* and *Hurricane Season,* on *The Heart Between Us*

"A sweet story of sisterhood, familial bonds, sacrificial love, and finding your own identity amidst the storms of life. Poignant with tender moments, as well as laughter, *The Heart Between Us* is a touching novel that is sure to please."

—Catherine West, author of *The Memory of You* and *Where Hope Begins*

"I love this story of facing our fears. Harrel pens a clever, well-written love story between two sisters, the men in their lives and the dreams of a heart donor. Life is more fleeting than we know and this timeless story reminds us to love well."

—Rachel Hauck, *New York Times* bestselling author, on *The Heart Between Us*

"*The Heart Between Us* is an absolute gem of a story. The intriguing premise drew me in from the start, but it was the authentic characters and their relatable struggles that kept me reading. I especially loved getting to travel vicariously through Megan and Crystal! A heart-tugging, not-to-be-missed book from an author who belongs on your keeper shelf."

—Melissa Tagg, author of the Walker Family series

THE SECRETS OF PAPER AND INK

ALSO BY LINDSAY HARREL

The Heart Between Us

THE SECRETS OF PAPER AND INK

LINDSAY HARREL

THOMAS NELSON
Since 1798

The Secrets of Paper and Ink

Published in Nashville, Tennessee, by Thomas Nelson. Thomas Nelson is a registered trademark of HarperCollins Christian Publishing, Inc.

Published in association with the Books & Such Literary Management, 52 Mission Circle, Suite 122, PMB 170, Santa Rosa, California 95409-5370, www.booksandsuch.com.

Third party information is accurate to the best of author's knowledge as of the date printed.

Thomas Nelson titles may be purchased in bulk for educational, business, fund-raising, or sales promotional use. For information, please email SpecialMarkets@ThomasNelson.com.

Scripture quotations are taken from *The Message*. Copyright © by Eugene H. Peterson 1993, 1994, 1995, 1996, 2000, 2001, 2002. Used by permission of NavPress. All rights reserved. Represented by Tyndale House Publishers, Inc.

Publisher's Note: This novel is a work of fiction. Names, characters, places, and incidents are either products of the author's imagination or used fictitiously. All characters are fictional, and any similarity to people living or dead is purely coincidental.

Library of Congress Cataloging-in-Publication Data

Names: Harrel, Lindsay, author.
Title: The secrets of paper and ink / Lindsay Harrel.
Description: Nashville, Tennessee : Thomas Nelson, [2019]
Identifiers: LCCN 2018041167 | ISBN 9780718075729 (paperback)
Classification: LCC PS3608.A7794 S43 2019 | DDC 813/.6--dc23 LC record available at https://lccn.loc.gov/2018041167

Printed in the United States of America

19 20 21 22 23 LSC 5 4 3 2 1

For Kent Walker
Daddy, you've always been there for me,
always believed in me, and always modeled for me
how a man should treat and care for the woman he loves.
I love you more than words can express.

There is no greater agony than bearing an untold story inside you.

—Maya Angelou

PROLOGUE

Edward,

Hello, new friend. I must say, the hollow of this tree is the perfect location to leave you a note. Thank you ever so much for allowing me to share your special spot. It's nice to have a friend. All the children back home thought I wasn't a proper enough lady because I prefer climbing trees to needlework. I am glad you are not like them.

Cordially,
Emily Fairfax

Edward,

You will not believe what happened today. While waiting for you to come by after your studies, I climbed into our tree, higher than I've ever climbed—even past that large branch overhanging the ocean where you normally sit and try to frighten me—and I became so hypnotized by the waves that I slipped and nearly fell! It was quite an adventure, one I'm quite sure Captain Nathaniel Pike would have been proud of (if he was more than just a character in our favorite stories, of course). My mother would have had a few things to say if she'd seen me, though I believe she secretly likes my antics.

From the girl at the tree,
Emily

~ひ~

Edward,

Thank you for the note and the new book you left for me to read. I can hardly wait to dive into its depths and learn more about America. It looks to be a wild land full of adventure, one where people are not so constrained by decorum. I think I should like to see it one day. Would you care to go with me?

Your friend,
Emily

~ひ~

Edward,

It's hard to believe you've been gone for three months (you will have many letters piled up in the tree's hollow by now), but I look forward to Christmas holiday when you will return.

I have kept up my studies, and I read late into the night when I am able so you won't have an advantage over me. I may never be able to go to a fancy school like you, but that does not mean I'll let you whip me so easily! Be prepared to match wits upon your return, my friend.

With affection,
Emily

~ひ~

Edward,

I leave tomorrow to begin life as a governess. I do not love the thought, but 'tis the way of things for girls whose fathers are poor reverends, and I am proud to begin earning my own wage. Now that you are away at Oxford, life around here has grown quite dull, and I am thrilled to see what excitement this new life will bring.

My sister has already been gone from home for two years. Can you believe it? Mother has spent that time teaching me all she knows. As always, she has encouraged me to remember that what others see as my faults may be my greatest strengths. Oh, how I pray that is true!

I do not know when next we will meet in person, but perhaps you will find this note before then. Whenever I do return for a visit, I will run immediately to our tree to see if you have left me a note of your own.

I have come to love our exchanges. You challenge me more and know me better than anyone else ever has, or ever could.

Your friend always,

Em

~ઝ~

Edward,

Mother is gone. My sister too. Cholera has taken them both. My life is not what it once was. Father is a shell of a man, and I have moved home to care for him.

I have turned to writing more than merely letters. Every night I sit at my desk and pour out my pain from pen to paper. Stories of every variety gather inside and beg for release, so I obey.

And I have found the one subject that brings me joy—you, dearest Edward.

Because I love you.

I think I always have, ever since at age eleven you told me that you thought ladies were dull and you much preferred being in my company. You scampered up our tree, pausing and asking me to follow. And follow you I did. And follow you I would, if only you would ask.

But I know that will never occur.

I can never admit my feelings to you, and because of that, this is the one note that will never find its way into our tree. But I will burst if I do not at least express it somehow.

And so I turn to the written word, and my love for you is a secret I will keep hidden, forever etched only in paper and ink.

Yours ever truly,

Em

1

SOPHIA

When life was busy, three months had a way of flurrying by.

But Sophia Barrett's last ninety-two days had passed in a drizzle of constant monotony. She'd spent them curled up napping on her leather couch, reading well-worn novels, and sitting in a slew of therapy sessions.

Thank goodness today was day ninety-three and she was finally standing in front of her office. She straightened her freshly pressed blazer, adjusted the strap of her laptop bag across her shoulder, and blew out a breath. At long last, a return to normalcy. Her trembling hand pulled on the large black door to Suite 608 and swung it open.

Sophia walked through the door and did her best to pretend like she was still the strong, confident woman whose mission in life was to help others through their pain.

The waiting room smelled like lavender as always, the view of downtown Phoenix from the window behind the secretary's desk remained unchanged, and the wall fountain to her right still had a way of soothing her nerves.

But something about being here felt different. Maybe it was simply Sophia who had changed.

Kristin's head popped up from the large, oak secretary desk. "You're back!" The intern unhooked her headset and rushed from behind the desk, throwing her arms around Sophia. "We've all missed you."

"I've missed being here." Sophia released a breath she didn't know she'd been holding.

"You chopped your hair!" Kristin tilted her head and chewed her gum as she studied Sophia. "I love it."

"Thanks." Sophia reached up to tug at the shorter strands, which now barely reached her shoulders. David had always liked her hair long. "It was time for a change."

Kristin's smile turned sympathetic. She squeezed Sophia's shoulder. "Good to have you back. I know Dr. Beckman has been going crazy without you."

"I'm sure Joy has survived just fine."

"No, Joy has not. But that's beside the point."

Sophia turned to find her best friend standing in the hallway, hands on her hips. Joy Beckman stood at barely five feet tall, but what she lacked in height, she made up for in personality. From her blond pixie haircut to her outlandish jewelry and bright-colored clothing, no one could accuse Joy of not being her own person. Sophia, on the other hand, was much more comfortable in her black pants and cream-colored blouse, perfectly content to not stand out.

But despite their differences and the nearly ten-year age gap between them, Joy was more friend and pseudo big sister to Sophia than a boss.

"Hey." Sophia leaned down to hug Joy. "It's not like it was my idea to sit at home for the last three months. You're the one who banished me."

Joy rolled her eyes. "Come on. I'll brief you on your schedule for today." The phone rang. "Kristin, can you get that, please?"

"Of course." Kristin scrambled back behind the desk and slid her headset on. "LifeSong Women's Counseling. How can I help you?"

Sophia followed Joy down the short hallway into her friend's office. She picked a photo off Joy's cluttered desk. "You got new pictures done." In the photo, a jubilant Joy sat surrounded by five dogs.

"I couldn't very well have a photo without Lion. He'd be offended." Joy took the photo from Sophia's hands and glanced at it briefly, a small smirk playing at the corner of her lips.

"Lion is a tiny, nine-year-old dog with one eye that you rescued in his old age. I think it would take a lot to offend him." Sophia plopped into the seat opposite Joy, who slid into the office chair behind her desk. "So, do you have any appointments scheduled for me today? I wasn't sure whether you decided to transition my former clients back to me or keep them with Veronica." Though she'd seen her outside the office several times a week, Joy had always refused to discuss work, believing it would only stress Sophia out more to know what she was missing.

Joy searched the piles of paper on her desk and finally pulled a piece loose. "Here. I sent this via e-mail but thought we could chat briefly before you got all settled in."

Sophia took the paper from Joy's hand and studied it. She raised an eyebrow. "There's only one name on this list."

"You should start slow." Her friend worried her bottom lip. "I'm still not sure you should be here. Three months isn't that long."

"Three months is plenty long. I was wasting away on that couch and you know it." Sophia tried hard to keep the accusation from her tone, but it slipped in anyway.

"Nobody said you had to spend the three months twiddling your thumbs."

"I didn't." At Joy's pointed look, Sophia huffed. "Okay, fine. I guess I did. A little." At first, it'd been so hard to deal with the fact that she'd had a mental breakdown—in the grocery store of all places—on the first anniversary of David's death. Somehow she'd managed to hold it together for a year—denial was a many-faceted

beast—and seeing the expensive brand of protein powder he had liked on the clearance shelf had just set her off.

How embarrassing to think back to the way she had taken every single container, unscrewed the lids, and dumped the contents onto the floor, not stopping until she was sobbing in a pile of powder and empty tubs.

Needless to say, she hadn't been back to that particular grocery store, even though she'd apologized profusely and paid for the mess she'd created.

After that, facing anyone other than Mom, Joy, and Cindy—the therapist who had walked Sophia through the worst of it—had been too difficult. It had seemed easiest to bury her nose in her favorite books and just grin and bear her sentence as quickly as possible: three months' paid leave from work.

Most people would find that sentence glorious. But most weren't trying to forget a dead fiancé and all the complicated feelings his death still raised in her, now more than a year after a car accident had taken him from this life into the next.

"I'm not judging you. I'm just concerned. You know that. David did a number on you. And when he died, you stuffed all your feelings away and tried your best to pretend his death didn't affect you."

Right. The very opposite of what she'd learned in six years of school for counseling and countless practicum hours. "I know all of that. But going to therapy with Cindy was just the thing I needed to get past it all. I'm better now."

Well, she would be, once she relearned how to stand on her own two feet.

And part of that meant facing the world again. "I need this." Sophia gestured around the room. "To return to something familiar. To keep busy." To help other people. Mom always said that was the best way to get out of your own head—and Sophia was so tired of being in hers.

Joy rubbed her forehead. Clearly she wasn't finished, despite all the protests she'd already laid in the weeks leading up to today. "I'm just afraid that being here will trigger—"

"I do appreciate your concern, Joy. I do. But please. Just trust me." Sophia stood and straightened her shoulders. "Now, it looks like my client will be here at nine, so I need to get to my office and prep." She walked toward the door and turned. "Goodness knows I wouldn't have survived without you. But I'm ready. I can do this."

Joy's smile appeared forced. "Okay."

Sophia stepped across the hall and rummaged through her bag for her keys. She unlocked the door and flicked on the fluorescent lights. The air smelled stale, tinged with disuse and the remnants in her apple-and-spice diffuser. Someone had cleared her desktop of any paper. Sophia slid into her chair and fired up her computer for the first time in months.

Her eyes roamed the office as she waited for her e-mail program to load. In the corner sat the most comfortable couch she'd ever had. Pride pricked her chest as she studied her master's degree and the certification that named her Sophia Barrett, Licensed Professional Counselor in the state of Arizona. No matter what happened, no one could take that away from her.

Finally, Sophia reached across her desk and snatched the photo frame that had sat there ever since she'd started working here half a decade ago. At first, the picture inside the frame was a family photo—just her and Mom. Then a few years ago, she'd traded it for an engagement photo—only four months after she'd met David.

The picture in the frame showed Sophia on his back, her long, black hair flowing down her shoulders, pale blue eyes trusting and full of love, her arms wrapped around his neck with his grasped under her knees, a tangle of love and obsession that had grown since that first time she'd seen him at the coffee shop and he'd actually noticed her somehow.

His brown eyes stared at her from the photo. They'd always called to her as if he were a Siren and she Odysseus. His easy smile and thick hair had given him a Patrick Dempsey air, and his impeccable taste in clothing had spoken of the wealth he'd grown up knowing.

She'd fallen head over black Payless flats. Plain-Jane Sophia Barrett had landed a prince, a man all the women wanted.

A prince on the outside, anyway. The inside was another matter entirely.

Sophia opened a desk drawer and stuffed the photo inside. There. Progress.

She worked through a slew of e-mails until Kristin buzzed her office, informing Sophia of her client's arrival.

Ugh, she hated the first-day jitters that flew through her whole being. But surely they'd go away once she set aside her own emotions and focused on someone else.

With a deep breath, Sophia rose and headed to the waiting room. "Patty Smith?"

A mousy woman who looked to be in her late thirties stood, her shoulders stooped and brown hair hanging limp in her face. "Here." Her voice squeaked.

Sophia extended her hand. "It's a pleasure to meet you. I'm Sophia Barrett."

The woman avoided her gaze, but shook her hand and murmured a return greeting.

Sophia led her back to her office and gestured to the couch. "Please, have a seat."

Patty did as she asked, sitting on the very edge of the couch. Her build was difficult to determine thanks to the oversized sweater she wore. In Phoenix. In late May. Her sneakered feet tapped against the carpeted floor in quick succession.

Sophia's heart squeezed. "Patty, I like to record my sessions so I can take fewer notes when I'm with you." She made sure her voice was soft, as if soothing a child, but without patronization. "Would that be all right?"

Patty's eyes darted upward. "I don't want anyone knowing I was here."

The way she said "anyone" sent a chill up Sophia's spine. And suddenly, her behavior made sense. Why she was here made sense.

Had Joy known when she'd given Sophia this client? Her friend wasn't that cruel, was she? But perhaps she was testing Sophia, making sure she was really as ready as she'd claimed.

"No one but me will ever listen to these tapes. I promise." The words stuck in her throat.

Patty tugged at one of her long sleeves. "I guess so."

"Great." Sophia clicked Record on her device. "Now, why don't we start by simply getting to know each other? I'm Sophia and I've been a licensed professional counselor for eight years, working here at LifeSong for the last five. I have a cat named Gigi, I love taking walks in the park when it's not a thousand degrees outside, and I simply adore British literature. How about you?"

The woman blew out a breath. A series of emotions flew across her features, finally settling on determination. "I'm Patty. I've been married to Jack for eleven years. We have two young children, Turner and Sabrina. I stay home with the kids, and Jack works construction."

"And what do you like to do for fun?"

"Fun?" Patty looked completely bewildered, as if nobody had ever asked her that. "I . . ." She stifled a sob. "I'm sorry."

"There's nothing to be sorry about. This is a safe space." Sophia snatched a tissue from a box next to her chair, leaning to hand it to Patty.

"Safe. What does that mean, really?" Patty wiped underneath her eyes and blew her nose. "I lied about why I made this appointment. I told your secretary I was here for anxiety."

The chill returned to Sophia's spine. "Oh?" It was the only word she could manage.

"I'm here because . . ." Patty's hand trembled. She rolled up her sleeve, revealing at least a dozen bruises, all in different stages of healing. "This."

Nausea rolled through Sophia's stomach. "Who—" She cleared her throat. "Who did that to you, Patty?"

"I don't think he means to." Patty let her sleeve fall back into place. "He just gets so angry when he drinks."

I'm sorry, baby. That wasn't me. Not the real me. It was the scotch talking.

No. His voice was not welcome here. Not now. Sophia reached deep inside, pulling from the strength she'd gained in the last few months. She gripped her pen tighter. "Your husband?"

A slight nod. "He's a good father. And a good husband. Most of the time. I just make him mad sometimes. I try not to, but maybe I'm just not grateful enough for what I have, you know?"

I've done nothing but love you, you ungrateful—

"That's called victim blaming, Patty. Tell me, do you believe those things?"

The words burned her tongue. How could she ask that?

After all, she'd let David sweet-talk her into loving him—preying on her vulnerability and the fact that she'd been too focused on school and then work to date much and experience real love—then stayed with him even when he began putting her down, a little at a time, then all the time, until her self-confidence was zilch and her emotions frayed.

And though he'd only hit her once, right before he died, how could Sophia sit here and ask this woman if she believed the lies her husband told her?

Because *she* had believed them, despite everything her textbooks had ever taught her.

Hypocrite.

Patty shrugged with one shoulder. She leaned forward. "All I know is, I can't live like this anymore. The other day, I actually had the thought—" Another sob wrenched from her throat.

"What thought, Patty?" The words came out tense, strung together of desperation. A physical aching filled Sophia's bones.

"I wished . . . I wished he was dead."

A flood of memories rushed in, David's voice at the forefront of them all. Pointing fingers, flying fists, nasty words—all aimed her direction.

The strength she'd imagined holding her in this chair left her body.

She couldn't stay here. She couldn't help this woman. She couldn't even help herself.

"I'm sorry, Patty. I have . . . I have to leave."

Sophia rose from her seat and raced out the door.

2

GINNY

So much of her future hinged on the twitch of an eye.

Ginny Rose folded her hands and placed them in her lap. The small office where she sat across from Reginald Brown felt stuffy despite the cool May temperatures outside. A droplet of sweat ran down the side of her face. Perhaps she should have worn her long, brown hair up in a bun like Mother would have. But these days, she tried to avoid doing anything like Mariah Bentley.

Not that it mattered how professional and grown-up she looked. Though the people of Port Willis had embraced her as one of their own five years ago when she'd trailed Garrett Rose from America to Cornwall, England, it was a small town. Mr. Brown knew her situation, no matter how she'd tried to put a positive spin on it.

He cleared his throat as he studied her application for a loan. "I apologize I didn't have a chance to review this before now. My secretary squeezed you in last minute as a courtesy."

"Oh, I completely understand. And thank you. Again."

His long, bony fingers tapped the edge of the multipage document in front of him. Mr. Brown adjusted his spectacles, and a slight frown overtook the corners of his droopy lips.

Just as long as his eye didn't twitch. According to her brother-in-law William—who had grown up in this town and had known Mr. Brown all his life—if that happened, she was done for.

And she couldn't bear to consider the possibility of that happening. How would Rosebud Books ever survive without this loan?

The better question was, how much of this was her fault—and how much was Garrett's? He'd always been in charge of the money side of things, despite the three years of business courses Ginny had taken before dropping out of Harvard. Numbers had never really been her passion, so she'd been more than happy to let him handle the bookstore's finances. Perhaps that had been a mistake. Or maybe she'd simply spent too much during the six months since he'd been gone.

How embarrassed her parents would be if they knew. Not that she could really do much to "humiliate" them further, according to her mom. She'd already chosen to do things far differently from her older siblings Sarah and Benjamin, who had followed in their parents' footsteps—she a high-powered attorney, he a vice president in a subsidiary of their father's company.

Ginny's knee began an up-and-down motion of its own accord. Her attention moved to the picture window behind Mr. Brown. From here, she could glimpse High Street, where the 9:00 a.m. bustle had taken over the previously quiet main road. Next door, the bakery's quaint wooden sign banged against the whitewashed siding. The wind must be blowing down from the bluffs again. She imagined she could hear it whistling through the narrow streets.

But she couldn't. In here, there was nothing but Mr. Brown's clock ticking away Ginny's fate.

The silence became as stifling as the humidity in the office.

"Mr. Trengrouse was baking something new today." Ginny couldn't keep the words in. They tumbled out as if pulled from her throat by some invisible force. "A sort of fancy raisin croissant with frosting. I can run next door and snatch one for you if you'd like."

Her outburst was met with the raise of one bushy eyebrow. But no twitching of that right eye. Yet. "No, thank you, Mrs. Rose. I'm quite all right." Mr. Brown moved his eyes back to her application.

The document sat there, stark white and vulnerable against the deep brown of his desk, which she recognized as a Huntington. Her father had one in his own study in Boston. Business at the bank must be booming with the recent economic recession of Port Willis and many other villages along the northern Cornish coast. She couldn't be the only business owner desperate for a loan.

But maybe she was the only one foolish enough to not quit when all signs said she should.

Ginny smoothed the edge of her polyester business suit skirt, a gift from her mom that had somehow ended up in the suitcase she'd packed when she'd followed Garrett to this tiny town. A wrinkle in the deep-green fabric remained, despite three attempts at ironing. Mother would have never left the house in such "disarray."

She bounced her knee faster, banging it against the desk's overhang and stifling a moan.

Mr. Brown glanced at her. "Are you all right, Mrs. Rose?"

She had a feeling he wasn't just asking about her knee.

"Yes. Perfectly." Ginny flashed a grin that likely resembled more of a grimace. "Just anxious to hear your verdict."

"I'm hardly a judge."

Oh, but didn't he realize that he was? His yea or nay affected more than just Ginny. After all, it was Garrett's bookstore too—their dream together. Well, more his, but she'd thrown all she had into it and it had become their baby together, a blessing since they hadn't yet been able to have actual children of their own.

If she gave up on the bookstore, then what did it say about the state of their marriage? Garrett may have needed some space to think, but once he returned from London, ready to embrace her once again, he would not be happy if she'd let their dream die.

Of course, it would have helped if he hadn't drained half of their accounts before he left.

But he'd see the error of his ways. He had to. Mother couldn't have been right about him.

"Hmm." The deep-throated mumbling in Mr. Brown's throat grated against the silence that hung in the office.

At long last, he removed his spectacles and sighed. "Mrs. Rose, how do you suppose this loan would help you? Yes, in the short term it can help pay some of your costs, but what is your long-term plan for overhauling your business? I know you've submitted the paper here, but I'd like to hear it from your lips."

"I've been brainstorming ways to bring in extra revenue and build some momentum for future success." She outlined her ideas, and unfortunately, it didn't take long. "I just need a leg up right now. A little wiggle room to get through the slump the economy has brought to us all. I've run the numbers and am confident that the extra revenue brought in by these changes will allow us to pay back this loan in record time."

She almost believed herself.

Mr. Brown folded his hands on the desk and leaned forward. His chair squeaked with the movement. "I'm not sure what numbers you've run to come to that conclusion, but I have to look at the facts in front of me."

His right eye—was that a twitch? Ginny held in a groan.

"According to the documents you've submitted here, profits at Rosebud Books have dwindled drastically in the last six months. I understand that part of that is the normal ebb and flow that comes with the lower tourist interest Port Willis has pulled in recently, but . . ."

Oh, that was most definitely an eye twitch.

Ginny slumped in her seat. "But what?"

"Well, my dear, it also accounts for the time you have been running the store . . . on your own."

The groan moved into her chest, threatening to escape. "He'll be back."

Had she really just said those words aloud? If only she could hide under the table, sink through a hole in the floor, disappear with a wriggle of her nose. Anything. "That is, I was a bit . . . taken aback by the circumstances I found myself in. But I know that a loan could be just the blessing I need to keep going."

Holy cow, she sounded desperate. This man had no reason to help her. Despite her five years of living in this town, some people held her at arm's length now that Garrett had moved to London temporarily. After all, he was the town's golden boy, and naturally some people made assumptions that she'd been the one to chase him away. Perhaps Mr. Brown was one of those people.

"Look." Mr. Brown's gray eyebrows bunched together and his lips puckered, as much a sympathetic expression as he could muster. "I know it can't be easy with everything you have going on. But I'm running a business here and can't hand out money. I'm afraid I can't offer you this loan."

The groan flew out of Ginny's mouth, deep and pathetic and embarrassing. "What can I say to change your mind?"

Mr. Brown's eye twitching picked up speed. In fact, wait . . . Was his left eye twitching too? That was bad. Very bad.

"I'm sorry, Mrs. Rose. My mind is made up. Perhaps you should give up and go home where you belong."

3

✿✿✿✿✿✿

SOPHIA

"Can I help you find something?"

Sophia dragged her gaze from the rows of books in front of her to face a teenage girl in a red shirt. The girl wore an employee badge that read, "My name is Lauren, and my favorite author is Rae Carson." Her face was apple shaped and innocent, and she looked at Sophia with a mixture of curiosity and dismay.

And no wonder. Sophia's eyes stung from the litany of tears she'd cried. They probably looked atrociously red and smeared with mascara. "No, I'm just browsing. Thank you."

The girl quirked an eyebrow and nodded. "Just let someone know if you need help finding a particular book." She wheeled her restocking cart around the aisle of the bookstore and disappeared.

Sophia had the sudden urge to run after the girl and make her promise to be careful out there, to not give herself away to the first guy with a cute smile she met, to—

Oh brother. *Snap out of it, Sophia.*

She turned back toward the selection of Robert Appleton novels, running her fingertips over the spines of her favorites: *Moonbeams on the Moor, Whisper Across the Bluffs, A Path Unwinding.* Though she owned copies at home, their pages stiffened from the oils on her fingers, she loved to come here and experience them afresh. There was just something about the way they spoke to her, instilling hope through the strong heroines who faced great odds to find love and happiness. She snagged *Moonbeams*, then headed for the circle of overstuffed leather chairs at the front of the bookstore.

The store was fairly empty, which made sense given it was a Tuesday at eleven in the morning. A few college-age students adorned the wooden tables in the small café and bar, their earbuds in and their laptops out. Two moms with young tots in strollers chatted over iced drinks, their hair thrown back in messy buns and flip-flops dangling from their feet. The smells of coffee and wine mingled in the air.

Sophia chose her favorite chair next to the window and settled in, cracking open the book in her hands. In moments, she was lost in the story, in the cadence of Cornish waves crashing against bluffs, in the way Julia's hands brushed across the tops of long grass as she moved through the moor, contemplating Martin's declaration of love.

The story was as familiar as breathing, and it calmed her.

"You know your lips move when you're reading, right?"

With a start, Sophia lost her grip on the book and swung her gaze upward. Joy plopped into the seat next to her.

"What are you doing here?" Sophia leaned over and grabbed the novel, which had slipped to the floor.

"You always come here when you're upset."

Did she? She only knew that being at the bookstore felt better than being at home. Something about the books, the stories—they spoke to her, whether they were nearly two centuries old or brand new. Each one had something to say, and she longed to absorb the wisdom held in the secret places of each page. The ink soaked from the pages into her soul.

"Did you hear me?" Joy's voice broke through her reverie.

"No, sorry."

"I said, what happened today? I came out of my nine o'clock and Kristin told me you'd run off about ten minutes into yours. Just left, without a word to anyone. I had to see my ten o'clock and then asked Kristin to rearrange my schedule for the next few hours." Joy played with her oversized orange hoop earring.

For a moment, Sophia considered lying. Joy would never let her come back to the practice if she told the truth. But other than Mom, there was no one Sophia trusted more in this world than Joy, and Sophia couldn't repay her with falsehood. "I panicked. My client . . . She was an abuse victim."

Joy's fingers stilled. "No, she said she suffered from anxiety. I thought . . . but of course she lied. Oh, Soph, I'm so sorry."

"It's okay. Of course you didn't know."

Nearby, one of the children in the strollers started to cry. One-handedly, the mother unstrapped the girl and pulled her into her lap, where she played happily with a plastic straw wrapper as her mom continued her conversation.

"Come on. I need coffee." Joy stood and tugged on Sophia's arm. She grabbed the novel and placed it on a shelf for restocking, then poked Sophia in the ribs with a good-natured smirk. "Your obsession with those novels is getting a bit extreme."

With a gentle push, she nudged Sophia toward the eating area, where a wooden counter outlined the bar and café. Wineglasses hung from a rack on the ceiling, creating a crystal halo above the bartender's head. A gleaming espresso machine sat on the counter behind a barista working to fill coffee and pastry orders.

While Joy ordered an iced coffee, Sophia ordered hers hot and black. Once the drinks were delivered, they selected a small table in the corner for privacy.

Sophia took a sip of her coffee, scalding her upper lip with the hot liquid. "I know I let you down." What else could she say?

"You absolutely did not. You just weren't ready."

"Guess this is the part where you say 'I told you so.'"

Joy reached for her hand and squeezed. "Best friends don't say that. And it's not like I'm glad to be right. Soph, you've got to heal more yourself before you try to help others do the same. Otherwise, their pain is too great. It latches onto you and threatens to pull you under. If you've still got all of your own pain attached . . ."

The visual left Sophia nearly gasping for air. She wrapped her hands around her cup. "I really did think I was ready. Now I wonder if I ever will be. I mean, what client wants a domestic abuse victim counseling her? It's hypocritical." Of course, when it was happening, she'd made excuses. Stuffed the abuse in the closet of her heart, telling herself it wasn't real. That the love story between her and David was the reality.

She'd told no one about it when David was alive. And once he'd died, no one but Mom and Joy—and now Cindy—even knew. Everyone still assumed her breakdown had everything to do with David's death, not the strange mixture of intense relief and over-whelming grief she'd felt after it happened.

"Hey." Joy waited till Sophia looked up at her. "You will get past this. And when you do, you'll have such a wealth of knowledge and empathy for these women that you'll be the best therapist they could possibly find. But until then, maybe you could take some of my advice."

"What advice is that?"

"Journal your story." Her friend had even given Sophia a beau-tiful notebook for just that purpose.

"No. I've already told you. I couldn't do that. The idea of putting the words on a page—I just can't." The pain she'd experienced—her confusion, her guilt, her everything—written in ink felt like a vise gripping her throat.

"But isn't that often the very tactic that helps so many of our clients experience a turnaround? Sure, it isn't instantaneous, but something about writing it out means you can't hide from it. It means you can't lie to yourself anymore."

"Is that what you think I've been doing?"

Joy shrugged a shoulder. "I know you're desperate to be strong, even though you don't have to be. He's not here to hurt you anymore, Sophia."

"You don't get it, Joy. He is. He's still here. Everywhere I go, I feel him. Like a ghost I'll never get rid of. His voice, in my head. His words, forever ingrained on my heart."

"And so you escape into your novels."

"No, that's not . . . I don't know, maybe. But counseling is helping me, though maybe more slowly than I'd hoped."

"Your story is worth telling, Soph."

Her friend's words were a barb to Sophia's tender heart. But maybe she was right. At this point, shouldn't Sophia be willing to try anything if it meant she could stop relying on other people and finally be the independent woman she'd always been . . . before? "Okay, fine. I'll try it."

"And another thing." Joy reached for her arm and squeezed. "You're not going to like it. But you have to take more leave from work. At least two or three more months. Maybe even take the whole summer."

Joy was right. Sophia knew it.

Though she couldn't help but wonder if she'd ever be strong enough to help anyone else ever again.

4

※※※※※

GINNY

". . . go home where you belong."

Mr. Brown's words pounded through Ginny's head with every step she took down High Street. The smell of fish and salt permeated the air the closer she came to the harbor. The scent of it churned in her gut as she marched past galleries filled with vibrant local art, pubs serving Cornish mead and saffron cakes, and specialty shops designed to appeal to tourists. Within weeks, the official summer season would begin, and the winding streets of Port Willis would fill with visitors on the hunt for a bit of Cornish magic.

They'd come to her bookstore, perhaps to find the perfect souvenir to take home—would she still be open by then?

". . . go home where you belong."

Didn't Mr. Brown realize? Ginny didn't know if such a place existed. She'd thought it was in Garrett's arms, but now . . .

No. She couldn't give up. Because then what would she do? The one course in life she'd finally chosen for herself would come to a dead end. And she would have used up all of her family's goodwill on the wrong one.

As Ginny made her way toward the bookstore from the bank, a sudden break in the buildings left her with a spectacular view of the bluffs. Grass waved along the ocean-battered coastline, a friend begging her to slip off her clunky heels and go for a run.

But she turned her gaze toward the street once more, watching granite-and-slate-fronted houses and buildings seem to grow around her as the street dipped downward into a valley. The harbor was close, and with it, her lifeblood. Nestled between the newly updated Port Willis Pottery Club and the ever-cozy Loretta's Bed & Breakfast, Rosebud Books stood sentinel. She and Garrett had fallen in love with the eighteenth-century shop, which had been vacant for several years after the last bookstore owners decided to move to Ireland for retirement. The lease had been affordable and the landlords were thrilled to have renters once more. Together, she and her husband had poured hours of sweat and love into this place, fixed it up, made it their own.

A tear began to roll down Ginny's cheek. Not again. She couldn't focus on the pain, the things out of her control. All she could do was hope for a brighter future. With a quick swipe across her cheek, she dipped her hand into her purse and pulled out her keys. Unlocking the cheery yellow door, she was met with the quaint jingle of a bell above her head.

The smell of old books greeted her, reminding her a bit of the *Beauty and the Beast*–style library at Wingate, her family's Nantucket estate. It seemed a lifetime since she'd been back there.

Ginny flicked on the lights and unloaded her purse onto the front desk counter, a large oak piece Garrett had created himself. His father had been a carpenter and passed his love of woodworking on to his youngest son. Though he hadn't been a rich man, the sale of his house and other belongings after his death had been divided between his two sons, and Garrett had used his as the seed money for the bookstore.

She ran her hand over the oak countertop, felt the dips and ridges in the wood—imperfect but beautiful, crafted from love.

Her fingers formed a fist and she pounded the desk. A sharp pang radiated through the side of her hand. She bit back a choice phrase.

"Gin?"

Her neck twisted upward. "William?" How had she not heard her brother-in-law enter? "What are you doing here?" She shook out her hand and winced.

"Checking on you. You okay?" He closed the door behind him and strode toward her. He and Garrett looked so much alike—well built and lean but not overly muscular, with sloping noses and dirty-blond curls cut short. Today he wore his dark-rimmed glasses, making him appear every inch the literature professor he was.

"I'm fine." Her hand fairly throbbed, but hey . . .

"You don't look great."

"Just what every girl wants to hear." She lifted an eyebrow, then added a little smirk to show him she really was fine. People who weren't fine didn't kid around, did they?

But William clearly wasn't in a joking mood. He folded his arms across his chest. "What happened? Why are you crying? Did Garrett—"

"No. I haven't heard from him." In weeks. "I requested a loan from Brown & Brothers. Mr. Brown denied my request."

William groaned. "I'm sorry, Ginny."

She flexed her hand. It was finally starting to exhibit a dull pain instead of a sharp one. "It'll be okay." Determined to avoid further inquisition, she snatched up an old rag and some furniture polish. She hadn't cleaned the shelves in . . . oh, a day or so. As she headed toward the nearest bookcase, which towered over her five-seven frame, Ginny squirted some polish onto the rag, then rubbed it into the wood.

"How bad are things?" And there was William, at her back, his question boring a hole into her attempt to distract herself. "And don't say they're 'fine' or 'okay.'"

Didn't he understand that if she was going to stay upbeat about all of this, she couldn't get into the nitty-gritty? "It doesn't matter.

You can't help anyway." Ginny rubbed the bookshelf until the sun from outside was reflected in the wood.

"I have a little saved."

"No. That's the money for your sabbatical." William had been working as a professor in the nearby town of Danby for years, and planning his time off to travel and write a book for just as long.

"We're family. What's mine is yours. Especially since that no-good brother of mine left you high and dry."

Her hand stilled. "William, he didn't leave me high and dry. He just needs time. I'm trying to give him that." Of course, there had been the times when she'd caved and called him anyway—telling herself it was to discuss the future of the bookstore, and not to beg him to come home.

He'd never answered those calls.

The scent of the furniture polish burned her nostrils as she fired another shot of it onto the bookshelf and scrubbed for all she was worth.

His lips flattened into a frown. "You're so much better than he deserves. I still can't believe he did this to you." The pain that flashed across his face tore at Ginny's gut. "My brother was never the most selfless person, but he seemed a changed man when he married you."

"He never struck me as selfish, just driven to achieve his dreams."

"How can you of all people defend him?"

Didn't he get it? Garrett was all she had. Him . . . and this bookstore.

She shifted the conversation slightly. "Have you talked to him yet?" After his initial attempts to talk sense into Garrett, William had refused any further communication with his brother.

"No." William fidgeted with the strap of his messenger bag. "I know I should, but I can't forgive him for leaving you, Ginny. It's wrong."

"For the last time, he didn't *leave* me." Why wouldn't anyone believe her? Garrett had not filed for divorce yet. Wouldn't he have done so if he was leaving for good? "We're just taking some time apart . . ."

"Time where he does whatever he wants and lets you keep running his business on your own? He's abandoned his responsibilities. And for what?"

"To find himself." The words squeaked out of Ginny's throat. Even six months later, she still didn't understand. Garrett Rose had always seemed so sure of himself and what he wanted. For a girl who'd spent her whole life doing exactly what her parents had demanded of her, Ginny hadn't stood a chance against Garrett's charms. He was all the things she'd always wanted to be, and he'd inspired her to finally take a leap down her own path.

Ginny swiped at her eyes. "He needs to know who he is without all of this . . . even me. He assured me he'd be back when he could get it all sorted. Do I wish he'd let me help him? Yeah, of course. But he's asked me to give him space, so I am."

Her voice sounded much harsher than she'd intended. She considered apologizing, but squirted more polish onto the rag. The hiss of the can filled the silence. Ginny rubbed until the ache from her hand spread up her arm.

"I'm just sorry he's putting you through this." William leaned against the bookcase. "I'm praying that he'll see what he's doing to you and come home soon."

She'd never really given prayer much credence—it wasn't how she'd been raised—but the gesture was well meant and appreciated.

"Thank you." Ginny sighed and put the rag and polish down. "You've been a good friend and brother to me. Even my own parents would love to see me fail if it'd mean slinking home with my tail between my legs, admitting I was wrong."

"Have you considered asking them for a loan?"

The caustic laugh from her lips attacked the air. "George and

Mariah Bentley have disowned me until I 'come to my senses.' They don't even know that Garrett has . . . that things are the way they are. I haven't spoken to them in a long time. There's no way I can ask them for money. Even access to my trust fund has been frozen until I 'cooperate.'"

"What other options do you have? How long until you're out of money?"

Should she tell him the truth? But why not? He'd find out soon enough if she had to close her doors. "Let's just say my need is immediate. I have to brainstorm some ways to make extra money, pronto. I've got a few ideas, but have no idea if they'll make a difference or not."

"Like what?"

"I put an ad on *B&B Today*."

"The vacation rental site?"

"Yes. I thought I'd rent out the flat over the bookstore. It's got a bed, bathroom, and small kitchenette. And I posted it with the opportunity to work in the bookstore for lower rent. I figured I wouldn't have to hire summer help if I could keep a steady enough flow of visitors."

"Nice way to think outside the box. What else do you have?"

"Not much else. A few marketing ideas, but finding a way to afford them might be tough."

At this point, with no loan and no prospects for financial windfalls, she had to admit it—she needed a miracle to keep this bookstore alive. It seemed everyone in town knew it.

Why couldn't she accept the truth too?

Ginny took up the rag and polish once more, moving on to the next bookcase.

5

SOPHIA

Heat hit Sophia's face as she entered her home through the garage door. She'd set the air conditioner to kick on in an hour or if it got too hot for her cat. She hadn't anticipated being home this soon, but she'd killed as much time as she could at the bookstore.

She moved forward through the arched hallway tiled with travertine until she reached the thermostat and turned on the AC. Then she headed toward her huge kitchen. Setting her bag on the granite countertop, she stared at the gleaming stainless steel appliances, the oversized farm sink, the designer cabinets. What a pity no one had cooked here since she and David had moved in a month after getting engaged—unless using the microwave to reheat leftovers counted.

A light pressure grazed against the bottom of her pants. Sophia bent down and snatched Gigi into her arms. "Hey, girl. Looks like you're going to be seeing more of me. Again." The vibration of her Persian's purrs rumbled through her arms.

With a quick pat, Sophia put Gigi down and explored the refrigerator: a half-full container of milk, one apple, and some lunch meat that may or may not be expired. She sighed. "Should have bought some dinner on my way home, shouldn't I?"

Her voice seemed to echo in the cavernous space. She closed the fridge and headed to her bedroom upstairs. Why had she and David purchased this monstrosity of a home? It was so different from the modest, two-bedroom house she'd grown up in. Two people and a cat didn't need four thousand square feet. But David had said it was a home befitting a lawyer, and hadn't he worked hard to make partner by the age of thirty-five? He deserved it.

In some ways, she'd been attracted to his power suits and flashy cars. But she'd never quite fit in with his affluent crowd. And when he'd died and she'd inherited all of his money, she'd paid off the house and stuck the rest in her savings account and hadn't touched it since.

Sophia replaced her work clothes with yoga pants and a T-shirt. Gigi followed her and settled onto the quilt laid on the edge of the California king-sized bed—Sophia's attempt to make the black-and-white designer room feel more . . . her.

She plopped onto the bed and scratched Gigi's head. Joy's words from earlier this morning replayed in her brain on repeat. Should she give journaling a shot? Maybe the words would flow faster than she thought. Maybe she'd find the healing that seemed to elude her. Wasn't it worth the risk?

Her eyes swung to her nightstand, where the white leather journal Joy had given her sat buried under a few other books. Sophia leaned over and dug it out from the pile. It was gorgeous, with her name in pink threading across the front, along with a design of sunbursts and flowers.

Every time she'd attempted to write in it, it had ended up tossed across the room. Yet somehow, the leather cover remained nearly pristine, with only a smudge on the lower right corner indicative of all it had been through.

But perhaps she'd never been able to write in the journal because she hadn't been ready. Maybe now she was.

She licked her lips and grabbed a pen, poised it over the first page. Closed her eyes, visualized the words spilling from her.

Nothing.

Who was she kidding? She wasn't a writer. Had never aspired to be. She just loved reading—seeing words come to life on a page. Would she ever be able to string them together for herself?

As if sensing her need for companionship, Gigi moved to curl up next to her, rubbing her nose a few times against Sophia's knee.

Maybe this was a horrible idea. Sophia gripped the pen in her fingers, shuffling it back and forth against the upper part of her middle finger and the pad of her thumb. She studied her room: the overstuffed chair in the corner, the shutters, the floor vase filled with fake calla lilies, the large mirror over the vanity . . .

And suddenly, violent images shuddered through her.

Her head slamming against the edge of the vanity. Blood everywhere. She'd had to convince the carpet cleaners that she'd tripped over a pair of boots . . .

No. Too much.

She slammed the journal shut, repressing the urge to hurl it. Instead, she placed it firmly on her nightstand. "Come on, Gigi." Sophia grabbed a Robert Appleton novel and headed out of the room and down the stairs, ready to sink onto the couch and pick up the story where she'd left off.

Her phone jangled from her purse, which still sat lonely on the large kitchen island. She rummaged through her bag till she found it. "Hey, Mama."

"I'm guessing you don't have anything for dinner?" Mom's voice lit the line with humor.

"You'd be correct. And your timing is impeccable." She plopped onto the couch. It was old and floral-patterned, a Goodwill find from six months ago. She and Joy had been shopping for something "vintage" for Joy's new apartment, and Sophia had grown weary, sitting on the couch as she waited for her friend to dig through a pile of clutter. The couch had been so comfortable, she'd sunk into it and nearly fallen asleep.

Joy had joked that Sophia should just buy it. Pointed out how much David would have hated it.

And now, here it was, her tiny act of rebellion. Too little too late, but it was something.

"How about I come over with some pizza?"

Sophia tucked her feet underneath her body. "Aren't you busy with that really big wedding? I thought you had a meeting with the bride tonight." Despite her meager beginnings as a secretary at an event planning corporation, Mom had really made something of herself after Sophia's dad had decided that being a family man was no longer appealing. Now Sandy Barrett was a sought-after wedding planner with a busier schedule than her daughter. But she never complained about her late hours or long days because she saw it as her calling in life to help brides have the perfect Big Day and do anything she could to serve them.

"She got sick and canceled, so my evening is wide open."

"Why don't you go out on the town with your friends from Bible study? You're all empty nesters now." The group of women from Palmcroft Baptist Church had raised their kids together and supported one another through multiple crises. They'd even brought Sophia meals after David died. "I'm sure you have better things to do than come hang out here with your boring daughter."

"Sophia Lynn Barrett, don't you ever say that. A mother's greatest joy is being with her children. Especially when they are no longer throwing tantrums, clinging to her legs, or begging for the latest toy."

"I make no promises that I won't do those things."

"I'll risk it. Be over in an hour with your favorite sausage and pineapple pizza in hand."

"And you won't even call me a weirdo like Joy does for liking that particular combination." Sophia pulled at a loose thread on the couch.

"Doesn't mean I don't think it."

"Ha-ha." The thread unraveled a bit more. "Hey, Mom, speaking of Joy—did she call you?"

"No. Why?" There was a hitch in her upbeat tone.

"Never mind." Mom just had a sixth sense about these things. Or maybe she knew that Sophia was always in need of her these days.

"Thanks, Mom." A sudden clog of emotion made her throat dry.

Sophia knew Mom wanted to rescue her—goodness knew she understood how it felt to be mistreated by a man. Even though Sophia's father had never spoken harshly to or hit Mom, his abandonment when Sophia was a child had dealt her mother a heavy blow that had taken years of recovery and healing.

Still, no matter how many nights Mom spent letting Sophia cry on her shoulder, the next day always came, and here Sophia would be, alone in this big house.

But it wasn't Mom's job to protect her. That had been Sophia's job, and she'd failed.

After all, from a young age Sophia had known the truth—that a woman had to learn to stand on her own two feet. Her mother had, and Sophia had put her all into doing the same. Until she met David.

Then she'd melted into a puddle of weakness, and her resolve had become wisps in the wind, floating away at the first knee-trembling smile he'd turned her way.

Pathetic.

Her therapist, Cindy—and Joy too—would have a conniption if they knew how much self-loathing she still secretly harbored. In her brain, she knew it wasn't healthy.

But how was she supposed to let it go? All she could do was make sure it never happened again.

She hung up with Mom and settled back into the book. Maybe she *was* escaping, but if she had to escape, then there was no better place than Cornwall. She closed her eyes, pictured herself walking where Julia and Martin walked, taking in the gorgeous sunsets off the bluffs, surfing in the probably very chilly ocean. She laughed at the absurdity. As if she could ever surf, despite the fact her father had been a surfer once upon a time. When she'd confided her desire to learn, David had scoffed, called her a city girl who had no business doing anything adventurous, said—

"Enough."

She looked up, startled. Had . . . had she said that? Had that word come from her mouth? That sentiment from her soul?

Yes, it had.

Because what was so absurd about her surfing in Cornwall? And what was so impossible about her lying in the tall grass, staring at the sky and dreaming of a better future?

Maybe even . . .

No.

But perhaps . . . yes.

And then a feeling overtook her, one that smacked of holiness, if she really believed in that sort of thing—like she used to. A moment that felt ordained. An idea. A way to move forward, when here she was basically stuck.

But maybe in Cornwall she could get unstuck.

Not as if there was anything magical about that place. Not really. It was just dirt and sun and sky and water like anywhere else. But for her, it was also the home of amazing authors like Robert Appleton, the place he'd been inspired to write, the place he'd described as "the most freeing, most alive realm in all the world—and I have the privilege of calling it mine."

Could it perhaps be Sophia's too? At least for a time? Two weeks, maybe? Three? The whole summer?

Could it inspire even the most frightened and hesitant of wannabe storytellers?

Before she could talk herself out of the idea, she ran to the den that functioned as her office down the hall. She snapped on her computer, pointed her browser to Google, and, fingers trembling, typed in words that just might change her life forever.

Vacation rentals in Cornwall, England.

6

SOPHIA

It was even lovelier than in her dreams.

Sophia climbed from her rental vehicle—somehow she'd survived driving on the opposite side of the road—and stared at the adorable town spreading out below her. She stood at the top of a hill in the large community parking lot, or "car park" as it was labeled. It sounded so . . . British. A thrill of excitement ran up her spine.

Was she really here?

The breeze brought a whiff of briny ocean and fish. It was an altogether different smell from the mingling of dirt and smog she was used to as a native Phoenician. Sophia stepped forward to glance below. She could make out the harbor with at least two dozen sailboats and other ships docked tightly near the pier.

Despite the flurry of hurried prepping for her trip in a matter of days, she'd managed to do a bit of research on the town and had read that Port Willis survived largely on fishing, crabbing, and tourism, though it had suffered lower tourist numbers the last few years. Sophia's eyes closed as she imagined the fishermen's boats nestled against the coastline, waiting to bring in an exciting catch each day.

Her mouth watered at the thought of tasting fresh-caught crab, a surprise given her pure lack of appetite over the last several months.

Back home, she constantly felt hemmed in by the heat, the continuous rush of people and cars on the freeway, the houses crammed together in massive subdivisions that spanned the entire "Valley of the Sun." But here, the water stretched beyond her sight, whispering freedom to her soul.

"Would you mind moving a bit to the left, love?"

Sophia's eyes popped open, and she realized she was standing in the exit to the car park, where a man in a small car was attempting to leave. He'd leaned out the window to speak to her, and instead of the annoyance she would have expected, his eyes lit with humor, his lips with a smile—a very attractive one.

"Oh my. I'm so sorry." She moved out of his way in a flash, then looked back toward her car. How far had she walked without realizing it?

"Not a problem. Are you lost?" This time his English accent caught her attention. The sincerity in his tone again surprised her. How sad, really, that kindness from a stranger should.

"Just taking in the view." Sophia spread her hand out, indicating the town. "I guess I got a little carried away."

"It's easy to do." The man smiled again, a dimple appearing in his right cheek. "Enjoy your time in Port Willis. It's a lovely little town."

"I will, thanks." As the man drove off, Sophia returned to her car and lugged her overstuffed suitcase from the trunk. When Joy heard she'd booked a trip to England, she was delighted. At first, she'd suggested that Sophia continue her therapy sessions with Cindy via Skype, but Sophia had decided a complete break from the therapy process was in order. She just needed to fully escape, press reset on life. She'd promised to resume sessions with Cindy in September when she returned, though.

Mom had been a bit more concerned than Joy, especially when

she'd heard how long Sophia would be gone. She'd even offered to come with her. But this was something Sophia had to do on her own, and Mom had understood.

Of course, part of Sophia wondered if she was crazy, or if escaping for months really was healthy. She'd be away from everything and everyone she knew. But staying put in a place where David and her memories haunted every room hadn't done much for her psyche either.

And when she'd found a place with rent for next to nothing, plus the opportunity to work in a bookstore of all places, it had seemed like fate. She'd booked the rental through the end of August and decided to leave in less than a week—why stick around Phoenix when nothing was stopping her from going immediately? The thought had crossed her mind that the bookstore could be owned by complete psychopaths, but she hadn't had to pay much of a deposit in advance, so she could always leave early if things felt shady.

As Sophia wheeled her suitcase down the pavement toward the centuries-old village below, she felt, in a strange way, that she was coming home. Cornwall was the same as novels had always described it, though the sky was a brighter blue, the air saltier, and the breeze fresher than even words could bring to life.

She passed strangers on the street, and each one tipped his head or waved her hand in greeting. It was a Saturday, so children played in huddles or ran in happy groups down the streets, which bustled with activity the closer to the town center she came. Sophia passed pub after pub, each advertising a special catch of the day. There was a Cornish pasty shop on the corner she promised herself she'd try right away. She stopped at the fudge shop and peeked in the window, amazed at the large variety of flavors she could see even from here. The enticing scent of chocolates, peanuts, and cinnamon drifted from inside as a man led his young daughter out the door, ice cream dripping from her cone.

Her phone dinged inside her purse. Sophia dug it out and saw a text from Joy: *Wanted to see if you'd made it okay. So excited to hear about all your adventures and praying you're able to find and tell your story at last. XOXO*

Sophia fired off a reply: *Just arrived. Walking to the bookstore now. It's gorgeous here. I feel like I've stepped into a novel and I never want to leave.*

She pulled up the e-mail on her phone and looked once more at her *B&B Today* confirmation with the bookstore's address. From what she could tell from the map, she was close. Sophia rounded the corner and there, tucked between two more modern-looking shops, sat Rosebud Books. The wooden sign's paint was peeling around the edges, but in a quaint way, and it beckoned to her.

Suddenly, her heart picked up speed. What would she find inside?

"Books, silly." She whispered the words under her breath. Books, the things that had always brought her comfort whether school was easy or difficult, whether she'd found the perfect job or not, whether her fiancé was alive or dead, a monster or her personal hero.

Books had always been her escape. Here, she hoped they'd become her healing.

Sophia took the handle of the door and swung it open. Immediately, she was surrounded by her favorite smell in the world—that of old pages and book spines, slightly musty but not in a stuffy way. No, this mustiness was an old friend, one that spoke of stories told and untold, of age and wisdom and love and passion and history and . . . everything.

"Welcome to Rosebud Books."

Sophia's head snapped toward the front counter, where a twenty-something woman wearing a faded Beatles T-shirt stood behind a computer. Her brown hair was pulled back in a ponytail off her long neck, and though her dark eyes were friendly, Sophia sensed an exhaustion behind them. Despite that, her smile took up nearly half of her face, and her dimples made her more adorable than drop-dead gorgeous, which also put Sophia immediately at ease.

And wait—she sounded American. "Thank you. Are you Ginny? I'm Sophia."

"Hi!" The woman made her way from behind the counter, revealing a casual pair of jeans and purple Chucks on her feet. "I'm so pleased to meet you. Nice to have someone else from the States here." Yes, definitely American, with a Boston lilt.

"I agree." How had this woman landed here in this tiny English town? She must have an interesting story to tell.

"Would you like to see your room now? I'm sure you must be tired from your travels."

"Sure. That'd be great."

"Follow me, then." Ginny led her toward the back of the store, wringing her hands ever so slightly. "I'll of course give you a proper tour later, but in case you're curious, over there is our new book section. We specialize in older editions, but also sell modern books to keep up with the times. Back that way is our used section, and then you have our rare books all the way in the back."

Sophia took it all in while Ginny chattered on. If Port Willis felt like home, then this store would be her sanctuary. Yes, she could picture it.

Ginny stopped at the base of a staircase and pointed up toward a door. "Your apartment is just above. As listed in the advertisement, it's a study with bedroom furniture and a small kitchen and bathroom. Oh." She dug into her pocket and pulled out a key. "You'll need this. And if you need anything else, I live in the cottage behind the store and I'm usually up late. So don't be afraid to text me, and I can be right over."

Sophia took the key. "Thanks so much. And when do I need to report for duty? I know part of the deal is working at the bookstore."

Ginny folded her arms and leaned against the stair rail. "Right. You'll have Fridays through Sundays off, so you don't need to report till Monday."

"Will I be working by myself or with another employee?" The idea of running the bookstore by herself was a bit overwhelming.

"I'll work alongside you."

"How will the other employees feel about me taking hours away from them?"

"It's just me right now." The woman's smile faltered.

Hmm, curious reaction. Sophia needed to shut her therapist's brain off. She was not here to take on anyone else's burdens—she had enough baggage of her own. "Perfect."

The woman's shoulders seemed to relax. "In the meantime, go out and enjoy yourself. Explore the town. There's plenty to do, and I can offer some suggestions if you'd like. I've lived here for five years, so I know a lot of stuff the guidebooks won't tell you."

Sophia bit her lip and stared up at the door above them. She longed to go upstairs, unpack, curl up with her novel, and fall asleep with the window open, the salt-tinged air lulling her to sleep. But she'd also come here to break free of the mold, to write her story. And part of that meant discovering, digging in, doing what wasn't the most comfortable.

She turned back to Ginny. "Would you happen to be free for dinner? I don't know anyone and would love to hear more about the bookstore and the town." It seemed like a small step forward, but she'd already taken the large leap in coming here. Small steps were enough for now.

Sophia's question seemed to take Ginny by surprise, and it took a moment for her to respond. "I—"

"Of course, you're probably busy. Forget I asked."

"No, it's not that. I just don't have anyone else to cover the bookstore. But I can close a bit early tonight. It's not like we get much business on a Saturday night anyway." Ginny's lips tightened and her jaw twitched. "Plus, it would be good to get out."

Sophia couldn't help but put her hand on Ginny's upper arm and squeeze. Perhaps that was a strange thing to do for someone she'd just met five minutes before, but Sophia's therapist instincts kicked in. Despite Ginny's brave front, she could tell this woman was hurting—and Sophia could relate. "It's settled then. I'll go put my things upstairs, you get everything sorted out, and we'll go eat a delicious dinner somewhere."

7

⟨⟨⟨⟨⟨⟨⟩

GINNY

At least one of Ginny's ideas for helping the bookstore seemed to be working out well. Her first renter was almost too good to be true.

Ginny opened the door to the Village Pub, a Port Willis classic frequented by locals and tourists alike. Enticing scents of roasted lamb, frothy Cornish beer, and sizzling butter nearly knocked her over. It had been hours since she'd last eaten. Sophia followed her inside, taking in the well-lit pub with its wood-paneled walls and nautical decor as if she was a child at Christmastime and this the North Pole.

Open fireplaces lit several cozy snugs where patrons enjoyed cask ales and lagers. "This way." Maneuvering around the crowded room toward her favorite table in the back, Ginny nodded to villagers as she passed. She plopped into a white wooden chair in front of a long window overlooking the harbor.

Sophia sat across from her and folded her hands in her lap, eyes glistening as she took in her surroundings. "This place is so amazing. How long has it been in business?"

Ginny had always liked it here, but she'd largely avoided it the last six months—just like she'd avoided most public places. She hated feeling like people were whispering about "poor Ginny Rose."

But she'd forgotten the charm of this particular pub, the first Garrett had taken her to when they'd newly arrived in Port Willis together. Looking around the room, she studied the nooks and crannies, the way the tables sat intimately but felt communal at the same time, how the little trinkets and displays on the wall set the fishing village tone without overdoing it. "I believe since the eighteenth century. Rumor has it many a prime minister has dined here in the last few centuries."

"I can't even imagine that kind of history. Arizona only became a state a little over a hundred years ago." Sophia tucked a strand of jet-black hair behind her ear. Despite having just traveled all day, she looked put together without seeming like she was trying too hard: her slacks only slightly rumpled, her blouse chic, but more Target than Barneys, her makeup pretty but minimal.

The woman seemed pleasant, if not a bit on the quiet side, and the fact that she was staying for the whole summer meant Ginny would have some steady help in the bookstore—especially if first appearances meant anything.

Ginny pulled a menu from between the salt and pepper shakers and handed it to Sophia. "They're known for their roasted artichoke and garden pea tagliatelle, but the stargazy pie is supposed to be good as well."

"You haven't tried it?" Sophia opened the menu, her white-painted fingernails tapping the plastic cover.

"Ugh, no. I actually hate fish."

"Has it been hard living here then?" Sophia cracked a smile.

"I actually grew up near the water." Ginny shrugged and leaned back in her chair. "My dad worked all the time—still does—and my mother was the president of a million charity organizations, so she didn't ever have time to cook. So I'd just either request something non-seafoody from our chef or whip something up myself." Shoot, she'd let it slip that they'd had a chef. What would Sophia think of Ginny now?

But she wasn't that person anymore—the kowtowing daughter of a millionaire with a trust fund that would set her up for life. When she'd come here, Ginny had left behind the Bentley name and all it stood for.

Thankfully, Sophia didn't seem to have a reaction to that tidbit of info. "I'm sure I would accidentally poison someone if I tried to cook. Despite my mom's best efforts to teach me, I'm horrible in the kitchen. I did much better in the classroom."

"It's actually quite fun." More than fun—once upon a time, she'd dreamed of going to culinary school. But her parents had shot that idea down as soon as the words left her lips.

Mary Patrick, whose family owned the restaurant, approached their table, a tentative smile in place. "Hi, Ginny. How are you? We haven't seen you in a while."

She and her husband, Blake, had been friends with Garrett since high school, and the four of them had enjoyed many a pizza and movie night together. Until Garrett left. Then, when Mary had tried to call, Ginny couldn't move past the question of whether they were really friends with her . . . or just Garrett.

But seeing Mary now, she realized how much she'd missed having a friend all of these months. "Hey. Yeah, things have been . . . you know." She cleared her throat. "This is Sophia Barrett. She's renting the room over the bookshop for the summer."

"Ah, I'd heard something about that. Welcome to the Village Pub. I'm Mary." She leaned in close to Ginny. "We're all hoping you and Garrett can work this thing out between you. It must be hard."

"Thank you." Ginny gripped her menu a bit harder, flicking her eyes toward Sophia. Had she heard the exchange? But if she had, she pretended otherwise and kept studying her menu.

After a slight hesitation, Mary turned to Sophia. "Do you know what you'd like to order?"

Sophia bit her lip. "I'll take the roasted lamb, please." She flashed a smile at Ginny, something hidden in the depths of her piercing blue eyes. "I'm not much for being adventurous."

"Excellent choice. My da makes the best lamb on the northern shore. And for you, Gin?"

"The normal, please." She couldn't go wrong with shepherd's pie. "Thanks, Mary."

The waitress bit her lip and patted Ginny's shoulder. "It'll be right up." She left them.

Ginny swallowed, her throat dry. She took a sip of water.

"So, tell me more about the bookstore and the town." Sophia's gaze moved to the window and settled on something in the distance.

Whew, yes, please. "What do you want to know?" The things she loved about it couldn't really be explained and would never be written in a guidebook. At first, Port Willis had represented an escape, a new life for herself with Garrett by her side. It was all about a feeling she got when she waded in the brisk water overlooked by the bluffs, the pride when she sold a book and built on Garrett's dream, the sweet memories of Garrett chasing her along their favorite hillside trail, making love in the tall grass where no one could find them.

"I suppose I know a lot of the basics about the town itself. I'm a bit of a research nerd." Sophia picked up the saltshaker and ran her fingers over the grooves in the glass surface. "So how did you end up here, so far from home?"

Ginny winced. She hadn't intended to mention Garrett. But Sophia was going to be here for months. She'd learn about Garrett sooner or later. "My husband was born here." The memories were sweet and painful all at once. "He was working at a bookstore in Boston, and I was in my junior year at Harvard when we began dating. We met through mutual friends. He always intended to come home and open a bookstore eventually, then a chain of bookstores throughout England and maybe all of Europe. It had been his mother's dream to do that, but she died when he was young, so the dream became his. He'd planned to get some experience, earn enough money to do it, but then his dad passed away suddenly when we were dating. He asked me to come home with him for the funeral. I did, and I never left. We married a few weeks after we arrived here."

"That's such a sweet story."

Sophia's words startled Ginny. She'd lost herself in the reverie for a moment. Remembering how broken Garrett had been over his father's death, how determined to find some purpose in the pain. He'd clung to her, and she'd never felt more needed or more beloved. For the first time ever, she'd belonged.

"My parents didn't think it was so sweet. But that's a story for another day."

Sophia reached across the table and squeezed Ginny's arm for the second time tonight. The touch was surprisingly comforting, and another tear sprang to Ginny's eyes.

"When did your husband pass away?"

"What?" Ginny nearly jerked from Sophia's touch. "He isn't dead." Her new tenant must not have heard Mary's comment about Garrett after all.

"Oh. I'm so sorry. The way you talked about him, I assumed . . . but I was probably projecting my own experience onto the situation."

"What do you mean?"

Sophia's lip quivered. "My fiancé . . . He died recently. Well, a year and a little over three months ago." She looked out the window once again. "But that too is a story for another day."

"I'm so sorry, Sophia." The pain of being separated from Garrett was bad enough. To imagine him dead—the thought punched her in the gut and stole her breath.

"That's one reason I'm here. To heal. Finally move on, if such a thing is possible." Sophia pulled her gaze back to Ginny, and she put on a brave smile. "Let's change the subject to something less dreary. What's your favorite thing about owning a bookstore?"

"I thought you wanted a less dreary topic. The truth is, the bookstore was more Garrett's dream than mine. I'm afraid I'm not very good at it. We're . . . I'm kind of in trouble. Financially, I mean."

"That's awful." Sophia tapped her fingers on the tabletop. "I'm aware I just arrived and don't know much about running a bookstore, but I do love books, so if there's anything I can do to help, I will."

"Thank you. That's very kind." Ginny paused. She hated to burden a virtual stranger . . . Oh, why not? Sophia would be involved in the day-to-day operations of the bookstore anyway. "Actually, I'd love your help in brainstorming some ways to make the store more attractive to patrons or turn a bigger profit."

Just then, Mary delivered their food. Steam rose from Ginny's shepherd's pie, a lovely mixture of potatoes, vegetables, and lamb. Personally, she'd have added a bit more onion and thyme, but this version was nearly as good as her own.

Ginny filled Sophia in on the things she'd tried already and what issues she'd run into.

Sophia swallowed a bite of her lamb. "This is just a fleeting thought, but as we were walking through the bookstore, I noticed the rare books are buried in the back somewhere. Is that intentional?"

Ginny shrugged as she moved her fork through her mashed potatoes and snagged a carrot. "That's just where they've always been."

"But your specialty is rare books, right? Then maybe those should be front and center."

"Wow. Why have I never thought of that?"

"Also, your website really could use some work." Sophia waved her fork in the air. "Before I booked the reservation, I looked it up. It's fairly basic, but it doesn't offer any opportunities for people to buy online. And you know with Amazon and other internet giants that online is the wave of the future. Well, it's the wave of the present, really."

"That's a really good idea too. I know a guy in town who builds websites." Steven was another of Garrett's chums from school, and he'd always been kind to her.

They continued tossing ideas around, putting their brains together and creating a storm of thoughts that started a stirring in Ginny's soul. A stirring that looked and felt a lot like hope.

And Ginny knew she might have just met the answer to her many prayers—someone to help shoulder her burden and bring success back to Rosebud Books.

8

✦✦✦✦✦✦

SOPHIA

Most people wouldn't voluntarily spend their days buried in the back room of a bookstore, sorting through dusty editions of classics and non-classics alike. After all, it was ill-lit, the dust bunnies caused frequent sneeze attacks, and she hadn't seen another soul for hours.

But Sophia was not most people.

She hummed as she sat cross-legged on the wood floor, piles of books surrounding her. Volumes large and small, some with torn jackets and frayed covers, threads coming loose, others in more pristine condition, as if they'd never been cracked. The poor dears. To never have fulfilled your purpose, even if you were only a book . . .

Of course, in Sophia's mind, there was no such thing as "only a book." Books were whole other worlds wrapped in cardboard and parchment.

"You're ridiculous, Sophia." Her whispered words echoed in the storeroom, but no one was around to hear them. Ginny was up front working the desk.

It still came as a surprise to Sophia how quickly they'd become friends, though it was clear that Ginny didn't want to discuss her husband and their current situation. Sophia had heard others around town whispering about it, but she'd closed her ears to the gossip. If Ginny ever decided to tell her what was going on, Sophia would be there to listen. Even though she'd initially planned to focus solely on writing her own story while she was here, something drew her to Ginny. She wanted to help the woman, and not just as a therapist, but as a friend.

It was why Sophia had offered to help any way she could—thus, how she'd landed the task of sorting through books that had been donated or purchased and then shoved in boxes and stuffed in the back for who knew how long. Ginny hoped to get their entire inventory up online as soon as possible, but she was so busy managing the other aspects of the store, she hadn't had a chance. And Sophia really didn't mind, although she looked forward to this weekend when she could explore more of the area surrounding Port Willis. She'd spent most of last Sunday getting settled in and acquainted with Port Willis itself.

Sure, she'd been here five days and still hadn't written a word of her own story. But she had time. She only had to wait for inspiration.

"How's it going back here?" Ginny poked her head through the door.

The light from the doorway hurt Sophia's eyes. She waved her hands at the piles of books. "I've made decent progress. Of course, in order to determine pricing on them, I have to examine them thoroughly, including skimming the pages for blemishes, which inevitably leads me to reading . . . so I'm afraid I'm a bit slower than others might be."

There were just so many new-to-her authors and books she'd never heard of, each one fascinating. Even with boring titles like *Horticulture in the Eighteenth Century* and *Cornish Mining History Explained*, each book held secrets she longed to discover.

Ginny laughed. "You're likely more effective at pricing than I am. I'm not much of a reader."

Sophia lifted her eyebrows and wiped her dusty hands on her jeans. "And you run a bookstore?"

"It's business, and it was my husband's dream before it was mine." For a moment, a flash of sadness passed over Ginny's face, but it was quickly replaced with a smile. "When I have free time, I'd much rather experiment in the kitchen or binge watch *The Great British Bake Off.*"

She squatted next to a pile of books, picked up the one on top, and flipped through it. "Oh, snore. I feel so guilty giving you this job."

"Don't. I'm loving it. How do you have so many unique books I've never heard of?"

"Families from all over Port Willis and surrounding areas donate books to us, or we buy them for a pittance when they want to clean out their attics. Our policy has always been to take them, sell what we can, and then donate any leftovers to the public library or school system. Of course, some are in such deplorable condition, that's impossible." She picked up a bound notebook. "And then we get stuff like this, which isn't even a book. Is that the toss pile?"

"No, that pile isn't sorted yet. I can't bear the thought of tossing any of these books." Sophia took the notebook in hand. She flipped it open, finding pages and pages of three-hole-punched, 8.5" by 11" printed paper.

Sophia's eyes skimmed the first page. "Oh wow. This one seems to be a story or something."

Ginny held out her hand. "May I see?"

Sophia handed it over. Ginny perused the pages briefly. "Maybe a school project?" She gave it back to Sophia and stood.

"I wonder if whoever donated this box knew this was in here. They might be sad to have lost it. Do you keep a record of donors?"

"We probably should, but no."

Sophia cracked the spine of the notebook once again. Just because something wasn't published didn't mean that what she held in her hands didn't have value. What a treasure. "Do you mind if I buy this from you?"

Ginny looked at her as if she'd gone mental. "Just keep it. And if you come across any other books that don't meet our criteria for selling or donating, you're welcome to those as well."

"Really? Awesome. Thanks." Sophia moved the notebook aside and created a new pile.

"I'd better get back up front. Thank you again for all your hard work. You haven't even been here a week and you're already making my life easier."

Sophia picked up a new book and began examining the cover. "I'm happy to help."

Ginny left the room, shutting Sophia in half-darkness again.

Dust kicked up from the door's movement and Sophia sneezed. She refocused on the book in front of her, but her thoughts kept drifting to the notebook. Finally, when she couldn't stand it a moment longer, she penciled a price into the book she held, set it in the sell pile, and picked up the notebook.

Sophia opened to the first page and began reading:

On the outside, I was a simple woman, with a simple life.

The words, the tone—something about the writing resonated with her. Perhaps Sophia could see a bit of herself in this unnamed author. How could anyone have given this away? And was it a work of fiction or truth?

Whatever it was, one thing was certain. The "simple woman" had a story worth telling.

Oh.

The truth smacked her between the eyes. Joy's words flooded back to her: *"Your story is worth telling, Soph."*

Sophia breathed in deep. This girl had a story worth telling—and so did Sophia.

It was worth telling.

It *was*.

Why did she have to try so hard to convince herself that her story was worth it, when she could so easily find worth in anyone else's words, even this faceless somebody she'd discovered by accident?

Because she shouldn't have had a story in the first place. It was her fault for letting it happen. For staying. She knew the signs, what they'd eventually lead to.

No, it wasn't *my fault.*

Frustration clawed up her throat and came out as a groan. Even after months of therapy—even after being a therapist and knowing what she "should" feel—her insides were all mixed up.

Because some days, she missed David with a fierceness that surprised her. But then it was followed by relief. Then anger at herself. Then guilt. Then a tumult of other emotions.

But no matter what she felt, she knew deep down that her story did matter. She had to fight against the lie that it didn't. And if she didn't protect her own story or have the courage to write it down, no one else would.

No one else could.

Sophia set aside the notebook, dusted off her jeans, opened the door, headed up the stairs to her bedroom, and found the white journal and pen she'd brought all the way across the ocean. She curled up in the window seat, which overlooked the street below. For a moment, fear fought to overtake her. She heard David's words: *Not good enough. Not strong enough.*

If she didn't fight for herself, who would?

So with the slash of her pen across the page, she finally joined the battle.

9

EMILY

DECEMBER 1856

On the outside, I was a simple woman, with a simple life.

I did not, however, have simple dreams. And in that moment, as I imagined each breath might be my father's last, they seemed most impossible.

The candle flickered on the table next to my father's bed, the yellowish hue of his skin lessened in the dim lighting. I laid aside the book I'd been attempting to read and poured myself a glass of water from the pitcher on Father's nightstand. I hardly felt the cool liquid slide down my throat.

It, like the rest of me, was numb.

Rain pattered on the house, bringing with it wind that rattled the windows and howled as if a specter roamed outside—appropriate weather for such a night as this.

I leaned over Father, trying to discern whether his chest still moved.

It did. But for how long?

I inhaled a sob, trying to hold it back tight inside, determined not to let it loose. For what good would that do? It wouldn't bring back the father I had loved. He had been gone for two years, since the day Mama passed from this life to the next, and Father had traded his Bible for the bottle.

A knock sounded on the door.

"Who would be out in this weather?" I don't know why I said it aloud. Father had been unconscious for days, and I had not left his side but for a few moments at a time.

The last words he'd said to me were forever etched in my memory, as I knew they could be his last. I'd thought he was sleeping, so I jumped when he latched onto my hand as I read. He'd inclined his head toward me, but had not seen me. Not really. *All we have in life are the choices we make. We must make choices we can live with—and die with, if it comes to that.*

Did that mean he believed his choices to be right? Or the only ones available to him?

Perhaps I might never know.

The knock came again, heavy against the door. "I will return shortly, Father. Someone is here. Perhaps the doctor again."

I did not believe the words as they left my mouth. Dr. Walter Shelley had come but once, looked Father over, shaken his head, and muttered about what a shame this all was. Hardly helpful, but he required payment all the same. I had given him the last two farthings I possessed, hidden away in my apron so Father could not find them and use them for something unsavory.

I grabbed the candlestick and left the room that smelled of death and malcontent. The parsonage was not the smallest I had seen, but I was still able to cross from my father's bedroom to the front door in a few steps. Before wrestling open the thick door, I pulled my shawl tighter around my shoulders. Since I had not been expecting visitors, especially at this hour, my hair fell in blond waves down my back instead of being pinned. At this point, it was of small concern to me what others might think.

I pulled open the door and peeked outside.

"Edward." The word carried more weight than I meant it to, but the days of caring for Father alone had removed the careful guard on my feelings that I had placed there years before.

He stepped forward, the moonlight glinting down behind him, granting him the appearance of an angelic being. His brown hair was plastered across his forehead, his coat splattered with rain, and his chest heaved a bit, as if he had run all the way here from the main house like he had countless times when we were children. He towered over me, not because he was terribly tall for a male, but because I had inherited my mother's slight stature.

"Louisa told me. I only just arrived home or I'd have been here sooner."

I confess I had wondered at his absence, had begun to assume the worst—that he, like everyone else in this town, despised us.

But when my dearest friend stepped forward and took the candle from me, setting it aside and encircling me with his broad arms, resting his chin on the top of my head, my doubts slammed against one another and shattered. If I had not the sorrow regarding my father filling up my heart, this moment would have been the culmination of so much joy—finally being in the arms of this man I'd loved for years.

This man, whom I could never have as more than a friend, and for the last few days, had thought perhaps a distant memory.

"I'm sorry for getting your clothes damp." Edward released me, and I suddenly felt the rush of cool air seeping in from the open door.

I hurried to close it. "Think nothing of it."

"How is he?" Edward removed his overcoat and slung it over a chair. Formality had never been a mark of our friendship, and it would not begin tonight.

"It's only a matter of time." The words I uttered were meant to be brave, but they only hung in the air heavy with loss. The sob I had been holding inside nearly escaped. The anger too.

"You don't deserve this, Emily." He took my small hand in his own and squeezed.

"What do any of us deserve, really?" I shrugged.

He stared at me. "You most certainly deserve better than to have a drunkard—"

"Edward. Please." I glanced toward my father's room. Though he seemed to lie unaware, perhaps some part of him could still hear us. I did not want his last moments to be filled with condemnation. "He was a good father to me, once upon a time. When he was able to be."

I tried desperately to hold on to those memories, to not become consumed with thoughts of betrayal and abandonment. No, my father had not physically left me, but he had, in a way, chosen this desertion.

He simply could not live in a world without Mama.

And though I couldn't understand it, I could not hate him for it either.

Edward sighed, pushed his hand through his hair, a gesture he had always made when feeling chagrined. "You are right. I was only thinking of you. You have endured too much already. It is not fair. Why must you also endure this descent into despair and poverty?"

Poverty did not concern me, so long as I had all the essentials. It was the impending loss of my father, my home, Edward, our tree . . . everything I loved. My throat tightened as I forced the sob back down. "You have always been a good friend. I will carry fond memories of our childhood capers with me wherever I go."

"Go? Where are you going?"

The sharpness in his tone caused me to look up into his eyes, those eyes I knew so well—brown with flecks of gold, a strange assortment of colors to create the perfect combination of kindness, passion, and brilliance. "When . . . all of this is over, I must find another place to live. Your parents have already been too kind to allow us to remain here, despite the fact my father could no longer fulfill his duties as reverend." Or *would* no longer, rather.

"Why would I want to praise the one who hurt me, Emily?"

The anguish in my father's voice still haunted me because I did not know how to answer his query. My faith had never been as strong as his once was.

"But where?" Edward broke into my thoughts. "You don't have any other family, do you?"

I winced at the reminder. "None that would assist me. I'll find a job as a governess again."

"You despise teaching."

"What choice do I have?" I picked up the candle once more.

"You could marry."

The candle nearly slipped from my grasp. A caustic laugh rumbled from my lips. "You know how I feel on the subject, Edward." If I could not marry him, then I would have no one. Not that I'd told him that. He merely believed I preferred my independence. "And who would marry the daughter of the town's fallen preacher?"

Certainly not Edward, who came from a fine family with connections and prospects. To him, I had only ever been like a younger sister who lived at the parsonage on his family's estate, who could best him at tree climbing and every other rough-and-tumble thing it was not right for a "proper lady" to do.

"*You* are not fallen, but I do see your dilemma." Edward's lips pressed together. "All right, then what other skills do you possess?"

I looked away. I had never told him of the way I spent my evenings, pouring from my soul onto paper with a pen. No one knew, though I intended one day to tell the whole world. It would be my redemption, the only way to ever truly be free. But for now, I settled for a mild joke. "I can make up beds and sew with the best of them."

Edward's brow wrinkled but then flattened again. "Do be serious, Em. You could not stoop to becoming a common servant."

In moments like this, I had to forgive Edward for his snobbery. He was born to it and perhaps could not hear how he sounded. "Hard work is never stooping. And I may not have much choice. Which is why I've settled on becoming a governess again."

I turned toward the bedroom. "You came to see him, did you not?"

"I . . . well, of course I will see him, but it was my main purpose to check on you."

"Come, then." I led him to the bedroom. He followed me through the doorway, where once there had been laughter and love and now there was only a diseased man who had abandoned his faith and all his hope.

Though I had tried to be, I was not enough to bring the light back to his eyes.

"Father." I took his cold hand in mine. The veins under his sallow skin resembled a spider's web. "Edward is here to see you."

No reaction.

Edward came closer and cleared his throat as if to speak. Then he paused. "Emily." He reached his fingers to my father's neck, then turned his brown-gold eyes toward mine. "He's gone."

"No." My eyes flew to my father's chest, the one that had risen slowly up and down before I had set foot from this room.

And the sob that had been lodged inside me forced its way upward from my chest, ripping my insides with violent strength.

10

⚜

GINNY

Ginny's thumb hovered over the Send button. All she had to do was press down, and Garrett would know she was thinking of him.

But reason won out and she deleted the text, one character at a time.

He had asked for space. Others thought she was crazy to give it to him, but weren't spouses supposed to give each other what the other needed?

She shoved her phone into the back pocket of her jeans, catching a glimpse at the time before it disappeared. Oh! Her appointment with Steven was in five minutes.

Ginny grabbed her purse and slung it over her shoulder. Of course, there was no one to usher out of the bookstore. In fact, she'd only had two customers the entire day. With a sigh, she walked to the bookstore's front door and flipped the sign to indicate they'd be open again tomorrow morning.

Granted, tourist season would be in full swing soon, but if she didn't do something to get more customers, she might be flipping that sign for the last time before it even began.

She exited the bookstore and locked up, then turned and started walking toward Steven's place.

When Sophia had first mentioned improving Rosebud Books' website last Saturday, Ginny had tried to look at it with fresh eyes. After a few minutes, she concluded that Sophia was right—it was difficult to navigate. The design, which had seemed so state-of-the-art five years ago, now felt outdated and clunky.

She'd tried to fiddle around with some of the design and figure out the best way to add her stock online—but the minutiae had soon given her a headache. As she rubbed her temples, something she'd heard her father say growing up came to her mind: *Hire someone else to do what you can't do well.*

But that required money. In fact, a new website or even an update to one could get quite costly.

Of course, to make money, sometimes you had to spend money. But how did one know when the cost was worth it and would actually lead to more sales?

This was one of those times she wished she'd paid better attention in Harvard business school, a place she'd never wanted to be in the first place.

Her head had pounded all the more. And her fingers itched—to get into the kitchen and bake something, anything. Escape.

Think, Ginny. Think.

Steven.

Yes, Steven. Garrett's old friend was exactly who she needed to see right now. He'd started a web design business a few years ago, and he probably wouldn't charge her quite as much as a London firm. Besides, she'd much rather go with a company she trusted than some random one she found on the Internet.

So she'd called and made an appointment.

And now, she finally reached the tiny house where Steven lived near the docks. Ginny knocked.

The door opened and Steven appeared. His red hair was slightly rumpled and he wore low-slung gym shorts and a white T-shirt. "Hey, Gin. How are you?"

Nearby, she heard the call of seagulls and the clanging of boat bells.

"We have a meeting, right?" She eyed his apparel. "Because it looks like you're ready for a workout—or bed." Steven had always been easy to talk to and tease. He and Garrett had been friends since Steven's family moved to Port Willis in grade school.

Steven laughed. "Yeah, but I like to be comfortable while I work. Come on in."

She followed him inside the obvious bachelor pad. Laundry sat piled in baskets and draped on the arms of the couch, half-folded and forgotten. An empty pizza box from Valero's adorned the coffee table, and the television droned from its spot hanging on the opposite wall. His horrid putrid-green leather sofa was the worst eyesore, though it competed with a few abstract paintings that made her nauseated if she stared at them too long.

But while slightly messy, the house was not dirty. It didn't smell bad either—more like fresh soap and spice mixed together.

She'd missed the smell of clean man in her own house.

Ginny swallowed a knot in her throat and sank onto Steven's couch. "Thanks for squeezing me in. I know you're busy."

He sat next to her, angling his body toward her and leaning back against the arm of the sofa. "I told you I'm here if you ever need me."

"I appreciate it. Like I said on the phone, we . . . well, *I* need to figure out some ways to bring in more customers. Sophia, my summer employee, recommended revamping our website."

"Right. Did you take a look at some of the sample sites I've done?" He pulled his laptop from a bag at the foot of the sofa and opened it.

"Yes. I liked a few of the options. Specifically, the third option, I think. But . . ." Oh, this was awkward. "How much would something like that be?" If it was beyond her budget, she couldn't accept his help, not without being certain she could pay him.

Steven waved a hand, dismissing her question, then pulled the site up onto the screen. "Don't worry about that right now. What did you like about this design?"

She looked once more at the site on his screen. "I like the clean lines, but the creative bent to it too. It seems like it'd be easy to find your way around, but it's not boring either. The plug-ins you have for keeping track of inventory sounded intriguing, too, and just what I'd need." Ginny paused. "But I can't not worry about the cost, Steven. Things are . . . tight."

He shut the lid of the laptop and studied her. "Then why redo the site? What's your vision here?"

She explained her goals for the project. "Sophia is funny. She loves books. Like, loves them the way macaroni loves cheese. The way noodles love spaghetti sauce. The way—"

"I think I get the general idea." Steven smirked.

"Right. Well, anyway, she talks about books as friends who need a place to belong, a new home. And . . . I guess it's kind of silly, but I sort of relate to that. So the idea of getting them online, where we can hopefully sell them more quickly, really resonated with me and seemed to be one of the best ways to turn our business around."

Wow. Funny how her brain worked sometimes.

"What?" Steven lifted an eyebrow. He must have noticed her awe.

She shook her head. "I just don't think I'd made that connection until right now. I've always been a verbal processor, but boy—thanks for asking me that. So many things lately have been purely about getting the bookstore out of the red, but this . . . this goes a little deeper, I guess."

The serious weight of her thoughts hung heavy in the air.

"I *am* pretty amazing like that." Steven winked at her, grinning.

She let loose a giggle. What a nice friend to make her laugh when she should have been crying. "Well, yes, that too."

·He sobered. "But really. If you do ever need to verbally process, I'm a pretty good listener."

"You are. That's it—I'm finding you a woman, pronto. Oh! Sophia's single. Maybe I should set you two up." Ginny nudged Steven with her elbow.

He put his laptop away, chuckling. "I'm going to be too busy designing your site to date anyone right now."

"Oh, come on. There's always time for a little romance. But you still haven't told me how much it will be." She twisted her hands in her lap. "I'm not sure—"

"I'm doing it free of charge."

"What? No, I couldn't accept that. That's not why I came to you. I refuse to take advantage of our friendship."

"But you did come to me, and I want to help your vision come alive." His teasing eyes turned serious once more. "No matter what happens with Garrett, you'll always have friends here. Though I do hope you two can work things out. I'm rooting for you."

She swallowed hard. "Thank you. That means the world."

11

SOPHIA

Today was the day. She was finally going to finish writing her story.

Sophia settled on a blanket in her chosen spot near Chaser's Beach about a half hour's drive from Port Willis. She'd promised herself that she'd branch out a bit and see more of England, and this was a start. It was still early on Saturday, so the beach wasn't very crowded yet, though research had told her it was a popular spot for surfing.

Not that she'd be partaking in that—not today. But maybe someday soon.

She sat on the grassy headland that overlooked the golden sand below. There were already numerous surfers plunging their arms through the water, paddling out on their boards to catch the next wave. Some rode monster waves back toward the land. What would it be like to feel weightless, to let the water carry her, to be one with the surf and sea?

The clouds from yesterday's storm seemed to be lingering just enough to make it a bit chilly. She zipped her jacket and pulled her white journal from the bag that sat next to her. Last night, she'd reread the story in the mystery notebook for the tenth time. Something about the author's yearning spoke to her soul, and she knew she had to get away and write more than the few pathetic pages she'd penned since first finding the notebook three days ago. Her fingers itched to sketch the words of her heart onto the paper, like Emily had in the story.

With trembling fingers, Sophia opened her own journal. Her eyes flitted over what she'd already written. The words fell flat. All she'd managed to say was a whole lot of nothing.

Why was this so hard? She knew what she felt, didn't she?

She ripped the two pages from the journal, balled them up, and stuffed them inside her bag.

"I thought you seemed a creative soul when we first met."

Her head turned and looked up to find a man standing over her, a surfboard in his hands, a wetsuit covering his body—his quite sculpted body. She blinked and shook the thought from her mind.

"Um, hi." He looked familiar. "Do I know you?"

"Car park. You were blocking the way . . ."

The kind, handsome stranger. "Right. Hi."

"You said that already." His grin was contagious. "I'm William."

"Sophia."

"I know." He crouched down so he wasn't towering over her anymore.

She raised an eyebrow. "Should I be worried?" How did he know who she was?

"Port Willis is a small town. Also, you're working for my sister-in-law."

Ah, yes, Ginny had mentioned her husband's brother a few times in passing. "The lit professor, right?"

"My reputation precedes me."

For some reason, the comment made her giggle. She never giggled. There was just something so . . . cute about this guy. "I suppose it does."

"Mind if I sit for a moment?"

She eyed his surfboard and apparel. "I don't want to keep you from surfing."

He shrugged. "I come out here as often as I can. It's all right if I'm a bit delayed today."

"Okay, then sure. Sit on down." She scooted over so he could join her on the blanket. "And what do you mean, I seem like a 'creative soul'?"

He pointed to her journal. "I saw you ripping pages from your diary there. Only intensely creative people get frustrated enough to do that."

"Oh." If only he knew how wrong he was. She was no writer, though writer's block had become her frenemy. Sophia closed the journal and pushed it back into her bag. "I thought this would be an inspiring place."

"And is it?"

"I've only just arrived, so I'm not sure yet. But it is gorgeous and so different from home."

"Where is that?"

"Arizona. Phoenix, to be precise."

"The desert, then."

"You know American geography. Have you ever been?" She pulled her knees into her chest and studied him. He didn't seem much older than her, though Ginny had said he was a tenured professor already. Maybe thirty-five?

"Sadly, no. I've always wanted to, but my travels have stayed on this side of the pond."

"I haven't traveled much, but in college, I took a trip to London with students and faculty from my university the summer before my junior year. We visited the British Library and I was forever ruined for American literature. From that moment on, all I wanted to do was read what the Brits wrote."

William's mouth curved into a smile. "See? Creative soul. I knew it. And who are your favorite authors?"

"Of course there's Austen, the Brontës, Dickens, and Hardy. But an author whose work has really spoken to me lately is Robert Appleton."

His eyes brightened, and he shifted his body to face her more. "Most Americans have never even heard of that particular author."

"One of my professors who chaperoned the trip abroad was obsessed with him. Of course, Dr. Rosenthal was convinced 'he' was really a 'she.'"

"I actually focused on Cornish authors for my dissertation. Robert Appleton was one of my key focuses. And I tend to agree with your professor."

She'd considered the possibility but wasn't sure which way to lean. "So little is known of his life, so what makes you think he wrote under a pseudonym?"

"That's one of the main reasons. Why wouldn't more be known of him? Just look at how much is known about Charlotte Brontë and her sisters, who wrote around the same time. But not one single letter or piece of information was ever recovered about Robert Appleton. Of course, for many, that adds to his appeal. Still, outside of Cornwall, his is a quiet fame."

"Once my professor introduced me, I fell in love." Sophia leaned back on her hands. "I've read each of his books at least twenty times."

"Which is your favorite?"

"That's like asking a mom who her favorite kid is. Impossible to decide. They each bring something different to the table. Each one speaks to me in different ways. Like *Whisper Across the Bluffs*. It's a story about courage and becoming someone new, and goodness knows I need to be more like Margaret." She sighed, her eyes studying and following the horizon. "And then there's *Moonbeams*. A great love that conquers all, even death? How could that not speak to someone?"

"Indeed. I love how Appleton took so much inspiration from the Bible, don't you?"

She pulled her gaze back to William. "Did he?"

"That's what my dissertation was about, actually. Biblical symbols and parallels in Cornish fiction."

Ironic what a pull Appleton's stories had on Sophia's soul then, given her own wavering faith. She shrugged her shoulders. "Regardless of what inspired them, they've in turn inspired me. It's why I'm here." Partly, anyway.

For a moment, they were quiet. Then he started chuckling.

"What?"

"Outside of my colleagues at the university, I've never met someone who enjoyed reading as much as you. It's refreshing."

Sophia found herself laughing along. "I'm definitely a book nerd."

"Do you like the show *Unsolved Mysteries of a Literary Nature*?"

"I'm sorry, what?"

"You mean you don't have it in America? I never miss an episode. It's brilliant. They discuss all the theories of mysteries within and surrounding literature. For instance, who wrote *Beowulf*? Or in James's *The Ambassadors*, what was the 'little nameless object'?"

Sophia couldn't keep a grin from spreading across her face. "Okay, you officially win nerd of the year right there."

William laughed. "Don't pretend that you're not going to go look it up when you return home."

"You got me." Actually, the show sounded right up her alley. It was the kind David would have mocked her for liking, so she would have waited until he went out with his buddies on Friday night and snuggled up on the couch to watch it.

"So how long do you plan to stay in Cornwall?"

She snapped back to the present, with thoughts about her fiancé souring the beauty around her. "Three months. Then I have to return to my job."

"Which is?"

She picked at her cuticles. "I'm a women's therapist." That was all she could manage. Why was she able to go on and on the moment anyone mentioned books, but when asked about her own life, she shut down? If she'd been psychoanalyzing someone else, she'd have said perhaps they were not able to face the pain of their past or present and so avoided those topics altogether.

But she'd been in counseling for months now. She'd talked ad nauseam about how David had made her feel, how she longed for a fresh start.

So why was there still some sort of blockage there? It wasn't just with William. He was actually fairly easy to talk to. Of course, she wasn't used to talking much to men other than David. He'd grown into a jealous person the last few months of his life, constantly accusing her of things she hadn't done, so it'd been easier to just avoid other guys.

She could hear David's voice in her head now, all the lies—what she knew were lies—raining down on her mind:

Slut.

Seductress.

Cheater.

Nonsense, all of it. They'd been lies when he'd thrown them in her face, and they were lies now. But even things she could identify as lies held weight sometimes.

"Well, I'll let you get back to your journaling then."

William stood, snatching up the surfboard in his hands.

It'd be easy to let him walk away. To dismiss him and not engage. To push away anything she really felt, to bury it deep inside and never go digging for it again.

But the path toward healing wasn't an easy one.

"No. Stay, if you like. I'm sorry. I was just thinking about things."

A smile graced his lips, and he plopped down once more. "Like what?"

Then they chatted for hours, till the sun was about to set and she realized she hadn't eaten a thing all day and he hadn't surfed and she hadn't written a word. But that was okay. Because she'd cracked the door to another friendship—let someone in. A man, no less. This was progress, whether she'd reached her "goal" for the day or not.

Her eyes scanned the beach, where a photographer set up his camera, ready to capture life in stillness. But life could not be captured that way, not really. A photo would always lack a little something, however beautiful, because a photo couldn't capture what the sprinkles of salt water felt like against the skin or how the warmth of the sun crested over her face and soaked itself in.

And if a camera had been pointed her way, it wouldn't be able to show how her heart was beating wildly at the way a man she had just met looked at her like she was more than just a little interesting—or how the equal fear and exhilaration of something new swept through her veins.

12

EMILY

AUGUST 1857

When I wrote, the dark days of my past obscured around the edges, and I was capable of forgetting for just a moment the pain of losing nearly everyone I have ever loved. Whenever I poured myself out on the pages and invited myself into a story, I found the kind of life I had always longed for.

If only that sort of magic could be translated to the rest of life.

My pen flew across the page as quickly as I could manage it, thoughts streaming from my mind through my hand and becoming etched onto the page. I spent every spare moment here at my desk, though those moments seemed few as of late. Being a governess to Edward's sisters had proved quite challenging at times, but he had been so kind to arrange it. I had no right to complain.

A knock sounded at my door, and a servant girl stepped inside. "Your presence is requested in the sitting room, Miss Fairfax."

"Thank you. I'll be there in a moment." Perhaps Edward's mother had more to discuss regarding the upcoming school year. I had already been tasked with making sure Edward's sister Louisa was as "accomplished" as possible, given that she would be presented during this year's social season.

The servant curtsied and closed the door behind her as she left.

I placed the pen on the desk and rolled my head either direction, rubbing the sore muscles at the base of my neck. How long had I sat here? I'd ended the school day early, given the children's desire to have a picnic and roam the countryside this afternoon.

In the schoolroom, I counted the seconds until we were finished. But when I held a pen, hours could pass without my notice.

I rose and checked my appearance in the ornate looking glass—a luxury I'd never had in the parsonage—and was astonished at how visible the sadness in my narrow brown eyes had become. Other than the freckles dotting my cheeks and a small ink stain on the front of my frock, I seemed presentable enough with my blond hair pulled back into tightly pinned plaits. Of course, I was not a great beauty like my mother and older sister had been, but I had always enjoyed the noble slope of my petite nose and the fact I could eat as much dessert as I liked and not worry about my dress becoming too snug.

With a quiet step, I left my room and walked down the long hallway of the house toward the sitting room. Before becoming the governess, I had only set foot inside the house on the rare occasion when the family had invited mine to dine with them. Edward and I had done most of our childhood romping outdoors on the family's grand estate.

Finally, I reached the sitting room. But when I stepped through the door, Edward's parents were nowhere to be found. His mother had recently hired a new decorator to adorn the room in the latest styles— red silk window treatments, gold-framed mirrors, damask furniture, wrought-iron candlesticks. A large chandelier overhead boasted the simple elegance of this home and its occupants.

The servant *had* said the sitting room, hadn't she? I turned back toward the hallway to inquire—and nearly collided with a tall figure.

"You simply couldn't wait a few extra moments so I could surprise you, could you?"

The voice brought to life every fiber of my being, and my eyes swung upward to find Edward standing before me. Edward, in the flesh. Edward, whom I had not seen since my father's funeral eight months before. He had been away at school and then living in London to help his father run some aspects of business after graduation.

I couldn't contain my grin. "When did you arrive?"

"Only just. I had to see how you were faring."

I forced myself to ignore the connotation of his words—that he had sought me out immediately upon arrival. It meant nothing to him, and everything to me. Even if he never loved me as I did him, to at least have his friendship was of paramount importance. I do not know how I could have survived my family's deaths without him. "I am well, thank you."

"Come. Let's wander the garden. It's such a lovely day." Edward ushered me through the door and outside, where the sun hung low in the sky. Dinner would be served soon, but for a few moments we could enjoy the glorious crispness of the air, an indicator that autumn would soon be upon us.

"I didn't know you had planned to come home."

We descended the steps leading from the house into the extensive gardens below. Rhododendrons, Himalayan magnolias, and more than 120 species of cream-and-white magnolias brightened each step we took. They were arranged in an orderly way, but I could imagine them longing to burst from their constrained beds and twirl about once they found their freedom.

"Really? I told Mother to inform you." Edward placed his hands behind his back as he walked. His top hat sat slightly askew on his head, and I had the urge to tip it off entirely. It was strange to see him dressed so formally when not so very long ago we scampered about in play clothes together, seeking adventure around every bend. "In any event, my business concluded sooner than I thought, so I was able to return a week earlier than intended."

"Perfect." We continued to follow the walkway, where orange exotic plants such as Kniphofia and Strelitzia reginae came into view, along with the blooms of Erythrina and Echium and the green pods of the okirah bush. Their brilliant colors drew my eye, and I stopped to gaze upon them. It had been too long since I had enjoyed a walk here. The outdoors used to invigorate me, provide my only solace, but I had allowed my circumstances to tame me. I did not much care for the weak and weepy woman those circumstances had left in their wake.

"You are very quiet. Again I must ask you . . . How are you faring?" Edward's question seemed to erupt in the silence.

I peeked at him. "I truly am well." His raised eyebrow gave me pause. "Most of the time."

"And the other times?"

"I have forgiven Father as best I am able." I began following the curve of the path once more. "As for being a governess, it is a lonely sort of life. The other servants do not interact with me, yet I am not on equal standing as your family. When I am not teaching the children, I take most meals in my room and spend the other hours either reading or . . ."

I clamped my lips shut. I had almost revealed my secret. Though Edward and I had always been forthright about everything, for some reason I held this particular secret back from him. He would not understand the desire to do something one was not "supposed" to do. His future had always been clear—heir to his family's business and estate, the only son upon whom the responsibility of caring for several sisters would fall. He would marry a wealthy woman of gentility who could increase his standing in society, father several sons, and be the sort of man everyone in the county respected.

I could not bear the thought that he would disapprove of the dreams of a poor woman who wanted to write and be published—something only a man generally succeeded at, at least in name—or worse, that he would not believe I could achieve it.

"Or . . . ?"

Quickening my steps, I pulled away from his gaze and rounded yet another bend in the garden, which opened up into a view of the tree where I'd first met Edward so many years ago. It sat rooted on the edge of the bluffs, the ocean crashing far below. No other trees, nor any plants, grew in the immediate vicinity, which only made its unfurling branches even grander. Despite its obvious age, the gnarled branches still sprouted new life, gorgeous greenery against a darkening sky peppered with clouds. In the distance, a new lighthouse watched over the bluffs below.

My breath left me. I had forgotten about this view—how, I do not know. For how could one forget something so reminiscent of heaven?

I walked toward the edge, where our tree was anchored, the place of a thousand memories between us. We would climb into its branches and sit for hours eating plums, watching the water swirl far below. Being in those branches had felt unsafe and like a cocoon all at once.

Now, the sea-sprayed wind hit my cheeks, and I determined to come back here with a journal to record the sights and sounds before me. Without translating my words from my heart to the page, I felt incapable of truly making sense of the heady feeling buzzing inside.

"Is my family treating you well?"

I spun at the sound of Edward's voice, took in the clean lines of his jaw, the way his brow crinkled in his worry. "Yes, of course. Your mother has been nothing but kind to me." Ever since my midwife mother had saved her life when Louisa was coming into the world, the two women had become friends. Before my mother passed, Edward's had promised to look after me. Hiring me as governess, I assumed, was her way of doing so.

"Good." Edward nudged me with his elbow. "Earlier I said I'd just arrived, but I did manage to make a quick stop before coming inside the house."

My eyes widened and I flew to the hollow of the tree, reaching inside in one fluid motion. I pulled from the depths a new edition of *Pride and Prejudice*. "Oh, Edward." It was a favorite of mine, and his family's copy had been lost for some time. I stroked the cover and imagined reuniting with Elizabeth and Mr. Darcy once more.

"It's yours to keep."

"Truly?"

He laughed. "Of course. My mother and sisters do not read much, and Austen is not quite in line with Father's tastes."

"It's perfect. Thank you." I plopped myself down in the tall grass not far from the tree. "Come. Tell me everything about how life has been these eight months."

Laugh lines formed around Edward's lips as he watched me. "Don't you think we should return to the house?"

I eyed the sun—it *was* growing late. But perhaps for a few minutes, I could pretend that life might bring me more than my destined loneliness. For I knew that my time with Edward, like this, just the two of us in the lingering sunlight, was limited. Once he grew old enough, his parents would ask him to seek a bride.

And though I loved him more than anyone else ever could, that bride would most certainly not be me.

13

SOPHIA

It had been a week since the discovery, and she couldn't get the notebook and its contents off her mind.

Sophia walked up the winding path that led into the hills surrounding Port Willis. The tall grass bowed to her as she passed, dancing a ballet so sweet and subtle she wished she could linger just to watch. But she also wanted to check out the old lighthouse up this way, because there was a mention of one toward the middle of Emily's mysterious story—whoever Emily was. Something within urged Sophia to see if she could discover more about her.

It was foolish, really. She didn't even know if Emily was a real person or a character dreamed up by some random author.

"Why does this matter so much?"

No one was around to hear the words she'd spoken, and yet she seemed to feel a deep stirring, almost like the muffled whisper of a voice trying to get out.

She polished off the last bite of a muffin she'd purchased at Trengrouse Bakery this morning. The wrapper crinkled as she shoved it in her pocket. Sweetness lingered on her tongue as she looked out over the bluffs. To her right and down a ways, the ocean spilled onto a rocky beach, soaking between the stones and retreating.

Sophia's short hair fluttered in the wind, her bangs flicking across her eyes. She pushed them away with one hand.

The lighthouse finally came into view. Ginny had said it was no longer in service but was open for exploration by the public. The lighthouse stood a few stories high, its outer walls whitewashed and wind battered. Craggy rocks surrounded the bluff on which the lighthouse perched. As Sophia approached, it seemed the smell of the sea was stronger here.

She looked both ways down the shoreline, but didn't see any tree that could have been the one Emily wrote about.

Sophia headed toward the door of the lighthouse, which was painted a bright red and propped open. She paused, listening, hearing nothing.

She was alone.

Taking another look at the ocean, she closed her eyes and let the breeze whisper across her cheeks. Then she ducked inside and began climbing the stone steps. Worn with age and use, they twisted upward in a spiral shape and ended in a room where the light operator must have worked. There was a large window that displayed a magnificent view of the Port Willis harbor and coastline.

It was impossible to tell if this was the same lighthouse as in Emily's story. What had she expected? Some sort of cosmic sign? Of course, there were something like eight to eleven lighthouses around Cornwall—depending on which website could be trusted—and that was assuming Emily's story even took place here.

Keen disappointment flooded her heart. But why? It wasn't like unlocking the mystery of the story would help to unlock her own in any way. Not when she thought about it logically.

Yet her heart rebelled at that idea.

Footsteps sounded on the steps below. Sophia turned to find

Ginny emerging at the top. "Hi." She checked her watch. "I'm not supposed to be on shift yet, am I?"

Ginny shoved her hands into the pockets of her zipped-up Harvard hoodie. "No, not at all. William stopped in and said he'd cover for me for a few minutes so I could get away. I think he was hoping you'd be there, though." She winked.

"Oh." Sophia looked at the ground, a blush attacking her cheeks. She'd seen him a handful of times since the day at the beach last weekend. And every time, he captured her attention in a way that reminded her all too much of her attraction to David.

That had been a fast and furious fall, and she was not anxious to repeat it.

Besides, could she really trust her own taste in men? The only one she'd ever seriously dated had ended up being emotionally abusive, jealous, and controlling.

"I hope I'm not intruding on your solitude. It's been forever since I've been up here." Ginny reached for the window, tracing a G in the condensation left over from the morning dew. "It's where Garrett proposed, you know."

"Oh, wow." Was Ginny finally ready to tell her what was going on with her husband? Sophia leaned against the lighthouse wall. "I'm sure it brings back a lot of memories."

Ginny's finger stilled. She stuffed her hand once again into her pocket. "Yes." Silence hung between them for a few minutes. "You're probably wondering about him."

Sophia smiled softly. "I'm here if you want to talk."

Ginny blew out a breath, hard. "Let's just say he's been gone for six months." Then she detailed the rest of the story for Sophia.

There were so many things Sophia could say. So many strategies she'd learned for helping people through trials like this one. As a therapist, she knew how to help Ginny process the emotions she was feeling.

Sophia opened her mouth to employ one such strategy—but something entirely different came out. "I told you my fiancé died." What was she doing? One thing she never did as a therapist was share her own story. This was Ginny's time. It was about her, not Sophia.

Yet that same muffled voice inside of her seemed to be nudging her toward sharing. Because after all, today she was not a therapist, just a fellow sojourner on the path from pain.

"What I didn't tell you is that I waver between being sad about it . . . and glad for it."

As her own story came spilling out, Ginny moved closer, grabbing her hand and clutching it, not taking her eyes from Sophia's. "Oh, Sophia." Her eyes filled with tears. She blinked and they spilled onto her cheeks. "I've only known you a little while, but I already can tell you're an amazing person. You deserve nothing but happiness."

"A lot of people deserve happiness and don't get it."

"But a lot do. Maybe we just need to keep walking, even when it takes us somewhere we don't want to go. Maybe on the other side, that's where the happiness is found. But if we give up when we're wading through the muck and mire, we'll never discover . . ." Ginny paused. "Come on."

Then she tugged Sophia gently back down the stairs and out of the lighthouse. They walked a short path to the railing where the coast dropped off into rocks below.

"The ocean here is gorgeous, isn't it? So different from the view from my home on Nantucket, which is also beautiful. But it always signified imprisonment. A taunting of what could be but never was, not until I had the nerve to cross it and look for a different view. So, in a lot of ways, the ocean is a symbol to me, the thing that separates me from my old life. It's given me a new future." Her friend turned to Sophia. "If we give up hope, we'll never discover the ocean of possibility spread before us, or what it could hold."

Sophia squeezed Ginny's hand. "I don't know how you're able to be so optimistic with everything you're going through."

"My only other choice is to give up completely and admit defeat. And I can't, not when the stakes are so high."

They both fell into quiet reverie. The ocean rose and fell in the distance. Even though it smacked against the rocks every time it came ashore, it managed to get up the courage to come back. To give and take another thrashing. And it occurred to Sophia suddenly—over time, the rocks had been changed by the waves. Worn down.

Change was inevitable. But like Ginny, Sophia had a choice. How was she going to respond?

Emily's story.

There was that voice . . . again. It grew less muffled with every word it spoke. Would Ginny think she was crazy if she brought it up? She leaned on the wooden railing. "You know how I said I was here to write my own story?"

"Yes."

"I know this is nuts, but I feel like this journey is somehow linked to that notebook I found last week in your storeroom."

Ginny's eyebrow lifted. "What about it?"

With an inhale of fresh air, Sophia launched into an explanation. "It's filled cover to cover with elegant prose. I devoured it all in a few sittings. It's either about or written by a young woman who wants to be a writer. And the story she has to tell—it's one of love and loss and heartache and bravery and all kinds of things that hit me right here." She thumped her heart.

Ginny chewed her lip. "I wonder . . . I mean, William is a lit professor. Maybe he could help you find out more about it."

She allowed the idea to simmer, then brought it to a full boil in her mind. "What if it's just a novel?"

"It might be. Or it could be someone's true-life account. Wouldn't it be fun to find out?"

"It could be a wild-goose chase."

"Or it *could* be the adventure of a lifetime." Ginny pointed once more to the view in front of them. "It could be your ocean."

~✑~

Ginny's words reverberated in Sophia's mind all day through a Skype session with her mom, a shift at the bookstore, and dinner out with Ginny at the Cornish pasty place she'd seen her first day in Port Willis.

That night, she read Emily's story from cover to cover once more. Then she leaned back against her bed's headboard, sighed, and looked at the clock on her bedside table—an antique oak piece with intricate carving that matched the designs on the bedposts and the dresser. It was late, and she should just go to sleep. With a tug on the lamp cord, she snuggled down under the covers. But sleep wouldn't come, her mind swirling instead of shutting down.

"Or it could *be the adventure of a lifetime. It could be your ocean."*

Was it the most ridiculous notion in the world, trying to find the author of this story? Wouldn't it be just another distraction on her journey to write her own story and find healing?

Sophia turned the lamp back on and grabbed her phone, hitting the second number on speed dial and waiting with the device pressed against her ear until she heard Joy's voice.

"Hey, Soph. How are you? It's been too long."

"It really has." Try five or six days—they'd never gone that long without talking. "What have you been up to?"

"It's too hot to do much of anything. I'm on lunch break right now, but after work I fully intend to laze around with my dogs and marathon watch *Dr. Who.*"

"And you say I have a boring life." Sophia snatched a nail file off the side table. "Why not go out, meet some handsome doctor?"

"I like my dogs better than any of the men I've met lately."

"I hear you." Except, that wasn't entirely true. Because now there was William.

The file whizzed over the edges of her nails.

"What aren't you saying?" Joy's voice interrupted her thoughts.

"Nothing."

"Spill it, girlfriend. You've got something juicy to tell me, am I right?"

Sophia laughed, though it felt forced. "You're crazy."

"Wait. Have you met someone?"

"What? No." She cringed as the file slipped slightly and attacked her cuticle. "Well, kind of. But no." She filled her friend in on William and their brief interaction at the beach. "He showed up at the beach where I was attempting to journal. We talked for . . . a while." It had been amazing. And terrifying.

"As in . . ."

"All day." She still couldn't believe how easy it'd been to chat with him. Of course, it was easy to talk literature with anyone. But then they'd gone deeper, talking about their travels and chosen professions. They'd briefly hit on the topic of their families, but William hadn't mentioned his brother at all.

And Sophia hadn't mentioned David.

"And have you seen him since?"

"He's been by a few times." Sophia couldn't help the way her heart skipped at the memory of his visits. "He's only teaching a few summer classes, so his schedule allows him to pop in and help Ginny with the bookstore when she'll let him."

"Girl, I'm—"

"I know, I know, it's too soon." At least, that's what Mom had implied when Sophia had slipped up and mentioned William during their talk this afternoon. Her mother wouldn't rest until she heard every last detail, then reminded Sophia that she should remain cautious given her proclivity for making bad choices.

Well, she hadn't said that last part. Instead, she'd asked if Sophia would like her to come out to Cornwall at some point during her stay, which probably meant she didn't think Sophia could handle herself. And who could blame her? Of course, Sophia had refused and Mom had seemed to accept that. But still.

"That's not what I was going to say. I was going to say I'm happy for you."

"Oh. Well. It's nothing . . . really."

"Uh-huh. Okay, so switching subjects then. How has the writing gone?"

Sophia set aside the nail file and stood, the wooden floorboards cold against her toes. "It hasn't. Much." She walked toward the refrigerator, opened the door, and searched for a soda. She found one in the very back and pulled it out.

"Still stuck?"

"That's one way of putting it." She popped the lid of the soda can and took a swig. The liquid sloshed down her throat, hard and biting. "I thought I'd have found some inspiration by now."

"Sounds like your rut followed you all the way to England." Joy paused. "I told you when you left that it would be good for you, but only if you aren't using your trip to escape. Because even though you're not in your house right now, the memory of David follows you wherever you go."

Sophia leaned against the counter, letting the soda fill her empty stomach. Ugh. That wasn't going to feel good in an hour. But she guzzled it anyway. "You don't think I realize that? I have the same degree you do. I understand how all of this works psychologically."

"You understand from a provider's perspective, but not from a client's. We can have all the head knowledge in the world, but our hearts are often what lead us toward destruction—or healing."

Sophia let Joy's words soak in. She walked to the window and peered through the curtains. In Phoenix the entire horizon would be dotted with lights—people up late, out on the town. Here, the only lights on were streetlamps and the occasional window like hers, where people shuffled about their homes and enjoyed the quiet.

"I do feel different here. I'm starting to let my memories find me instead of running away. Nothing major, I guess. But in little ways." A boat horn sounded in the distance, low and guttural. "I haven't totally retreated into my shell like I've been doing for the past fifteen months."

"Listen, you know I love you." Another pause. "But, Soph, you've been retreating for far longer than that."

Her words hurt, but they were true in many ways. No matter how many times Sophia had gone over it all in her head, no matter how many hours she'd spent in therapy or talking about it with the people closest to her, she still couldn't get past one fact. "I knew better, Joy." She finished off the soda and crushed the can in her hand.

"I don't know how else to tell you this, but I'll say it again—it's not your fault."

"Whose fault is it, then?"

"David's. Would you dare tell a client that it was her fault her boyfriend or husband abused her?"

"No, but they're not therapists. I am. I should have . . ." Sophia sighed. Once again, there was no right answer. Like Joy said, she knew the answer in her head, but her emotions were telling her something different.

"Any one of us can become a victim, Sophia. Abuse does not discriminate, and neither do abusers." Joy had said these same words to her before. What a patient best friend. "When you and David got together, he tried to mold you into the person he wanted you to be. He trapped the real Sophia. She's been buried for so long you don't remember who she is. I think you get little glimpses of her, but then you start to feel ashamed about it."

"He may have buried me, but I handed him the shovel."

"He manipulated you. Called it love and then did the very opposite of real love. It. Is. Not. Your. Fault."

"I really do know that. But my heart won't listen. And I can't figure out how to forgive myself for it."

"Start by reclaiming your life. It's not enough to know in your head that you're hearing a lie. You have to actually replace that lie with the truth."

"But how do I know what's the lie and what's the truth?"

"By realizing that you're not the source of either one."

"I don't understand." The ocean frolicked just outside her window. The waves sang her a lullaby, like it was trying to soothe a baby to sleep.

"I know, friend. I'm praying that someday, you will."

Sophia wandered back to the bed, got in, and sank under the quilt. She was so tired of it all—the thinking, the crying, the futility. "Ginny thinks we should try to locate the author of the story I found. She thinks it'll be an adventure."

"What do you think?"

"I worry that it could be a distraction from the reason I'm here."

A tapping filled the silence—Joy always drummed her pen against her desk when she was deep in thought. "You know, when authors have writer's block, they go take a shower, or a walk, or watch TV. Basically, they do something else to get their minds off their stories, off of trying so hard to produce it. But their minds are always mulling over the story subconsciously. Maybe that's what you need to do. Get your mind off of the trying, and in the meantime, you'll give your heart room to heal."

14

❦

EMILY

NOVEMBER 1857

"Charlotte, come away from the window, please." I tried to keep the exasperation from my tone, but given the scowl the seven-year-old sent me, I was not successful. She crossed her arms over her chest, stuck her bottom lip out as far as she could manage, and flopped into the chair next to me as if anchored by a great weight.

With a sigh, I tapped the book in front of her. "This work would not take quite so long if you did not wander to the window constantly."

Across the table, her sister—age nine—snickered. I shot her a look and her eyes swiftly found her book once more. In the corner of the room, their oldest sister practiced writing French. She sat so elegantly, so poised. Though five years my junior, Louisa far surpassed me in grace and etiquette. If only she applied as much energy to her schoolwork as she did to dreaming about her upcoming season. I had only been teaching her half as much as usual, as her mother had hired a special tutor to help her put the finishing touches on her social graces education.

I tapped the page again. The seven-year-old's lip quivered and she looked up at me with eyes full of tears—eyes that reminded me so much of Edward's.

"Please, Miss Fairfax. Can I go outside soon?"

The plea cut at my core, for it was a question I had often asked my mother, who taught us at home as long as she was able. She had always indulged my love of the outdoors, and my education had not suffered for it. I glanced down at the young mistress once more and narrowed my gaze, trying not to smile. "If you finish this page of work, then you may take a short break to explore." It was a rare dry day in the very wet month that was November; in fact, the sun shone without clouds to dim its light. "Perhaps we can convince Cook to pack us a picnic. What do you say to that?"

Her eyes brightened and she began completing the work with fervor. I couldn't keep the chuckle inside. It had been too long since I'd really laughed, and I missed that part of me. Once upon a time, I'd been full of more than gloom and misery.

An hour later, we were spreading a blanket on the ground and pulling sandwiches and fruit from a basket. Edward's and my tree would have been the perfect spot for a picnic, but it did not feel right taking others into our realm, so we settled for a spot near a cluster of trees on the lawn.

Louisa had decided to stay indoors so she did not freckle, but I turned my face to the sky. Though a bit on the chillier side than most picnic days, the sun did its work in warming me.

If I had been alone, I would have removed my bonnet and let my hair loose. Something about the day seemed destined for joy—a thing I had not felt in a long time, that I'd only had a slight taste of that day three months before when Edward and I had talked on the edge of the bluff until it was dark and he said we must return in order to protect my reputation. If it had been up to me, I'd have stayed in his company, talking until morning about the dreams in our hearts.

Perhaps I would have even revealed my own—my dream of becoming a published author, not the one that began and ended with him.

That dream I would take to my grave.

We ate quickly, so I pulled a book from my bag, soon engaged in a story of adventure and buried treasure, and the girls chased the family dog. Then they were begging me to climb trees with them—Edward had told them I used to be the best tree climber around.

I glanced about and had my boot in a foothold on the lowest limb when a servant approached. He cleared his throat and looked at me pointedly, letting me know the missus wanted to see me. I should have been embarrassed, but a silly grin fixed itself to my face and would not leave me. The girls giggled and I winked. I felt more myself than I had in years.

After dusting a few stray leaves and twigs from my skirt, I followed the servant inside and he led me to the drawing room, where Edward's mother sat in a high-backed chair sipping tea. Her skin was pale like porcelain, and her cheeks perfectly rosy, her hair perfectly coiffed. A pearl necklace adorned her graceful neck, elegant and stately just like her. Every movement she made reflected her genteel upbringing.

"Miss Fairfax, please sit." She indicated the chair across from her, next to the fireplace, and set her teacup onto a tray. With the ring of a bell, a servant moved from the edge of the room to whisk the tray away.

I did as she asked, smoothing my dress and twisting my hands into my lap as I sat. Despite the many times I'd been in my employer's presence, something about this meeting produced unexplained nerves. The heat from the fire roared at me and flamed my twitter of emotions.

"Miss Fairfax, I wanted to let you know about a change in plans and see if you were amenable to them." She paused and tilted her head to look at me.

"Yes, ma'am."

"Miss Hayworth has given her notice, effective immediately."

"Oh?" Miss Hayworth was Louisa's companion. "That is poor timing indeed." The unofficial season began around Christmastime, and the family was scheduled to leave for London in a few weeks' time to settle in and begin preparations that could not be made until then. It would be my first visit to the city, and while I looked forward to seeing Edward again, my duties as governess would keep me busy and far from most of the excitement.

"Yes, I am well aware. That is where the change of plans comes in, and why I needed to speak with you."

Something about her perusal caused me to finally look away, into the fire. The orange flames leapt and disappeared, reappearing in a random, undulating pattern.

"I have great regard for the way in which you conduct yourself, Miss Fairfax."

I nearly reacted, but managed to remain unaffected by her comment. If only she had seen me ready to climb that tree not moments before. "Thank you, ma'am."

"And while I know you must adore teaching, I wonder if you might set it aside and claim the position of Louisa's companion for the duration of the season. After that, you may resume your current duties."

My eyes snapped back toward her. Before I could react to her false perception about how much I "adored teaching," the rest of her words caught up to me. She was asking me to take part in a world to which I had never truly belonged. Though my family had genteel roots, my father's decision to follow God's leading and become a preacher placed us outside of his own father's will. My grandfather had disinherited him and refused to ever meet his only grandchildren.

Surely Edward's mother, who cared a great deal what others thought, could not truly want me as a companion for her daughter, especially given the way my father's life had ended. "I'm flattered, ma'am. But—"

"I know how your family is viewed by society, but by now we must let your conduct speak for itself. You are not your father."

For Edward's mother to look past the scandal of my father's last years in this world, she must have been desperate indeed. Perhaps all the other suitable candidates for a lady's companion were already committed for the season.

The thought of being judged by others made me equal parts nauseated and bellicose. I opened my mouth to refuse, but another thought came. Being a lady's companion would provide me with more experience to put into my writing. My novel was almost complete, but I could still benefit from the knowledge when writing future stories.

Perhaps I could even find the time to visit a few publishers and present them with my manuscript. I would perhaps have more flexibility in my schedule as a companion than as a governess.

And best of all, being Louisa's companion would allow me more time with Edward, who spent most of his time in London these days.

"If it pleases you, ma'am, I am happy to relinquish my duties as governess and become Louisa's companion."

Edward's mother clapped her hands with pleasure. "Wonderful. This eases my mind greatly." Her shoulders relaxed, as if she had been afraid I would say no. "I must be able to trust that she is in good hands when I am not present."

This was the highest praise Edward's mother had ever bestowed on me. For a moment, I could not speak. Even though she likely had no notion of the way her words had affected me, something in me chose to believe her maternal instinct was rising up in favor of me.

I pushed the thought aside and straightened in the chair. "I will do my best, ma'am." With a pause, I considered my next words carefully. "Do you intend to pursue a match for her this season, or will you wait another year for that?"

"What a thoughtful question. Yes, you would need to understand our intent on that matter. No, we do not intend that, as she is still quite young and both her father and I feel she would benefit from another year of tutelage in the domestic arts." A smile flitted across her lips. "However, we have already spoken with several families interested in forming an alliance with ours."

The way Edward's mother spoke made me feel a part of her inner circle of friends—a confidante. I leaned forward ever so slightly. "Louisa will make a wonderful match, that is certain."

Edward's mother let loose a trill of laughter. "Oh no, dear. You misunderstand. We have been approached about matches for Edward, not Louisa."

The heat in the room suddenly seemed unbearable, and black clouded the edges of my vision. "Edward?"

His mother's smile shone like a million tiny stars lined up in a row. "Of course. It is our wish that he finds a wife and settles down, that he begins a family as soon as possible." The stars went dark. "You look quite pale, Miss Fairfax. Are you quite all right?"

"Yes." I squeaked the word out and excused myself as quickly as I could. When I was free of the room, my feet would not carry me unless I was running, so I sprinted through the hallway, past surprised servants, out the servants' exit, and down the garden path to our tree.

I fell to my knees. Here on the edge of the bluff, a breeze stirred, first quiet, then like a storm raging around me. Dead leaves on the ground blew out, out, out to the embrace of the ocean.

Why was I reacting so strongly? I had always known Edward would marry someone else. Had schooled my heart into submission, told it to enjoy our friendship for what it was, to cherish our fleeting moments together.

But my heart did not heed my instruction, an errant pupil determined to misbehave.

I stood, not bothering to brush off my skirt. I walked back to my room, picked up my pen, and poured my heart into the only thing that would ever be my salvation.

15

GINNY

Ginny groaned as she pulled the tray of cookies from the oven. Instead of succulent and soft, they appeared dry and hard. What had gone wrong with this batch? She set the tray on the counter of the tiny kitchen, where Sophia sat at a barstool. Her new friend eyed the cookies and reached for one tentatively.

"You're kind, but I won't let you try that one."

Sophia withdrew her hand. "I hate to see home-baked food go to waste. I don't get it anymore unless my mom brings something over."

"But bad home-baked food is much worse than takeout. I can't believe I messed these up. I'm just off today." Ginny took a spatula and tossed the cookies one by one in the garbage. She pointed to a platter of cranberry-orange muffins she'd baked early this morning. "Have one of those if you'd like."

"You sure?"

"Of course I'm sure. I'm baking plenty. Always do when I'm stressed."

She'd spent the day trying to eke out as many extra dollars as she could from the bookstore's budget in order to pay her landlords, as rent was due soon. And then there was Steven and his generous offer. How would Garrett feel about her accepting free help from him?

Of course, he was the one wasting who knew how much money living in London of all places when he could have been "finding himself" here, with her.

She slammed the lid of the trash can shut.

"I'm sorry you're stressed." Sophia continued their conversation as if Ginny wasn't behaving like a child throwing a temper tantrum. "Want to talk about it?"

"Not really." Denial clawed up her throat, but she swallowed hard. She did want to talk about it, in a way. She normally didn't have trouble opening up about stuff, but this . . . this was different. He was her husband. The one person who wasn't supposed to fail her. And fail her he had. She only wished she understood why.

Time to change the subject. "Oh, by the way. I talked to William this morning, and he said he's happy to help you find the author of the story. Has he told you how much he loves that TV show where they do all this literary research and stuff?" Ginny made a face. "He talked my ear off about it. Apparently he loves stuff like this."

Originally she'd thought Sophia and Steven would make a good couple, but after seeing the interest in William's eyes when talking about Sophia, Ginny had changed her mind. Plus, with how much they both loved books, it seemed a no-brainer.

"Oh. Thank you for asking." Sophia blushed.

Ginny could sense the hesitation in Sophia regarding William— and who could blame her, given what she'd gone through in her last relationship? But William truly was one of the good guys. Hopefully Sophia could see that in time. This project would be the perfect excuse for them to see more of each other. If Ginny had to nudge things along a little . . .

"I'm happy to help too if you do any research at night or on a day when I can close up shop early."

"Thanks. I might take you up on that. I'd definitely feel more comfortable with you there." Sophia gobbled up the rest of the muffin. "That was delicious."

Guess they were both good at changing the subject. "Eh, it's nothing special. Mr. Trengrouse—have you met him yet?—makes one with frosting that is to die for."

"Yes, he keeps trying to ply me with pastries. Says he wants to fatten up the American before I leave." Sophia hopped off the stool and headed to the sink to wash her hands. "And I've had his muffins and find them a bit dry, to be honest. Yours was moist the whole way through. If I didn't know you'd be baking up more treats tonight, I'd grab another one right now."

Ginny snatched a new recipe card and flashed it at Sophia. "Next is something you can really help me with: chocolate chip cookies. Everyone here considers them an American delicacy, so I haven't been able to perfect mine. No one has anything to compare it to. It's hard to even find decent chocolate chips at the market. I've had to order them online. I won't tell you how much they cost. It's been a nightmare."

With a snort, Sophia dried her hands. "I'll bet." She returned to her stool.

Ginny grinned and stuck out her tongue. "I know, I know, I'm being dramatic, but seriously. They're my favorite treat. I came up with my own custom recipe and think I have it as close to perfect as I can make them."

"As long as they're ooey and gooey and chocolaty, I don't think you can go wrong."

"If only that was the case." Ginny gathered the ingredients and began mixing them together with an electric beater. Her entire body began to relax, getting into the rhythm of the flour blending with sugar and butter and . . . ah. If only she could live life here, in this place, and forget she ever owned a bookstore, ever married a man named Garrett who was breaking her heart . . .

With a sigh, she put the mixer down. "Where would you be right now if you'd never met David?" She couldn't keep her denial tamped down any longer—didn't want to. The question had just flown out, but she really wanted to know, so she didn't take it back.

Surprise flitted across Sophia's features, but she recovered quickly, folding her hands and placing them on the countertop, leaning forward on her stool. "Not here, I guess." A sad smile lifted the right corner of her lips. "And neither would you if you hadn't met Garrett."

"I never would have heard of Port Willis before, much less left everything behind to move here."

"Do you ever consider going home?"

Ginny scooped a bit of the soft dough with a spoon, dropping it onto a parchment-lined cookie sheet. "It's not really an option. Not if I want to maintain any sort of independence." Ginny's hands created lines of dough rolled into balls. The parchment rustled as the dough fell. "Besides, if I left, then the bookstore would close."

"But you said it was more Garrett's dream than yours. How can he bear to leave it behind?"

Sophia's words held such a double meaning—probably not her intention at all, but Ginny's eyes grew wet all the same. Talking about it was one thing, but she was so sick of all the tears. She willed them to stay put. "Maybe . . ." Her lips trembled, and she nearly reached up to steady them. She continued to spoon dough onto the sheet. "Maybe the reality was not as glorious as the dream." Saying it was like stabbing a soufflé to see if it was done—it deflated all the breath from her lungs.

"Hey."

Ginny looked up at Sophia's soft voice, her heart trying to gallop away from her.

Sophia's eyes held such compassion, such understanding. "If that's the case, then it's truly his loss."

Oh boy. Ginny nodded, because what could she say? Words stuck in her throat like peanut butter on little-kid fingers.

"And as for your question, where would I be if I'd never met David? I really don't know. Maybe I'd be the same person I was back then—extremely focused and stressed out all the time from trying to be successful, trying to help as many people as I could, trying desperately to make my life count for something, to live up to my mom's level of awesomeness." Sophia tugged on the ends of her short hair. "I do know that without my experience, I wouldn't be who I am today. Or rather, the person I hope to become because of this. Right now I feel like a shallow shell of a person sometimes. Other times I feel so full of emotions, I'm like an overstuffed Easter egg that won't close. But eventually, if I let it, all the pain will lead to a better me. I hope. That's what I hold on to when all of this gets too rough."

"I like that perspective." Ginny scraped the last bit of dough from the bowl and made one more cookie. It was smaller than the rest, but it would still taste just as sweet. She stuck the cookie sheet in the oven and set the timer.

Sophia pointed to an apple-strawberry pie Ginny had made yesterday. "Okay, now that we're both all depressed and stuff, can I please try the amazing-looking piece of heaven over there?"

With a chuckle, Ginny found the pie knife and server. "Be my guest. I'll join you."

They dished up the pie and each took a bite. Sophia closed her eyes and moaned. "This is seriously the best thing I've ever tasted. Why aren't you selling your baked goods at the bookstore?"

Ginny choked on her bite. "What?" Sophia's nonchalant comment had the makings of a very workable idea.

Sophia seemed to realize it too. "You totally should. A café would be amazing too, though that would take some renovation. But for now, maybe set up a few tables and chairs in the corner. You know, where the nonfiction overflow is? And I'll bet you could easily add a display case on top of the desk up front. There's plenty of room. Ooh, and do some promotions—buy a book, get a muffin free, things like that—to give customers an extra incentive."

"You are a genius." Ginny snatched a piece of paper and started recording ideas.

Finally. A way to marry her skills with Garrett's dream.

It wasn't guaranteed to succeed—but trying was much better than the alternative.

16

EMILY

Today perhaps, my luck would finally change.

Wind whistled through my bonnet, and dirty snow crunched under my boots. I clutched my manuscript with both hands, determined to keep it from falling from my grasp into the puddles on the London street. All around me, people bustled to and fro—servants running errands for their masters, daughters of fine families stepping out of their carriages to shop, vendors plying their wares on the corners, inviting potential customers into their warm stores.

Why did society love London so much? The smell from the sewage, the factories pumping out smoke, and the horse droppings left along the road were enough to make my eyes water. My senses rang with the cacophony of the muffin man's bell, the clamor of the clarinet player on the corner, and the clickety-clack of the pattens on ladies' feet.

I wished Edward's had been like other families who stayed in the country until after the Easter holiday, but his mother did not want to miss any part of the season—unofficial or official—the latter of which would not truly begin for another few months.

But London did afford me one thing I could not get in the country—access to publishing houses. The thought brought renewed vigor for my mission. I passed storefronts for the *Daily Telegraph and Courier*, a popular dressmaker's shop, and a small millinery.

But I only had eyes for Smith & Richards Publishing.

I had already been turned away from two publishers since arriving in London two months ago, but a fellow author I had been communicating with suggested I try Smith & Richards, a fairly new publisher that might be open to female authors. Given the extent of my duties and the fullness of Louisa's and, thus, my schedule, I'd been unable to find the time to visit and inquire regarding the submission policy. However, this morning I was informed that Louisa had a headache and would not be venturing out.

It came as no surprise. We had stayed at the latest ball until four in the morning. The constant parties had grown tiresome for me, except for the bright light that was Edward. Of course, seeing him dance with so many young ladies vying for his attention gave me physical discomfort every time. But I stored all the stolen moments of laughter and teasing between us away in my heart.

Smith & Richards came into view. It had only taken approximately five minutes to walk here from the family's London home, but I still shivered—from the cold temperature or from nerves, I did not know. The building in front of me boasted a brick exterior that was clean but neither modern nor old-fashioned. There was no indication of the power held within its walls—the power to change lives, both mine and those of readers.

I inhaled, exhaled, and saw rather than felt my gloved hand push open the heavy door in front of me. Once inside, a quiet hum filled my ears. The room I'd stepped into was quite small, with several hallways leading in various directions. A young woman sat at a desk near the door. She glanced up from her pen and smiled at me, eyeing the manuscript in my hands. "G'day to you, miss. How can I help you? Are you here to drop off a manuscript?"

"I am." Her friendliness took me aback. I did not expect such a warm welcome. I stepped forward and carefully laid my manuscript on the polished desk. "Is it possible for me to speak with the person in charge?"

"Mr. Richards is very busy today. Is he expecting this manuscript? Is it Mr. Joseph's or Mr. Langley's?"

A niggle of doubt blossomed in my mind. "No, he's not expecting it. I heard you accepted unsolicited submissions."

"We do. Though of course there is no promise of publication. Only the best are selected."

I had placed my very heart into this manuscript. "I believe this will meet your standards."

The girl smiled again, though this time I could sense an underlying haughtiness that had not been there before. Or perhaps it had. "I am sure you think so, but Mr. Richards will be the judge of that. How can he get in touch with your employer?"

"What does my employer have to do with this?" It was preferable that they never find out—not because I was doing something unsavory, but because Edward's mother in particular was the type of person to base everything on reputation. And while some women had succeeded at this profession before, they were not always respected by members of well-bred society, many of whom believed women should be spending their time in other ways.

The woman at the desk lifted an eyebrow. "Is this not your employer's manuscript?"

The humming in the room seemed to grow louder. I straightened my shoulders. "No. It is mine."

A giggle bubbled up from the woman. "I see. I regret to inform you that Smith & Richards does not accept unsolicited manuscripts."

I couldn't help the way my mouth fell open, how my hands automatically found my hips. "You told me only moments ago that you did."

"Yes, from the best." The woman looked like she might begin snorting in delight, her lips twitching from holding in more laughter.

I could have handled her censure. But her mockery? Nothing was worse than that. My hands became fists clenched at my sides. "And why should mine not be one of the best?"

"Look at you, my dear. You are clearly a servant of some kind—"

"I am the companion to the daughter of one of the most respected families in the county." My voice shot barbs at this woman, and I prayed one would hit her square in the nose. "But why should my station or my gender"—which was obviously a problem for her too, despite her also being female—"matter when a great story should stand on its own?"

The woman shook her head, and a look of pity replaced the ridicule. I had been wrong. There was something worse than mockery. "I—"

Before she could get out another word, I snatched the manuscript from her desk and flew out the door. Warmth gathered behind my eyes, threatening to leave and burn a trail down my cheeks. I began weaving in and around the crowd on the street outside. In my distressed state, my foot slipped on a patch of ice and I fell, watching in horror as my manuscript slid from my hands into a slushy pile of days-old snow. People continued to move around me, either unaware of or unconcerned about my fall. I dove for the manuscript and lifted it from the snow, nearly weeping at the sight of running ink and sopping parchment.

"Emily?"

I looked upward from where I crouched on the dirty London street, holding the remnants of my heart in my hand. Was any of it salvageable?

"Emily." A girl crouched next to me and placed her hand on my arm. "Emily? Are you all right?"

I blinked. "Louisa? I thought you were staying abed today."

Behind her stood a friend I recognized from last night's party.

"Here." Louisa tugged me to my feet, surprisingly strong. "I decided that nothing would better cure my headache than being out among society in the fresh air."

I nearly laughed at her depiction of London and how very different our perspectives were. Though we'd grown up on the same land, Louisa and I had never been particularly close—she the very essence of propriety and decorum, I the girl who did not care one whit for the rules. And when I became her governess and then her companion, there was a certain professional relationship that had developed, a wall between us that was the consequence of our different classes.

One I suddenly realized I had erected.

Now, though, the concern in her eyes made me wonder if I had written off a potential friendship. Though she tended to be much more vivacious, perhaps the joy she exuded would be a good thing, if I allowed it to affect me.

"Thank you." I tucked the manuscript under my arm, praying she would not notice. I may have been ready to attempt befriending her, but divulging my secret was not the beginning I had in mind.

But some prayers do not come true.

Louisa's friend stepped forward and snatched the manuscript from my hands. At my cry of protest and Louisa's scolding "Hattie!" she rolled her eyes and tossed it back in my arms, but not before she glimpsed the first page.

The sneer on Hattie's face told me exactly what she thought of my endeavors. "Have you written a story?"

I lifted my head in as regal a manner as I could. "That is none of your concern."

Her eyebrows rose. "Louisa, dear, are you going to let your companion speak to me that way?"

Louisa bit her bottom lip, studying me. She must have decided something, for her shoulders rose ever so slightly. "She may speak however she wishes. Who am I to censure her?"

Before I could send her a grateful smile, Louisa turned to her friend and took Hattie's hands in her own. "Be a darling and let's keep Miss Fairfax's secret, hmm? It's rather exciting to know an authoress, isn't it?"

Hattie tipped her nose a bit. "I suppose so."

"Good. Now, I promised Mother I would be home for tea, so I'd better leave. Emily? Do you mind accompanying me?"

"Of course not."

Louisa waved good-bye to Hattie, who had seen another acquaintance down the street, and she and I climbed into the family's waiting coach.

"Thank you, Louisa. For not saying anything to anyone about this."

"Your secret is safe with me." Louisa smiled and looped her arm through mine.

17

✧✧✧✧✧✧

SOPHIA

Stepping inside a library always toasted Sophia's insides, plying her mind with beautiful memories of Saturday mornings spent lounging in beanbag chairs, reading the latest Baby-Sitters Club books, and getting lost in someone else's dream world.

But being inside the depths of the Port Danby University Library lit an inferno of joy in her soul.

"Just this way." George, a librarian in his forties with a thin frame and oversized, horn-rimmed glasses, led Sophia, William, and Ginny through the stacks.

Sophia breathed in the scent of old books—distinguished somehow—and allowed herself to be enveloped by the pure quiet surrounding her. Most students were away on summer "holiday," and the stillness was enchanting.

As if reading her thoughts, William turned his head, looked down at her, smiled, and winked.

Ginny nudged her. "This place is kind of creepy, isn't it?" Her whisper broke the enchantment.

But Sophia couldn't be upset with Ginny, not when she had closed up the bookstore a bit early to tag along. Her friend had sensed that being alone with William again made Sophia all kinds of nervous. She just didn't know how to feel about him and this blossoming . . . something . . . between them. Ever since the day at the beach last weekend, she'd second-guessed everything she'd said to him. Had she come off as flirty? Had she sounded like a complete idiot? Was William here because he thought it might score him points or because he was genuinely interested in the mysterious notebook like she was?

Sophia pulled her gaze from William and leaned toward Ginny as they walked. "I love old libraries. And this one isn't creepy, not by a long shot. You should have seen some of the libraries at my university."

The archives room at that library was located in the basement with no natural lighting and a smell that rivaled a men's locker room. But as they approached the Port Danby University Library's Archives and Special Collections room, her breathing hitched. Four stained glass windows adorned the walls, and an arched Tiffany window over the door welcomed visitors. Three sturdy, large oak tables and twelve chairs provided ample space for researchers to spread out and linger over their findings. Bookcases and a few exhibit cases lined what was left of the wall space. Other than the two state-of-the-art computers lingering in the corner of the room, she could almost imagine she'd stepped back in time.

"This university is five hundred years old, so 'old' is quite accurate." The amusement in William's tone made her blush.

Her whisper must not have been as quiet as she'd thought.

Sophia caught Ginny watching them both, a small smile playing across her lips.

Once they were all inside the room, George turned to them. "Now that we are inside the room, feel free to converse as much as you'd like." His pointed stare shot Sophia with a twinge of guilt for her earlier failure to observe the librarian's golden rule of silence.

But William stepped forward and clapped a hand on George's

shoulder. "Thanks for agreeing to help us out today, George. We'd be lost without your expertise."

His flattery seemed to puff George up a bit. The librarian pushed his glasses onto the bridge of his nose and nodded. "Why don't we all take a seat and discuss your search."

At first, Sophia hadn't wanted to accept William's help in searching for Emily Fairfax. After all, something about the whole thing felt intensely personal. But William had access to the university's resources, including a research librarian who specialized in genealogy. George had agreed to give them a quick overview of the process of tracing ancestry and help them figure out where to begin.

They all slid into seats at one of the tables.

George sat ramrod straight and picked a piece of lint off his polyester suit. "So William told me the basics of your search."

She'd loaned the journal to William to read yesterday, when she'd finally accepted his offer of help.

"And I have to warn you that it will be difficult. In fact, maybe impossible."

The words splashed icy water over the hope that had been lit just being here in this place. Sophia couldn't help the way her shoulders fell. "Oh?"

"Come on, George, old chum. There is some chance, isn't there?"

The librarian straightened his glasses. "There is always some chance. But even with a lot of information to begin your search, it can be difficult. All you have is a single full name. No date. No place of birth."

What had she been thinking? This was a mistake. "We're sorry to have wasted your time."

William held out his hand. "Just wait, Sophia. George, we may only have one full name, but we have a few context clues to help us with the other things. Thanks to the reference to the *Daily Telegraph and Courier*, we know the story had to have taken place after 1855, when that newspaper was founded. Of course, we don't know exactly how old Emily was, but it's likely she was in her late teens to midtwenties. And there are several other clues that point to this story taking place during the Victorian era. So that at least gives us bookends for our search."

Sophia flashed him a look of gratitude. "And while we don't know for sure the county of Emily's birth, we do know the setting of the story or journal is England, so that's likely where she was born too. We don't *have* to have all the specifics, right? Isn't there a way to cast a wider net for the search?"

"Yes, of course. It will just take you much longer to wade through the entries."

"That's fine." William glanced once more at Sophia. "Right?"

Sophia couldn't hold his gaze for long. "I'm here all summer, so long as my landlord doesn't kick me out." Her poor attempt at a joke fell on deaf ears, though. Ginny sat next to her writing in a notebook. A quick glance at her scribbles showed a bunch of numbers. Poor girl. Sophia should have let her stay home to brainstorm ways to save her bookstore instead of having her come here. Next time, she'd find the courage to come alone with William.

If there was a next time.

Sophia cleared her throat and redirected her attention to George. "So what do we need to know about this process?"

"It's tedious and takes patience. Always begin with what you do know. You'll mostly be searching birth, death, and marriage certificates. In England, civil registration did not begin until 1837 and was not compulsory for births or deaths until 1874, so there are some gaps in those records. Reporting marriages was compulsory, so those records are a bit more reliable."

George paused to be sure she and William were tracking with him. Upon their nods, he continued. "After 1837, the government divided England into registration districts and subdistricts, where records of marriages, births, and deaths were kept. Each quarter, the districts submitted an index of these events to the central registration office. But an index only includes the most basic information. Here is where your search can get tricky."

Then he rattled off a list of resources, as well as possible complications—indexes could have errors in transcription, some records might have been lost due to fire or other issues in the districts, names might be spelled incorrectly, the records might not yet be available digitally, et cetera.

As he spoke, Sophia's shoulders continued drooping until they felt like they were hitting the floor.

If it was possible for a task to be more than impossible, this was it.

"Any questions?"

William glanced sideways at Sophia. "I think we're good for now. I'll let you know if any come up, though. Thanks so much, George."

George nodded, stood, and left.

Just then, Ginny's phone rang. "Oops. I forgot to silence it." She pulled it from her purse. "Sorry, I have to take this." She left the room.

For the first time since that day on the beach, Sophia was alone with William. Out of habit, she scanned for exits—the entrance they'd come through was one. And there, an emergency exit door to the right.

Get a grip, Sophia. Don't be weird. He's not going to hurt you.

She just needed to rediscover the camaraderie they'd found so easily on the beach.

"So, should we get started?" William sat back in his chair. "The computer has several of the databases George mentioned we should try."

Sophia couldn't hold in her doubts any longer. "This is totally ridiculous. We don't even know if this story is fact or fiction. It's silly to spend so much time chasing a ghost who might never have existed in the first place."

"But it's fun. And it seems important to you."

"I don't know why I can't just let it go. I mean, it's a cool story.

And I definitely connect with a lot of what the author says. But it feels like more than a normal novel, you know? It feels . . ."

"Real?"

"Yes." And familiar. But why?

He leafed absently through the book on the table again. The thick pages swooshed as he turned them. "There's definitely something special about the story. It is of course well written, which begs the question of why it was buried in a box of books donated to the bookstore in the first place."

"I know. And I did a Google search of some of the key phrases and came up empty, so it's not a published book that was somehow printed off someone's home computer. Unless it's published but not on the Internet." Sophia stood and paced. She'd thought a lot of this through already, but it helped to talk it out with someone else.

William pulled a pad of paper and a pen from his messenger bag. "That's a possibility if it's older, but the notebook itself doesn't appear to be more than ten years old. So the real question is, was this something someone wrote originally on a computer, printed out, and accidentally placed in a donation box? Or was it copied and typed out to preserve an original document that was written by someone in the past?"

"Ugh. George was right. This is impossible."

"If you recall, he also said there's always a chance. Let's just take it one step at a time, all right? Follow the clues. If we are meant to figure this out, we will. Have faith."

Have faith in who? Herself? That had been a dismal failure considering all she'd been through.

Nodding, she shoved the thought from her mind. "You're right. Let's get to work." Sophia headed to one of the two computers, sat, and maneuvered the mouse. "Looks like I need a login."

"Right." William got up and came to the desk. He leaned over her, placing his hands on the keyboard.

As he typed in his username and password, she couldn't help but take in the faint scent of lemon that gave him that fresh-out-of-the-shower smell—one she liked very much.

David had smelled like citrus too—oranges. Clean. Always clean.

Suddenly, the air closed in around her, claustrophobia looming. She wanted to move out of William's way, but the wall on her other side boxed her in.

The last time she'd been this close to a man, she was pressed against a wall, held there with one hand around her throat and . . .

She stood abruptly, knocking over the chair behind her.

"Whoa, you okay?" William tried to steady her, but she backed away from him.

William is not David. William is not David.

"I'm sorry. I just—"

"Sorry, guys, that was Steven with an update on my website." Ginny breezed back into the room and halted as she looked between the two of them. "What did I miss?"

"Nothing." She felt William's concerned gaze on her as she righted her chair and sat down again. "William is just helping me sign in to the computer so we can start our search."

Without another word, he signed in to Sophia's computer and navigated to the correct collection they had planned to use. He then did the same for the computer terminal next to hers. "Okay, Gin, here's one for you all queued up."

"Thanks, bro." Ginny slid into the seat next to Sophia. "Now what in the world am I looking for?"

Sophia kept her eyes on the screen. Her heart rate was finally returning to normal.

William spoke from behind them. "Right now all we really have to go on is Emily Fairfax, since all the other names in the story are first names only. You two look for any Emily Fairfaxes, circa 1830s to 1890s in England. I'll browse through census information like George suggested, and we can cross-reference any information we find."

Ginny saluted. "Aye, aye, Cap'n."

Yes, she was very glad Ginny was here. So far, William had remained completely respectful, never even flirting, except for that wink on the walk to this room. He seemed to be a genuinely nice guy who was going out of his way to help her. And she'd reacted like a fool. At least Ginny helped to diffuse some of the tension in the room, and maybe her presence would keep at bay William's questions about what had just happened.

Sophia grabbed a water bottle from her bag and took a sip, swallowing hard.

Ginny raised an eyebrow. "How will we know if we have the right Emily Fairfax?"

According to George, the only information they'd find on the databases was the index, which listed basic information. "We won't necessarily. William and I think that maybe she was from Cornwall, since the notebook was found here, but there's no way to be sure of that. But George said we can send away for a birth certificate if an entry looks promising. That takes time, of course, but it might give us a context clue. We know her father was a reverend, so that information might be included on a birth certificate."

With that, Sophia input the information they had and hit Search. Over a thousand Emily Fairfaxes in England alone during the Victorian period. "Must have been a popular name."

"You seeing what I'm seeing?" Ginny peeked at her screen. "Yep. Okay, should we split them up and start investigating one by one?"

"Sure. Let's keep a list of any Emilys in Cornwall specifically. Then we can narrow from there." Or something.

After several hours of searching, Sophia tucked her hair behind her ear. "Maybe we're going about this wrong. Is there another starting place we haven't considered?" An idea formed. She snapped her fingers. "William."

His head popped up from his laptop. "Hmm?"

He'd put on reading glasses, the thick-framed kind. Whew. She'd always been a sucker for the professor look.

Sophia cleared her throat. What had she been about to say? Oh, right. "What about looking for landmarks? Like Edward and Emily's tree? Maybe that's a real place?" But was it unique enough? Maybe combined with the fact it had been part of a larger country estate and was close to a lighthouse . . .

William's mouth flattened, and his brow wrinkled. "That's a good thought." He paused, as if heavily considering his next words. "Actually, I know a professor in London who has intensely studied the terrain of England. We haven't spoken in a while, but . . ."

"Do you think this professor might be willing to help us?"

"Perhaps. Like me, she enjoys a good intrigue. She can be rather difficult to get ahold of, though. Very old-school in that way. She hates talking on the phone."

"I'll take it." Perhaps a little help was all right now and then.

18

GINNY

Every day just before closing, Ginny cheered on the inside.

The clock tonight read 6:59 p.m. Only one more minute and she could close up shop for the day, go home, and do something that didn't remind her of the gaping hole in her heart.

The clock's hands clicked into place. Hallelujah. She moved from behind the desk toward the door and flipped the sign. Then she closed out the register. It wasn't all that different from this morning, though the promo she had run for a free muffin with each purchase had attracted some new blood. A few of the tourists who had come through had raved about her chocolate scones, buying up every one and some other pastries too, giving her at least some sense of accomplishment.

It still wasn't enough to make a difference financially in the big scheme of things, but it was a start. And tourist season was bound to pick things up. She just needed to think positive.

Ginny hummed some song she'd heard on the radio this morning while she unloaded the display case—a couple of oatmeal raisin cookies and three blueberry muffins. Perhaps she'd bring them by

William's house later. They hadn't had a chance to talk much after their library adventures last weekend.

A knock sounded at the door. Huh. Everyone around here knew she closed at seven, but maybe this was something important. Had Mr. Albert forgotten his wife's birthday and needed a last-minute gift?

Zipping up the plastic baggie containing the pastries, she placed it on the counter and returned to the door. She peeked out through the glass. Why was her landlord here?

Ginny unlocked and swung open the door, then put on her best fake-it-till-you-make-it grin. "Julia, hi."

The woman held a baby in one arm and had a toddler clinging to her leg, with two more school-aged children standing behind her. "Sorry to disturb you, Ginny. Can we talk?" Her limp brown hair hung around her face, a sincere but cautious smile on her face. The woman looked just plain tired. Ginny couldn't imagine—well, she had imagined, but when she and Garrett hadn't gotten pregnant . . .

"Of course. Come on in." Holding open the door wider, Ginny reached for the hand of the toddler. "Hi, Rosie. Would you like to see some of the new toys I bought?"

The little girl's eyes widened and she nodded, breathless, dried peanut butter flecked above her upper lip. She and her two older brothers raced off to the kids' corner.

Julia blew out a breath and switched the baby from one hip to the other. "Thank you. They've been quite the handful today. We ate an early dinner, and I needed to get them out of the house for a bit. Plus, I've been needing to talk to you."

Ginny reached for little Sammy. "Here, let me hold him." Before Julia could protest, Ginny took Sammy in her arms. Whew. He was a hefty guy. She looked the gurgling eight-month-old in the eyes and made a funny face, earning herself a hysterical giggle. When she moved her gaze back to Julia, the corners of the woman's eyes were crinkled, almost as if she were in pain. "What's going on, Julia? I'm not late on rent, right? I thought it was due next week. Of course, Garrett was the one who always handled the lease agreement and payments, but it's just me now and I'm doing my best to make sure . . ."

Shut up, Ginny. Not everyone needed to know every thought that popped into her head.

"No, you're not late." The woman sighed. "I don't exactly know how to say this."

Sammy snatched a handful of Ginny's hair and tugged. She bit back a yelp and gently unwound his hand from the strands still attached to her head.

"You're making me nervous." She added a light laugh to urge Julia on, but on the inside, her stomach roiled.

"Aldwin says things are tighter because of the economy." Julia fiddled with the buttons on her shirt, which looked stained with something orange. "So we must start charging more for rent at all our properties. He's already spoken with Mr. Trengrouse and Mrs. Lincoln. So it's nothing personal, I promise."

The news caused acid to climb up Ginny's throat. She could hardly afford the lease as it was. "How much?"

Julia named the price.

"But what about our lease agreement?"

"It's time to renew the lease."

It was? "Oh." Ginny absently stroked Sammy's soft arm. He snatched at her necklace and started sucking on it. "I'm not sure—"

From the other side of the store, loud voices interrupted her words. Julia heaved a sigh. "Would you please excuse me for a moment?" She marched off toward the children's section.

"Sammy, what am I going to do?" Ginny snuggled the infant close, breathing in the scent of him—was that milk and sweet potatoes? But he pushed away from her chest, clearly not wanting to be restrained.

Julia strode back, holding each of the older kids by an arm. Rosie toddled after them, crying huge crocodile tears. "I'm sorry, Ginny, we need to go." She crouched and gave the boys directions in a very firm but quiet voice. They both nodded, solemn, and headed toward the door. Julia took Sammy from Ginny and ushered Rosie to the exit as well.

Before she stepped out the open door, Julia turned again. "I really am sorry, Ginny. I know things are rough for you right now. I pleaded with my husband, and he understands your predicament, but . . ."

"It's all right, Julia. You have a family to take care of. A beautiful one."

Julia's shoulders relaxed a tiny bit. "Thank you for understanding. Aldwin will be contacting you about whether you are able to renew the lease or not. He offered to contact you initially—he was always the one to deal with Garrett on this—but I said I would be able to break the news in a more . . . personal way."

"I appreciate that."

Once Julia and the children left, Ginny gathered her things, walked out the door, locked up again, and headed around back to her cottage, which she also rented from Aldwin and Julia. If she couldn't renew the bookstore's lease, she might lose her home too—the first place where she'd ever had any say in the decor, in the things that were purchased. The Bentleys may have been loaded, but never once had Mother asked her opinion on anything, from her room design to her clothing to her first car. In fact, an interior decorator had done up the pink-and-lace shabby chic room where she'd spent eighteen years of her life.

Ginny hated pink.

She set her keys on the counter and looked around the gray-and-black modern kitchen that Garrett had let her redesign—not in an expensive way, but in an it's-all-yours-and-I-trust-you kind of way. He had given her a place to belong and let her stretch her wings for the first time in—ever.

Oh, how she missed him.

If he was here, they'd be able to figure this out together.

Anger and raw hurt flared anew. Why wasn't he here? He'd never given her a solid reason, just vague generalities and cliché statements. And despite all the people who raised an eyebrow and clucked their tongues—who thought for sure his absence meant he was having an affair—she'd believed him when he said that wasn't what this was about. She'd known it was possible to need time to discover yourself. She'd been patient.

But now, the bookstore was going to close if something didn't change. Fast.

She'd tried to pretend she could manage it on her own, that she could handle the burden without him and give him the space he'd requested.

But if he came back and his beloved bookstore was closed . . . Well, he needed to know. He *did* still care about what happened to it, didn't he?

Oh please, let him still care.

Her hand slid into the pocket of her purse and pulled out her phone. She dialed his number. It would probably go to voicemail . . .

"Hello? Ginny?"

"Garrett." She breathed out his name like an amen.

"Wow. It's a bit like fate that you called. I was just going to call you."

"You were?" Relief surged through her. Her body sagged as she sank onto one of her kitchen stools—*their* kitchen stools. He missed her. Perhaps he was ready to come home at long last. His voice sounded hesitant, but there was no need.

"Yes." He paused. "I'm not sure how to begin."

"It's okay, Garrett." The past was in the past. "Of course you can come home. I forgive you."

"You what?" A deep breath. "I wasn't going to . . . That's not what this is about."

She grabbed at a napkin sitting on the counter, began tearing it into long shreds. "Oh? Well, how's London? Is it raining a whole bunch? We've had beautiful weather here. A few scattered storms, but nothing like last year." Her own reason for calling had flown completely out of her mind.

"Really, Gin? The weather?" Agonizing moments walked laps around her. Finally, the words she'd dreaded and thought impossible came from his lips. "I'm filing for divorce."

A gentle knocking. The murmuring of her name, muffled. An ache in her neck.

Ginny groaned as she roused from sleep. Where was she? Cold pressed against her cheek as she opened her eyes and lifted her head. She'd fallen asleep at her kitchen bar, the granite countertop her pillow, the stool her bed.

No wonder her whole body screamed at her.

But why had she . . . ?

Memories of her conversation with Garrett flooded her mind and stole her breath. After she'd begged him to reconsider and he'd once again given her hardly any information to go on, they'd hung up.

Ginny glanced at the stovetop, where she'd left a cherry pie, snickerdoodles, pumpkin muffins, and a bowl with chocolate cake batter—evidence of her post–phone call baking frenzy. Around two in the morning, she'd collapsed on the stool for a rest and must have fallen asleep altogether.

"Ginny?" Again that muffled voice.

She rubbed the sleep from her eyes, wishing she could head straight to her bedroom. A yawn forced its way out. Wait. What time was it? Ginny squinted at the clock on her microwave. Great. She'd been due to open the bookstore almost an hour ago. Thankfully, Sophia was working it today . . .

Rap rap rap. "Ginny? Are you okay?"

Sophia? Ginny raced to the door. Opening it, she found her pseudo employee standing there, questions in her eyes. "Why are you here?"

"Good morning to you too. But you didn't answer my question. Are you okay? You look awful."

"Thanks a bunch. But you didn't answer my question either. Why are you here and not the bookstore?" She hated the accusing tone snapping from her tongue.

"When you didn't show up, I called William and asked him to come in. He's got it handled."

Thank goodness for her brother-in-law and Sophia. She'd have been out of business already if not for them.

"Sorry. I didn't mean to snap at you. Thanks for arranging that." Ginny tried to laugh, but her throat rumbled. "I'm okay."

Sophia cocked her head. "Something's wrong."

Her new friend was far too perceptive.

Maybe if she acted like everything was fine, it would be. "Just overslept." Ginny headed to the fridge, opened it, and pulled out a bottled water. She twisted off the cap and took a sip, cleansing her body from all the sadness, all the tears, all the . . .

"C'mon, Ginny. That's not the truth and we both know it."

Ginny's fingers tightened around the bottle, crunching the plastic a bit. She sighed. "Guess I can't fool the shrink."

Sophia closed the door and came inside. "I'm a therapist, not a shrink." She smiled and placed her hand on Ginny's upper arm. "Right now, though, I'm just a concerned friend. What's going on?"

With quivering lips, Ginny downed the rest of the water. She did not want to think about this anymore. Last night had left her with more questions than answers. "I have to get to the bookstore."

Sophia pointed to the kitchen table, another of Garrett's creations. It was small and round—their "eat-in" kitchen wouldn't fit anything larger than a two-seater—and shoved up against the window. "Sit."

No, no, no. When she sat, she wallowed. "Want some breakfast? I have pie. And I can make some coffee."

"Sure." A picture of calm, Sophia settled into one of the chairs.

Ginny felt her friend's eyes on her as she pulled two plates down from the open-faced cabinets. "Any word from William's friend about Emily's story?" Sophia had been so bummed when more information hadn't turned up.

She unwrapped the cellophane from the pie, cut two generous slices, and placed them on the plates.

"Yes, actually. I think we're going to go meet her in London this weekend." A pause. "I know you've got your own stuff going on, so you don't have to come this time if you don't want to. Of course, you're welcome to. That's not what I mean."

"I don't feel like I was much help last time." After all, she hadn't read Emily's story, so she hadn't had any thoughts to contribute. She'd really just gone to make sure Sophia was okay being alone with William. "That reminds me, though. What happened at the library? When I came back into the room after my phone call, you looked white as a coconut cream pie."

It took a moment for Sophia to answer. "To be honest, William got a little close to me when we were signing in to the computer. It was all very innocent, but I had a flashback." She sighed. "I kept having to remind myself that he is not like David."

Ginny brought the plates to the table and set them down. "I'm so sorry." Maybe her friend did need her to go to London after all. But it took about four to five hours each way to drive there, and she couldn't really afford that much time away from the bookstore.

"Thank you." Sophia pursed her lips, but Ginny saw the tremble there. Then she seemed to compose herself and eyed the pie. "Seeing all this food reminds me. A few customers came in wanting muffins this morning, but the display case was empty. So we should probably take some over once we're done here. It looks like you have plenty."

"That's what happens when you're up past midnight stress baking." Wincing at her own remark, Ginny turned on her heel. Coffee. They needed coffee. She practically scrambled to her espresso machine—a gift from Garrett for their fourth anniversary.

"Not able to sleep?"

"Something like that." Ginny filled the machine's reservoir with cold, filtered water. Then she groaned. That's right. It took nearly fifteen minutes for it to heat up. Out of excuses. She flicked on the machine and faced Sophia once more.

Her friend studied her. How was it possible that Ginny was closer to her—whom she'd known not even three weeks—than to her own brother and sister or anyone else she'd met in the last five years living here?

But there was something about their mutual hurt that drew them together. And that meant Sophia was a safe place. Perhaps she could give her some ideas about how to make Garrett see reason.

Ginny grabbed two forks from the silverware drawer and handed Sophia one, then slid into the seat across from her.

With a sigh, she set her fork down on the table and stared at her pie. The flaky, golden-brown crust housed the beautiful red filling. The arrangement looked almost too perfect to eat. "My landlord came by. It's time to renew my lease, but she's nearly doubling the monthly price of rent if I want to renew."

Sophia frowned. "That's awful."

"It gets worse. I called Garrett to let him know, to see if he had any solutions."

"It must have been difficult to talk to him again."

"That's the thing. I was nervous, yes, but excited to talk with him. It's like I finally had a real excuse to do so. Imagine, feeling like you couldn't talk to your husband without bugging him."

The garden box outside the window caught her attention. She'd always taken such pride in working the soil, planting gorgeous local flowers and watching them bloom. This year, however, she'd been far too busy with the bookstore and Garrett's absence to tend to the tiny garden. Weeds grew in place of many of the pretty plants. The flowers that did grow were stunted from lack of care—the only water they'd received was what had fallen from the sky this winter and spring.

"So did he have a solution?"

"I never got to tell him about the bookstore. He . . ." She expected a flash flood to issue from her tear ducts, but none came. Must have dried up after last night. "He said he was filing for divorce."

Sophia dropped her fork and reached for Ginny's hand, giving it a gentle squeeze. "Oh, Ginny."

"I was in shock at first. It seems dumb, right? I mean, he's been gone for more than six months and it's been weeks since we've even spoken. But I kept telling myself that he'd come home when he was ready." Ginny picked up her fork again and poked a cherry tucked inside the pie. It tumbled out in slow motion, stuck in the gelatinous filling. "You can ask me what I know you must be wondering."

"And what's that?" Sophia's voice remained tranquil and low.

"Aside from 'What kind of idiot are you—'"

"Stop right there." Sophia folded her hands and looked Ginny straight in the eye. "I understand that this kind of pain and grief leads to self-doubt, but negative self-talk gets you nowhere. Believe me. I know from experience. I fight it every day. A lot of days, it wins."

Ginny's chest squeezed. The sun began to rise higher outside the window, casting part of the garden box in light. One flower—a bright-yellow vetch—seemed to almost lean toward the lit section from the shadows.

"I tried to ask him why. I just want to understand. Maybe if I do, I could fix it for him. Bring him home. Remind him that we belong together."

"What did he say?"

"He said he hadn't been happy for a while. That he didn't know if he loved me anymore." The words had been like using a butter knife to slice steak—just plain wrong. Impossible. That couldn't be how he truly felt. "I just don't get it. He loves this town, this bookstore. He always has. And despite what he says, I *know* that he loves me. How could he just leave?" A tear finally slid from her eye and plopped onto her pie, soaking into the crust.

From across the table, Sophia handed Ginny a tissue.

She used it to wipe her eyes.

Her friend sighed. "I don't have the answers. Sometimes it's easier to leave than to deal with your emotions."

"But at some point, you do have to deal with them, right? I never thought he'd stay away this long or that he'd decide not to return."

"So he said he's staying there?"

"For now."

"You didn't get to talk about the bookstore at all?"

"No. He wasn't exactly open to discussing the particulars. Just said his lawyer would be contacting me."

What did she do now? Give up on the bookstore? Give up on Garrett? Go back to the States, where her parents would surely lord her failures over her?

The light drifted away from the yellow flower, pulled in the other direction. And yet still the flower seemed to lean.

"Wait. When are you guys leaving for London?"

19

fffffff

EMILY

MAY 1858

I never would have believed it possible, but I missed being a governess.

As a governess, I could hide away from society for the most part. My behavior wasn't under constant scrutiny, since children were my main observers. They didn't care whether I was entirely proper or said the right things.

But as a lady's companion, I felt constantly trapped, like an insect whose wings were pinned to a board. I accompanied Louisa to parties and called on countless families with her, slipping into the background while she flitted around like a butterfly, free to flirt, prattle, and preen with the rest of them.

In some ways, I envied her. In others, I could not imagine being like her.

But I did miss freedom.

Not that being a governess was truly freeing either. I would have no true freedom until I called myself a published author and began receiving payment through which I could live my own life, doing what I loved. In the few months since my manuscript had fallen in the snow, I had used the dying flames of my candle every night to reconstruct the ending of my story—and in doing so, discovered that second chances were often the most beautiful. The story was richer now, fuller. Experience had added to its flavor.

And one unexpected thing that had come from my new position was a blossoming friendship with Edward's sister. Ever since that day when Louisa had discovered my secret, we had become much closer—not as close as Edward and me, but closer than any female friend I'd ever had.

I dreamed of such things as I placed a bite of lamb into my mouth and chewed. All around me, forks scraped plates and conversation droned. Edward's family had invited a few families to dine with us this evening. The women looked divine in their gowns, especially a young woman named Rosamond, whose deep brown hair reminded me of spun silk in its soft appearance. Her waist appeared to be half the size of my own, but she did not seem weak as many petite women did. Whenever she laughed, joy seemed to spread throughout the room, though I could not fathom why—it was not a kind-natured laugh, but a rather obnoxious one.

My view of her may not have been entirely unbiased, I admit. For this was not the first time her family had dined with Edward's, nor the first time she had been seated next to Edward and engaged him in conversation for the entire meal. In fact, rumors had swirled among the servants that their parents were intent on arranging a union between them.

I dug my fork into a pile of peas and stabbed one. The clang seemed to reverberate around the room and a few heads turned my way, including Edward's and Rosamond's. Edward smiled at me. Rosamond did not.

I set my fork down and dabbed my lips.

"How are you enjoying London, Miss Fairfax?" Rosamond's

mother asked. I had been seated between her and Louisa. Though she'd been speaking to the guest on her other side, she must have noticed my embarrassment. Bless her for attempting to cover my faux pas.

"It is perfectly lovely."

"Oh, come now. You infinitely prefer the countryside."

I glanced up at Edward's teasing words. His eyes sparkled with mischief.

"I can't imagine what you mean." I felt the corners of my lips lifting.

"Why would anyone prefer the country to the excitement of London?" Rosamond's laugh grated against my ears.

Why must she become involved in the conversation? "I merely prefer the quiet. I'm not much for socializing."

"How can that be? Socializing is the height of enjoyment." Rosamond glanced between me and Edward, a sliver of annoyance simmering beneath her composed façade.

"Our dear Miss Fairfax here much prefers the company of books."

"'Tis true. I have always been guilty of that. Of course, you indulge my tastes by giving me plenty to digest."

"I can hardly keep up with your voracious appetite for books now." Edward turned to Rosamond, breaking the spell between us. "Miss Fairfax here is a very accomplished reader, and her tastes span the gamut."

I raised my cup to my lips in an effort to keep a full grin from spreading across my face.

"How interesting." The words slid from Rosamond's perfectly shaped lips as she turned her attention to me. "I hear that you are not merely an accomplished reader, but also an authoress."

Several drops of water dribbled from my lips. I set my cup down and quickly dabbed my face with a napkin. The other guests stopped speaking and turned their heads of one accord to me.

My gaze shot back to Edward's, and this time his look was one of confusion. "You must be mistaken. Miss Fairfax is no authoress."

"Oh?"

How did one word, spoken with such false innocence, have the power to shake me so? And why was I finding it difficult to speak?

"I am sorry, Miss Fairfax. I had it on good authority that you had written a novel and were attempting to have it published. I wanted to wish you luck in that endeavor."

Who had told her? But only two people could have done so. I turned my head to Louisa, and when she refused to meet my gaze, I knew it had not been her friend Hattie. Her fingers trembled slightly as she sipped from her glass. Betrayal sliced through my gut.

"Really? I am most surprised." This from Mr. Banks, a wealthy barrister who lived in London year-round. He and his wife had climbed high in the social sphere, and Edward's mother had been thrilled when they'd accepted her invitation to the dinner party. "Young women should be spending their free time learning the domestic arts or attending to the duties they already have."

"Quite right, dear." His wife eyed me with suspicion. "Young lady, if you have enough time to pen a novel, you must be neglecting your duties in some way."

My cheeks were on fire now, but this time it was not due to embarrassment. How dare this woman who did not even know me say such things—she, in her finery, with her well-padded life, who likely knew nothing of suffering? I folded my hands in my lap, and it took every fiber of control in my body to keep from throwing my goblet at her.

"Now, now, let's all calm ourselves. Miss Fairfax has been a very attentive companion to Louisa. You must have misunderstood." Edward's mother came to my rescue.

It was Rosamond's turn for a reddened face. Both of her parents appeared slightly alarmed at the turn in conversation. "I do apologize, ma'am. It was not my intention to stir up trouble, merely to congratulate Miss Fairfax on such an achievement. Is it not an admirable thing to write an entire novel? The self-discipline, the talent it must take to weave an entertaining tale when your own life has been so misfortunate—does this not warrant congratulations?"

I was not the only one with talent. The way Rosamond managed to compliment me and insult me in the same breath was talent indeed, all while making herself appear naive and blameless.

Surely Edward could see through her act. But his smile at her words appeared genuine, as did his sadness when he looked my way.

I had hidden a deep part of myself from him, and now he knew it.

"You're a dear girl." Edward's mother smiled at Rosamond, and the young woman beamed. "Now, let's discuss the upcoming ball at Camden Hall."

The conversation spiraled away from me and my chosen *hobby*—as if that was all it was—and onto frivolous topics.

As we adjourned from the room, Edward's mother approached me. "Miss Fairfax, I must know. Is it true?" The other guests were out of earshot, and it was only the two of us and a few servants standing in the corner of the room.

I may have been able to avoid directly answering the question at dinner, but that was not an option available to me now. "It is. But I promise I have never once neglected my duties. When I was the governess, I wrote in the evenings after the children were in bed. Now I write each day once Louisa no longer needs me."

She considered me for a moment. "I admit, I have never taken such a hard line regarding female authors. However, you heard Mr. and Mrs. Banks tonight. There are those in our circle who would look down upon us for employing you—especially as a companion to our daughter. Your father's indiscretions are one thing. This is something you are choosing to participate in yourself. I cannot abide it."

I opened my mouth to speak, then shut it again. What could I say? It would probably not change how she felt on the subject because it would not change the perception of female authors overnight. But there was one sentiment I needed to express. "I will respect your decision, whatever it is. However, I cannot stop writing. It is a physical ache, and if I do not let it out, I will die inside."

She reached out a hand as if she might pull me into a hug. But she must have remembered I was only a servant, and her hand fell to her side once more. "I cannot pretend to understand the losses you have endured and the pain you must feel. Your mother was a wonderful woman and a good friend to me. I see she taught you to be strong and mindful of your own needs, and I do admire that. If writing helps you in your sorrow, then by all means, write. However, I cannot allow you to seek publication while in my employ. It might reflect poorly on us."

Her words were a balm to my soul and a chisel all at once. I nodded, because what else could I do? If I could have afforded to refuse her terms, I might have done so. But I needed the pay this position provided.

We joined the rest of the ladies in the parlor. I found my place beside Louisa, who turned to me with tears in her eyes.

"I'm so, so sorry, Emily. I did not mean to tell. Rosamond was simply asking about you and I was so proud of your accomplishments that I just . . ." Louisa's voice squeaked. "Can you ever forgive me?"

Why would Rosamond have been asking about me? But it was no matter. The damage had been done, and Louisa clearly had not let my secret slip out of malice. I patted her hand. "All is well, Louisa. Of course I forgive you."

She visibly relaxed and smiled at me.

When the men joined us, I saw Edward coming toward me, no doubt to ask me about what we'd discussed at dinner. Rosamond intercepted him. I'd never been more grateful to her.

I rose and made my way to the opposite side of the room, where there hung a few paintings I could pretend to study. One depicted a man riding atop a horse, adorned in a military uniform, a sword pointed in the air. Soldiers marched on the ground, following him to war. His posture was that of one confident in a win.

The war that waged inside of me felt impossible, with no win to gain. How could I maintain my position here—and thus my income, my livelihood—and still be true to my own heart?

Footsteps approached behind me. Had Edward finally been loosed from Rosamond's clutches?

But as I turned, it was Edward's father I saw. "Good evening, sir."

He smoothed his mustache and nodded at me, once, twice. "Indeed." His mannerisms had always been a bit strange, methodical and slow. In my experience, it always took him a long time to say what he wanted to say—or his wife just said it for him.

We looked at the paintings together for a full minute before he finally spoke again. "I think . . ."

"Sir?" I peered up at him.

He cleared his throat. "I think, were you to use a pseudonym in your professional pursuits, my wife would have no objection, so long as nothing could be traced back to her. Ever."

"Truly?"

A nod.

Finally, a bit of hope. "That is very kind. Thank you, sir."

"Do you promise?"

"I promise. I will never publish under the name Emily Fairfax."

~∘~

I'd managed to avoid Edward all the rest of the evening, which was not terribly difficult given Rosamond's interest in him.

But the next morning, as I walked toward Louisa's room to begin the day's duties, Edward appeared, almost as if he'd been waiting for me.

"Emily."

"Hello, Edward." He looked even more handsome than usual in the dim hallway, though he wore the same thing he always did—a brown waistcoat and long, cream trousers. The smell of the cigar he had smoked last night still clung to him, a sweet, potent scent that was entirely too manly.

And though I had seen him in all kinds of situations throughout our lives, standing here with him in the early morning hours—the bustle of other people seeming far, far away—brought with it an intimacy that was different and new.

He tilted his head and gazed at me. "Why did you not tell me?"

Unexpected tears filled my eyes at the grief in his. "I'm sorry. I did not tell anyone. Not on purpose anyway."

"I did not think I was just anyone to you."

Not for the first time, I wondered if Edward was aware of the way I felt about him. If so, he was cruel to say what he did. But that was not Edward, which meant he must be blessedly unaware of my love. "You're right. You are my best friend." That I *could* tell him. "And I am afraid that is all about to change."

"It is." His lips fell into a straight line and he leaned against the hallway wall. "But what does that have to do with you not telling me about your writing?"

"I suppose . . . perhaps I was beginning to pull away." It had not been intentional at first, but I recognized now the truth in the statement. "This is the most personal thing I have ever done. And when you are married, we will no longer be able to share such personal things."

"I wish it were not so."

"As do I." I settled against the wall next to him, my arms aching to touch him.

"But I'm not married yet. And I so want to know what is in your heart. Will you tell me?"

If he knew what he was asking . . . but he did not. So I told him as much as I was able—that writing had saved me when nothing else could, that it was where my future hopes were pinned, and that I would fight with all my being to see my dreams realized.

Nothing else in the world may be certain, no one else might fight for me, but I would remain steadfast in my pursuit of some greater meaning in my life.

As I spoke, something lit in Edward's eyes. He seemed to move closer to me, intent on every word I said. His gaze did not leave me once, and his lips parted ever so slightly when I finished.

Silence buzzed between us as we stared at each other—and something seemed to shift. I didn't know how to define it, but it was as if he suddenly saw me differently, noticed me for the first time as someone other than his childhood playmate.

It might have been my imagination run away from me, but the tension between us was palpable. My heart pounded.

"Would you . . . show me?" His whisper trotted into the silence but did not break the spell. "Can I read your book?"

And in that moment, I squeezed my eyes shut.

Because this was reality, and reality dictated that I take a step back. Much as I wished he would sweep me up in his arms and kiss me soundly, declaring his love, I knew he never would. He was the only male heir to a fortune, one that required him to marry well. And while I was not lowborn, my fortune was nonexistent.

"I . . . can't." How could I explain to him that handing over my book would be like handing him all of me? I would be his—mind, body, and soul—and would be left with nothing in return but memories and even lonelier nights than I already experienced.

"Em . . ."

I opened my eyes once more and realized my mistake. His fingers approached my cheek and wiped at a tear I had not realized I'd cried. Edward's touch was so gentle, amazing for the boy who had been as rough-and-tumble as they came.

But he was no longer a boy. I was no longer a girl. We were no longer children.

And we could no longer pretend to be so.

"Oh. Pardon me, sir."

A voice snapped me from the whirlwind of emotions churning inside of me. Edward lowered his hand fast as lightning and nodded at a maid, whose features had communicated surprise but now were void of expression.

She cleared her throat. "Miss Fairfax, the missus is asking where you are. Louisa is awake and needs your assistance." She walked away.

"I must be going." I flashed Edward a tentative smile, but his frown followed me all the way to my rightful place serving his sister.

20

SOPHIA

The last time she'd been to St. Paul's Cathedral in London, Sophia was a college junior—full of hope for the future, with a driving desire to help others and a naiveté that rivaled Giselle from that Disney movie *Enchanted*.

Now here she was again, stronger in some ways and beat down in others, trying her best to chase the inspiration to write her story.

Sophia stood next to William in the cathedral's nave, her gaze taking in everything from the black-and-white checkerboard floor tiles to the dome decorated in brilliant frescoes three-hundred-something feet overhead. Visitors moved throughout the nave in hushed reverence. Some sat in the chairs, heads bowed. The sight stirred something within her chest.

"It's so beautiful." She murmured the words as she and William continued to wander, taking in each monument, plaque, and statue.

William remained quiet. From the short time she'd spent with him, she knew being reflective was not unusual for him. But something seemed off.

"You okay?" She felt the urge to give his arm a squeeze, but gripped her purse strap instead.

He continued to stare at a carved marble statue of two women before a tombstone.

"William?"

His head shot up, his gaze finding hers. "Sorry. What?"

"I just asked if you were okay. You were studying this statue with intensity. And, I mean, it's a cool statue, but not overly unique from what I can tell."

The lines around his lips were more pronounced when he frowned like he was doing now. "I suppose I'm just worried about Ginny."

When they'd heard from William's professor friend in London, who thought she could help if they were willing to visit, Ginny asked if she could come too. At first, they'd assumed she merely wanted a distraction, but this morning—much to William's protest—she had declared that she was going to see Garrett. William had insisted on going with her, but she said it was between her and her husband.

"I'm worried about her too." Sophia had also offered to go with Ginny for emotional support, but she understood Ginny's desire to do this alone. In fact, she admired it. "Hopefully the face-to-face time will help. Communicating over the phone isn't all that conducive to resolving things."

Since William's friend couldn't see them till this afternoon, and there was no point in coming to London and not going sightseeing, Sophia had begged him to take her and Ginny to some of his favorite sites in the city before their appointment. After Westminster Abbey, Ginny had split off from them, and they'd come here for a quick peek around.

With every interaction, she was loosening up around him. Hearing all the good things Ginny had to say about him sure hadn't hurt.

"It's probably better I don't see Garrett right now anyway. I'd be liable to clock him."

Sophia's hand tentatively found his shoulder. "You don't exactly strike me as the punching type."

"Anger and disappointment can make you do things you might not normally consider."

"True enough." Sophia considered her words carefully. "I know you probably don't want to hear this, but whatever happens between him and Ginny, he's still your brother. You'll have to talk to him eventually—probably without the punching part—or you'll be miserable. I can tell you really love him, or you wouldn't be so angry."

William studied her for a moment, his look so intense she couldn't interpret how he'd taken her words. But then he noticed Sophia's hand on him.

She yanked it back to her side.

He frowned again, something he did far too often. He had a nice smile. And Sophia wanted to see it again.

"Come on." She reached out her hand, and after a moment of studying her, he took it. His hand was large, slightly calloused—not smooth like David's had been. But William's father had been a carpenter, and his sons had grown up working alongside him. Of course, William had confessed he hated woodworking, that he much preferred reading and studying. He'd only done it to be close to his dad.

David had grown up the entitled son of a wealthy businessman. His idea of using his hands was doing the dishes, and he hadn't even done that. *"But, baby, why should I do them when you're so good at it?"*

She couldn't keep comparing the two men. It wasn't fair to William. He didn't even know about David.

But she didn't know how to stop.

Let yourself enjoy this moment.

So she put her worries and fears from her mind as best she could and focused on more pleasant things, like the gentle pressure of William's fingers entwined with her own and the way he allowed her to lead the way up the steps to the next floor. They emerged and stepped out into the circular gallery, which overlooked the cathedral floor below. The last time she'd been here, it had been super crowded, but only a few others milled about at the moment.

Sophia walked to the iron railing, catching sight of the same checkered floor where she'd been standing moments before. Something like a sunburst graced the center of the flooring. If she looked long enough, it almost appeared to be spinning.

William leaned over the railing, angling for a better view. "This is called the Whispering Gallery."

"I seem to remember something about that. We took a tour here during my college trip."

"It's fun. The acoustics are such that you and I can stand at opposite sides of the gallery and whisper something for the other to hear."

"Oh yeah! My classmates spent ten minutes whispering crude things to each other after the tour guide told us that." Sophia rolled her eyes.

William turned to face her, leaning one hip against the railing, his hand still gripping hers. "I would love to remake your memory of this place, but I'm hesitant to let go of your hand."

Her cheeks likely betrayed her mixture of pleasure and embarrassment. "I agree. That is a dilemma."

"Perhaps if you promise that we can re-create *this* moment when we're done?" He smiled, and a pair of dimples appeared.

"Perhaps."

"I'm willing to risk it then." William tugged her gently to the bench that sat flush against the wall and wound its way around the gallery. "You sit here."

She did as he asked, then watched as he walked around the ring of the gallery. When he was directly across from her—the gallery was over one hundred feet in diameter, from what she'd read—he sat too. Sophia leaned back against the wall and waited.

There came a low, soft whisper that tickled her ears. "You're a mystery to me, Sophia Barrett. One I want very much to solve."

A tingle ran up her spine. She steepled all her fingers together and placed them over her mouth. What should she say back to him?

Inside, a voice taunted her. She'd never been good at flirting. How she'd ever attracted David was a mystery. Then again, maybe he could see what a weak person she was, how much she depended on others in her life to lift her up.

"Lie."

Joy's voice resounded in her head. So what was the truth?

"You there?" William's whisper, a gentle prodding, took precedence.

"I hear you."

"That's a relief. I thought I might just be talking to a wall."

"At least you wouldn't be the only one to do so in this place."

"True, true. So want to tell me your deepest, darkest secret?"

If only she could.

And for the first time, she almost wanted to. Not simply because he was so easy to talk to. But because the idea of opening up to him felt . . . freeing.

And William was sweet and he was steady and . . .

David had been all of those things once upon a time. But looking back, there had been signs of his true character. Mom had always warned her about men like him—like her father—but she'd chosen to ignore her. And she refused to let it happen again.

Best to stick with lighthearted whispers than ones that could shatter her soul.

"I hate English tea. Give it to me iced, not hot. And just the tea. No milk or sugar."

"That is a dark secret indeed. I don't think you should share that with anyone here. You might be banned from England forever."

A giggle escaped. "That would be sad now, wouldn't it?"

"I think so." And suddenly, his voice no longer held a tease.

She swallowed. How had this man gotten under her skin in such a short amount of time? Emotions filled her, taking up room in her toes, her fingertips, her chest, her brain. As a therapist, she knew what she should do—allow herself to feel them. But they were too over-whelming. Perhaps she could merely examine them one at a time.

Right now, she'd leave the feelings of guilt and shame inside. Instead, she'd choose to let herself feel the joy of new beginnings. "I think so too, William."

It took a while for another whisper to come round the gallery. "You didn't ask about my secret."

She lifted her eyes to the domed ceiling, saw the scenes from the life of St. Paul depicted in the paintings high above her. "What's your secret?"

"I'm falling for you, Sophia."

Something about talking to William this way, where he seemed far away but could still hear her heart, gave her courage. "I think I'm falling for you too."

21

❦

GINNY

This was where Garrett preferred to spend his time?

Ginny continued her walk from the Underground stop toward the address William had given her. Even in the broad daylight, she hugged her purse close. Her jeans and shirt clung to her body, a byproduct of the humidity harassing the city. The buildings she passed were in various states of disarray and abandonment. Groups of men leered at her as she hurried toward Garrett's flat.

Maybe she should have taken William up on his offer to come with her after all.

But she'd wanted the time alone, didn't want to stir up any extra drama between the brothers. They had their own issues to work out. Today was about convincing Garrett to come home and figure out what to do about the bookstore. She needed her teammate.

Finally, she reached his building, an old Victorian that had clearly seen some decay over the last hundred-plus years. The brick crumbled, the slate roof clearly needed patching, and the sash windows were caked with dirt. His flat was on the ground floor, so at least it was easy to find.

Ginny stood in front of the red door with peeling paint and lifted her hand to knock, then lowered it. Pulling a compact mirror from her purse, she stared back at her reflection—smudged mascara surrounded her brown eyes, wisps of untamable hair framed her face, and an indent in her pale pink bottom lip showed where she'd been biting it all day.

Good thing their relationship was built on more than looks.

Before she could stop herself again, she knocked. A fluorescent light buzzed and flickered down the hallway.

The door opened. "Did you forget your—" Garrett stopped and blinked. "Ginny?"

She'd expected to find him unshaven, wearing nothing but basketball shorts and a stained T-shirt, with bloodshot eyes and maybe a beer in his hand—the result of not working and trying to figure out what was wrong with his life. Instead, he was dressed in pressed slacks and a collared shirt, his cheeks and chin smooth and his features well rested. He'd cut his hair short, cropped close to his head. It looked good.

"Hi." She ran her fingers over the rope-like strap of her purse.

He peeked out into the hallway. "What are you doing here?"

The sharpness in his tone made her wince. "I couldn't . . . I didn't know what else to do. Things have been so horribly wrong, and I just wanted to see you and I knew that if I did, it could all be okay." Her chin trembled. "Garrett, I . . ."

His features fell. "I'm sorry, Gin." Then he stepped forward and enveloped her in his arms, where she'd always fit, where she was meant to be. A new scent—spicy, like cinnamon—surrounded her. He must have stopped using the cologne she'd bought him for his birthday.

She held on tight, all reason leaving her. If only he'd tip her chin up, kiss her . . .

Wait. The word breathed a warning to her heart. This was not why she'd come. Yes, she wanted to reconcile. But she also wanted an explanation.

Ginny pried herself from her husband's arms. "Garrett, what's going on?" Surprised by the strength in her voice, she straightened.

He looked at the ground, a grungy carpet that had maybe once been a brilliant blue but now appeared dull and worn out. "You shouldn't have come."

"I didn't have a choice. The bookstore . . . Well, I needed to talk to you. Plus, you hardly gave me anything to go on. We've been married for five years. I deserve to know why you're filing for divorce."

He wore his decision-making face: pursed lips swung to one side, brow furrowed in concentration. Then he nodded. "Come in."

Was it her imagination or did he take another look down the hallway as he was ushering her inside and closing the door? Why would he be embarrassed to be seen with her?

The flat must have come furnished because he couldn't have bought all of this since he'd left. She'd assumed it would be a sty—this man never even managed to get his underwear in the hamper—but other than a bit of clutter, it was neat and tidy. As they passed the kitchen, she noticed a pile of dishes in the sink, including skillets and pans. Since when did Garrett cook? Perhaps it was part of "finding" himself.

He led her to a small living room and waited for her to sit on the sofa. Then he lowered himself into a recliner. His hands gripped his kneecaps as he leaned forward, rocking his feet ever so slightly. Clearly, he was just as nervous as she was.

She longed to put him at ease, but she had to remember why she'd come. "I'm sorry to show up unannounced, but you weren't really returning my phone calls."

"I know, but you just kept asking the same thing over and over again. I couldn't handle it." He glanced at the clock, squeezing his hands open, shut, open.

"It's just . . ." Her eyes burned. "Why?" There was no possible way the wrenching word could sound more pathetic.

He did not answer right away. "I've already told you—"

"Yes, you said you weren't sure you loved me anymore."

"It's not just that." He made a fist with his right hand and punched his left hand, frowned. "I'm not sure I ever really loved you."

Her jaw fell open. "Wha—"

"Let me finish. It's taken me a while to process this, but I know this is the first time you're hearing it. So I apologize if I sound . . . unemotional about it. The fact is, my father died, you were there to help me through, and I thought it meant you were the one for me. You really were amazing to me, but that doesn't mean we were meant to be together."

"But we *are* together. Does it matter if it's 'meant to be' or not?" How could she articulate how she felt when she was with him? "You are everything to me, Garrett."

"And do you know how much pressure that puts on a man? I'm not perfect, Ginny. In fact, I'm a pretty royal screw-up if you haven't figured it out by now." He'd said he wouldn't be emotional, but she glimpsed an undercurrent of grief and anger in him.

"I never meant to put pressure on you. I'm not perfect either."

"Aren't you, though? You are truly what every man could want: intelligent, beautiful, kind."

"If you feel that way, then why are you divorcing me?"

And there were the tears, unshed but glimmering in his eyes. "Because it's not enough." He punched his hands together once more. "I'm sorry. I never meant to hurt you."

"But what about the book—"

"Honey?" The front door creaked open and slammed, and a disembodied voice floated through the room. A female voice. "Can you come help me with the groceries?"

It took Ginny several moments to process what she was hearing and seeing.

Garrett's face draining of color.

147

The rustle of paper bags.

A petite blonde walking into the room clutching said paper bags, a look of surprise on her face.

A low moan slicing through her whole being.

She was the worst kind of fool.

"Ginny . . ." Garrett slid off the recliner and crouched in front of her.

"What is going on? Who"—Ginny pointed to the woman, whose eyes had flown to the ground—"is that? And why is she calling you honey?"

Her husband reached out as if to grab her hand, but stopped himself. "I'm so sorry." His words sounded anguished, genuine even, but the apology could not compute with the lie in the form of the blonde standing ten feet away.

"You lied to me."

"No. Yes." Garrett sighed. "I truly did come here to find myself. There wasn't anyone else. But in the midst of my sorrow, the first week here, I met Samantha and we formed a friendship. And it turned into more." He paused. "You have every right to hate me."

Samantha approached them, set the bags down on the coffee table, and placed her hand on Garrett's shoulder—whether to claim him or comfort him, who could tell.

Ginny didn't look up at her to find out. "So why didn't you come home, ask me for forgiveness? I would have forgiven you."

And she would have. The thought surprised her. Would she have taken him back without question? Yes, there would have been hurt, but was she so desperate that she'd trust him right away after such a huge grievance against her?

"I know, and I considered it. But then . . ." He cleared his throat. "Samantha and I fell in love. I didn't mean for it to happen. It just did. And it felt different from what I've ever felt for you. It's not your fault, Gin. You've been a good wife. But . . ."

And then she understood fully.

It didn't matter that she loved Garrett with every breath of her being, that she'd given up her own dreams of culinary school to pursue what everyone else wanted of her, that she'd worked her rear off trying to save Garrett's dream.

She was no better off now than five years ago because she still didn't know where she belonged.

22

SOPHIA

When William had described an "old-school" contact in London who was difficult to reach, Sophia had pictured an elderly woman with an eyeglass chain and a poor sense of style—not the long-legged beauty wearing a flowy top and Gucci jeans standing before her.

Professor Abigail Wentworth opened the front door to her flat a little wider. "William. Come in." She stepped forward and wrapped him in an enthusiastic hug. Her blond hair fell in waves to her waist and she smelled of eucalyptus. A tiny surge of green besieged Sophia at the sight of William hugging her back.

William pulled away from his friend's embrace, smiling. "So good to see you again, Abigail. It's been too long." He turned to Sophia. "This is Sophia Barrett."

Abigail seemed to consider her, and her gaze penetrated Sophia's armor. After a moment's glance, her features softened, as if she'd discerned something about Sophia just then. "Welcome to my home, Sophia. It's a pleasure."

Though the tinge of jealousy from earlier still remained, Sophia couldn't justify it. There was a softness, a friendliness to Abigail that was unusual upon first meeting someone. "Likewise."

Abigail turned on her heel and headed down her hallway. "Come," her voice called back to them.

They stepped across the threshold, and William shut the door behind them. He cocked an eyebrow at Sophia. "Well? I told you she was unique."

"She is. But you didn't mention she was so . . ."

"Rich?" The flat was a well-positioned home in Chelsea.

"No. Beautiful."

William looked amused. "Is she?"

"Never mind." She flicked him on the arm and strode past him, following Abigail's path. She heard William chuckle as he hurried to catch up.

Large oil paintings lined the hallway walls, everything from Monet to Picasso to some modern art pieces by artists Sophia was not familiar with. The hallway split. To the right, Sophia spied an elaborate dining room, or what was supposed to be one. Instead of a formal table and chairs, however, the room held display cases featuring a variety of artifacts. She wasn't close enough to make them all out and would have gone inside if Abigail hadn't called to them from the left side of the hallway.

She turned from the display case room and followed William into a library with at least twenty tall bookcases stuffed to the brim. In the corner of the room, next to the expansive window with floor-length curtains, sat a ten-foot white statue of Buddha, his eyes closed in meditation. Crucifixes peppered the walls that weren't covered with bookcases. Incense burned on a coffee table in the middle of the room, where Abigail sat on a regal-looking sofa.

William lowered himself into an overstuffed leather chair. "I could spend weeks in this room. It's quite something. You've added even more books."

On her way to join them, Sophia passed a display case, catching sight of a very old edition of the Quran. "Are you a professor of religion, Abigail?" She joined her on the sofa, leaving ample cushion space between herself and William's friend.

"Oh no. Geography." Abigail's light laugh floated on the air. "I'm merely interested in the spiritual. William, do you remember that retreat we took in uni? Ah, it was so refreshing. I now try to get away like that at least once a year if I can."

"I do remember. If I recall, that's when you first convinced me to try yoga. It was not pretty."

"Oh, I'd forgotten! It was quite amusing, I'll admit. But you didn't come here to discuss that." Abigail swung her smile toward Sophia. "William sent me a copy of the written material in question and I think I might be able to help."

"That's wonderful." Hope zinged through Sophia's heart.

"Before I do, though, let me serve the tea." Abigail stood and left the room for a moment, then returned carrying a tray sporting a teapot, three cups and saucers, milk, sugar, scones, cream, jam, and small finger sandwiches.

Placing everything on the coffee table, Abigail sat once more. She bent forward and poured milk into each of the cups, then added tea from the teapot. The way her lithe fingers moved nearly hypnotized Sophia. There was an aura of calm surrounding Abigail. "Let's get to know each other a bit before diving in, shall we? Sophia, I sense that your profession has something to do with helping people."

She *sensed* it? "Y-yes, I'm a women's therapist."

Abigail slid Sophia a cup of tea, holding out a sugar bowl with a small set of tongs. "Hmm." Abigail tilted her head and studied Sophia as she dropped two cubes of sugar into her tea. Maybe it would mask some of the tea's flavor. "What drew you to that profession in the first place?"

"I guess I just wanted to help people." Sophia raised the cup to her lips. It would be rude not to try it. She caught William watching her and remembered he knew her "secret" about hating English tea. She lifted the cup slightly as if to say, "Here goes nothing."

His lips curled into a grin.

As the tea flowed into her mouth, she held back a grimace.

"Yes, that makes sense." Abigail's voice brought her back to the present. "As soon as I saw you, I could tell you felt sympathy for others. But it's more than that, isn't it? You feel empathy, because you've also been a victim. But you don't want to be one. Still, your body language and everything else tells me this desire in you is making you closed off."

"How . . . ?" Sophia couldn't get the question out. Without thinking, she sucked down a full mouthful of the tea. The hot liquid burned the roof of her mouth and throat. She coughed.

"Are you all right?" William reached into his bag and pulled out a water bottle. "Here."

Sophia waved him off. "I'm okay. Thanks." She turned once more to Abigail, who lifted her own cup to her lips and sipped, her back poised and straight, the perfect picture of harmony. "How did you know all of that?" From across the table, she could feel William's questioning gaze burrowing into her.

"Oh, I'm just good at reading people." Abigail set her tea down, then brushed her hair behind her shoulders. "Your mother plays into it, doesn't she? Your decision to be a therapist, I mean." Her ability to read people bordered on the bizarre, but maybe she was one of those Sherlock Holmes types who could simply pick up on context clues.

Still, Sophia considered the question. "In many ways, yes, I suppose so. She has always been a huge influence in my life. She remained strong in the face of her trials, and she's always put others first."

"You can put others first without counseling them, you know." Abigail raised an eyebrow.

Of course she knew that. But being a therapist was a surefire way to make sure she remained others-centered—and that she didn't descend into the depths of self-pity that could easily become her home at any moment if she thought too hard about her past.

Abigail continued. "Can I ask you something? Why are you here today?"

"I'm confused. You said you might be able to help us."

"Yes, but I mean why are you on this quest to begin with?"

Sophie shrugged. "To be honest, I don't know why I'm doing this. I came to England to . . . well, to overcome the past. And something tells me that finding out more about Emily's story is part of that, though I don't understand how."

Taking a biscuit in hand, Abigail dunked it, then tapped it against the side of her cup. She took a bite and chewed, thoughtful. "If I've learned anything, it's that life is often a puzzle. We have the right pieces, but they're all jumbled up. Sometimes we try to complete the puzzle in a hurry, and pieces that don't really belong together get shoved into place. Then, frustrated, we tear it all apart once more. My mother and I loved doing puzzles together. But she always had to remind me to put together the frame first before filling in the middle. That's like life too. What you're doing is good. Take it one step at a time. The picture on the puzzle might not even make sense until the last piece is popped into place. Then it will form a beautiful picture."

Abigail stared at Sophia like she expected a response. But how was she supposed to respond to that? The analogy had stirred something within her, but she wasn't sure what. Longing, perhaps? Gratitude?

"Abigail." William's gentle voice broke the tension.

His friend seemed to shake herself from intense focus. She inclined her head to him and smiled. "Have you tried the scones, clotted cream, and jam? If not, you must."

He picked up a scone, cut it open, and placed a dollop of cream and red jam inside. "Now, fascinating as this conversation is, we've come to discuss the story by or about Emily Fairfax. What help can you offer us?"

"Of course." Abigail wiped her hands on a napkin. "You'll forgive my rambling, Sophia. My spirit is just very drawn to yours." She smiled softly. "But I did promise to help. When reading over the pages in question, one thing stood out to me. There's a mention of the okirah bush."

"What's that?" Sophia scoured her memory. "That was something that grew in Edward's family gardens, right?"

"Exactly. The okirah bush went extinct in the early twentieth century. The only known observations of it were in Cornwall, and its popularity peaked in the Victorian era. It was a plant that took a skilled hand to maintain. Only the wealthy could afford to hire gardeners with the expertise to do so."

Finally a clue, however small. Leaning forward, Sophia's knee bumped the coffee table, sending her tea spilling over the edges of the cup onto her saucer. She snatched a napkin to clean the mess, but mostly kept her eyes on Abigail. "Anything else?"

"Yes. The fact that it's mentioned at all is surprising, given its virtual anonymity and obscure existence. Other than the fact it's extinct now, there is nothing extraordinary about the bush. This leads me to believe that the story might not be fiction, unless written by a Cornish botanist or horticulturist."

"How do *you* know about it then?"

Abigail averted her gaze, staring off toward the window behind Sophia. "Nature has always allured me. As a girl, I became something of a fanatic, studying all manner of geography, botany, geomorphogeny, and geology. My parents gave me a large encyclopedia of plants in primary school. I have a very good memory, so . . ." She shrugged. "The okirah bush is stuck in my brain somewhere between oak leaf hydrangea and ornamental onion."

"I see." Sophia smiled.

William folded his hands together and bounced a knee. "What about the tree? The one where Emily and Edward meet up? Do you recall any mentions of trees such as that one in the area where the okirah bush was known to grow?"

Abigail's lips tucked into a slight frown. She leaned back in her chair, her shoulders crunching downward. "Not immediately, but something is niggling the back of my mind. Give me some time to do a bit of research and I'll get back to you. I have your e-mail."

Another disappointing halt to their search. While Abigail had provided the grain of a next step, there was nothing concrete in the information she'd provided. They'd just have to wait and see if she came up with any other information.

～✺～

"Well? Not so bad, is it?" William leaned forward, elbows resting on the pub table, a huge boyish grin plastered on his face.

Sophia forced herself to keep chewing, then to swallow. She inhaled a half glass of ice water before she could answer. "That. Was. Disgusting."

"Oh, come on." He took another bite of his haggis. "It's Scotland's national dish."

After they'd left Abigail's, William had given Ginny a call—no answer. They'd headed back toward their hotel, which was located in Piccadilly Circus, and wandered the area until dinnertime, when they'd stumbled across a quaint Scottish pub.

"It's made of sheep innards. But at least I can now say I've tried it." She speared a turnip and dipped it in her mashed potatoes—or neeps and tatties, as the menu had proclaimed the side dishes to be— and took a bite. Thank goodness this part was edible. "I can cross that one off the bucket list for good."

"Ah, there's a list?"

Wood-paneled from ceiling to floor, with an arts-and-crafts feel, the pub was dimly lit, with soft Scottish folk music lilting from speakers Sophia couldn't see. Though the bar area was crowded with patrons, the small corner where she and William shared a booth was tucked away enough to feel private. Intimate. Almost like a date.

Was she ready for that?

"Doesn't everyone have a list? I recently read a blog by a woman who had a heart transplant and later fulfilled her donor's bucket list. She traveled all over the world doing the things this girl never got to do. Isn't that neat?" Sophia took another sip of water.

"That is indeed very neat." William set down his fork and wiped his mouth with his black paper napkin. "But I want to know what's on *your* list."

"Just the usual stuff." The things that had been on her list before she'd met David seemed so trite now. And the ones she'd placed there after he'd died seemed too personal—frankly, even somewhat impossible. "How about you?"

With a swig of wine, William's face grew thoughtful. He took her avoidance in stride. "I've been planning a sabbatical sometime in the next few years. I'd like to travel a bit, do some research in the old cathedrals across Europe, that sort of thing."

"Sounds amazing."

"I think so. But ultimately, I want to take the time to write a book."

"Like Emily?"

Smiling, he shook his head. "Not exactly. I want to write a book about how grace has changed my life."

"Grace? Who's that? Or do you mean grace with a little *g*?"

A short red candle on the table between them flickered.

William smiled. "Little *g*. The man you see before you is not who I used to be. I was fairly obedient as a child, but when I went to uni, I abandoned my faith and pursued my own pleasures." His voice was matter-of-fact, but his facial features strained against the words. "It wasn't until my father died that I truly began to realize that the way

I'd been living my life was not right. I was in a pit of despair, with no way out—and God rescued me with grace."

Things about William were beginning to add up—the topic of his dissertation, the fact he'd taken her to see both Westminster Abbey and St. Paul's Cathedral out of all the other sights in London, the way her heart felt so comfortable with his, despite her reservations. She'd believed in God, too, once upon a time. "But . . ."

"But what?"

"Well, no offense, but I've always thought if you get yourself into a mess, you're responsible for getting yourself out of it. Why would God become involved?" She'd grown up with faith, sure, but Sophia had since seen how the world worked. People made decisions, and those decisions had consequences. End of story.

"I think sometimes he's just waiting for us to realize our own limitations."

Sophia snatched up a dessert menu, ran her fingertips over the smooth, glossy surface. A lump formed in her throat.

William reached across the table, tentative, and squeezed Sophia's hand. "If you want to talk . . . well, I'm here."

What would it be like to tell William everything? Would he think less of her?

Weakling. You're nothing. David's whispers still haunted her from the grave. But she was slowly getting better about recognizing his voice and the lies he told.

She'd told Ginny the truth about her past, and her new friend had been nothing but supportive. Maybe the same would be true of William.

Raucous laughter from the next booth over invaded their quiet bubble.

She looked down at William's thumb stroking her hand. It was always a risk to open herself up to someone new. But opening up to someone didn't have to be the equivalent of losing herself—not this time. "Let's get out of here."

They paid the tab and left the pub. The night air was brisk against her skin, filled with promise. It had grown late while they'd chatted inside, though that didn't stop the sidewalks and streets from being crowded. Being a Saturday night in London, it shouldn't have come as a surprise. The moon radiated down its light, and black lampposts lining the streets provided even more.

Turning onto a quieter street situated in a neighborhood, Sophia worked up the courage to begin.

"I'd like to tell you a story." As she spilled about David and why she'd come to Cornwall, they entered a small square lined with benches. Rose beds and grass verges surrounded the perimeter, and cascading trees marked the various entry points to the square. A statue stood in the middle, raised on a paved area. Other flowers bloomed in gardens planted around the statue. Reds, blues, and yellows splashed color into the night.

William tugged Sophia down onto a bench while she spoke. He watched her with careful eyes, sympathetic eyes—eyes full of something akin to . . . what? Was it respect?

How could he possibly respect her? But maybe he respected her desire to become someone new. To rise from the ashes.

If only she knew how.

When she finished, Sophia took a shuddering breath. "So I guess that, even though I feel half the time like I'm stumbling with no direction, I've made some progress toward healing. But it's hard to know when that healing will be complete, or if it ever will be. I refuse to be a victim, though. Not anymore."

A breeze rolled past them and made her shiver.

William moved his arm around her shoulders, and instead of making her feel hemmed in, the gesture brought comfort. "I cannot even imagine what you've been through. You should have been treasured, cherished. But I so admire how strong you've been throughout this whole ordeal."

"Did you hear the part where I didn't leave David?"

"Sophia, you survived. Survivors are strong. You want healing. You want to move on with your life. You have not let this define you—or at least, you no longer want it to."

Sophia shrugged, unable to speak.

"There's nothing shameful in accepting help, you know. We were designed to need each other."

"That's so not what I grew up believing. At least on a subconscious level."

"Oh?"

How could she explain what she meant? "It's hard to believe that when you see what 'love' has done to people. I still remember my mom right after my dad left. I hid on the stair banister and saw her huddled against my aunt, her breath shuddering. Then all of a sudden, she drew herself upright, wiped her tears away, and you know what she said? 'They say it's better to have loved and lost than never to have loved at all. Well, that's not true. I loved deeply and now he's gone, and I'm a simpering sack of potatoes. I refuse to let a man make me feel like this. I won't be this weak ever again.'"

It took William a moment to respond. "Did you ever ask her if she really meant that?"

The question rattled the cage surrounding Sophia's memory. "I've never mentioned to her that I was there, no."

"Maybe it was a gut reaction to her immediate circumstances. Perhaps she didn't really mean it."

Whether she'd meant it or not, Sophia could now see how that moment had shaped how she saw her mom . . . and how she'd seen her own failures where David was concerned.

"Did your mom ever remarry?" William must have sensed her reticence to discuss these new thoughts.

"No. She never even dated again." A light huff of laughter blew from her mouth. "Though ironically enough, she's a wedding planner now."

"So maybe she still believes in love." William's breath hovered above her brow, a gentle warmth in the midst of the chilly night air. "What about you? Do you still believe in love despite all you've been through?"

It was something she had not really let herself consider. But she felt the answer in her spirit. "Honestly?"

"Of course."

"When it comes to others, yes. But as for myself . . . I'm not sure if I believe." She paused. "But I want to."

William didn't say anything, just rested his head against hers. She'd never met anyone who made her feel so much like she was stepping into a judgment-free zone, free of the shackles of her past. Like she was stepping toward something and not running away.

It was both unnerving . . . and reassuring.

Sophia snuggled into the crook of William's arm, quiet for a moment. Then she took one more proverbial step forward. "So, my bucket list. You still want to know what's on it?"

"I do."

"It's changed over the years, of course, but one thing has always been at the top." Sophia took a deep breath, praying William wouldn't laugh like David had. "I want to learn how to surf. Does that surprise you?"

"I'm surprised by you every day. And I love it." He pressed a kiss to her forehead and she could feel the smile in it. "So, why surfing?"

"My dad surfed, and I guess in a way I feel like it's in my blood. Or it should be. Or maybe I just want to find out if it is." She traced a figure eight on William's arm. "I know it's strange, but I never allowed my dad's leaving to make me doubt myself as a person. Instead, I was just angry that he put Mom and me through that, especially Mom. Eventually I learned that hating him was only hurting me. I also started thinking that maybe not every part of him was bad. He wasn't pure evil, even though he made mistakes. I have a few good memories from childhood. So in a weird way, I think learning to do something he loved would almost be like forming a new good memory with him. Taking back what the anger stole from me." She blew out a laugh. "That probably only made sense in my head."

"It makes perfect sense." William squeezed her shoulder. "And if you want to learn how to surf, then learn to surf you shall."

23

EMILY

JUNE 1858

I closed the book I was reading and sighed. The main character had ended up with the right woman.

My shoulders slumped as I leaned against a chair in the sitting room. If only real life mirrored fiction.

Enough of this drudgery and dwelling on things I could not change.

The children were on an outing with their mother, so I had the rare afternoon to myself. I'd thought reading would brighten my mood, but perhaps I'd have better luck with the great outdoors.

Outside my window, the London sky was painted a striking color—if I stared at it long enough, shades of purple began to appear. Tiny wisps of clouds teased me with the way they flitted through the sky, changing shape and becoming whatever they wished to be.

I hooked my cape over my dress and left the room, maneuvering down the hallway and through the door that led to the small garden behind the house.

The light from the outdoors exploded all around. Blankets of colorful flowers greeted me. Spring had asked winter to step aside and had fully bloomed in its place.

After a few moments of walking, enjoying the breeze upon my cheeks and the bright splashes of evergreen grass and bluebells, I stopped at a plant with beautiful white flowers hanging down like bells. Struck by their beauty and their alluring fragrance, I reached out to touch one. But then I recalled something Edward had told me when I had first seen them at his family's estate in the country: *"The plant is called angel's trumpet. However, do not be fooled by how stunning it is. The blooms are poisonous."*

I heard raised voices around the bend, one of them Edward's. My hand dropped, and I walked quickly toward them. Were Rosamond and Edward arguing? I couldn't keep glee from being my first emotion at the thought.

As I came upon the scene, I slowed my pace. It was not Rosamond but Louisa who was crying and yelling at her brother. When she saw me, she put a hand over her mouth and hurried past, leaving Edward standing there, a hand gripping the back of his neck.

"What's happened?" I strode forward. "Is someone ill?" I had never seen Louisa act that way and could not imagine what else would have caused such behavior.

"No, nothing like that." Edward blew out a breath and paced.

"What then?"

"Charles Miller has made an offer of marriage to Louisa, and she fancies herself in love with him." Edward practically growled the words. "Has she said anything to you about him? Have you noticed them together much?"

"Not any more than a handful of other men who have paid attention to her. Louisa is a beautiful girl."

"Beautiful and naive." Edward started down the garden path, hands clutched behind his back.

I hurried to match his steps. "I suppose I'm not seeing the problem. I know your parents had intended for her to look for a husband next year, but it's a good match, is it not?" The Millers were one of the wealthiest families in all of England, and Charles was considered to be devastatingly handsome. It would not be the basis of marriage for me, but I stood apart from the rest of society.

Edward stopped and turned to me. "Charles Miller is a scoundrel. Everyone knows it, but because of his money, no one in polite society cares. I won't go into the particulars, Emily, but trust me when I say that no sister of mine will be shackled to a man like that."

His chest heaved at the passion his words produced, and it only made me love him more. "How did your parents feel about the match?"

His expression darkened. "Father was all set to agree to it until I persuaded him otherwise. He is so desperate . . ." He trailed off.

"Desperate for what?"

"Let's return to the house, shall we?"

"What are you keeping from me, Edward?"

With a sigh, he plucked a flower from a nearby bush and twirled it, staring at the bloom. "My father has made some poor investments and soon we will be bankrupt if something does not change. It's why I agreed to find a bride this year when I had hoped to put it off a while longer."

I could not move. "Why did you not tell me before now?"

He lifted sad eyes to me. "You have such high ideals, Em. In a world that is defined by marriage, you refuse to marry because you want your independence. And you have no idea how much I admire you for it."

If only he knew the truth. I had only ever pretended to reject marriage because I could not bear the thought of Edward rejecting me.

He moved toward me and reached for my hands. Placing the flower inside, Edward closed my fingers around it. "I do not wish to disappoint you by marrying for money. But it's required of me. The responsibility is not one I take lightly. I have at least tried my best to find a bride whom I believe I could one day love."

I swallowed, my throat suddenly dry. My heart stampeded in my chest as Edward and I looked at each other for a long moment.

At last, he let go of my hands and looked away. "What do you think of Rosamond?"

"She's lovely." What else could I say? He likely heard the lie in my words. I rushed on. "Does her family not care that yours is in trouble financially?"

"Her father is well aware of our circumstances, and is willing to rescue my father. Apparently their business pursuits are aligned, and my father's good reputation would be of great value to him. Together, they would make formidable partners."

"I see. Well, it sounds as if it's all arranged." I could not keep the tightness from my tone as we walked toward the house.

As we passed by them, the angel's trumpets taunted me in the breeze, whispering a song only I could hear.

24

GINNY

Ginny grasped the vintage ring between her fingers, holding it up to the light from her bedroom lamp. Its large center diamond was nestled within a square bezel setting, flanked by delicate latticework and smaller mine-cut diamonds.

Her eyes threatened tears for the hundredth time that morning since she'd made her decision.

Before she could change her mind, Ginny shoved the ring into the pocket of her jeans, threw on a sweatshirt, stuffed her feet into a pair of ratty sneakers, and made her way down the stairs into her kitchen. She considered stopping to eat a little breakfast, but no—she might lose her nerve if she waited too long.

Her hand slid into her pocket again, and she brushed her thumb along the edge of the platinum band. Her paternal grandmother had willed it to Ginny, since her father didn't have any sisters and Ginny's sister Sarah preferred more modern jewelry. But Ginny had always loved the ring, and when her grandparents had died within a few months of each other, it had come to her.

It was not the size of the diamond or high value of the ring that mattered to her. Instead, it was a great symbol of her grand-parents' everlasting love. Unlike Ginny's parents, Grandmother and Grandfather had found a way to let love and family trump money or status as the most important things in life.

When Garrett had proposed to Ginny, all of their money had been tied up in the bookstore, so he didn't have a ring. But she didn't mind because Ginny had always loved the idea of wearing her grand-ma's ring. So she had.

The thought of selling it turned her stomach cold, but what other choice did she have? None, if she wanted to keep the bookstore afloat.

Ginny walked through her front door and straight toward Mrs. Lincoln's antique store. The cloudy sky darkened the day. As she entered, the bell above the door jangled a merry greeting. Ginny got the urge to grab it from its perch and toss it violently across the room.

"Hullo." Mrs. Lincoln's gravelly, disembodied voice rose from somewhere in the back of the store. "I'll be there in a moment."

"Take your time." Ginny peered through a maze of antique objects—from old doorframes to furniture, knickknacks to cloth-ing. Somewhere, the scent of lavender rose to meet her. Its purpose was to relax the customer, but being here only set Ginny even more on edge.

If she could convince Mrs. Lincoln to buy it, her ring was going to join the ranks of once-loved items now entombed in this chaos.

She could do this. She must do this.

Mrs. Lincoln bustled around the corner. She reminded Ginny of Mrs. Claus, complete with rosy round cheeks, an ample derriere, and a shock of white hair. Her smile brightened a bit when she saw Ginny. "My dear, what brings you by today?"

"I . . ." She hesitated.

"What's going on, love? You look like a bee without a flower to land on."

Ginny reached into her pocket and pulled out the ring. She kept her fist closed around it for a few extra moments, savoring the feel of it in her palm. She'd had dreams for this ring—dreams of forevers and I do's, just like her grandparents.

But those dreams had come crashing down around her five days ago when she'd met Garrett's new flame and had found out they planned to marry as soon as Ginny's divorce from him was final.

After that, she'd wandered the streets of London, aimless in body and mind. She'd finally ended up at the hotel before William and Sophia, snuck into her bed, and wrestled with sleep all night. The next morning, they'd all driven home, Ginny not saying a word about seeing Garrett except "He's found someone new."

William's face had blanched and Sophia had reached back to squeeze her knee. When they'd returned home, Sophia held her hand while she spilled the whole awful story.

All Ginny had left was the bookstore. She wouldn't lose it, not while she had breath in her body. But somehow she had to pay for the increased rent and other expenses that kept rolling in. She just needed enough to get her over the hump until her website was up, and she'd employed all her ideas for bringing in new customers.

Ginny opened her fist, revealing the ring in her palm. "I've come to see if you would like to purchase this from me."

"Isn't that your wedding ring?"

"It is." Ginny held back tears. How she could possibly have more after nearly a week of off-and-on crying was a mystery. "Are you interested?"

"It's quite lovely. I've always admired it." Peering closer, Mrs. Lincoln extended her hand. "May I?"

"Of course." Ginny dropped the ring into the woman's palm, feeling part of her heart break with the motion. A tear escaped down her cheek, but she swiped it away before Mrs. Lincoln could see.

"What do you know about it?"

"It's from the Edwardian period, and the center diamond is 2.2

carats. My family—the Bentleys of Boston, Massachusetts, in the States—has owned it since it was made in the early twentieth century." A stab of guilt shook Ginny. Was this a mistake?

"Impressive." The shop owner ambled toward the microscope she kept at the jewelry counter for product inspections. She placed the ring underneath and studied it for a very long few moments. The time ticked by slowly. Ginny's toes curled in her sneakers.

When Mrs. Lincoln finally glanced up, she looked over her small-rimmed glasses at Ginny. "How will Garrett feel about you selling this?" Her voice held no judgment or scolding, merely questions.

"He shouldn't care one way or the other." And clearly didn't.

The memory of the ring on Samantha's finger—a full carat at least—jabbed against Ginny's brain. How had Garrett afforded the purchase? Was he blowing through money he didn't have? Or was he using the part of the cash he'd cleared out from the bookstore account before skipping town? It should have run out by now, but maybe Samantha was supporting them.

"I'm sorry, dear. I was hoping the best for the two of you."

"Thank you."

A few moments of awkward silence ticked by. "How much are you looking to get for it?"

"I need—I mean, I'd like . . ." Ginny cleared her throat, then named her price.

Mrs. Lincoln picked up the ring again and held it out toward Ginny. "It's worth double that. A piece this fine should continue to be handed down through the generations."

Ginny shook her head, refused to take the ring back. "I'd like nothing more, but . . . I'm in a bit of a pinch. Financially." Her cheeks burned with the admission.

"I'm sorry to hear that, love." Mrs. Lincoln moved around the register. "Perhaps you could try selling it somewhere you might make more. There are many options online, or so I'm told by my nephew.

I simply can't afford to pay what it's really worth, and I don't want to rob you."

The woman's sweet words pricked Ginny's conscience. Grandmother would be so sad if she knew what Ginny was doing. But hopefully she would have understood. "I can't wait for any other options. I need the money now."

With lips pursed in thought, Mrs. Lincoln finally nodded. "You've got yourself a deal." She pulled a ring box from behind the register and placed the ring inside. "Do you prefer cash or check?"

"Either is fine." Ginny fidgeted with her sleeves. "Thank you so much, Mrs. Lincoln."

The elderly woman wrote her a check and before she could beg for the ring back, Ginny forced herself to leave the shop. She turned in the direction of the bank—and ran smack into Steven.

"Whoa." He held out his hands to steady her. "You all right?" His smile filled her heart.

"Fine, thanks." Ginny attempted to return the smile, but it fell short. "I've gotta go." Any moment now, she was going to lose it. "I'll watch where I'm going next time." She took off toward the bank, the soles of her feet burning with the effort.

"Hey, wait up." She heard him jogging behind her. "Where are you off to in such a hurry?"

She waved the check in the air. "The bank."

"I didn't know anyone still wrote checks these days."

"Mrs. Lincoln does." Too late, she realized her mistake.

"Did you sell her something?"

She avoided his gaze. "Yes." Aaaaand, there came the tears. Ginny kept moving up the steep street, where the bank sat at the top of the hill.

"Ginny, are you crying?"

However nice his concern, she couldn't stop.

But Steven was persistent. He gently tugged on her arm, turned her toward him. "You *are* crying. What's wrong? What did you sell? And why? I mean, you don't have to tell me, but I'm here if you need to talk. Remember? Good listener."

The months of feeling completely alone, of crying into her pillow at night, of missing Garrett with a ferocity that astounded her after his betrayal, of hating him for leaving her to manage all of this by herself, of loving him still—it all came spilling out. "I'm crying because my husband found a new woman and is divorcing me, and the only thing I have left is a stupid bookstore I didn't want in the first place. But it's the only place that's ever felt like home, and I can't let it go. I can't."

Her raised voice was attracting attention, but for once she didn't care. "So I had to. I sold my wedding ring, which was also my grandma's ring and has been in my family for over a hundred years. The one I'd hoped to wear forever. Now it's over. It's really over."

She ran her fingers underneath her eyes, pushing away the wetness that clung there. Now she'd done it—let loose all of her failures to this man who would probably side with her soon-to-be ex, who was surprisingly still standing there in front of her, hands in his pockets, his mouth downturned.

But in an instant, his hands were wrapped around her, pulling her to his solid chest as she released a fresh torrent of tears.

How embarrassing. Ginny sniffed, but her nose was clogged from all the crying. She coughed. "I'm sorry." Her voice came out hoarse and muffled against the soft cotton of his shirt. "You didn't want to know all of that."

"Ginny."

She looked up into the clearest and sweetest eyes she'd ever seen. The thought was disconcerting. She pulled away from his embrace. "Yeah?"

"I'm sorry. About your grandma's ring. And about Garrett."

Words suddenly failed her. She shrugged.

"And I'll double my efforts to get your website up as soon as possible, all right?"

"I feel so bad, you doing it for free. It's taking you away from other money-making projects."

"I'm happy to help. I'm sure others would be too, if you asked. You're not just Garrett's wife around here, you know. People love and respect you."

She kicked at a rock. "Thank you." In her fist, she still clutched the check from Mrs. Lincoln. "I had better get this to the bank."

Steven studied her for a minute, then nodded. "I've got an errand to run too. Chin up, Gin. It's gonna be okay."

As she watched him walk away, the ends of the check fluttering between her fingers in the breeze, the tiniest bit of hope broke through the clouds, shining sunlight on the cracks in the street in front of her.

She had friends who cared.

And she had a small influx of money.

For now, that was enough.

25

❦

SOPHIA

The sound of the surf had never been so sweet.

Or so frightening.

Sophia stood on the secluded beach, warm sand between her toes, the wind teasing her bangs. It blew just enough to create beautiful white waves on the water, but not so much to turn her first day of surfing disastrous.

She might do that all on her own.

No. She could do this. After all, she had William here to teach her.

There was no denying how handsome he looked in his black-and-gray wetsuit, and Sophia was transported back to their first meeting. Was that only a month ago? How had they become close so quickly?

It happened quickly with David too.

Sophia slammed the thought from her mind. Of course she was growing close to him. For the last two weeks since their London trip, she'd done nothing but work in the bookstore and hang out with William and Ginny. They hadn't heard a peep from Abigail, so they'd spent their time playing cards, watching movies, talking books, and taking walks around town in the evening. She'd even "introduced" him to Mom and Joy on separate Skype calls. Afterward, both had given their thumbs-up of approval.

It was the most at peace she'd been in a long time.

She folded her arms across her body. "So, are you sure you want to do this?"

He looked down at her, something alight in his eyes. "I couldn't be any happier to do this. For one, it's a good distraction from what's going on with my brother."

Poor William. He'd called Garrett and yelled at him as soon as they'd returned from London, but still felt like he needed to do more for his sister-in-law. Over the last few weeks, Sophia had tried her best to comfort Ginny, who had every right to be falling apart. But something she was coming to learn—and admire—about her friend was her sunny disposition despite rotten circumstances.

Sophia looked down, tugged at one of her two short ponytails. She smiled. "Well, I'm happy to provide said distraction."

"And look, it's the perfect day for surfing too." The sun shone bright but not hot, and the beach was peppered with a handful of surfers. However, the water wasn't crowded like some of the more popular beaches. William had brought her to one of his favorites, which wasn't overrun by tourists or vendors.

It was indeed perfect.

"What are we waiting for?" Sophia turned to pick up the foam board Ginny had loaned her.

"Hold on there." William chuckled. "Before we dive right in, so to speak, we need to practice on shore."

He set his board on the beach and indicated she should do the same. She did. Then he got on his knees behind his board, and Sophia followed suit.

"When you lie down on the board, you need to hold both sides. You don't want to be too far forward, or you'll nose-dive, and being too far back will make it really difficult to paddle through waves and get up on the board." He indicated the right positioning on his own board. "This wooden line down the center is called the stringer. You want your body to be centered along that line so you don't tip to one side or the other."

She practiced the positioning. It felt so foreign. The thought of doing this out in the waves, where things were uncertain . . .

Her hands flexed into fists and she tried to shake the sudden clamminess from them.

William reviewed a few other surfing tips and facts. His explanations were efficient and not overly detailed, but Sophia struggled to keep them all straight in her mind. "I think I've got it." She tried to infuse confidence into her tone.

Why was she so nervous? Having success at this shouldn't mean so much.

But in truth, she didn't have to have a degree in counseling to understand why. David had told her she couldn't do this, that it was stupid of her to want to. And somehow along the way, she'd started to believe it, allowing the lie to become more powerful than her desire to connect with her father in this way.

It was time to break free of his lies. All of them. For good. "Let's do this thing."

"All right. How about first we just go in the water and practice getting on and off the board?" William pushed himself up, then offered her a hand.

She grasped it and stood, scooping up her board. They headed into the water. Even with a wetsuit on, the initial splash of cold made her gasp, but soon she became acclimated to the temperature. For half an hour, William helped her practice getting into position.

Then he grabbed his board, and they paddled and rode the waves in on their stomachs, just so she could get a feel for the rhythm of the water beneath her.

"Be sure to keep your feet together and your core tight." William demonstrated the basics on his own board.

"Like this?" Sophia tried to mimic his paddling position.

"You look great."

She tried not to read too much into his words—or the way he was looking at her. He'd already confessed he was falling for her, so why was William's attention so hard for her to handle? Refocusing on making big, long strokes, Sophia cupped her hands and kept her chest lifted as she cut her arms through the water.

Next, William showed her how to duck dive under a wave. After another half hour of practicing her navigation of the water, they came back to the beach to rest.

He pulled a water from the cooler he'd brought from home and handed it to her. "How are you feeling?"

She unscrewed the cap and took a sip. "Good, I think."

"I know it can feel awkward when you're first learning, but I've got to say, you look like a natural."

Perhaps she'd inherited her father's skill after all. *Take that, David.* "Thank you. For the compliment and for taking the time to do this. I know there are many other ways you could be spending your day."

"None so pleasant as this." William stared off into the waves. "Not only do I get the pleasure of your company, but there's something about the water that has always beckoned to me. When I'm out there, it's pure poetry—the same thrill I get deep in my soul when I read Dickens or Keats. Like a universal truth calling to me."

"What's it saying?" She didn't know anyone else who connected with literature as much as William. And to know he felt the same as she did about nature, the water . . .

A tingle raced up her spine.

"Something different every time, but with the same undertone. Freedom. Grace. Love." He brought his gaze back to her. "Are you ready to get back out there and try standing?"

"Yes." And she was.

Still on the beach, he showed her the proper standing technique and she practiced getting up into that position.

The time had come to try it in the water. Her heart beat wildly against her chest as she paddled out to the waves. He'd taught her as a beginner to look for foamy waves breaking parallel to the shore. She duck dove under several waves as she made her way out into the open sea, William somewhere nearby.

Right now, it was just her and the ocean.

A wave started rolling toward her. She turned to catch it, and as it broke, she pulled herself to a standing position on her board. For a few sweet moments, she rode the wave. Though it was small, the power of conquering it filtered through her whole being, filling her with inexplicable joy.

As the wave petered out, she abandoned her board. Coming up for air, her feet found the soft bottom of the ocean below, and she heard William's whoop and saw him swimming toward her, boardless.

"That was amazing! Your first try. I'm so impressed."

"I have a great teacher."

The water—which only reached their chests—was calmer here, the bobbing up and down less jostling than farther in. "I'm ready to do that again." Sophia started to pull herself up onto the board from one side.

William moved directly across from her, the board between them. "Not so fast." Water dripped from his hair, which curled when wet. She could smell the coconut sunscreen on his skin.

"What? Do you need to correct my technique or something?"

But his eyes told her exactly what he was about to do—and though part of her brain protested that this was far too fast, that she was leaving in a few months so what was the point, the other part told it to shut up.

William placed his elbows on the board and pushed himself up, closing the gap between them. For a moment he waited, studying her, silently asking permission. When she didn't protest, he kissed her. It was soft and sweet, and she wanted more—more of this beautiful man and his beautiful soul. She slid from the board, unhooked its Velcro leash from her ankle, and pushed the board toward shore.

This time she closed the gap between them, throwing her arms around William's neck and kissing him more deeply. He wrapped his hands around her waist and tugged her close.

As the sun caressed their surroundings, they stood together against the waves that broke gently toward the shore.

He finally pulled away, placed his forehead against hers. "See? Poetry."

26

EMILY

AUGUST 1858

I only had to make it through one more ball before the season was over—before we would return to the trees and the splendor of the coast.

A maid helped me slip into my gown, a relic of my mother's that was so painfully out of fashion I ought to have been embarrassed. But there was something special about this dress. I had saved it for the last ball. It was not likely I would ever have occasion to wear it again in the future. Though Louisa's family seemed pleased with my last-minute service as her companion, the plan was for me to return to my previous position as governess, and a new companion would be secured for Louisa as soon as we left London.

Once my hair was properly arranged, I left my room and walked down the hallway to Louisa's. I knocked and peeked my head in. She was surrounded by three maids, who fussed over her and made certain her beautiful brown head did not have a single hair out of place. Her blue gown had been commissioned and created by one of the finest dressmakers in London.

"Emily, isn't this dress divine? I have been aching to wear it, but Mother made me promise to wait until the end of the season." She powdered her nose and dotted perfume on her wrists, doing her best to pretend away her sorrows. Her effusiveness had been much dimmed since her family's rejection of Charles Miller two months before.

"Rosamond is going to look like a goddess. She showed me her dress last week." Louisa fluffed her dress. "And it's a good thing because Edward plans to propose tonight, or so Mother tells me."

I had to whirl away from her so she could not see my face. What was wrong with me? Why this gut-wrenching dread coiled in my stomach like a snake about to strike? I had known a proposal was coming. Had avoided being alone with Edward since that day in the garden, though he had attempted to pull me away from the crowd a few times.

Once he was engaged, he would likely stay in London or travel to Hertfordshire where Rosamond's family had a massive estate. Whatever the case, it would be some time before he returned home. That would give my heart time to heal. It was for the best.

I repeated those words to myself as I followed Louisa down the staircase where Edward's family waited. My eye caught Edward's as I descended. The look in his was indefinable, but even from a distance I could see him swallow hard. Perhaps he was nervous about proposing to Rosamond. He needn't be. It was clear she was enamored with him and would say yes in an instant. And though she had not shown me any particular kindnesses, neither could I find any discernable flaw in her character that should prevent them from being a good match.

When we reached the bottom step, Edward's father kissed Louisa on the cheek. "You look lovely, my dear." He took her and his wife, one on each arm, and escorted them from the room toward the front door.

Edward and I were alone.

I stepped forward, head down, walking as quickly as I could— but he grasped my elbow.

"Emily Fairfax, if I didn't know any better, I would think you were avoiding me. Though I cannot think what I have done to deserve it." His voice echoed in the cavernous room where the ceiling arched overhead.

"I don't know what you mean." I pulled my elbow from his grasp and kept walking toward the front door.

He stepped in front of me, and I could see the frustration on his face. "We have hardly spoken since that day in the garden."

"Edward, please. Your family is waiting for us. We cannot be rude."

He gave me a look—one that conceded only temporary defeat but promised more argument to come—and extended his arm. I took it, and we walked together through the door. Before we reached the carriage, he stopped and leaned down. "You look more beautiful than I can ever remember seeing you."

My pulse skipped. I glanced up at him, my mouth falling open slightly.

His eyes were serious but his mouth twitched. "It's difficult to reconcile the sight of you now with the tomboy I knew growing up."

"Do not fret. I'm still the same girl underneath all these frills."

"That is what I love best about you."

As he helped me into the carriage and climbed in after me, his words struck something deep in my soul. It was probably the only time I would hear him utter the words "love" and "you" in the same sentence when referring to me. How pathetic of me to mull his phrasing over and over in my mind, and yet that is exactly what I did all the way to the ball.

A few hours later, after dinner had been served and couples spun together on the dance floor, I sat in a high-backed chair keeping a close eye on Louisa, who danced with Andrew Forsight, a dull young man who was harmless enough. Blessedly, Charles Miller was nowhere to be seen.

The air around me was punctuated with laughter as guests socialized and young people flirted. A mixture of perfumes and colognes mingled together in the grand hall, creating a cacophony of fragrance that had given me a slight headache.

Louisa seemed content, so I stood and made my way to the balcony for a bit of fresh air.

Out here I was alone. The sound of the strings and other instruments was dimmed, though still vibrant. The air felt full of rain and portent. I stood at the edge of the balcony, wrapping my arms around my waist and swaying to the lovely tune drifting from behind me.

Though the party was inside, I wasn't eager to step through the glass once more into a world where I would never be more than a spectator. But then and there, I vowed to be part of their world in another way—these people who did not think me their equal would one day find my words in their homes, in the form of their favorite books.

"Come, the party is not so bad, is it?" Edward joined me next to the railing.

Had he followed me out? "It is not bad at all."

"You're lying. You hate it in there. You hate anything having to do with fine society, do you not?" A hint of jest mixed with something else—a real question, perhaps?

"That is not true. I simply don't belong in fine society."

"You belong with me, so you belong here."

I shut my eyes, not daring to look at him. Once again, the power of his careless words to both enthrall and cut me reigned supreme. "We are friends, it is true. But no one in that room thinks of me as an equal."

"You are not their equal, Emily. You are better than all of them combined."

I finally looked at him. He wore that serious expression again, this time without a hint of teasing.

I could not help myself. "Not better than your Rosamond, surely."

He frowned.

"I hear congratulations are in order."

Edward shifted from one foot to the other. "Nearly. I plan to pro-pose tonight, if I can locate Rosamond. She seems to have disappeared."

"I will not keep you from your search, then."

The music changed from a quadrille to a waltz. Edward tilted his head, then extended his hand. "First, might I have this dance?"

I couldn't help the laugh that escaped my throat. "Don't you remember what happened the last time we tried to dance? I stepped all over your feet. It was rather humiliating." Granted, I had only been twelve when Edward tried to pass along what he'd learned from his dance instructor.

"I recall that it was charming."

"You have a very poor memory then."

"Nonsense." He stepped closer to me and placed his hand in mine.

My heart beat out a warning to me. *Stop*, it said. I did not listen. Instead, I allowed Edward to take me around the waist and lead the way through the waltz.

A few times I did step on his toes—but it was different from when we were children. I looked up at him, expecting us to laugh together, but he was gazing down at me as if he had never seen me before now. His lips turned downward at the corners, his eyes locked on mine, and his hand seemed to pull me closer. We were tucked together as tight as was proper, moving around the balcony as one, completely in step with each other, completely in tune to us and us alone.

So when the music halted, we kept dancing. I was afraid to stop, afraid this world I had fallen into would shatter.

But it was Edward who finally quit the dance. Both of us were breathless as if we had run, and we maintained eye contact. What was he thinking? Was he feeling what I was feeling—the light and joy and passion welling up inside of me, bursting and begging for freedom to finally whirl outside of myself?

He spoke first. "I'm sorry."

"For what?" For finally realizing that it was me, not Rosamond, whom he longed to marry?

"You're all wet."

It was then that I realized a gentle rain was falling from the sky. But it should not have been gentle. If it was going to match what shook inside of me, the lightning and thunder should have been terrorizing us, the rain pelting our skin, the wind pulling our hair in every direction.

And I could no longer be silent. "Do you love her, Edward?" The whispered words did not reveal everything, but it hinted at it all the same.

Rain dripped from the tip of his nose. "It doesn't matter." He turned to go back inside.

I snatched at his jacket. "You did not answer me."

"Don't, Em." He would not look me in the eye when he said it. "Please."

My pride would not let me stay there any longer. I wouldn't beg him for more than he was willing to give. The time for us to share our hearts was past—perhaps had been for a while, and I had just been too full of wishful thinking to believe it. "Be happy, Edward. No one deserves it more than you."

I smoothed the wet hair from my face and headed back toward the ballroom. It would look scandalous to enter with Edward alone, drenched as we were, so I found a side entrance that took me down a separate hallway. It was not such a long walk back to our house, and I prayed Edward's parents would not think I had neglected my duties where Louisa was concerned—though that was exactly what I had done.

But my heart was bursting. I needed to return to my desk so I could process my emotions with my pen.

Not thinking clearly, I became turned around in my flight to find the exit. Strange that I had not come upon a single servant or guest who could direct me to the right location. I stopped to assess my whereabouts. Everything looked the same to my muddled brain.

Finally, I heard low voices as I rounded the corner. I saw movement in a dark alcove and couldn't help the small gasp that left my lips.

A man had Rosamond pressed up against a wall, her skirts lifted in a most unladylike manner, her arms entwined around his neck. She moaned as he kissed her, then kissed him back with a fervor not meant for anyone else's eyes—especially mine.

Edward's conduct was what surprised me most. And how had he found her so quickly after leaving me? Whatever the case, he evidently had proposed and she must have said yes.

I backed away, my heart sinking at the sight before me. But in my attempt to escape, my foot hit something that clattered to the ground, alerting Rosamond and Edward to my observation.

Rosamond jerked away and saw me. Edward did the same—but indeed, it was not him! Instead, she'd been in the passionate embrace of one of the footmen who'd served us dinner earlier that evening.

How dare she do this to Edward! I knew that even if he did not love her completely, he would always be faithful to her. That was his way. Obviously the same could not be said about Rosamond.

She strode toward me, an accusing glare accompanying her. "You will speak of this to no one."

I should have closed my mouth and continued walking. But my bruised and battered heart would not allow me to do so. "Edward has been looking for you all evening, and yet *this* is where you've been? It's deplorable."

"Do not pretend you are perfect, Emily Fairfax. I see the way you look at him." Her lips turned upward into a wicked smile. "And no matter what you say, he is mine. It must break your heart to know you have no claim on him."

My lip quivered, but I would not cry—not in front of her. "He is my friend, which is more than I can say for you. You are merely an adulteress."

She laughed, and the footman silently approached her side. "I'm not married yet. I plan to have my fun while I can."

"Perhaps Edward should hear what kind of woman he is planning to propose to." I knew I shouldn't have said it, but I could not allow Edward to be shamed in such a way.

The accusing glare returned. "If you say a word to him about this . . ."

"He would believe me, you know."

I turned on my heel and raced away before my mouth could get me into even more trouble than it already had.

~ ✺ ~

My eyes were bleary the next morning. I'd stayed up all night after the ball, my headache and heartache raging as my fingers flew across the page. Should I tell Edward about Rosamond's indiscretion? Was it something he would appreciate knowing, or was it simply a normal part of society and I was naive about such matters? I dreaded the idea of being the one to bring him pain.

My fingers were hopelessly smudged with ink, and I still wore my mother's old gown when I received the summons to meet Edward's parents in the sitting room.

"Did they say why they wanted to see me?" I asked the maid who had delivered the message. They had never called for me at this early hour before.

"No, miss." Her eyes darted from me to the floor.

A chill shook me. The fire had gone out in my room a few hours ago, but I didn't think that was the cause of the sudden cold. "What do you know?"

"I should not presume—"

"Please. What can you tell me?"

"Only that the missus did not look happy."

Perhaps she had noticed my abandonment of Louisa after all. This did not promise to be pleasant. "Thank you, Bridget. Would you mind assisting me with removing this dress?"

The servant hurried to help. I thanked her and changed into my day dress, then left my room and walked to the drawing room, each step heavier than the last. To think about having disappointed Edward's family—who had been so good to me in my time of need—brought me very low indeed. But I would take whatever punishment they saw fit. I only prayed it was not the loss of my employment altogether.

I knocked and entered the room. Edward's parents sat in chairs pushed close to each other. They held their voices to a whisper. Though the room was decent in size, it felt suddenly small and crammed. I longed to run to the large window behind them and throw open the burgundy drapes so more light could shine through.

"Good morning, sir, ma'am. I heard you needed to speak with me."

Now alerted to my presence, Edward's mother looked at me. Her features tightened. "Miss Fairfax, thank you for coming. Please, sit." She indicated the sofa across from them.

I followed her instructions and folded my hands in my lap, bracing myself for the blow.

Edward's father cleared his throat. His mustache twitched, but not in amusement. "There is something quite urgent we need to speak with you about. And it is . . . delicate in nature."

Delicate? Perhaps I had been called here to discuss something else entirely. "Go on."

Obviously reticent to do so, he turned to his wife and they exchanged a look. She sighed. "It has come to our attention that last night at the ball, a young woman was observed in the arms of a servant. Her behavior was . . . unbecoming."

They knew about Rosamond? Relief flooded my entire body.

"You've heard then? Who told you?" Perhaps they were attempting to find the best way to tell Edward, and sought my assistance because of our friendship.

Edward's mother seemed to slouch in her seat. Her hand fluttered to her mouth. "So it's true?"

"I'm afraid so." As much as I despised Rosamond, confirming her poor behavior to Edward's parents brought me no pleasure. They were sure to be embarrassed by their choice for their son.

"I am astonished," Edward's father piped up. "I expected better."

I didn't want them to believe it was in any way their fault for not seeing through Rosamond's façade. "It came as a surprise to me too."

"That is no excuse." Edward's mother's cheeks had reddened. I suddenly felt quite warm. Why were they both glaring in my direction? Had I unwittingly become some sort of target for their anger?

"I quite agree." I chose my words carefully.

They exchanged another look, and Edward's mother nodded once. His father studied me, deep disappointment etched into his features. "In that case, I'm afraid we have no other choice than to ask you to seek employment elsewhere. Immediately."

Seek employment . . . ? "What do you mean?" I had clearly misunderstood something during the course of our conversation.

"We owe your mother a great debt, and we have attempted to repay it by taking you in, giving you a position in our household. But you do not imagine that we could continue to employ someone—a lady's companion to our daughter, no less—who behaves in such a manner?" Edward's mother fanned herself as the words sliced through the air. "It would be scandalous."

"You believe *I* was the one caught gallivanting with a footman?" I couldn't help the screech leaving my lips.

"That is what was reported to us, yes."

"By whom?" But I knew. I could picture her accusing glare as it had been in front of me last night. "Rosamond?"

"She came to us with her concerns, yes." Edward's mother narrowed her gaze at me even more. "Now you wish to deny it?"

"I do deny it, yes. I was there, but—"

"What is going on in here?" Edward charged into the room, his eyes flashing, hands balled into fists. He took in the sight of me facing inquisition and raised his eyebrows to his parents. "Louisa informed me that you were accusing Emily of something awful, but I didn't believe her. Yet here I find you doing just that."

"Edward, please. This doesn't concern you." Edward's father held up his hand, as if by doing so he could silence Edward. He did not know his son very well.

"If it concerns Emily, it concerns me."

His mother lifted an eyebrow. "*Miss Fairfax*"—she emphasized my name—"has found herself in a compromising position, and we will not be embarrassed by having such a servant in our household."

Even though it was indeed my role, I winced at the word *servant*, especially given her caustic emphasis on the word. I couldn't sit there with my hands in my lap any longer. Standing, I worked to control the shaking in my voice. "I told you, I deny it."

"See?" Edward crossed the room and stood next to me. He looked at me. "Emily only ever tells the absolute truth."

My chest squeezed, and I looked away. He believed that, but I could not tell him about Rosamond. If he had read the truth of my love for him in my eyes last night—and I did not see how he couldn't—then he might think my story one born of vengeance.

"We have proof, son." His father remained calm, even while his mother observed the two of us, panic building in her eyes. It both pained me and gave me a slight nudge of satisfaction to see it.

"What proof?"

"The man she was seen with came forward and confessed to Rosamond."

Incredible. What had she promised the poor footman in exchange for this lie?

"Why would he do that?" Edward seemed to be calming too, attempting to resolve this with logic instead of emotion.

"Exactly. What would possess him to lie?"

"Em?" Edward grabbed my hand and squeezed—a gesture as familiar to me as breathing. "He is lying, isn't he? The footman?" His eyes were full of such trust in me, such love for me. Even if it was brotherly love, he was the only person left in this whole world who truly cared for the real me.

At last, I found my voice. "Yes, of course. He's lying."

"There." Edward fixed his gaze once more on his parents. "I will hear no more of such accusations against Emily."

His father studied him, then nodded. "Very well. Miss Fairfax, you may go. We apologize for the intrusion into your morning."

"It's no trouble, sir." I turned to leave. But before exiting, I leaned toward Edward and lowered my voice. "Thank you."

"Of course."

I made my way out the door, but stopped once in the hallway, leaning my head against the wall, breathing deep. Rosamond was even more cunning than I had given her credit for.

From inside the room, I heard raised voices.

"Since when are you and Miss Fairfax so close, Edward?"

"Mother, we have always been friends. You know this."

"I knew you had a childhood friendship, yes, and that you cared for her family. But the behavior I just saw . . . Tell me I am wrong to be concerned."

"Concerned about what?"

A disbelieving laugh. "You were quite protective of someone who is just a friend to you, Edward. You are engaged to another, are you not? You're not turning your attentions another way? Because you know what is at stake here."

"Yes, you know I am engaged to Rosamond." A pause. "And how could I forget what is at stake? I am reminded at every turn."

"You did not answer my other question."

Edward sighed, and from experience, I knew the sigh to be tinged with frustration. "Em—Miss Fairfax and I have only ever been friends, Mother. You have nothing to be concerned about on that account."

27

GINNY

"I can't believe we did it."

Ginny stared at the bookstore's upstairs loft, transformed before her eyes. From the time she and Garrett had started renting the building, the loft had been crowded with junk. She'd always seen the potential in it but had never taken the time to do anything about it. Now, it would make the perfect reading nook to encourage patrons to spend more time here.

Aldwin and Julia had gladly okayed the changes. Gone was the rickety railing, replaced with sturdy wood. The steps that had been too unsafe to climb could now be used. Broken bookcases had been repaired. All thanks to William and Steven. They'd spent the full day working, while Ginny and Sophia cleared away boxes and covered furniture with drop cloths to protect it from the paint they were about to apply to the loft's walls.

William had to finish up some grading, so he'd had to cut out a few minutes after finishing the construction, but Sophia and Steven had claimed to be up for helping her paint.

"Thank you both so much. I'm so pleased with the result." Tears clogged her throat. After her torrential downpour in front of Steven two weeks ago, she had no desire to repeat Hurricane Ginny. She swallowed hard. "Just, thank you."

Steven lightly twirled the hammer in his hands. "We were happy to help."

Sophia smiled. "Yes. So glad we could."

"Even on your day off?" Ginny hated that, but Sundays were the only day the bookstore could be closed for part of the day. The whole town usually shut down on Sunday afternoons, giving families time to eat, laugh, and spend time together. "Count this as one of your working days, please. Take tomorrow off."

Sophia tilted her head and chewed her bottom lip. "I might take you up on that. William just told me he finally heard from Abigail—the friend we met up with in London. She's got a tip for us about the story. Although if you want to come, we could wait until next weekend to go."

"Oh, I wouldn't want you to wait that long. I know you're dying to find out more if you can." Besides, she didn't want to interfere with whatever was developing between Sophia and William.

"I'm available if you need an extra hand in the store." Steven placed the hammer in the toolbox. Garrett's toolbox. Her husband should have been the one here doing this. But he wasn't. His friend and his brother had stepped into that role, helping her refurbish the bookstore one project at a time. Helping her create something new and improved.

Steven removed a screwdriver from his pocket and placed it in its proper spot.

Not for the first time ever, Ginny noticed how handsome he was, even wearing sweats and a stained T-shirt, with flecks of construction dust in his hair.

What was wrong with her? She wasn't even divorced yet, and already her heart was latching onto the nearest guy. But she'd learned her lesson. She could not find her belonging in a man. "That's too generous. I'll be okay. But thank you."

Ginny maneuvered to the back storage room and emerged with two cans of paint: one a vintage blue and the other a cream color. "Shall we?"

Steven snatched the cans from her. She and Sophia followed him up the stairs, where they'd already placed the paintbrushes, rollers, tape, and pans. Sophia, the self-proclaimed Queen of Taping, grabbed the tape and started working.

Ginny jimmied open the first can of paint. She tipped it, and a waterfall of blue became a pond in the pan. Though Sophia had suggested the color, Ginny had gravitated toward it anyway. It reminded her of the wallpaper in her parents' bedroom at home. Was it possible she actually missed the place, just a little?

"What's the saying? A penny for your thoughts?" Steven nudged her with his elbow.

"Glad to know my thoughts are worth so much to you." The rollers leaned against the wall, so she picked up two and held one out toward Steven.

"Ha-ha." He took it in hand. "But seriously. You've got something on your mind."

"I was thinking about my family." She dipped her roller in the paint and told him about the estate where she'd grown up. "I haven't seen any of them since I came here with Garrett. And we rarely speak." A light tap of the roller against the pan sent the excess paint dripping off. Ginny moved to the nearest wall. The roller glided across, leaving gorgeous blue streaks behind.

"They must miss you."

"Maybe." She shrugged. "Or they're just mad they missed the chance to marry me off to some wealthy Campbell or Livingston."

"Hmm. Well, I admire the courage it took to move to a completely new country without knowing hardly a soul." Steven began rolling paint next to her, covering the higher parts of the wall she couldn't reach.

The paint fumes began to tickle her nose. "Looking back, it doesn't feel very courageous. Maybe I was just running away."

"So why are you staying?"

Ginny's hand stilled, and her head snapped toward Steven.

He scrunched his nose and studied her. "Don't mistake my meaning. I'm happy you are." He held his roller suspended in the air while he talked. A glob of paint slid from it onto the floor, which was covered in plastic. "But doesn't this bookstore remind you of Garrett? Why subject yourself to the memories?"

She gripped her roller hard and pushed it at the wall. These streaks were noticeably darker than the ones she'd painted just a few minutes before. The old familiar ache rose toward her throat. "Of course it reminds me of him. But I've fought so hard for a place to call my own. I won't give it up so easily."

Behind them, Sophia flicked on some classical music.

"Is it really giving up when it's not something you wanted to do in the first place?" Steven re-dipped his roller before starting to paint again.

"I've asked myself that a thousand times. But what else can I do? Go home? Then I'll just end up working for my father in some Bentley-run corporation, never measuring up for the rest of my life, just like the first part of my life."

She pushed the roller toward the edge of the wall, covering the final patch of white. But it didn't matter how many layers of paint were put on top. She could try to make it flashy and new, but it would always be the same underneath.

Maybe she was stupid to have tried to change her fate. Maybe she should just go home and surrender to her family's will, try to bend herself into the mold they'd created for her. Perhaps then she'd finally feel like she belonged, even if the belonging wasn't totally real.

Fake was better than alone and desperate, wasn't it?

At that moment, the phone in her back pocket started buzzing. Ginny placed the roller on some newspaper on the ground. Her nail beds were flecked with dried paint.

She snatched the phone and stared at the caller ID.

Mother.

She only called when something was wrong. "Sorry, I need to get this."

"No problem." He stood, heading back toward his paintbrush.

Ginny inhaled and answered the phone. "Hello?"

"Virginia Bentley, what is this I hear about a divorce?"

Ginny groaned. With quick steps, she walked down the stairs into the main part of the bookstore, finding herself in the Travel section. How she wished she could charter a flight to anywhere but this moment. "How did you find out?"

"Your husband's lawyer contacted ours, that's how."

"What?" How did Garrett even have their contact information?

"Yes, apparently that no-good man of yours thinks he can squeeze us for money."

"He wouldn't do that." Ginny massaged her temple.

"He only married you for your money in the first place, darling, in case you haven't figured it out yet."

The words sliced through Ginny's heart. "That's not true." No, Garrett had loved her, once upon a time—no matter what he'd said. If he hadn't, then her life had been a lie for the last five years.

"Regardless, our lawyer informed him that we had cut you out of our will long before this day, unless you decide to come to your senses and move back home where you belong."

It shouldn't have come as a surprise to her. But still, that her parents were placing conditions on her inheritance felt like they were placing conditions on their love for her too.

And no matter how hard things had become here, she couldn't return to that.

"I'm sorry he bothered you, Mother. I'll call him and make sure it doesn't happen again."

"If it does, we'll sue him for harassment." Even from thousands of miles away, Mother's familiar harrumph made Ginny wince.

"I apologize for the inconvenience." She couldn't keep the bitterness from her tone. "And I'm doing great, thanks for asking."

The line went silent, and she could almost imagine Mother rolling her eyes. "Don't be so dramatic, Virginia."

"Okay, then. Well, I need to go. I have a bookstore to paint."

"You aren't seriously staying, are you? Why? I thought you'd be coming home now that your pathetic excuse for a marriage is over."

Ginny gripped the phone so tight she thought she might snap it in half. As much as Mother's digs hurt, the thing that hurt more was that she'd actually, for a moment, considered doing exactly what her mom had suggested.

It was time for Ginny to carve out a place for herself in this world. *She* would decide what she needed. She would create a home for herself. By herself.

This time, she wasn't running.

"I'm afraid you're wrong, Mother. I have no intentions of leaving."

28

SOPHIA

William parked his car at Elliott Manor, an estate near the town of Wendall, not eighty kilometers from Port Willis. He turned off the ignition and reached a hand toward Sophia's, grasping it. "Ready?"

After Abigail had called Saturday to let them know she'd located an estate with both a famous tree and a lighthouse in the area, Sophia and William had spent their free time researching as much as they could about the place. Elliott Manor was now used as a wedding and corporate retreat venue, and locating the previous owner had proven difficult. An online gallery showcased the estate's beauty and various venue setups—including a ceremony held at the "Story Tree."

The tree stood on the edge of a bluff, stretching its leaves over the grass and ocean alike. It certainly looked like it might have been the tree Emily spoke of.

But that didn't prove Emily was real.

"It's a long shot. But I'm ready." Sophia plastered a smile across her face, then climbed from the car.

"You never know what we'll discover." William met her outside, and they turned together to face the enormous hall.

They'd driven several hundred acres of the gorgeous grounds

before arriving here at the enormous house built of gray slate and granite. The sun shone bright, speaking hope into the day. They approached the large front entrance, framed by grand windows on either side and a stone staircase in front. It felt strange to simply walk inside, but William had called ahead and been told to do just that.

Before Sophia could fully take in the beauty of the regal foyer—tapestries stretching high to the ceiling, a staircase splitting off into two wings of the house, large columns creating various focal points in the room—a petite brunette in a pencil skirt and ruffled blouse rounded the corner from what appeared to be a small office off to the right. "Hello. Welcome to Elliott Manor." She stuck out her manicured hand, which William shook first, then Sophia. "I'm Claudia Vetters, the event director here. Are you Mr. Rose and Ms. Barrett?"

"We are," William said.

"Wonderful, wonderful. Are you ready for a tour?"

"That would be lovely, thank you."

Claudia flashed a smile. "Anywhere in particular you'd like to begin?"

William snuck his hand around Sophia's waist. "How about the Story Tree?"

"Oh yes." Sophia couldn't stop the shy grin that came from feeling his arm around her. "I'd like to see that too."

"Fabulous choice." Claudia ducked into the small room to the right—her office, probably—and emerged carrying a binder. "Follow me, please."

She led them through the foyer, down a few hallways, and out the back door toward the gardens, all the while spouting various facts about events at Elliott Manor.

Sophia drowned out what the woman was saying. All she could think about was Emily. Had she walked these same halls? Was this where her love of Edward had grown, been nurtured? Where her heart had been broken? Where she'd decided that enough was enough?

Or was it all fiction?

And why did the answer matter so much? She wasn't really here for this—she was here to focus on her own story. And yet, as she'd discovered when she'd surfed for the first time over a week ago, maybe this was part of her story. Maybe her story hadn't begun and ended with David. In some strange way, perhaps the weaving together of her life with Emily's mattered.

It was mysterious and magical and she didn't understand it. But maybe she didn't need to in order to accept that it simply . . . was.

"Soph."

William's voice pulled her from her reverie. Her breath hitched as they came upon the tree—larger than she'd imagined, some of its deep roots threading through the ground.

She stepped forward and looked east. When she glimpsed an old lighthouse, a peace settled in her soul. "This has to be it." Sophia turned to Claudia. "Do you know why it's called the Story Tree?"

"Rumor has it some famous author used to write here."

Her eyes widened. "Do you know who?"

She watched Claudia's lips, waiting for the name Emily Fairfax to emerge. But instead, Claudia said, "I'm sorry, no. Like I said, just rumors."

"Right."

"That would have been too easy, right?" William nudged her.

"Yeah."

Claudia turned on her three-inch heels. "So, the officiant would stand in front of the tree, and you two would face the audience, so the ocean would be behind you. When the sun sets across the waters, it's simply gorgeous. Now, what date were you looking to book your wedding?"

"I'm sorry, what?" Sophia quirked an eyebrow at William. "Our wedding?"

William laughed. "Ms. Vetters, there must be some mistake. We aren't getting married. When I called, I mentioned we were doing research into the family who might have owned this house in the past. I thought you knew that. We wanted a tour to see if we'd located the right home."

"Hmm." Claudia's back straightened and she smoothed the front of her blouse. "My assistant who made the appointment failed to mention that."

"I'm sorry." William rubbed the back of his neck. "I hope you don't mind helping us."

Claudia sighed, clearly disappointed she wouldn't be booking an event today. "No, of course not, although no one here knows much about the history of the house. I can tell you that the company I work for purchased it twenty years ago and has been using it as a retreat center and wedding venue ever since. It had fallen into disrepair, all the valuables sold off."

"What a shame." Sophia worried her lip. "Is there anyone who can tell us anything more about it?"

"I'm not positive, but I could make a call for you. My boss might know the name of the person we purchased the home and land from."

"That would be wonderful. Thank you."

Claudia pulled her phone from inside her binder. "One moment." She dialed and stepped away.

While she spoke to someone on the other line, Sophia stepped toward the tree. She reached out her fingers and stroked the bark. "I can't explain it, but . . ."

"This feels like the right place." William placed his fingers next to hers on the tree.

"But what do we do if she comes back with no answers?" Sophia looked up at him. "Where do we look next?"

"Don't worry. I'm sure someone at the Land Registry office could help us."

"That might take time." And she was growing impatient.

He leaned down and pecked her on the lips. "It will all work out."

Sophia wanted to believe that. So badly. Not just about discovering more about Emily and her story, but about . . . everything. Her soul felt closer to healing than it had in months, but what came after this? Especially when she had to return to reality, to work—a prospect that for some reason brought with it a heavy feeling of dread? Maybe her "healing" was only happening because she was away from home. Maybe this thing with William was just a fling.

Maybe, maybe, maybe . . . The unknowns were enough to drive her batty.

"Got it. Thanks." Claudia hung up. "My boss said the former owner of the home was Hugh Bryant. He had some major debts and apparently used the money to pay them off. As far as my boss knew, Mr. Bryant still lives in the village."

"Perfect," William said. "Thank you."

"I'm going to head back to the house. Feel free to wander the grounds if you'd like. We close at five tonight." Claudia took off.

Sophia turned to William and squealed, throwing her arms around his neck and landing a kiss on his lips.

"What was that for?" He pulled her closer to him. "Not that I'm complaining."

"That was for believing when I didn't. We have the next step."

She didn't know where it would lead . . . but for now, just having one was good enough.

29

~~~~~

EMILY

MARCH 1859

We returned to the country soon after Edward's engagement was announced. He did not accompany us, but instead left to visit Rosamond's family estate. I felt his absence acutely, though he did write to me a few times to inquire after me and my writing.

I did not respond.

It felt so foreign to ignore his letters, but I could not truly be happy for his impending nuptials, knowing the character of the woman he was marrying. Further, I knew that were we to communicate, he would sense my reticence and would question me—Edward had never held back when he wanted to know something, and he would have pursued the issue rather doggedly. I couldn't lie to him, but neither could I tell him the sordid truth in a letter.

Looking back, I wished I had told him in person, but my emotions had been so contorted, I did not know how to identify what was right.

Upon our return to the country in August, I resumed my governess duties and gave all of myself to my work and my writing, starting to compose another novel and a book of poems, while simultaneously sending the first manuscript to several editors, seeking publication.

Then the rejections came.

Upon reflection, the first rejection had come as no great surprise, for was not everyone's manuscript rejected at least once? The second stung a bit, but I still carried hope for the future. Something felt different about the third, though I didn't know what. Perhaps it was simply the timing—it came a week before Edward's March wedding, which was to be held at his family's country estate.

For that reason, the house had been in a dither for the last month. The family had even held off going to London for Louisa's second season until after the wedding.

I had not seen Edward in months. He was due to arrive with Rosamond and her family a few days after I received my latest rejection. I alternated between longing to see him and considering the idea of hiding in my room all day—nay, for the next week. However, my pressing need for fresh air won out.

I crept down the hallway and toward the staircase, and there they were. He and Rosamond stood arm in arm, laughing at something his father had said. Even in traveling clothes, Rosamond struck me as a great beauty, not a single hair out of place despite the often uncomfortable experience of riding hundreds of miles via carriage.

And then there was Edward.

They made a handsome couple indeed.

My heart lurched. I started to inch backward, but somehow Edward saw me. I wanted to believe his eyes sought me out in a crowd the way mine always looked for him, but it was more likely the fact that my boot squeaked on the wooden floor as I attempted to turn and flee.

"Emily." He glanced down at Rosamond, then back to me, his eyes full of raw grief and anger. "I mean, Miss Fairfax. How are you?"

"I am well, thank you." He must have hated me for failing to respond to his letters. A tiny part of me was glad for it. It would make things easier.

Rosamond's grip tightened on Edward's arm. "Yes, hello."

I scurried back to my room. This was most certainly going to be the longest week of my life.

~~~

I don't know why I did it, except that I simply could not allow things to remain strained between me and Edward. Not when he was getting married the next day.

Leaning against our tree and hugging the package in my arms, I stared out at the blackness beyond. Everyone had been in bed when I had snuck from my room. The moon's fullness had lit my way here, though I would know the path with my eyes closed.

A twig snapped behind me. I turned to find Edward approaching, lantern in hand.

"You came."

He drew closer, and even in the darkness, I could sense the tension in him. "Your note commanded it." The teasing in his voice mixed with an underlying sarcasm. It was justified—I had avoided him since he'd arrived at home with Rosamond.

It was becoming easier and easier to pull my heart back from the clutches of his unwitting grasp.

But then, tonight I realized, not for the first time—though it was the first time I had allowed myself to truly think on it—that never again could we meet like this, free to be just the two of us. Even now, it was highly improper in society's eyes. But were he to be married, it would be downright shocking.

And so, with all the memories of us twirling in my heart, I had penned a quick note in the language we had made up as children and sent it to his room via an unsuspecting maid.

"What is this about, Emily? I have an early morning if you weren't aware."

Edward's words pulled me back to the present. I bit my lip and extended the package in my arms toward him. "I wanted to give you this gift." I could not bring myself to say *wedding gift*.

He placed the lantern on the ground and took the package from me. The brown wrapping paper crinkled under his hand and he peeled it back. Edward pulled the small gift from the paper, raising his eyebrows at me. "You hate needlepoint."

"You're right." I pointed to it. "But it's a poem. One . . . one that I wrote. For you." It may not have been my novel, but I had finally given him what he had asked of me: a sample of my writing.

His features instantly softened and he gazed intently at the needlepoint, which was very poorly made indeed. It was too dark to read it, and yet he stared at it anyway. "Thank you, Em."

"You're welcome. And, Edward." I paused. "I'm sorry. For never writing you back."

Edward studied me in the dark, then placed the needlepoint in his jacket pocket. He took off his cloak, spread it on the ground, and sat down. I hesitated for only a moment, then joined him.

Out across the ocean, the heavens spread before us, a vast array of bodies that kept going beyond what even I could see or imagine. The ground was cold beneath me, but this moment warmed me enough that I didn't care.

"Why didn't you? Write back, that is."

The waves crashing against the cliff below lulled me to a contemplative place, one that charged the night with some sort of magic. Only in the dark could some words be spoken, it seemed. "You know how I've always had an aversion to marriage? I lied, Edward."

"What do you mean?"

"I would marry if it was the right person. If it was you." I had not come here to say it, but the words leaving my lips felt right. He should know the truth at long last.

His sharp intake of breath was all the proof I needed. He had not known how I felt.

What was he thinking?

He scooted closer to me, and his arm moved around my shoulder, pulling me close, tucking me in. I leaned my head against his chest, and we stayed like that for a long while.

Finally, Edward spoke. "I love the constancy of the stars. They never change. The whole world can be falling apart around us, and yet the stars show up every evening."

"That is a beautiful thought."

"There is only one other thing in my world that has been as constant. You, Emily."

I did not move, but Edward's heartbeat sounded steady in my ear. "Me?"

"You have been a constant friend to me, and it was only when I no longer had your friendship that I felt the gaping hole in my life—that I realized how completely you had filled it."

So I had only ever been just a friend, then. He was letting me down in the gentlest way he knew how. "I—" A sob came to my throat. Wrenching away from him, I stood and leaned against the trunk of our tree for support. I closed my eyes and took several deep breaths.

I felt rather than saw Edward come up behind me. "Em . . ."

Something about the way he said my name—an anguished groan—made me turn and look at him . . . really look at him for the first time that night. His hands were balled into fists. In the light of the moon, I saw the outline of his jaw, clenched.

Finally, he stepped closer, the tips of our boots touching. He placed his hands on either side of my upper arms and turned me to fully face him. "If only I'd figured out my own heart before I gave my promise to another. Em, I've been a fool."

His heart? Then perhaps . . .

I could not see his face with the moon shining brightly at his back, so I lifted my trembling fingers to his cheek and dared to trace his lips—a frown. The stubble on his normally clean-shaven jawline surprised me. For some reason, feeling it there seemed an intimate thing. He turned his lips toward my fingers and kissed them lightly. His hands left my arms and wrapped around my waist, pulling me close.

My lungs filled with air—with hope. "Your promise is not complete until you utter your vows tomorrow." Surely his parents would understand. After all, wouldn't they want him to be happy? "Edward . . ." I searched for his gaze, even in the darkness.

But instead of kissing me as I longed for him to do, he groaned. "What am I doing?" With agonizing slowness, he released me. "Emily, if I could change things . . ."

My arms ached for missing him. "You *can* change things. It's your life. Be your own person, Edward."

"I cannot be my own person when others are depending on me." He paced, running his hand through his hair.

"Don't you *want* to marry for love, Edward?" My words were potentially dangerous to my heart, but I said them anyway.

"It's not that simple. The debts . . . They've piled up. Don't you understand? My family could lose everything. My mother and sisters, they'd be penniless, and if anything ever happened to me or my father, what then? I shudder to imagine it. We can't all have the luxury of marrying for love, Emily."

"So you condemn yourself to a life without it?"

"Love is only part of a marriage." His breath shuddered. "I don't know what else to do."

My own heart broke seeing the man I loved warring between his own happiness and his family's well-being. "What you don't realize, Edward, is that life is not about money. Even if your family lost everything, they would still have each other, would they not?" I tried to keep the desperation from my tone.

His eyes pierced me. "You know my mother would rather die than become a pauper or lose her good reputation."

This was getting us nowhere. He'd clearly decided. But he didn't have all the facts. Perhaps it was a desperate attempt, but it was all I had available to me. "Rosamond is not worthy of you, Edward." The story of finding her and the footman together at the ball spilled from my lips.

"I suppose I deserve it."

I walked forward, grasping the lapels of his jacket. "What? Of course you don't."

"Perhaps she felt slighted because I had been harboring feelings for . . ." He couldn't even say it—that he loved me, not her. The Edward I loved was not a coward. What had happened to him?

How could he be defending her actions? "She's vile, Edward. She—"

"Don't talk that way about her, Emily." His voice was gentle but firm. "Whatever she is, she is my fiancée. And I am trying to do the right thing."

The word slapped me in the face. "The right thing for whom?" I imagined placing my heart in a box, closing it, throwing away the key.

"Em, if it were up to me . . ."

My cheeks were aflame. "Then what?"

"You must know."

"Say it anyway."

"I cannot."

"And I cannot stay here and watch you throw your life away." I released his jacket and strode back toward the house. Soon I was running, past the gardens and down the hallway to my room, where I threw myself onto my bed and screamed into my pillow.

But I could not hold on to my anger for long. Edward had always been loyal. I could not blame him for continuing to be the thing I loved most about him.

I only wished I had not fallen so completely apart in front of him. What must he think of me now?

The next morning dawned beautiful and bright—perfect for a wedding. I claimed a headache and clung to my bed all day long.

And as the church bells rang in the distance at midmorning, I discovered who the real coward between us truly was.

30

GINNY

Today, another victory would be had.

Ginny shifted from one foot to the other as she waited at Steven's door, a platter of chocolate chip cookies in one hand.

He opened the door. "Come on in."

"Thanks. Sorry I couldn't come right away. And sorry it's so late." He'd texted around six thirty—Sophia had closed tonight—and it was nearly nine now. "I was in the middle of a baking sesh when you texted. But I come bearing gifts, so hopefully it was worth the wait."

A huge grin lit his face. "What have you got there?"

As she moved through the doorway, Ginny handed him the cookies. "Just a thank-you for getting the website done so quickly. I love it."

He closed the door behind her and headed toward the kitchen, pulling the cellophane from the platter and snatching a cookie from beneath. "I'm glad you like it." When he took a bite of the cookie, his eyes closed briefly. "Mmm. These are way better than the treats Mum makes. Just don't tell her I said so."

Ginny laughed and stepped into the small kitchen, which smelled like cooked onions. The sink held several dirty dishes and inside the fruit basket rested a few spotted bananas. "My lips are sealed." Then she reached into her purse and drew out an envelope, slipping it under the basket with what she hoped was nonchalance.

But Steven caught her. "What's that?"

"Nothing."

Frowning, he set the platter of cookies down, grabbed the envelope, and opened it with his index finger, then pulled a stack of bills from inside. "Ginny Rose, what is this?"

"Payment." Not even close to what Steven and his work were worth, but all she'd managed to scrape together. "I can't let you do this for free."

Without blinking, he pushed the cash back inside the envelope and stuck it in Ginny's purse. "You're not *letting* me do anything. I offered." Before she could protest, he took her elbow. "Now let's go launch your website."

She set down her purse and sighed. "Fine."

He led her to his couch and they plopped down. The piece of furniture was so worn they both sank toward the middle, their legs touching. Ginny moved ever so slightly to the right, but the cushion beneath her just tilted her back toward Steven.

Steven rested his computer on his lap and navigated to the admin page where he'd been building her site. She'd looked everything over last night, offering only a few minor suggestions for improvement. "Ready?"

Ginny gripped her knees. "Ready."

Steven clicked something on the screen. "And you're live."

"Wow." Ginny felt a mixture of emotion, everything from relief to hope to sadness. She had updated the About section, and in it, she'd named herself as sole proprietor. Though Garrett technically owned half of the store, he was not here to claim it. He hadn't mentioned it in their handful of conversations—even the one where she'd called to tell him to back off on contacting her parents. He'd claimed that was his attorney's doing, not his, and that he had no desire to turn this divorce into something nasty.

Despite all he'd done to her, she believed him.

So now, all she could do was take the next step forward. Updating the website and putting their collection of rare books online was a start. "We should celebrate."

Steven closed the laptop and set it on the coffee table. "What do you have in mind?"

"I don't know. I just don't want to . . ." She was going to say "be alone." How pitiful did that sound? "I'd like to escape my normal life for a little bit."

He seemed to consider her, then hopped up and offered his hand. "I've got the perfect thing."

She let him help her stand.

He pulled on a lightweight coat and they walked out his door together. The sun had just lowered in the sky, light still hovering on the horizon, and with the harbor not thirty feet away, the sound of water lapping against boats permeated the air. A few townspeople sauntered down the sidewalks, but most people around here were tucked into bed by ten, even on a Friday.

Ginny zipped up her black jacket and shoved her hands into the pockets as they walked. "So where are we going?"

"You'll see."

They zigged and zagged up various small streets, finally stopping in front of a run-down diner. She'd been living in this town for five years and didn't remember ever being in this particular spot.

Steven opened the diner door, and jazz music spilled out. As they entered the dimly lit space, Ginny smelled hamburgers and . . . Was that sushi?

Steven watched her reaction and laughed. "The owner has quite eclectic taste."

"Clearly." As was also evidenced by the paraphernalia on the wall, showcasing everything from a framed marching band costume to guitars, bugles, and those cheesy motivational posters that littered the corporate world. The rest of the diner looked fairly normal, and a surprising number of the red vinyl booths were filled with customers.

A few people called out greetings to Steven. He waved and walked with purpose to the bar. While he ordered something to go, she caught a glimpse of the harbor from the window. The moon reflected off the ocean and several fishing boats bobbed in the water.

"Ginny!"

She turned toward the voice where Mary and Blake Patrick sat at a table with several of their family members. Mary slid from her seat and walked toward Ginny. She cocked her head to the side. "Haven't seen you back at the pub for a while."

"Yeah, life's just been super busy. What are you doing here? I wouldn't expect you or your parents to frequent another restaurant. Especially one so . . ."

"Strange?"

"Exactly."

"Oh, we love this place. The food is amazing. Our own menu gets tiresome after a while. And when we go out, we don't have to cook or clean."

"Makes sense."

"How are things?"

Ginny stuffed her hands into the back pockets of her jeans. "Things are . . . good. Okay. You?"

Mary smiled softly, placed a hand on her stomach. "Blake and I just told our family we're expecting."

How many times had she and Mary talked about raising their kids together? Though the thought sent a pang through her heart, Ginny was able to smile too. "Mary, that's so great. Congratulations." She threw her arms around her friend, who readily hugged her in return.

"I've missed you, Gin. We should get together sometime."

"We really should." First Steven, now Mary . . . proof that this wasn't just Garrett's town anymore. It was hers. His friends may have been his first, but they were also hers—with or without him in the picture.

She nearly jumped when Steven approached them holding two Styrofoam cups with lids. "Hey, you two."

Mary glanced between Steven and Ginny, a question in her eyes. "Hello, Steven. What do you have there?"

"Only the best hot chocolate in the world." He held one out to Ginny.

She closed her hand around the cup and the warmth penetrated her fingers.

"It was so good to see you, Gin, but I should get back to my family. I'm going to hold you to our date."

"You got it, Mary. Good to see you too. And congrats again."

Mary grabbed her hand and squeezed it, then headed back to her table.

Ginny turned back to Steven. "I can't wait to taste this hot chocolate. Cheers." She took a sip and nearly swooned at the gorgeous melding of sweet creaminess.

"Good, right?"

"Really good." Ginny lifted the lid and inspected the liquid. "I need to get this recipe."

Steven sipped his drink. "I'm sure yours is equally delightful. You're quite a good cook. I've heard your baked goods are flying off the shelf at the bookstore."

"Thanks." Her cheeks reddened with the praise. "I definitely enjoy baking. I even considered going to culinary school once upon a time . . ." Oh, there was no use in talking about *that*. "So, do you want to sit down somewhere?"

"I've got a better idea."

"Lead on."

So he did, all the way to the harbor. A few of the larger boats were illuminated, light laughter lilting from them across the water. The sand shifted beneath her feet as she walked, the feeling so familiar. She'd practically grown up on the beach, especially during summers at their Nantucket home. Memories of bonfires and roasting s'mores rushed her mind. Her parents had always been too busy to join them, but she and her siblings had gotten along once upon a time.

Until they'd done what was expected of them. And Ginny had not.

Now she was far, far away, struggling to save a bookstore that hadn't even been hers in the first place.

But while some might call it futile—or even call her a failure—something like pride warmed her even more than the hot drink in her hand. Because she was doing it. No, it wasn't perfect progress. More like imperfect. And she still might have to close the bookstore's doors if all her efforts didn't work.

But she'd stayed and she'd tried. Was there really failure to be had in that, no matter what the ending?

Maybe she needed to cut herself a little more slack.

Steven stopped at a small houseboat and climbed aboard. "Care to join me?" He put his drink down on a small table situated on the deck in front of the entrance.

"Whose boat is this?"

"Mine, actually. My grandfather left it to me when he passed."

"Oh, I'm so sorry." She let him help her over the lip of the boat, which rocked gently under her feet.

"Don't be. I have many fond memories of days at sea on this beauty." He lowered himself into one of the chairs flanking the table, and she did likewise.

They faced Port Willis, a town she'd never seen from this angle, down at the lowest end of Main Street looking upward. The hills surrounded the village and a few large homes dotted the ridges. Here there was such a sense of calm, the air so pure, the quiet so stirring. She could almost sense God in this moment.

That thought surprised her. After all, religion in the Bentley household had been all about what God could do for you. When Father had concluded a successful business deal, God was good and heaping blessings on their heads. When something fell through, God was unkind and unfair.

Ironic that she'd spent the last several years spurning her parents' ways, yet had still unintentionally absorbed so many of their beliefs.

"You look extremely serious right now. Not exactly in celebratory mode." Steven's words startled her back to reality.

"Sorry. I'm just . . . thinking."

He let it be, staying silent for several minutes. Then, "So what's next? You've got your website up. Any other projects going? Or are you planning to settle into your new normal and see how things turn out?"

"I'm not sure I have that option. I need to constantly be trying to improve my situation at the store."

"There's always an option." He picked up his cup and tapped his index finger against the lid. "I know you said you feel like you'd be quitting if you gave up the bookstore. But is there more to it than that? There has to be a reason you're fighting so hard to save it."

Ever since talking to her mother last weekend, she'd thought long about this. Would he understand? But perhaps for him to really get her, she had to go further back. "I've told you a little bit about what it was like growing up in my family. The pressure was intense. I always felt like I was one step away from failure, especially living in the shadow of two perfect older siblings who were everything my parents wanted in children. I was the misfit who would rather be baking than studying."

Her throat clogged, but she pushed her emotions down with a swig of the now-tepid liquid chocolate. "When it came time for college decisions, my parents had Harvard all picked out for me. But I had something else in mind. I prepared a fancy dinner for the whole family, complete with a beautiful cake. I spent weeks perfecting that cake recipe. It had to be just right because, after dinner, I planned to tell my parents I'd decided to go to culinary school. The cake was supposed to be for the celebration afterward, and was going to serve as the proof that I could be successful as a chef."

"I take it that conversation did not go well."

Ginny shook her head. "First, my father said he couldn't eat the cake because he had recently been declared a diabetic—no one had even bothered to tell me. I'd never felt like such a stranger in my own home before. That of course made me nervous when I was talking about my reasons for wanting to be a pastry chef. Mother let me get about two sentences out before she flew off the handle and told me that I was a disgrace to the Bentley name, that I needed to shape up and get my head out of the clouds, and that I'd never amount to anything or belong in our family if I didn't stop daydreaming and start getting serious about things." She couldn't stop the tear that rolled down her cheek. Even eight years later, her mother's words had the power to wound her fragile heart all over again.

"That must have been hard." Steven shifted forward in his seat, his brow furrowed.

She nodded. "The bookstore is the first place I felt like I really belonged. Like I had a purpose. Does that make any sense?"

"Of course it does. But . . ." He trailed off, moving his gaze from her to the sky. The stars made a canopy of lights above them.

"But what?" The anticipation of what he would say built within her.

When had this man become such a close friend that she would hang on his words in this way?

"I guess I don't think of 'belonging' being about a physical place. It's not even about family. It's more about embracing who we are. Identity and how we view ourselves is a large part of feeling 'at home' some-where. It doesn't change no matter where we are or who we're with."

The truth of what he'd said settled into her spirit, but an ache came with it.

Because how would she ever truly belong anywhere when she hadn't the foggiest notion who she really was? She'd been George and Mariah Bentley's daughter first, then Garrett Rose's wife.

Now?

She was a daughter disowned, a wife soon to be divorced.

She was Virginia "Ginny" Bentley Rose—and she had no idea what that really meant.

31

SOPHIA

"My head hurts." Sophia groaned after checking her e-mail for the millionth time. She lay her forehead against the cool wood of William's kitchen table. "I don't think Mr. Bryant is ever going to e-mail us." And calling him again would probably border on harassment.

William stretched. He sat in the chair next to her, laptop open in front of him. It was early on a Friday morning. She had the day off from working in the bookstore, and William's class didn't start until noon. "We're making good progress without him."

After they'd received Hugh Bryant's name from Claudia at Elliott Manor two and a half weeks ago, William and Sophia had headed to the local village pub and asked around about him. They'd heard many things—none of them good—and finally got an address, with a warning to keep away from the miserly hermit. Sophia had remained hopeful, sure that this couldn't be a dead end. But knocking and waiting and knocking again had done nothing. Neither had leaving a note asking Mr. Bryant to contact them via e-mail or phone.

"I know, but it's already the beginning of August." And she was leaving at the end of the month—a thought that churned her stomach.

The idea of leaving him behind, right when they'd started something, didn't sit well.

And then there was the question in the back of her mind, the one that had come unbidden more times than she wanted to admit—did she really want to go back to being a therapist? Yes, she was working toward her own healing, and that would probably be helpful in her pursuit to help other women. But the idea of being stuck in a room one-on-one, hearing grievance after grievance, remembering her own . . . Well, after working in the bookstore and interacting with people in their everyday lives, finding ways to bring smiles to their faces through a common love of literature, her chosen profession just did not seem as palatable as it once had been. Which was crazy, considering how many years of training she'd put into becoming a therapist.

But it was probably just nerves, the worry in the back of her mind that she'd fail the women she'd counsel, right?

William frowned. Did he feel the same way about her leaving? "We'll figure this out before you go. Don't worry."

"I didn't mean it like that. Just that we've been working so hard already."

In fact, they'd spent countless hours trying to fill in the blanks. It hadn't been easy. The land office hadn't been much help in learning the history of the title for Elliott Manor either, since the information wasn't yet available online and the waiting period for any sort of request was anywhere from two to eight weeks. So they'd decided to move forward with genealogical research by starting with Hugh and working their way backward. Because they weren't sure whether the manor passed via his father or mother's line, they had a ton of research to do. They did a lot of guesswork and had to backtrack frequently when they realized they'd followed the wrong trail. It was tedious work, but in between the research, she and William had grown even closer.

He'd taken her surfing again a few times, and every night when he didn't have a class, they ate dinner together at Sophia's kitchen table, usually takeout from a pub they both enjoyed. They took turns reading aloud from Dickens or Gaskell, and he introduced her to a few lesser-known authors like Braddon, Grand, and Edgeworth. Then, while the sun made its descent for the evening, they'd stand by the large window in her apartment, his arms wrapped around her shoulders as they watched, silently taking in life together.

And he was such a gentleman, kissing her softly, passion brewing just beneath the surface, a promise that he would always leave before things became too heavy.

She'd never been treated with such care.

And that made the thought of leaving Cornwall downright horrible. Sometimes, impossible.

Of course, when she'd told Mom how close she and William had gotten, her mother's pause said everything that her "That's wonderful, dear" did not. Or was she just reading her own fears into things?

Sophia only prayed she wasn't being naive or falling into some trap. But looking back, she realized David had never been this unselfish, this loyal. For some reason, she'd been too blind to see it then.

Hopefully that was not the case here.

Sophia shook off her morose mood. "Okay, so we ended on a marriage certificate for Henry Bryant and Vivian Sherwood in 1912." Sophia leaned against him to peer at the screen, her fingers curling around his arm. He felt sturdy and warm. "Should we start with a search of Henry's birth certificate?"

"Sounds good." William navigated to the site they'd previously used for research and typed in Henry's name. Several results popped up.

"Should I start searching for Vivian's birth certificate?"

"Sure."

She looked up at him, and he leaned in for a kiss. The jab of anxiety that had first come from being with him faded a bit with every kiss, every interaction with William.

They both went back to work, the room filled with the clacking of their keyboards. The smell of chocolate emanated from the box of Ginny's donuts Sophia had brought with her. Her eyes began to blur after an hour. "I need coffee."

"Hmm?" He sat up quickly, then winced and rubbed his neck.

"Were you asleep?"

His sheepish grin gave him away. "I've been staying up far too late grading papers after coming home from your place."

"Sounds like you need some coffee too."

He grimaced. "You know I dislike coffee the way you dislike British tea."

"And yet we get along so well. Maybe I can convert you yet."

"I'd like to see you try." William scooted his chair closer.

Oh, his nearness did something to her. She pushed him away, laughing. "Coffee it is." Sophia stood and stretched, then rubbed a sore spot in her lower back.

"I don't have any."

"Oh yes, you do. I brought some over last time I was here and stashed it in your cupboard for just such an occasion."

"You didn't." William tried to grab for her as she passed his chair.

She laughed and flitted from his reach.

Sophia strode toward the kitchen, amazed. She hadn't flinched at his playful grab. In fact, she hadn't had any sort of flashbacks of David in weeks.

His voice was gone.

A thought struck her. What if it had been her own voice in her head the whole time? Negative self-talk had been a part of her psyche for as long as she could remember—failure was not an option, and whenever it seemed near, she panicked—and yet she couldn't recall any major episodes of it in the last few weeks.

Perhaps she really had made more progress than she'd realized.

Sophia made quick work of putting the coffee together. William happened to have a small coffeepot, perhaps a housewarming gift from when he'd purchased his two-bedroom home. As the coffee brewed and dripped into the pot, the delicious scent filling the kitchen, her eyes were drawn to the side of the refrigerator, where a variety of pictures and fliers were affixed with magnets. One photo stood out in particular. William and Garrett stood with their arms slung around each other's shoulders. Garrett was saying something and William was laughing.

She'd seen William laugh—but not like this. His laughter always seemed reserved in some way. Maybe only his brother was able to pull pure joy from him like that. And his brother had betrayed him when he'd betrayed Ginny. William didn't talk much about Garrett, but when he did, a sadness overwhelmed everything about him—his voice cracked, his shoulders slumped, his mood darkened. He'd acknowledged he would have to forgive him someday, but didn't know how.

The people in their lives had such power to wound them. It was tempting to pull away from everyone when even one person hurt you because it might seem easier to not allow yourself to feel the pain ever again. Sophia had done that after David, in a way.

But she and William were both fighting through the pain, weren't they? They weren't letting the people who had disappointed or failed them run their lives.

Maybe it didn't even matter that she hadn't written her story yet. Perhaps she was healing without it. By trusting again. By letting love win.

Whoa there. Where had the L word come from? *Slow down, Sophia. You just mean love in the general sense.*

Sophia snatched two mugs from William's shelf and poured in the coffee, adding a dash of cinnamon to each. She carried them back to the table, where William was humming as he worked. Setting the mugs down, Sophia leaned over and tossed her arms around William's shoulders from behind. "Find anything good?"

"I certainly did." He twisted and pulled her into his lap, a crazy grin on his lips.

She giggled. "What?"

"Something I've been waiting for for a long, long time." His eyes grew serious as he searched hers.

Oh boy. Was she ready for him to look at her like . . . that? "I mean, did you find anything good about the Bryant family?"

"Oh, that. Not really."

"Bummer." She nestled back against him. Just then, her phone dinged, indicating an e-mail had come through. Reaching for it, she took a peek—and sat up straighter.

"What is it?"

She opened the e-mail and scanned it. "The Land Registry office addressed our request. They sent over the information on Elliott Manor."

"And?" Now William was leaning forward.

"There's a little note in the body of the e-mail and an attachment with the actual documents. Here, I'm going to get on my computer so we can see all of this better." She hopped off his lap and returned to her own seat, pulling up the information on her laptop screen. "The e-mail says that the Land Registry Act of 1862 allowed landowners to officially register their property titles, many for the first time. In 2014, the government released a bunch of digitized records of hand-written parchments they scanned in, but they still have more to add to the database. That must be why we couldn't find the information online."

Sophia's breath caught.

"Out with it, woman. What does it say?"

She swung her eyes toward him and smiled. "In 1862, a Randolph Bryant registered a deed for Elliott Manor. It's the same address."

"Brilliant." William's eyes scanned the deed and information on the screen. "So now we can narrow our research to the Bryant side alone. We just need to figure out if Randolph came before or after Edward."

"Exactly." She took a sip of her coffee. "I'll forward you this e-mail and we can look through the attachments to see if an Edward Bryant ever owned Elliott Manor, and if so, when. If we don't find one, we can assume he came before Randolph."

"How about you do that, and I'll search for Randolph's birth and marriage certificate and see what I can find that way?"

"Deal."

It didn't take Sophia long at all to locate the information they wanted. "It says here that an Edward Bryant owned the title for Elliott Manor beginning in 1878. So he must have been Randolph's heir. After him, it passed to a James Bryant."

"Nice work."

But where did they go from here? The dates and names and uncertainty of it all started to blur in Sophia's mind. It was difficult keeping it all straight.

Then, inspiration struck. Of course. "Should we maybe look for James's birth certificate and see who his parents were?"

William snapped his fingers. "And if his mother was Rosamond something . . ."

"Then we know they were real. Or at least that there's a strong chance. And if they were real, maybe Emily was too. Of course, everything we have is circumstantial. We're assuming we have the right house." Sophia tucked her lip behind her teeth and tried not to grin. "I hate to say this, but maybe we'll need to chop down Hugh Bryant's front door to get any legitimate information."

William laughed—and it was the happiest sound in the world. "Whatever we do, just stay beside me, okay?"

"I'm not going anywhere."

Of course, that wasn't entirely true, but Sophia wouldn't think about that today. Today belonged to progress and victory.

32

~~~~~

EMILY

SEPTEMBER 1859

I had not written a word since Edward married. At first, it took too much energy—surprising, since it had always given, not taken, strength. Then I told myself I was simply too busy. And I was. The children kept me so, as did avoiding Edward and Rosamond as much as could be managed during Louisa's second season, a difficult task since we lived in the same London townhouse. But Edward evaded me as much as I did him during those three horrible months. Now that we had returned to the country, I at last had some relief, as Rosamond preferred to reside elsewhere.

The note that came to me one night in September interrupted my carefully assembled routine. It requested my presence at the family's dinner party. Now that I had returned to my post as governess, I regularly took meals alone in my room. Why should I have been asked to attend that night? Since the incident in London over a year before, Edward's mother hadn't spoken to me unless absolutely necessary, and Edward's father was often away on business.

Whatever the reason, it would provide a nice distraction from the monotony of my existence. I dressed and forced myself to walk at a normal pace toward the dining room. When I entered, I saw Edward's parents and Louisa, whom I missed spending time with now that I was governess again. There were also several neighbors in attendance, as well as a few guests I had yet to meet, including a gentleman with spectacles and a white mustache and a woman with a high brow and silver hair done up in the latest fashion.

I lingered on the edge of the room until Edward's father saw me. "Ah, Miss Fairfax. Please, join us."

As I walked closer, Edward's mother raised an eyebrow my direction, almost as if she did not know I was attending. I hadn't mistaken the invitation, had I?

Edward's father ignored his wife's stare and guided me toward the unknown visitors. "Mr. and Mrs. John Davis, may I present Miss Emily Fairfax."

The woman's smile was kind. "How do you do?"

"Well, thank you."

Mr. Davis inclined his head. "Pleasure, miss."

"The pleasure is all mine." I looked at Edward's father, a question in my eyes. Why was he introducing me to such fine guests as these?

He winked at me. "I must speak with the serving staff, and I know you all have much to discuss. Please excuse me." And then he was gone.

What did he mean, we had much to discuss? Unsure what to do with my hands, I folded them behind my back and tapped my toes inside my slippers, staring at the ground.

Mr. Davis cleared his throat. "Our host tells us you are an authoress."

That caused my head to rise. It had been so long since Edward's father and I had spoken of it, I assumed he'd forgotten. "Y-yes."

"Have you met with much success?" Mr. Davis's tone did not indicate judgment.

"Unfortunately, no." I almost hated to disappoint him, though I hadn't met him until a few moments before.

He studied me. "Where have you submitted?"

I closed my mouth before it appeared I was gawking at him. Most people would have stopped their inquiry at this point. "Are you familiar with the industry?"

He stroked the ends of his mustache. "I am."

His wife leaned closer to me. "My dear, he is also an author. You may know him as Lionel Wilson."

"Truly?" I could not help the awe tingling in my tone as I breathed out the word. Lionel Wilson was a prolific author, one who had helped to shape modern British literature, and he was standing here in my presence. "I adore your fiction, sir." Edward's father allowed me to borrow books from his library, and he always brought home the latest from his visits to London. "You are brilliant. Your serials are my favorite."

"Now, now." Mr. Davis waved the compliment away.

"If you do not mind my asking, though, why do you use a pseudonym? You are a man, after all."

"Yes, well, John Davis is not a very memorable or unique name now, is it?"

I laughed softly. "I suppose not."

"Besides, I prefer anonymity." He eyed me. "Are you attempting to pursue publication using your real name?"

"No." The dream of using anything close to my name had died when Edward's parents asked me to use a *nom de plume*.

I detailed to Mr. Davis my attempts to pursue publication thus far—and the dead ends I had reached.

Just then, dinner was announced. I was escorted into the dining room by an unfamiliar male guest in his forties, who immediately turned to the lady on his left to discuss something of seemingly great importance. Thankfully, on the other side sat the Davises—Edward's father's doing, I suspected. We continued our conversation.

Mr. Davis told me about his journey toward publication and from where he drew his inspiration. "Life in every season is inspiring, is it not? And I do not mean in simply the highest highs and the lowest lows. There is something thrilling, almost miraculous, in the everyday things, in the mundane tasks we do. The small wonders found in nature. The way a child clings to his mother when he is afraid. The way a single flower bends to the will of the wind. All of it defines us, and yet none of it does. Life in all its glory and in all its plainness is what causes me to hold pen to paper and cull a story from within."

"But how . . ." I didn't even know the question I wanted to ask, not until it was on the tip of my tongue. "How do you wade through the emotions warring in your heart? How can you form a story when life brings you nothing but grief? How to create such beauty from the pain?"

He set down his fork and turned to me. "My dear, writing is the only way I have found to help the grief make sense. That, and knowing in my very core that there is a purpose in it."

I had thought that to be true, too, once upon a time. When my father died, I poured my pain out with my words, and they became a healing balm.

But when my friendship with Edward died, every word pricked my heart, scraping my insides raw until I was a hollowed-out shell.

I had always considered myself strong, but perhaps my strength had never truly been tested. Perhaps Edward had been my strength. I only knew that maybe this weak puppet of a person I had become was the real me all along. Without him.

What was I to do? How could I become something better than I was, on my own?

Mr. Davis seemed to take my silence as a sign I needed time to think, so he engaged others at the table in conversation. When the meal had ended, he turned to me once more. "Miss Fairfax, I know how difficult it is to begin in this industry, and our host has told me you are a very intelligent and hardworking young woman. I am happy to read a sample of your work and offer critique and feedback if you would find it helpful."

Then he stood, wiped the crumbs from his mustache, and left with the other men to smoke cigars.

And I sat there, keenly aware that something had changed.

Someone had finally noticed me drowning and offered to point me in the direction of the shore. Now it was up to me to keep stroking through the water until I reached the sandy beach beyond.

33

𝔀𝔀𝔀𝔀𝔀

GINNY

A knock sounded on Ginny's door.

She stopped rolling the dough on the counter. Who would be here at six o'clock on a Saturday night? Sophia and William had been out sightseeing all day and probably weren't even home yet.

Ginny ran her doughy fingers under the faucet and wiped them dry, then walked through the living room. Looking through the peephole, she saw Steven and opened the door. "Hey there." She'd seen him several times since that night on the boat two weeks ago, when he'd pried her heartstrings loose with his musings, but they hadn't had much opportunity to hang out one-on-one.

The last couple of weeks had been filled with further bookstore improvements, filling online orders, and trying new recipes for the store's pastry case—oh, and dodging calls from Garrett's lawyer. She just didn't have the mental or emotional energy to cope with the divorce stuff right now. Already her broken dreams for the future took up too much room in her heart and head space, and she fell into bed exhausted as it was.

"Hey." Steven glanced at her splattered apron and pink polka-dot pajama pants. "Sorry to drop in so late. Hope I'm not interrupting anything."

"You're not." Ginny swung her arm wide, indicating he should come inside. "I'm just trying to perfect my beignet recipe."

"Beignets? Don't think I've ever had those before." Steven closed the door behind him and shrugged out of his jacket, revealing a blue henley sweater that matched his eyes—too well.

She really wished she'd looked in the mirror before answering the door. With her hair thrown up in a messy bun, random strands hanging down and sticking to her sweaty forehead, she probably looked the very opposite of fabulous.

Not that it should matter. This was Steven. A friend.

Ginny swiveled on her heel and walked toward the kitchen. "You're welcome to have some when I'm done."

"I can help if you like."

Turning, she raised an eyebrow his direction. "Really?"

He rolled up his sleeves. "Just give me an apron, and I'm all yours."

He doesn't mean it like that, Ginny. Okay, it really was warm in here. She hurried to the window over her sink and pushed it open, letting in some fresh air. A cool breeze passed over her cheeks.

"So, what's up? Did you just happen to know I was baking? Looking to score more cookies?" She pasted on a smile as she headed to the pantry for an apron. The only options included a small flowery one and Garrett's grilling apron. She reached for the latter but her fingers twitched, changing direction at the last minute. Ginny turned to hand the smaller apron to Steven.

He pursed his lips, holding back a full smile. "Really, Ginny? C'mon . . ."

"What, not comfortable enough in your masculinity?" She looped the apron over his head, leaving the strings dangling at his sides. "Look, the color brings out the red in your hair."

"Everything brings out the red in my hair." He snatched the

strings and brought them around his trunk. Designed for a petite woman—not a well-built man—they were barely long enough to tie together. "And I'm here because I wanted to deliver some good news in person."

"Yeah? What's that?" Ginny picked up the rolling pin and finished flattening the dough till it was a quarter inch thick.

"You already made your five hundredth sale on the website."

Her head shot up to look at him. "No way. It's only been live for two weeks."

"I know. All the marketing money you've been putting into the launch has really paid off."

"Not to mention your amazing SEO and webmaster skills."

"Guess we make a good team, eh?" Steven cocked his head, then pointed to the dough. "Speaking of which, what do you want me to do? I didn't get all dolled up in an apron to stand here and look pretty."

She couldn't stop the unladylike snort. "Find me a dough cutter, would you? In that drawer over there."

He opened the indicated drawer and fumbled through it, various utensils scraping against one another as he did so. "I can't seem to locate it. Of course, it would help if I knew what in the world a dough cutter was."

"How do you survive without one?" Ginny tried to keep her tone serious, but couldn't.

He straightened and turned to face her, then winked. "I just trick females into thinking I'm helpless and they bake for me."

"Is that so?" She had to force a laugh—which was ridiculous. Why should the comment bother her? "Here, let me." She strode toward him.

"Okay, well, it's mostly just you and my mum." He flashed a mischievous grin as he tried to move aside for her, but this part of the kitchen was particularly narrow. Steven had to squeeze around her to switch places.

She flattened herself against the counter, but their arms still brushed. The contact unnerved her. Or maybe just the way it made her heart skitter.

When she reached the open drawer, her eyes flew straight to the dough cutter, tucked away under a few spatulas in the back right corner. "Found it."

"Ginny for the win." Steven wandered to an old radio sitting atop her microwave. "Mind if I put on some music?"

"Be my guest."

He flicked the dial on and a Rolling Stones song pulsed out, filling the kitchen with a lively tune. "Now, show me what to do."

She demonstrated how to cut the dough into one-inch squares. Then they put them on to deep fry, the crackling oil barely audible over the music. He helped to flip them in the fryer until they became golden brown.

As they worked, a familiar Beatles song came on the radio. Steven started singing at the top of his lungs, wiggling his hips in a ridiculous manner as he flipped beignets in the flowery apron. Ginny joined him, echoing the lyrics as she transferred the deep-fried dough from the stovetop to paper towels, then into a bag of powdered sugar. The powder leapt up in happy puffs whenever a beignet was plopped inside the bag.

One song rolled into another. Together they powdered the rest of the treats and sang until their voices were hoarse. Laughing, he took advantage of a moment when her hands were empty to spin her around the room, dancing to an upbeat song she'd never heard before.

They stopped spinning as the song ended. Her heart pounded with the exertion—and if she admitted it, Steven's nearness. She couldn't help but look up at him. Their laughter cut off. The moment seemed to last forever, hung in the balance between what was and what could be. The tension between them pounded in her ears.

He reached up and brushed his finger lightly down her nose. "You've got powdered sugar everywhere."

Her hand trembled as she watched it rise of its own accord to his hair, flecked with white. She pushed her fingers through it. "You too."

Steven's hands, which rested on her waist, seemed to tighten then, his fingers flexing. A breath shuddered in and out as he watched her. "I've never seen you like this before. So happy and lit up. It's as if you've been hiding and didn't even know it."

He got her, didn't he? Even when she didn't get herself.

And in a way, quite possibly, that Garrett never had.

What would it be like to kiss him? She closed her eyes, lifted up on her tiptoes—but something stopped her. She knew she'd regret it.

Part of her didn't care—she just wanted to not feel the emptiness inside of her anymore, the raw pain from Garrett's betrayal. Was there really anything wrong with that?

A sharp jab to her conscience.

Yes.

Because it wouldn't be fair to Steven. He was a good guy, one who deserved all of someone, not the broken leftover pieces.

She placed her hands on his chest, felt the rapid beating of his heart. "Steven . . ." The word came out strangled, a mixture of groaning and aching.

He studied her for a moment, taking a piece of her fallen hair and smoothing it down. "I really didn't mean to fall for you, Gin. I tried not to, but you have a way about you that draws a man in." Then he pulled her to his chest in a fierce hug, his whispered words hot on her forehead. "You aren't ready, and the timing's not good, and I get that. But someday, if you are, and it is, I'll be here."

Tears fell from her eyes and she nodded, burying her face in his strong chest. The soft cotton of his shirt grazed her cheek. He smelled sweet, like the treats they'd just created together. "Thank you."

"Anytime."

She pulled away and swiped at her tears. "Should we sample our handiwork?"

He stared at her for a moment, then nodded. "Yeah, of course. But I have to grab something first, okay?"

"Sure."

Steven left the kitchen and she turned to the cabinet, pulling down two plates and two glasses. After filling the glasses with water, she plated two beignets and waited at the kitchen table for him to return.

He finally did, and in his hands he held what looked like a brochure. Sitting in the chair next to her, he slid the brochure across the table. On the front was a picture of three people, each wearing a toque blanche on their head and a double-breasted white jacket. They posed in front of a stovetop. *The London Culinary Institute* flowed in cursive script across the top of the pamphlet.

"Why are you giving me this?"

Steven's fingers drummed along the rim of the ceramic plate in front of him. "I researched a bunch, and this is the best one in England. When I requested a brochure, I spoke with an enrollment adviser. There's still time to apply for the spring start in January. They have a fairly quick application process."

Whoa, whoa, whoa. "That's so sweet of you to do that, but I can't go off to culinary school. That ship has sailed. Like I told you, I've got the bookstore now and that's where my focus is."

"You've worked really hard at making a comeback with your bookstore, but it just doesn't seem to be something you enjoy. When you talk about baking, though—I don't know, you just light up. And then seeing you tonight just confirmed it for me." He considered her. "I'm sorry if I've overstepped my bounds . . ."

His words edged close to the wounds she carried inside. "Don't you think I can do it? Save the bookstore, I mean." She hadn't thought so either, but then her friends had rallied around her, helped her do more than she'd dreamed possible—and in such a short amount of time too.

"That's not it at all. You are more than capable of doing whatever you put your mind to, Ginny Rose. But there's a difference between merely existing and really living. We all need to stop caring what other people say about us. We need to do what makes us come alive, because that's where we will truly find joy."

He'd reached the wound, jabbing it and sending shooting pains through her heart.

"It's not that simple, is it?" Her thoughts turned to Garrett, her parents, her life from beginning until now. "I've been searching for that joy, and it comes in bits and pieces, but then always fizzles out. At least the bookstore is something tangible I can hold on to when everything else is crumbling around me."

"Maybe you're looking in the wrong place."

"Thanks, that's helpful." Anger surged—not really at Steven, but at the way he'd pulled the bandage off her wounds, exposing them to air. The sting was gut-wrenchingly painful.

He ran his hand over his jaw. "I'm just trying to help."

"I think you should go." She shoved the brochure back toward him.

Steven hesitated, then nodded and stood, leaving the brochure on the table. He walked toward the living room, but before he was out of her sight, he turned. "You are more than you think you are, and more than how others have labeled you. Don't be afraid to embrace that."

34

≈≈≈≈≈

SOPHIA

"Have a lovely day. And enjoy the rest of your visit." Sophia waved at the elderly German couple as they grabbed their purchases and headed out the bookstore's front door. The bell rang out a good-bye.

"Wow, that was like the twentieth customer to buy something already today." Pulling open the display case door, Ginny used plastic tongs to place fresh blueberry muffins inside. "Business is booming lately."

Ever since they'd opened the loft upstairs, locals and tourists alike had started drifting in and staying, purchasing baked goods and browsing the books downstairs when they needed a break from their work.

"It really is. I've hardly sat down at all." Sophia pulled a piece of paper from the printer underneath the computer. It had ten orders from the last twenty-four hours alone. "And I haven't had time yet to process these online orders. Would you like me to do that now?"

"That'd be great. I'm done baking for the morning, so I can man the front."

"Perfect." Sophia didn't mind interacting with customers—she'd grown to really love it, actually. But she relished being among the books too, so locating the stock and packaging it up for delivery was one of her new favorite things to do.

She headed to the rare books section, passing a teen wearing earbuds who snapped her gum as she thumbed through a copy of the latest McManus murder mystery. Then there was a man in a tweed jacket with patches on the elbows checking out the Philosophy section. His style and build reminded her of William. Sophia smiled.

Finally, she was alone with the books. The hustle and bustle of the front of the store became only a murmur here in this cocoon of shelves and pages. The sweet, musky smell, almost like vanilla, pricked her nose as she wandered the section, pulling the first few ordered books into her arms.

Her phone vibrated in her back pocket. Sophia placed the handful of books on the edge of a table and pulled her phone out. Joy. "Hey, girl."

"Hi! How are you?" Her best friend's voice lit the line, though something sounded . . . off. They hadn't communicated in at least a week, and that had consisted of texts sent back and forth over the course of several hours. She'd missed Joy—though she would see her in three weeks' time. The thought brought both comfort and heartache.

Because . . . William. And Ginny. And having to go back to work, resume normalcy, when this place and her time away had done so much to free her. She still had a long way to go, but the thought of returning seemed stifling.

But she didn't want to think about that now. "No complaints here. Oh, but William and I got one step closer to finding out about Emily's story."

It had been a little more than a week since they'd sent off for birth certificates for two different James Bryants who had been born in a plausible time frame. Normally, it only took anywhere from one to four days to receive the information, but the genealogical indices they'd searched had been sparse with information, so it was going to take longer for the General Registrar Office to track down the certificates. In the meantime, she and William had spent their time sightseeing or hanging out together, talking about deep subjects and falling for each other more and more.

Sophia sighed happily. With a quick glance at the paper still in her other hand, she started looking for the next book on the list. "How's it going out your way?"

"Well . . ."

Sophia stopped. "Is everything okay?"

"No, actually." Joy's voice shuddered. "It's my mom. She's got Alzheimer's."

"Oh, friend." Sophia slumped against the nearest wall. Joy's parents were just the sweetest. They always invited Sophia out to dinner with them when they were visiting Joy from Florida. "How bad is it?"

"In the early stages, but she was just diagnosed on Monday. And you know how much Dad depends on her. He's nearly eighty and his diabetes has gotten worse."

Despite being sixty, Sophia's own mother was the picture of health. She couldn't imagine what Joy was feeling. "How are your parents handling it?"

"Dad is being all optimistic, of course, but I can tell he's scared. And Mom . . . Well, I knew she had some dementia, but apparently she's been bad for a while. She just hid it from me until she couldn't anymore."

"I'm sorry. Are you planning a visit soon?"

"Of course. I'm going to leave today, in fact. But . . ."

Her friend needed Sophia. She owned the practice, but Sophia was her right-hand therapist—or had been, before she'd taken her leave. But Sophia was stronger now. No, she wasn't really ready to return, but for Joy, she'd do anything. "I'll book a flight." The thought of bailing on Ginny and William made her queasy, but Joy had been her family long before she'd met either of them. "I can be there tomorrow."

"No, you can't do that. I won't be here."

"Right, but you need me to return to work, don't you?" The air back here suddenly seemed heavy.

"Tracy—you know, the therapist I hired to temporarily replace you when you left for England?—is fine with taking on some extra clients, and between her and Veronica I think there's enough coverage until you return after Labor Day."

Relief flooded Sophia's veins. "Are you sure?"

"Yes. But, Soph, there's more." A pause. "With my parents' declining health, I've been thinking about this for a while, but didn't say anything because of all you were going through. And now with Mom's diagnosis, it's the final straw. I don't think I'm coming back."

"What do you mean?"

"I mean, who knows how long my parents are going to need me? My dad needs help, and I want all the good memories I can get with Mom. I've decided to move in with them for the foreseeable future."

She couldn't argue with her friend's compassionate heart. "I—"

"And I've decided to sell the practice to help my parents pay for the medical bills. They're on a limited income, and even with the insurance they have, the best treatment costs more than they can afford. Especially if Mom has to be moved to a nursing home. Of course, I'll do all I can to keep her home with us." Joy was sniffling now.

"Joy, you built LifeSong from the ground up. Are you sure about this?"

"I am. I have to be. I can always rebuild, but I can't ever get this time back with my parents. They've done so much for me over the years."

"Oh, girl. I wish I could wrap my arms around you right now. I'm coming to Florida. I insist."

"Don't you dare leave. You're finally finding yourself again, and I won't be the reason you don't. When I'm settled and you're back, you can come visit. Okay?"

When Joy made up her mind about something, it was best not to argue. Sophia rubbed her temple. "This doesn't feel right."

"I know."

"You tell me if you change your mind, and I'm there in a flash, okay?"

"Okay. Thanks." Joy sighed. "I do have one more thing to ask you, though."

"Anything."

"Do you want to buy LifeSong?"

"What?"

"You heard me. I know you never wanted to touch the rest of David's life insurance money, but maybe this would be a worthy cause. You could keep helping women who need it. Kind of poetic, really. And there's no one I'd trust more with my baby."

"Really? No one you'd trust more than the therapist who had a nervous breakdown and hid away reading books for three months?" Sophia's attempt to bring levity to the moment fell flat.

"You joke, but I'm serious. I trust the therapist who now knows from experience what healing entails."

She had to admit that she was better equipped now than she'd ever been to help women make it through their trying situations. Finally, Sophia understood that healing looked different for everyone—for her it had been a slow burn, the result of working in a bookstore, tracking down Emily Fairfax, befriending a lonely bookstore owner, meeting an amazing man, surfing, kissing.

Living.

But what would happen when she left England?

35

GINNY

"Be prepared for the best popcorn you've ever tasted."

Ginny clutched two bowls of her white- and dark-chocolate-glazed kernels in one arm and pushed through her kitchen door to the living room with the other.

Girls Night was officially under way. It was too bad Mary had to cancel at the last minute, but the time alone with Sophia would be refreshing.

"If you made it, I'm sure it will be." Sophia lounged on Ginny's red couch in her pajama bottoms and spaghetti strap top, her hair twisted back with bobby pins, her feet propped on the coffee table. She flipped through a stack of DVDs, but there was something about the way she shoved one behind the other that seemed to lack focus.

After setting the popcorn on the table, Ginny plopped next to Sophia. "Anything striking your fancy?"

Sophia shrugged. "I don't really care what we watch. I'm just glad we get to hang out. It's been too long since we did much other than work together at the bookstore."

"If only *someone* wasn't spending so much time with my

brother-in-law." Ginny winked, but the words she'd spoken socked her in the gut. William would soon be her ex-brother-in-law. Just another loss in the string of losses, thanks to Garrett's betrayal.

She snatched a handful of popcorn and shoved it in her mouth.

Sophia finished perusing the DVDs. "Do you have a preference?"

Ginny's eyes quickly scanned the titles she'd hastily thrown into a stack before Sophia came over. *Pride and Prejudice. While You Were Sleeping. Confessions of a Shopaholic.* All movies she'd normally love— but then again, they all ended in happily-ever-afters, didn't they? "Not really."

Where were all the movies about strong women who survived betrayal, had thriving businesses, and knew exactly what they wanted in life? That was what she wanted to watch.

Ginny took another fistful of popcorn and stared at the coffee table—yet another thing Garrett had carved. His handiwork was everywhere. How was she ever going to get over him, get past this hurt?

And yet, for a moment, with Steven . . .

"Whoa, what did that popcorn ever do to you?"

Sophia's voice broke through Ginny's thoughts. She looked at her fist to find broken pieces of popcorn spilling from between her fingers, chocolate melted against her skin. "Nothing. It was an innocent bystander."

Her phone buzzed next to her. Who would be calling on a Friday night? She wiped her hand on a napkin, picked up the phone, groaned, and pressed Ignore.

"You can get that if you want."

"I don't. It's Garrett's attorney." What more did he need? She'd formally acknowledged the petition for divorce he'd sent over weeks ago. She still had to secure her own attorney so she didn't get walked all over with the proceedings, but she couldn't figure out how she'd afford it. Mother had offered the services of the family attorney, but that was sure to come with strings attached. Ginny would rather eat a burned coffee cake. "I have no stomach to discuss anything with him right now."

"Want to talk about it with me?" Sophia curled her feet up underneath her, angling her body to face Ginny, leaning against the back of the couch.

Did she? "I know I'm delaying the inevitable, but I still can't believe I'm getting a divorce. It's not what I pictured for myself, you know? Garrett has been such a part of my life—this house, the bookstore, everything—that I don't know how I'm supposed to move forward without him in it."

Sophia took a moment before she spoke. "It was like that for me when David died. That's one reason I had to get out of that house and come here." A piece of her hair fell from its pin into her eyes. "In fact, I've been thinking that I might sell it. It's gone up in value since we bought it, and the money could give me even more freedom to buy Joy's practice."

When Sophia had found out about her friend's change in plans earlier this week, she'd seemed off-kilter. Now there was a quiet resignation in her eyes.

"So you've decided to purchase it? Move back?"

Sophia's eyes lit in surprise. "Of course I'm moving back. I never actually moved here. The plan was only ever to stay for the summer."

"Yeah, but William . . ." Ginny tilted her head. "I guess I thought maybe you might not want to leave because of him."

"I am sorely tempted to stay." A small smile twitched at the corners of Sophia's lips. In an instant, it was gone. "But he was never part of the plan. I can't make my decisions based on him. I feel like I did that with David. I can't do it again."

Maybe that was where it had all gone wrong with Garrett. "Hmm."

"What?"

"I . . . It's just, what you said. I think I built my whole life around my husband. And now he's being removed from the equation." No wonder it felt like life was crashing down around her, even with the bookstore thriving.

"You're not the first to do it. I'm guilty too. Of course, I allowed David to have complete control over my life. It seems like you and Garrett were partners."

"Until we weren't." Ginny pulled a green pillow to her chest. "Other than my grandparents, he was the only one who ever really got me, you know? He saw the real me—or I thought he did. Maybe I only showed him what I thought he wanted to see." After all, she'd still ended up here, running a bookstore she never would have dreamed up on her own. But spouses were supposed to support each other's dreams, weren't they?

Yes. She'd supported his dream.

Had he ever supported hers?

Then again, had she ever really expressed to him how much she'd wanted to become a pastry chef? Or had she allowed the thrill of being out from under her parents' thumb to be good enough? She thought she'd found contentment in her life with Garrett.

Perhaps it had only been a temporary salve for the deeper aches she hadn't been willing to address.

As Ginny chewed her lip, she caught sight of *My Fair Lady* peeking from beneath the other DVDs. She leaned forward and plucked it from the stash. She'd always bemoaned the utterly unromantic ending, but right about now, it was the only movie in her collection she'd be able to stand.

"How about this one?" Before Sophia had a chance to respond, Ginny got up and loaded the disc into the DVD player.

"Sure."

The TV whirred to life and soon the room was filled with music. Both Sophia and Ginny directed their attention to the screen. Sophia munched on popcorn, but Ginny felt her friend's eyes on her every few seconds it seemed.

Finally, Ginny turned. "Everything okay?"

Snatching the remote, Sophia lowered the volume. She seemed to consider her words before speaking. "I saw a brochure on your kitchen table when I first got here."

Ugh. Ginny hadn't touched it since Steven had left it behind on the table two weekends ago. She couldn't bring herself to open it or toss it. "Steven gave it to me. He thought I'd want to apply to culinary school."

"And do you?"

"No." On the one hand, part of her held out hope that Garrett would realize the error of his ways and come racing back to her. On the other, she longed to leave everything behind. But she'd already lived that way once. "He was trying to help, but I've kind of given him the cold shoulder since then." In fact, they hadn't even spoken.

"He seems like a good friend who wants you to be happy." Sophia speared her with a look. "Maybe even more than a friend?"

"He *is* a good friend. Just a friend." And she'd treated him so poorly.

Sophia pursed her lips like she didn't believe her—though given Ginny and Steven's near kiss the last time they were alone together, she was totally justified in her assessment of the situation. "I'll let that one go. For now. So . . . *do* you think culinary school would make you happy?"

"It doesn't matter. I have the bookstore now."

"What if you didn't?"

Dare she open herself to that dream again? To who she was when she had her own dreams?

In the background, Eliza Doolittle sang about dancing—how she could have danced all night if given the chance. How it wouldn't have been enough even then. Her heart craved more.

Ginny's own heart gave a little bump, as if trying to leap, but something held it back. She sighed. "There's no point in pretending

I don't. This may not be the dream I started with, but I'm making it into a place I can be happy."

Sophia squeezed Ginny's knee. "I think you will succeed at whatever you do, Gin. But you should still do something that makes you come alive. Don't settle for someone else's dream. Go after your own."

Steven had basically said the same thing.

She believed it for others. Why was it so hard for Ginny to accept that truth for herself? Maybe it *was* possible to make her own way.

"I'll think about it."

36

EMILY

FEBRUARY 1860

I made the final mark with my pen and placed it on my desk. There. My manuscript was finished at last.

Sitting back against my chair, I turned and stared out the window. A streetlamp stood guard, lighting up the darkness beyond. Snow fluttered from the sky, gathering in clumps on the ground. I longed to put on my cloak and run outdoors to spin in the falling fluff, but now that we had gone to London for Louisa's third season, neighbors were much closer than in the country.

And of course, I kept to my room as much as possible. Nearly a year after the wedding, it still hurt whenever I saw Edward and Rosamond together. Living under the same roof as him again—as them—had forced me back to my writing. That and the fact Mr. Davis had been true to his word. He had read my first manuscript and given me a detailed critique within a fortnight. I had spent all of my spare time considering and implementing his suggested changes—many of which had asked me to go deeper, to show even more of my heart.

And now those changes were complete, ready to be submitted once more. He had even promised to recommend my work to his own publisher.

I couldn't believe my good fortune.

But perhaps it had not been fortune at all.

Standing, I walked to the window, placing my hand on the pane. My fingertips became cold. For a long time, I had felt that way on the inside too. But now, with my story told, I was finally coming in from the chill to the warmth of the hearth. Each step was a tender one that I had fought to take. Facing the resistance had made me stronger.

My story had given me such a sense of self. Though it must be midnight at the earliest, I was far too stimulated to sleep.

I pulled my dressing gown on over my nightdress and walked down the hallway toward the library, my candle in hand guiding the way. The door creaked as I pushed it open. Moonlight spilled from the window, creating shadows in the room. A sofa sat against one wall, thick rugs covered the parquet floors, and a solid table and chairs stood in the middle of the room, ready for the next day's learning. While we resided in London, the library functioned as a schoolroom, my domain. However, it felt different during the night. Its broad, unbroken walls remained the same, as did the open-shelved bookcases filled with familiar and unfamiliar stories alike. But something about the quiet made the stories held within the books speak louder to me. I could almost hear their whispers shouting, begging for release.

I reached out to skim my fingers along the book spines, breathing in the scent of varnish and pipe smoke that always pervaded the library.

My hand stopped on a random book and I took it from the shelf.

"Emily?"

I dropped the volume, turning at the sound of the voice that invaded my thoughts every time my eyes closed at night.

Edward lay on the sofa and sat up at my perusal. Even from my spot across the room, I could see that his hair was in disarray and he wore no tie, jacket, or vest—simply trousers and a shirt. He ran his hands over his cheeks and eyes, through his hair, then he straightened once more. "What are you doing here?" He spoke as though he were ill—his voice hoarse, his nose stuffed.

"I could not sleep, so I thought I might read." As proof, I crouched to pick up the book I had dropped.

"Ah." He stared at me, expressionless.

I cocked my head. Though my heart told me not to approach him—remembering what had occurred the last time we were alone together—my feet moved of their own accord. "Edward, are you well?" I placed the candle on the table and sat on the opposite end of the sofa, my legs angled toward him. Upon closer inspection, I saw his eyes were rimmed with red, as if he had taken one too many glasses of brandy. "Were you sleeping in here?"

"Attempting to sleep is more like it." He leaned forward on his elbows, his face cradled in his hands. "You were right about Rosamond." His voice was muffled as he talked through his hands, but I still perceived its jagged timbre.

"What happened?"

"I . . ." He straightened. "I discovered a letter from a man who apparently was . . . is . . . her lover." He spat the words out.

My whole body twisted toward him and my hand found his. "I'm so sorry."

He offered a sardonic smile. "Why are you sorry? You tried to warn me. And I, in my self-righteous arrogance, ignored you." Edward sighed. "It doesn't matter now."

"Of course it matters. She has wronged you greatly." The feeling of his hand in mine, the darkness of the room, the sound of only a ticking clock and the two of us breathing—all of it was an overwhelming mixture. "Did you confront her?"

"I did." The words seemed to strangle him as they left his lips.

"And?" I scolded myself for the hope that once again soared in my chest. I had no place wishing that Edward would divorce Rosamond and run to me. And yet . . .

His eyes watched me. Slowly, he picked up my hand and brought it to his lips. He kissed my wrist, where he must have felt my pulse racing in time to my heart.

"Edward?" I could not utter another word. My mind buzzed like a thousand bees. Every breath in my being leaned into this moment.

He scooted closer to me on the sofa. "Emily. How I have missed you." His eyes searched mine, his fingers pushing a stray hair back from my face. Untying my nightcap, he tossed it aside, and when my hair fell around my shoulders, Edward moved his fingers through it. "I cannot tell you how long I have wanted to . . ."

All I could do was sit and wait, my body thrumming.

An inner voice screamed at me, but I did not have the strength—the desire—to listen.

"How did I allow you to slip away from me?" He drew closer, his face inches from my own, his breath warm on my cheeks. "I had everything in you. I should have found a way to save my family and have you as well. How could I have been so blind?"

When Edward's mouth met mine, I exploded in a mass of nerves and light. This was what a candle must feel like, flickering its brilliance against the darkness, allowing itself to finally be what it was created to be, fully unfurling its flame for all to see.

But every candle eventually burns out.

As this man whom I had loved for years explored my neck with his lips, the loud voice of my conscience finally returned me to reality.

"Wait." I gasped the word and twisted from him. "Edward."

His breath came heavy, and he ran both hands through his hair—hands that had just been where they should not have been. On me. Not on his wife. It did not matter that he was mine first—in friendship, if not in more.

He was hers now.

Unable to withstand the torture in his gaze, I closed my eyes. "What did she say when you confronted her?"

He didn't answer me.

I opened my eyes again. "Tell me."

"Emily . . ." The word, thus spoken, begged me to allow him to forget, to seek comfort where we could here in the darkness. But in the morning, he would still be married.

And I would be ruined—in every sense of the word.

"Tell me." This time, I forced my voice to be firm.

"She told me it was true, that she has been unfaithful." He sighed. "And that she is pregnant."

My hands trembled as I pulled them into my lap. "By him?"

A pause. "She claims by me."

"And is that a possibility?"

He knew what I was asking him. "Yes."

I nodded once, my cheeks burning. Before he could say another word, I stood, searching for my nightcap. When I found it, I wound my hair and attempted to yank it onto my head. My hands shook too much to tie it properly.

Edward joined me. He took the strings of the cap and looped them for me, never taking his eyes from mine. "I'm sorry, Emily. I never should have . . ." He looked away, but not before I saw a tear slip from his eye.

There was only one other time I had seen Edward cry—when his grandfather died.

Instantly, I moved back into his arms, my instinct to comfort my friend outweighing everything else.

He clutched me to his chest. "It's not fair."

"What?" Afraid to move, I spoke into his shirt and the word was barely audible.

"That she . . ." He steadied his voice. "I do not love her. I love y—"

"Don't." I swallowed hard. "Do not say it. Please. I could not bear to hear it only once in my lifetime." Pulling away, I looked up at him once more.

But he did not kiss me again. Something like resolve passed over his face, and he released me, grabbed my candle, and placed it in my hands. "Go, Em. Please. If you stand here for one more moment, I cannot promise to remain apart from you."

I nodded, a few tears starting to flow and blur my vision. With a last glance at him—my best friend, things forever broken between us—I flew down the hallway. Once I reached my room, I closed the door behind me. With a cry, I blew out the candle, threw the candlestick against the wall, fell on my knees, and let loose the torrent of tears that had been building for months. For years.

Edward was right. It was not fair. But it was still the reality of things.

When the torrent ended at last, I shuffled to my desk, bound up my manuscript, and walked toward the library once more. The light of a candle flickered beneath the doorframe and I heard Edward pacing. After slipping the package under the doorway, I scurried away.

Even without a note, he would know what this action meant.

And I prayed he would know what I needed, for I was just beginning to understand it myself. If ever the candle within me was to live again, I must light it with a different source.

The next morning, I found the manuscript returned under my door. A note adorned the top, slipped under the twine binding the pieces of parchment together. I picked it up, opened it, read it:

My dearest Emily,

Even if I had wanted to sleep last night, I would not have been capable. I was far too enthralled by your novel. You have a talent few can boast of and I am glad you are using it to make the world a better place. Thank you for sharing your heart with me. It is not merely the story that is beautiful, but the soul of the one who created it.

I wish our story had turned out as happy as this one. I take full responsibility that it did not.

I must apologize for my conduct. I did not behave as a gentleman should—but more so, I did not behave as a friend should. Please forgive me. To think you might be angry with me is a thing I cannot bear to consider.

When you read this note, Rosamond and I will be on our way back to the country estate. When the family returns at the end of the season, we will go to London or Rosamond's family's home. In doing so, I hope to cling to what I have and allow you to do the same.

Your friend always,

Edward

Though my chest hurt, I smiled softly, kissing the note. Then I wrapped the manuscript in brown paper and whisked away to the post office to post the parcel to M&L Publishing.

With a final hug of the parcel to my chest, I let go and gave my heart permission to fly.

37

SOPHIA

The moment Ginny walked into the bookstore with the manila envelope and stack of other mail, Sophia knew what it contained.

She kept ringing up patrons, trying to catch Ginny's eye as she spoke with a new mom, leaning over the stroller to say hi to the little bundle inside. The bookstore had played host to a whole slew of people today—Ginny had done such a nice job revitalizing this place—and there were three more people in line, so Sophia couldn't abandon her post.

But her fingers itched as she took one credit card after another.

Finally, Ginny approached the desk with the pile of mail. "How's it going in here?"

"Good." Sophia smiled as she bagged a copy of the latest Emily Giffin novel and handed it to the college student who had purchased it. "Is that for me?"

Ginny looked down at the envelope. "Yeah. Oh hey, the General Registrar Office. You think it's—"

"The birth certificates for James Bryant. At least I hope so."

"Here, open it. I can cover the desk for a bit."

"I can't. Not without William."

"Go find him. He should be home from work by now. I'll take over for the rest of the evening."

"No, no, I couldn't do that to you."

Ginny placed a hand on her hip. "Soph, I'm offering. This is my bookstore, remember? And you work more hours than I'd ever planned for you to work anyway. Go. Have fun. I hope you find some answers."

"Okay, but I'm taking your morning shift tomorrow." Sophia grabbed Ginny in a quick hug, then snatched her phone and the envelope and headed up the stairs to her room. She dialed William's number and found out he was at the post office and could stop by in a few minutes. Sophia didn't tell him why she wanted to see him. Surprising him would be fun.

Her nerves buzzed with anticipation. Another piece to the puzzle might be falling into place soon.

To take her mind off the wait, Sophia grabbed her laptop and slid into a chair at the tiny kitchen table. She navigated to Facebook, but all the images blurred as she scrolled.

A knock reverberated on the door. "Come in."

William entered. "So what's this surprise?"

"I think the GRO sent the birth certificates over." From where she sat, Sophia held up the envelope. Who knew that something so thin and light could be the answer they'd been waiting for?

"Yeah?" William strode over and sat in the seat next to her.

Sophia tore the top of the envelope and reached a hand inside. "Ready?"

"Yes." He gave her a quick peck on the cheek.

She turned, eyebrows lifted. "What was that for?"

"For being you."

Whew, this man. How could she be leaving him in ten short days? She studied him and abandoned the envelope for a moment, throwing her arms around his neck and pulling him in for a long kiss.

When he drew back, both surprise and joy lingered in his eyes. "And what was that for?"

"For being you." She winked, then focused once more on the envelope. Reaching inside, her hand emerged clutching three sheets of paper. The top one was their original search request and receipt. But the next page was a sort of salmon color, with darker and lighter shades of orange. All of the information was handwritten in cursive.

Sophia's eyes scanned the document. "Okay, this James Bryant was born in 1868 to a John and Elizabeth Bryant. Not our guy." As if in slow motion, she moved the last piece of paper to the front of the stack. Her fingers trembled. "William."

"I see."

This James Bryant was born September 13, 1860, in London—to Edward Bryant and Rosamond Turner Bryant.

"Soph, look at the residence of the person who reported the birth."

Though the day was warm, Sophia began shivering, goose bumps appearing along her arms. The birth certificate revealed that E. Bryant, James's father, had reported the birth—and his address matched that of Elliott Manor. "I can't believe it. Do you think we found them?"

"It sure seems that way."

But one glaring thought kept rippling in her mind. "We still don't know if Emily Fairfax was real, though." After seeing the possible results for James Bryant, they'd already done a search of Emily Fairfaxes born from 1830 to 1840 anywhere in England—and the results were inconclusive. William had reminded her that not all births were reported, they didn't know where Emily had been born, and something could have happened to the parish records.

Despite all their research, they were coming up empty. They didn't have any other information to go on.

"So. Are you content with knowing what we do, or do you want to try to find out more? We could try to hire a professional genealogist." William reached toward Sophia and encased her hand with his.

It should be enough, right? They'd done almost all they could. She should be satisfied they'd received as many answers as they had.

And yet.

That voice inside—the one she'd barely recognized a few months ago, but had slowly started listening to again—seemed to urge her to try for one more Hail Mary.

"Let's try to visit Hugh Bryant one more time. If he won't tell us anything, we back off. Leave all of this alone. Conclude that we weren't meant to discover anything else about it, and be grateful for what we've learned with this search."

And learn she had.

Because despite all the work they'd done to find the answers about Emily Fairfax, Sophia had a feeling that they weren't the ultimate prize.

∽᧬∼

The narrow roads of Wendall didn't leave much room for even William's car, but they managed to navigate their way back to the run-down flat at the end of Wellington Street. The shutters were cracked and peeling, and what had likely once been a prized garden in front now grew only weeds—dry, dusty, brown.

They climbed from the vehicle and walked to the front entryway. Sophia lifted the brass knocker and rapped it three times against the solid oak door. William grabbed hold of her hand and rubbed gentle circles into her palm.

A few minutes passed.

That was it. She had to call it—the end of their journey. "I suppose he's not home."

The door opened. A man who looked to be in his sixties stood on the other side.

Sophia held in a squeal.

"Hi, Mr. Bryant?" William stepped forward, hand outstretched.

The man lifted one bushy eyebrow as he studied them. Then he nodded, quick. "That's me."

There was nothing overly unique about his appearance—he had a slight beer gut, his hair had thinned up top and was peppered with gray, and he wore jeans and a plain white T-shirt. "And just who might you be?"

"William Rose, sir. And this is—"

"Sophia Barrett." Mr. Bryant hadn't bothered to shake William's hand, so she didn't offer hers.

The older man's lip curled. "Ah, the American who won't stop leaving messages on my mobile and notes on my door."

"Yes." Sophia couldn't help the blush that crept into her cheeks. "I'm sorry to have intruded on your privacy, but we have something very important to speak to you about."

"Let's get this over with." Hugh turned on his heel and disappeared down the hallway, his shoulders hunched and his steps heavy.

After exchanging a look of surprise, William and Sophia scurried after him. She was nearly bowled over by the strong scent of tuna that seemed to have leached into the walls. Boxes were piled everywhere, from floor to ceiling, with not much space available for walking.

"Are you moving, Mr. Bryant?" If so, they'd lucked out that he was still here.

"No, why?"

No pictures adorned the walls, almost as if he had never unpacked from his move there twenty years ago—just slid everything inside and kept his life boxed up.

When they reached the living room, they found Hugh already sitting in an overstuffed chair that was far too fancy for this ramshackle flat. Though old with a few scratches and cracks in the leather, it appeared sturdy, like it had weathered the test of time with dignity.

She and William sat on a sofa across from Hugh.

Sophia took a deep breath. "Thank you for taking time to—"

"Look here, missy. I don't know why you see fit to bother me, but I only agreed to talk so you'd leave me alone once and for all." He turned and lifted a small box from the side table next to his chair, opened it, and pulled out a cigar. Running it under his nose, he inhaled. "But while you're here, you might as well have a Cuban."

What an unusual man. "Thank you, sir. But we don't want to trespass on your generosity that long," Sophia said.

"Suit yourself." The man clipped his cigar and lit it. "So, what can I do for you?"

"A few months ago, I was working in my friend's bookstore when I discovered a notebook." She launched into her story.

Hugh took a puff from the cigar, held it in a few seconds, then released it. His eyes remained steady on Sophia as she talked. While he seemed to stay almost perfectly still otherwise, his right foot tapped up and down with fervor.

"So that's how we ended up here, Mr. Bryant. You appear to be the descendant of Edward Bryant and Rosamond Turner, and possibly our last hope for any sort of answer."

"I see." Though it was only partially smoked, Hugh extinguished the rest of the cigar. He leaned forward in his chair, elbows on his knees, and speared Sophia with an intense look. "Do you have this notebook with you?"

Though the man hadn't given any indication he knew what Sophia was talking about, his interest gave her hope. "I do." She pulled it from her bag. The corners of the notebook had begun to bend from being stuffed in there so many times.

He reached for it, turned a page, and studied the printed words. "I seem to recall my cousin—my father's sister's girl—bringing me a notebook like this years ago. She had the original, which was discovered in the parsonage attic on our land and passed down through the generations. What you're describing sounds like the contents of that notebook, though I couldn't tell you for certain. I never read it."

"Would it be possible to meet with your cousin to view the original?"

"She passed away a few years back."

"Perhaps her children have it?"

He shook his head. "Never married. And no siblings. Not sure what happened to all her belongings. Probably donated somewhere."

Another dead end.

William jumped in. "If this is indeed your notebook, do you have any idea how it would have ended up at the bookstore?"

"Earlier this year there was a young man who came by collecting donations for the library. I told him to take whatever he could find—I inherited a lot of books from my parents. I'm not a big reader myself." Hugh harrumphed. "I suppose he really did take whatever he could find."

Would they get *any* firm answers today? Sophia chewed her bottom lip. "I don't mean this in an offensive way, but I'm curious. Why didn't you ever read the notebook? Weren't you curious why your cousin brought it to you?"

He closed the notebook. "She was always prattling on about our family history, but I never cared for such things. The past is the past, and it doesn't affect me one way or the other. And like I said, I'm not a big reader." Standing, he pushed the notebook into Sophia's hands. "In fact, you keep this. It clearly means more to you than it does to me. Now, will you go on and leave me in peace?"

"Thank you." A weight pressed against Sophia's heart as she took the notebook from him. "I'm sorry. It's just . . . So you've never heard of Emily Fairfax?"

William put his arm around her, a reminder that whatever happened next, he was here. Even if Emily Fairfax wasn't real, he was. They were. This thing between them . . . it was too.

Hugh Bryant fixed her with a stare, but as he studied her, something around the edges of his eyes seemed to soften. "I didn't say that. According to my cousin, she was very much a real person. And this story wasn't just a story—it was her life. But I'm afraid I don't know much more than that."

38

ffffffe

EMILY

SEPTEMBER 1860

On a day in mid-September, when the birds sang in the bushes and the flowers swayed in the breeze, I learned my book would at long last be published. In addition, the publisher requested more manuscripts and offered me the chance to submit material for serialized penny novels, a possibility that could lead to a greater writing income.

My heart felt freer than it ever had. Not only had my dream finally been realized, but I had managed to move beyond the pain of what had occurred between Edward and me. Of course, his removal from the estate once we arrived—much to the protest of his parents— had helped immensely. Observing Rosamond's blossoming form every day, as well as his dotage of her, would have simply been too much.

As I walked toward my room, the publisher's letter in my hand, I heard an exclamation. Peeking over the railing, I saw Edward's mother waving a letter of her own in the air, running as much as was dignified toward the drawing room. "Rosamond has had the baby! A boy named . . ."

At that moment, my ears buzzed and my head grew fuzzy. I slumped against the nearest wall and heaved in air. Though my legs wobbled, I forced them to carry me back down the stairs, out into the light, onward toward the tree—the place where I had always been happiest.

But now . . . now Edward was a father. I pictured him cradling a tiny version of himself, kissing his brow, whispering that he would always love and protect him from the perils of the world.

I tore the letter from the publisher into hundreds of tiny pieces, continued tearing and ripping and shredding with my fingers as I flung each one into the ocean below. They were swallowed up and taken away, exposed to the elements and drowned in the roiling nature of the waves.

Why could I not escape this feeling of rejection, of failure? Was this always to be my fate? I had sought to save my soul through written words. I had bled myself dry with ink. I had allowed myself to dig deep as John Davis suggested—to give more of myself to the story.

And still . . . my soul continued to feel bereft.

What then was the purpose of it all? What would it matter if I poured out my story or kept it locked inside of me? What difference could it possibly make? Why was I here at all?

Such lofty questions could not be answered in one sitting, in one day. But I had finally come to the end of myself. I had offered all I had to give—and found my offering lacking.

Perhaps the striving had given me purpose. But once achieved, my efforts had proven to be in vain.

My father's final words came back to me then: *"All we have in life are the choices we make. We must make choices we can live with—and die with, if it comes to that."*

His choices had led him to death—both physical and spiritual. He had turned his back on his faith and his family, all because he could not live without the person he loved most, because life had turned out differently than he had imagined.

I did not want that for myself. And I knew what I needed to do.

"I surrender." The words returned to me on the wind.

Opening my arms wide, I twirled in the radiant sunlight, joyful and grievous tears streaming down my cheeks, a new sense of purpose burning in my soul.

39

❦

SOPHIA

"Holy cow, this place is gorgeous." Sophia had never seen water so turquoise-blue, so clear except for the spots covered in white foam as they hit the brown and black rocks.

"This is supposedly the birth place of the Arthurian legend— King Arthur, that is." William pointed toward Tintagel Island, which was just across a footbridge from where they stood.

"Thanks for bringing me here. I'd have kicked myself if I had missed a place full of such history and beauty—especially given how close it is to where I've been staying all this time." Sophia studied the map they'd picked up from the visitors' center. William had insisted they stop here on the way home from visiting Hugh Bryant. He'd said he didn't want their day together to end.

Neither did she. After all, she would leave England in a week.

In front of them, the island was covered in lush green grass and stone ruins from a castle built by Richard, the Earl of Cornwall, in the 1200s. The island was small, a peninsula, really, and walking paths led to various gardens, courtyards, and even down to a beach and Merlin's Cave. The sun was shining and the breeze fairly calm, and they had the whole afternoon to explore. They set out to do so, crossing the dramatic footbridge, a steel-and-oak structure that connected the mainland with the island.

As they walked, surrounded by the ocean and raw land on all sides, Sophia should have felt at peace. She should have been ecstatic.

Because as of an hour ago, she'd discovered that Emily Fairfax was a real person, that the story that had inspired her so much had actually happened. It wasn't merely the rendering of a novelist who had created a character she deeply connected with. An actual woman had survived heartache and come out stronger on the other side.

Together, Sophia and William had accomplished something she'd pretty much thought impossible a few months ago.

So why were her emotions all over the map? Instead of freedom and calm, walls closed in on her. The task that had distracted her all summer was over. She was now left to face the reality that Joy was counting on her to buy the practice. That she wasn't sure she really wanted to.

And that she'd unintentionally fallen in love with the man standing next to her.

A man who respected her, who understood her soul. A man she would do anything for.

That was probably what scared her most. Even though William was nothing like David, there was a time Sophia would have done anything for her former fiancé too. A time when she'd lost herself.

Figuring out how to move forward with William without that constant fear nagging her . . . In this moment, it made her feel like Houdini in an enclosed box filled with water, upside down, feet manacled. But unlike Houdini, she had no idea how to escape.

William paused on the bridge, turned to her, pulled her close to him, and softly touched her lips with his own.

The wind picked up, whipping her hair into her eyes as she pulled back and looked up at him.

He pushed her bangs aside and tucked them behind her ear. "We did it."

Sophia turned, placed her hands on the railing of the bridge, and stared out at the endless ocean. "We did."

William settled into the spot next to her, their shoulders touching. "Thanks for letting me be part of all this."

"I couldn't have done it without you."

How she would have cringed at those words three months ago. But it was the truth. She never would have learned all she did about Emily Fairfax and Edward Bryant on her own. Relying on William had made her stronger.

Still . . . What did that mean for their future? And her heart?

As if reading her mind, William cleared his throat. "So what now?"

"Now . . . now we soak in the time we have left together before I go home." She no longer wanted to linger here. Sophia reached for his hand and they began walking again, toward the castle ruins on the other side.

But William stopped in the middle of the bridge. His gaze penetrated her bravado, chasing it away, leaving only raw tenderness in its place. "I can't stand the thought of you leaving, you know. We haven't talked about it much, but . . ." He took a breath, grabbed her hands, held them steady in his. "I don't want you to."

"I don't want to either." She'd thought getting her answers about Emily would change things, give her sudden clarity about her future. But nothing had changed in her life, not really.

"So what can we do about that? Is this . . . good-bye?" The word held such a note of vulnerability, it made Sophia want to cry.

"I don't want it to be. These months with you have been wonderful. A dream, really. But I have to wake up from the dream and go back to reality. I have a job where I help people. And I'm planning to buy Joy's practice. I won't have the luxury of spending a bunch of time not working and pursuing whatever mysterious thing comes along next for the sake of my own curiosity."

"You weren't 'not working.' You worked all the time in the bookstore."

"That didn't count. That was for fun. For healing."

"Why does that make it any less real? What if this could be your new reality? For good?"

Oh, what a thought. But . . . "I—"

"I love you, Sophia."

The words made her world stop, lit it with fireworks, and thrummed a beautiful melody throughout her soul. "You . . . what?"

"I love you."

She'd known it, really. In the way he looked at her, in the way he kissed her, yes, but more than that—in the way he treated her like a delicate flower opening for the first time in spring, watering her with gentle, steady drops without drowning her, helping her blossom and grow one day at a time.

But it didn't change the facts. She couldn't stay, however much she might want to. Her plan had always been to return home, and she had to hold steady to that. And then there was the small fear in the back of her mind, one that had lingered with her all summer . . . What if her "healing" was only the result of running away? Would she still feel this whole once she returned home? Didn't she need to go back to Arizona to find out?

Perhaps they could do the whole long-distance thing, but for how long? Was that just delaying the inevitable?

"I'm sorry. I don't know what to say. I'm all turned around inside."

William's hand caressed her cheek, and his thumb swiped away a tear as it fell. "Sophia, you have to stop fighting."

"Fighting what?" It felt like she'd given up the fight a long time ago.

"Everything. Your past. God. Even me." At her attempt to protest, he held his fingers against her lips. "Maybe I'm wrong. But perhaps it's time to do what you came here to do."

"I came here to heal. And I thought I was heading that way." Then why this inner wrenching of herself in two?

"You are, love. But you specifically came here to write your story. And you chased Emily's instead. You found out as much as you could about her story. It's time to write the next chapter in yours. But how can you when you don't really understand how the past chapters have affected you? I think maybe you need to finish what you started."

"Don't you think I've tried?" Sophia turned, stared at the rubble of the ruins that stood in the distance. They had once belonged to a beautiful and grand castle, but had been reduced to a pile of rocks. People had been happy there once. Even sad. They'd experienced life.

But all of that was just a memory now.

"I can't do it."

"Yes, you can. You said you felt drawn to Emily's journal."

Sophia closed her eyes. "I do."

"Maybe you need to figure out why." Tugging her close, William pressed a kiss to her brow. "Pray. Search deep within. I'm betting the answers have been there all along." He reached into his pocket and pulled out his car keys. "I'll take a taxi. You take my car home when you're ready. And, Sophia?"

She sniffled. "Yeah?"

"When all is said and done, even if you do decide to go home, even if we . . ." He paused, his Adam's apple bobbing. "Well, I'll never stop loving you."

As he handed her the keys, their palms touched, sending a shiver down her spine. The scent of him lingered in the air around her even as he walked away.

40

GINNY

Apologizing to a friend was never easy. But Ginny missed Steven too much to let another day go by without making things right with him. Three weeks had been long enough. It was shameful, really.

She finished ringing up the last customers of the day and walked them out, flipping the sign on the door to Closed once they left. After she'd texted him earlier today, Steven had agreed to come over a little after closing. That meant she had about half an hour to figure out what she might say to him.

It wasn't as if she was still upset about him giving her the culinary institute pamphlet. She'd just gotten busy with the bookstore. And to be honest, whenever she thought about their near kiss . . . Well, it was better to give him some space, to let her feelings catch up with her head.

Ginny balanced the register, her knee bouncing up and down while she did so. Another great day of business. Hard to believe this was the same store that she'd thought might close at the beginning of the summer. Nearly three months later, it was a booming tourist destination on its way to being one of the top online sellers of rare Cornish books.

All of those years of Harvard business school had paid off in the end. That combined with the help of friends meant she hadn't failed after all.

Once she shut down the register and recorded all the information in QuickBooks, Ginny sat back in her chair and rubbed her neck. The day had grown quite warm—a storm was brewing outside and the humidity was at an all-time high—so she pulled her hair up. Her gaze landed on something sticking out from underneath her pile of business-related documents on the desk. The application for culinary school. She'd told Sophia over a week ago that she would think about it, and she hadn't stopped. When Steven got here, she'd discuss with him her thoughts on possibly attending culinary school and running the bookstore simultaneously.

How she'd missed their talks. Of course, she'd also missed his presence. The way he made her feel safe. Desired. Cherished.

Blood whooshed to her cheeks. Her emotions clearly had not received her brain's memo. Because she was still married, and it was much too soon to be thinking about another man in that way.

The bell over the door jangled and she smiled. "You're early—" Her words fell away as she looked up to find someone who was definitely not Steven standing in the doorway.

"Garrett."

In the two months since she'd seen him, she'd pictured a moment like this so many times. He would come to the bookstore and beg her to take him back. She would open her arms wide—she was much more forgiving in her daydreams—and they'd both cry for what they'd lost and what they'd gained.

But now that he was here, that was the last thing she felt like doing. In fact, she rather felt like threatening to call the cops on him if he took one more step inside the place. Of course, that was ridiculous. Despite the fact he'd taken a chunk of their savings to run off and do his own thing in London nine months ago, this place was half his. Still, his interest in the bookstore had clearly waned, considering he'd refused to talk to her about it, only saying his attorney would be in contact.

"Hi, Ginny." He pulled his eyes from hers and they swooped the landscape of the bookstore. "Wow. You've made some modifications."

Ginny crossed her arms over her chest. "I had to in order to keep the place afloat." She couldn't keep the tightness from her voice. So many months of pain and anger didn't just vanish overnight, especially when their target had been out of reach for most of that time.

Garrett's lips flattened and he pinched his earlobe. "Well, it looks nice."

"Thanks." She started toward the back of the store. "I'll show you the new and improved loft."

He followed without a protest. She led him up the stairs. This was a calm and quiet space, and it felt slightly wrong to be here with anger zapping her insides.

"This new sitting area has worked like a charm to bring new and old customers in." From the abstract paintings on the wall to the comfy couch, beanbag chairs, and small, round tables, each with a different board game on top, this sanctuary provided a haven for locals and tourists alike.

Immense pride ran through her veins. She'd stuck it out. It had been difficult to transform this place, but she'd done it. She was finally home.

And it had nothing to do with her parents or Garrett. It was about her. Finally, a success.

"I'm glad to hear you've done so well with this. I know I haven't been the best co-owner lately."

Garrett's words brought her back to the present.

"Yeah, well." Ginny headed back down the stairs before she could say something mean, her steps echoing in the space as she headed toward the front.

Garrett kept pace with her. When they reached the front desk, he pointed to the pastry case. "Oh, did you contract with Trengrouse to bring in pastries? That was a smart idea."

"No, I bake them every morning."

"Really?"

Ginny's mouth nearly fell open. What did he mean, *really*? "Why are you here, Garrett?"

He shoved his hands into his pockets and took a moment before speaking. "Samantha lost her job. She was a barrister with a big firm. They messed up a case, and she took the fall for it. So it's impossible for her to find something new now. She's been trying for a month with no luck. And I've been working as a clerk at a nearby grocer, but that doesn't pay much."

She pinched the bridge of her nose. "You need money."

He shrugged, a sheepish look on his face. "I waited as long as possible to contact you. But you know I poured my life savings into buying this place. I took a little to live on when I left, but I haven't asked for a cent before now."

"There wasn't a cent to be given until now." She swept her arm across the room. "And guess what? Because of my hard work, we're doing really well. No thanks to you."

She pulled up a document on the computer and pointed to the screen. "You left me with a mess. I turned it around. So yeah, I can give you some money, though I'll carefully record what you take and I'll fight for more than my fair percentage of bookstore earnings when it comes time for the divorce proceedings."

Garrett studied the computer screen, acting like he hadn't heard a word she'd said. Maybe he hadn't. "These numbers are awesome, Ginny." Then he turned and looked her square in the eye. "I want to sell."

Nothing could have sent a jolt of surprise through her the way those words did. "What?"

"I need the money, not just for the short term, but to invest in another bookstore wherever Samantha and I end up."

He dared to think that he could get rid of one bookstore in exchange for another? Just like that? "No, we are not going to sell. I've put everything I have into making this place successful. I had to sell my grandmother's ring to get us out of the red. I'm not just giving it up."

"It's my place too, Ginny. I appreciate all you've done for it, but I'll fight you on this. You can't continue to run it if I want to sell."

How was he so calm? "Watch me." Ginny felt like picking up book after book and chucking them at Garrett's stupid face. Maybe she should. She headed toward the nearest bookshelf, fists clenched next to her sides.

Garrett swooped in front of her. "C'mon, Gin, I don't want to fight. I figured you'd be glad to get rid of this place. But I don't want to kick you out if you really want to stay. Can you afford to buy me out?"

Her shoulders slumped. "No." It was possible for her to try for a loan again, but her first experience with Mr. Brown hadn't been overly positive. Even though the bookstore was doing much better now, there was still a lot working against her—including that she was American.

If she fought Garrett on this, would she even get a fair trial, being a foreigner? Would he have the hometown advantage?

But how could she let it go? It was one thing for her to work at making the bookstore a success and end up failing. At least she could have blamed that partially on the poor circumstances Garrett had left her in. But it was another thing entirely to have built something wonderful and still fail to hang on to it.

Once again, she was losing a home. Everything she'd worked for was being torn away.

Some might say this was a sign that she was supposed to finally pursue her dream of culinary school. But what if she applied and failed to get in? What if her "dream" was just a safety net for her excuses? What if she failed at the one thing she was sure she'd be good at? That would mean the problem wasn't people or circumstances—the problem was her.

Maybe the real problem was that she was a screw-up without a place to belong in the world.

Ginny squared her shoulders and brushed past Garrett. "You say you don't want a fight, but buckle up, buddy. A fight is what you're going to get."

41

41

SOPHIA

After William left, Sophia wandered Tintagel Castle for what seemed like hours, putting off just a little longer the task she'd avoided all summer.

Finally, she plopped onto a bench. The stone was cold beneath her, seeping through her jeans. Clouds gathered in the distance, threatening an evening shower. But she still had time before they reached her.

"You said you felt drawn to Emily's journal . . . Maybe you need to figure out why." William's words echoed in her brain over and over again.

What *had* compelled her to chase Emily's story? Had it just been a gut feeling? Or a distraction?

No. Emily's was more than just a tragic love story. The woman had a strength that Sophia couldn't help but admire. She hadn't let a lack of love destroy her.

In fact, when her own plans hadn't worked out, she'd surrendered.

Maybe William was right—Sophia had to stop fighting. Perhaps she really did need to write her story after all, to surrender to all the truth that she'd never wanted to face. The good, the bad, the ugly—and the beautiful too.

Her fingers itched as she reached into her bag. Of course. When she finally needed it, she didn't have any blank paper.

But wait.

Sophia pulled out Emily's notebook. Each typed page only took up one side of 8.5" by 11" printer paper. The backs were blank.

Yanking a pen from inside her purse, she finally stopped holding back. "God, if you're listening—if you care—then please, help me do this."

And then, finally, inspiration came.

She poured everything out, letter by letter, word by word, emotion by emotion.

> . . . *I may never understand why I let David in, why I let him control me like he did. I can see now that living a life where I tried to be "strong like Mom" didn't work for me. Could it be that I've been so focused on helping others that I forgot self-care? For so long, it felt like I was living outside of myself, a critical third party that saw but didn't feel. But when David came along, I finally let myself feel, and maybe that wasn't a bad thing in and of itself.*
>
> *Perhaps letting someone in never is.*
>
> *I think that I kind of reversed things then, feeling and not thinking. Or maybe just denying.*
>
> *Whatever the case, I feel stronger, more self-aware than I ever have. I can hear David's voice in my head and finally recognize whose voice it was all along—my own. And I'm not excusing his behavior. Not one bit. I'm finally able to accept that I was a victim and that doesn't make me weak.*
>
> *But I do recognize that it was easier to believe his lies because I already believed them about myself. That doesn't make the abuse my fault in any way—he's still responsible for that—but it's helpful for me to see how David did or didn't change me. To understand who I was before and who I am now, after.*
>
> *Thankfully, now I know the truth.*
>
> *I am strong, not because I steeled myself against love or because I went after*

what I wanted, but because I have finally learned how to be me—and to be okay with who that is.

Her pen stilled.

She'd done it. Her story weaved quite literally between the pages of Emily's—their lives intersecting despite their differences. Perhaps she'd never understand how she had come to have this notebook in the first place. It may have been coincidence. Maybe more. The important thing was it had helped her do what she'd been longing to do.

Her phone buzzed at that moment. She wiped away tears she hadn't known were streaming from her eyes. Sophia did a double take at the name appearing on her screen.

"Hello? Mr. Bryant?" Why was Hugh calling her? They'd left his house not five or six hours ago, and he'd made it clear he didn't want to be contacted again.

"Ms. Barrett, hi. I know you're probably surprised to hear from me, but before you left, I saw something in your eyes that . . . Well, I felt prompted to call the family attorney and inquire about my cousin's possessions."

"Oh?"

"Yes. He said they went to a friend of my cousin's. She runs a B&B not far from me. Name's Kathryn Forrester. Here's the address." He rambled it off and Sophia rapidly wrote it down on the bottom of the page where she'd just finished her story. "Not sure if she'd still have the original journal, but it's worth looking into. Oh, and my cousin's name was Evelyn Shoemaker. You probably need to know that."

"Thank you so much, Mr. Bryant. You have no idea what this means to me."

"Yes, well." He paused. "I hope you find what you're looking for."

"Me too, sir." She glanced down at the notebook. "In fact, I think I already have."

Sophia hung up the phone, stared at it, and laughed. It seemed providence had struck once again. With a quick swipe of her fingers, she pulled William's number up to call him . . . but stopped. How would he respond to a call right now, when she still didn't know what her future held? She didn't want to be unfair to him or get his hopes up.

Maybe she'd just drive to the B&B and scope it out first, then bring him back with her later if things panned out.

Sophia stuffed the notebook back into her bag as she walked down the pathway toward the parking lot. Finally, she reached William's car and climbed in. She pulled up the B&B on her phone's GPS, put the key in the ignition, and eased onto the narrow, two-lane road.

As she drove, splashes of water began to plink against her windshield, and fifteen minutes later, the trees lining the road thrashed in the wind, rocking William's small car. How had the day gone from perfectly brilliant to a raging storm? Sophia gripped the steering wheel and bit her lip. It was difficult to see with the water coming down, but the GPS showed she was getting close to the B&B. Thank goodness.

She rounded the corner and saw a sign that said Rambling B&B. Just beyond, she could make out the form of a two-story house. Her tires crunched over gravel and fallen branches as she drove the long driveway toward the house.

Sophia pulled into a small parking lot alongside a few other cars. Then, snatching her bag from the passenger seat, she got out of the car, wrapping herself deeper into her jacket as the wind and rain blew against her, and raced several feet toward the house. She walked up the wooden steps to a quaint porch and did her best to wipe her muddy shoes off on the welcome mat.

Before she could raise a hand to knock on the front door, she noticed a sign just above the doorknob that said, "Come on in." With a turn of the knob, Sophia entered. Instant warmth overtook her whole body, which was shaking with the cold by now—she'd been soaked through in a matter of seconds. A woman who looked her age sat behind a desk a few feet away. Was this Kathryn Forrester? She exclaimed when she saw Sophia and disappeared through a door behind the desk.

What now?

But the woman reappeared with a stack of towels. She bustled around the desk toward Sophia. "You must be freezing." As if she'd known Sophia her whole life, the woman threw a large, fluffy towel around her shoulders and pointed to a roaring fire next to a large dormer window. "Sit and warm yourself. I insist. I'll get some tea."

Before Sophia could respond, the woman was gone once more. But Sophia was so cold, she didn't protest. Instead, she moved toward the fire and plopped into a Queen Anne chair. The crackles and pops from the fireplace soothed the frayed ends of her soul, and the smell of burning wood took her back to Girl Scout camp all those years ago. The fireplace was flanked by two large bookcases filled with numerous volumes of all sizes.

But the book on the side table next to the chair where she sat was what stole her breath.

Sophia reached out and touched the spine of *Moonbeams on the Moor*.

"My mother's favorite author." The woman entered the room carrying a tray with tea and English biscuits.

Sophia gave a shaky smile. "Mine too. So few people have ever heard of Appleton, though I guess I shouldn't be surprised she's popular in Cornwall."

"Ah, you're one of the female theorists." The woman's eyes twinkled.

"My boyfriend made some very convincing arguments." The thought of William brought both warmth and heartache.

The woman set the tray down on the coffee table, then sat on the sofa across from Sophia. "I'm Alice Forrester. My mother and I own this bed-and-breakfast."

"Sophia Barrett. It's nice to meet you. I actually came to talk with Kathryn. Is that your mother?"

"It is. She's not here right now, but should be home shortly. Of course, with this weather, she might have decided to stay with my brother overnight in Camelford." Alice leaned over and poured the tea into a cup. "Can I pass along a message?"

"No, it's really something I need to ask in person, I'm afraid. Perhaps I'll come back tomorrow."

"Surely you're not going back out in that?" Alice's eyes widened.

"Well . . ."

"Do you live nearby? If not, stay the night. Mum will be home by the morning if not sooner. She has a daily routine and hates to get behind."

Sophia didn't have to work in the bookstore tomorrow. And she had to admit, the thought of not returning to Port Willis tonight— where she and William had created memory upon memory—was somewhat comforting. Besides, lingering here, with the fireplace and all the books, didn't sound half bad. And she could text Ginny and William and let them know she was all right. William shouldn't need his car tomorrow since church was within walking distance, and he could probably borrow Ginny's if he needed to go somewhere else. Other than that, she couldn't think of any reason not to stay.

"Okay, you've convinced me. I'll take a room for the night, please."

42

GINNY

Ginny marched from the bookstore. Rain bombarded her—perfect. It must have started sometime during her talk with Garrett.

"Gin—"

"I'm not doing this, Garrett. You can have your lawyer talk to my lawyer."

"Did you finally get one?" Frustration tinged his voice.

"I will. Just . . . leave me alone. Haven't you done enough?" She turned and started to run before he could say more. But Ginny didn't get far before she nearly plowed into Steven, who must have been on his way to meet her.

"Whoa." He put his arms on her shoulders to stop her from falling. "What's chasing you?"

The tease in his voice only made it all worse. She didn't deserve his good humor. "It's not funny."

His look turned serious. "What's wrong?"

Out of instinct, she threw herself into his arms. "I don't know what to do." The rain drenched them both, but she didn't care. Not now, when her world was falling apart. How was she going to get through this?

An answer came to her, and it made her stomach ache.

Her parents had money. And if she only admitted that they'd been right, and she'd been wrong, she could use their lawyers to crush Garrett into the ground and keep what had become rightfully hers.

Steven nestled his nose and mouth down next to her ear so she could hear him over the sound of the rain smacking the sidewalk. "Whatever it is, it'll be okay."

"Ginny—" And there was Garrett's voice again.

Ginny squeezed her eyes shut as she felt Steven stiffen. She pulled back from his embrace and avoided looking into his eyes. Instead, she lifted her gaze to Garrett, who stared at his friend, slack-jawed. "I don't have anything else to say to you, Garrett."

"What's going on here, Ginny?"

"Why do you care?" The fact Garrett thought he had any right to know anything about her life anymore . . . It burned.

"I definitely do care if my wife is taking up with my friend." Garrett looked like he wanted to take a swing at Steven.

"Hey now." Steven stepped around Ginny and held up his hands. "First, I don't feel like Ginny should have to explain herself to you. And second, don't insult her. She's done nothing wrong here, mate. You have."

Garrett's balloon deflated and he kicked at a rock.

On the one hand, Ginny hated seeing him brought so low.

On the other, she wanted to kiss Steven right here and now for the way he'd protected her. All she would have to do is grab him and pull him toward her, and he'd kiss her back—she knew it. And it would hurt Garrett, and maybe he'd know what it felt like to be punched in the gut.

Oh man.

Where had that thought come from? It wasn't her.

But it was something her mother would have done. Or her father. *Hurt people before they can hurt you*—that was their motto.

Or in this case, *Take revenge where you can.*

But that wasn't her either.

Or was it? Did she really know herself at all?

Steven turned to Ginny. "Do you want to get out of here?"

"Yes." She let him grab her hand and lead her around the corner, out of the rain, and to her front door, where the porch overhang provided temporary relief from the storm.

Since she'd run out of the bookstore so quickly, she'd left her purse behind, but going back now didn't seem like an option. She'd run inside and change, then go close everything up and retrieve her stuff when she was sure Garrett was gone. Goose bumps rose on her arms as she leaned down to the flowerpot next to the door and retrieved her spare key.

When she straightened, Steven was there, looking down at her. "What's going on, Gin? Talk to me."

"I . . ." She still needed to apologize to him for her rudeness a few weeks ago, but this didn't seem like the moment. Right now, all she could think about was how she was losing everything—including herself.

"I need to go."

"Where?"

"I don't know. I just need to get away." She placed the key into the lock and turned it. The metal click should have told Steven she was serious.

But he was persistent. "Gin, I care about you. Let me help."

"I can't."

Or, rather, she wouldn't.

Because she didn't trust herself. And if she couldn't trust herself, then who *could* she trust?

Ginny entered her home, alone, and closed the door behind her.

43

SOPHIA

The next morning, Sophia woke from a deep sleep. At first, her brain registered confusion at seeing the high-beamed wooden ceiling overhead, the four-poster bed, the pink walls, and the shabby chic curtains on the windows. But then she remembered. Alice had given her a room on the second floor and a change of clothes that were only slightly baggy on her.

Sophia stretched and sat up in bed, allowing her back to rest against the white headboard. Light streamed in from the window, and from what she could see, the sky was an azure blue, as if no storm had ever occurred.

She stayed in bed a few more moments before pulling herself up and over to where her purse hung on the back of a vanity chair. Snatching her phone, she hit the Power button. Since she didn't have a charger with her, she'd shut it off last night to preserve her battery. Now several text messages pinged at her. She scrolled through them. Both Ginny and William had responded to her group text last night when she'd told them she'd been held over due to the rain.

William's was just like him: *Glad you're safe. Don't worry about*

the car. I can take a taxi if I need to go somewhere. And don't feel like
you have to wait for me to find the answers you've been looking for. I'll be
anxious to hear what you discover.

He'd given his blessing, then, to learn what she could from
Kathryn about Emily's journal without him here. The thought was
bittersweet.

Sophia sighed as she put the phone down and wandered to the
window. Her jaw dropped at the gorgeous scenery surrounding her.
She hadn't been able to see it in the dark, but now that light had
come . . . Wow.

With a grunt, she worked the latch and pushed open her window. The cool air hit her cheeks, and she filled her lungs with it. Her
eyes wandered the landscape, from the assortment of tall and short
trees where the birds twittered, to the brightly adorned flower garden
below.

A rapid *thwack thwack thwack* rose from the melody of nature
beneath the window. Sophia angled her neck and saw a woman in a
wide-brimmed straw hat standing by some bushes, pruning shears in
hand. Gray hair fell around her shoulders. Perhaps this was Kathryn.

Sophia dressed quickly in her clothes—which were now dry—
and headed downstairs. She passed a man and woman on the stairs
who didn't even seem to notice her. They held hands and were softly
laughing together as they climbed. Honeymooners, maybe?

That could be her and William someday, if she could only figure
out what she wanted. What she needed.

Not now, Sophia.

Before going outside, she moved into the dining area and snagged
a mug, which she filled with coffee—thank goodness Kathryn and
Alice were catering to the non-tea-lovers among them.

She stepped into the sun, steaming mug in hand, and rounded
the house, where she found the woman she'd seen from above a few
minutes ago.

The rhythmic snipping ceased and the woman looked up. "Can I help you, my dear?"

Sophia knew next to nothing about gardening, but the plant the woman was working on seemed dry—maybe even dying. "Sorry. I didn't mean to interrupt."

The older woman used the top of her thick gloves to push back a chunk of hair that had fallen into her eyes. "You aren't interrupting. I'm Kathryn Forrester. You must be our unexpected guest who arrived last night."

"Yes, hi. Sophia Barrett. Nice to meet you."

"You as well, dear. My daughter said you needed to speak with me about something?" She resumed her pruning.

Sophia leaned against a nearby tree and wrapped her fingers around the warm mug. "I do, although I don't want to keep you from your work. Do you have time later this morning to chat?"

"I could clear some time this evening." Kathryn peeked at Sophia from under the brim of her hat. "But I don't mind you asking now. I sense you have a lot to say, and I'll be here awhile yet."

"Are you sure?"

"Try me."

"Okay. I'm looking for something Evelyn Shoemaker may have left with you. She was a friend of yours, right?"

"She was. What was this thing you're looking for?"

"A journal."

"Perhaps you'd best start at the beginning, dear."

Whether it was because she'd just relived everything by writing her story yesterday, or because Kathryn was simply easy to talk to—or maybe something else entirely—Sophia found herself spilling every relevant detail of her life to this woman she didn't know. In the middle of it, Kathryn handed her an extra pair of gloves and some shears. When Kathryn pointed to a shoot, Sophia cut as she continued to speak. Together, they pruned the dead or oldest shoots so new shoots could have room to breathe—and grow—in their next season.

"And that's how I ended up here, with you, asking about a journal I didn't even know existed until three months ago."

By now, Kathryn had a huge smile on her face. "What a lovely story."

"I only wish I knew how it ended." Sophia returned the shears to Kathryn and tugged off the gloves. Her fingers ached from the repetitive action they'd taken, but it was a good ache.

She was about to ask Kathryn about the journal once more, but the look on the woman's face—as if her mind was elsewhere, considering all that Sophia had told her—stopped the words before they left Sophia's lips. When someone wore a look like that, it was best to be quiet and let the revelations come.

Kathryn studied her a few more moments before speaking again. "Perhaps you're focused on the wrong thing. Life is more than a beginning, a middle, and an end. It's about the countless moments woven in between the lines, the growth, the pruning. Take these flowers, for example. I can't just sit around waiting for them to decide if they want to bloom or die. Growth won't happen without a little intervention. They were designed to bloom, yes, but circumstances and a harsh environment sometimes make it impossible for them to flower on their own. They can't prune themselves. And you can't prune yourself, dear."

Sophia squatted and picked up a dead shoot on the ground, one that had been clipped away and tossed aside. "It seems so simple when you say it like that."

Kathryn crouched next to her. "It *is* simple, but that doesn't make it easy." She placed a hand on Sophia's shoulder. "But you came to inquire about a journal. And it's your lucky day, because I have it."

"You do?"

"Yes. Evelyn was my roommate at uni and we remained close

for the rest of our lives. I was surprised when she left me all of her possessions—though there weren't many—since she still had living relatives. But apparently she feared they'd not appreciate the items she was leaving behind. She asked me to protect a few family heirlooms in case Hugh ever changed his mind about embracing his past."

"Would it be possible for me to see it?"

"Of course, dear. Give me some time to pull the journal out of storage and I'll let you peruse it as soon as I can."

"Oh, thank you. I promise I'll be very careful with it."

After a bit more chatting, Sophia went inside to eat breakfast, her conversation with Kathryn constantly on her mind, her fingers itching to hold the journal. When she returned to her room, something on the bed caught her attention. It was an archival box—she recognized it from the many episodes of *Antiques Roadshow* she'd watched in the long nights after David had died and she couldn't sleep—and there was a note on top:

Sophia,

Here is the missing piece to your puzzle. I think you will find it to be even more awe-inspiring than you've imagined. I'm here if you have any questions, but I thought you'd like to read it alone first.

Hugs,
Kathryn

Sophia's hands quivered as she set the note aside, sank onto the bed, and opened the lid of the box. And there it was, what she'd been looking for, the culmination of months of searching. The cover was bound in blue leather-backed stiff boards, and the word *Journal* was printed in small gold lettering at the bottom.

With care, Sophia opened the journal—and what she saw made tears spring to her eyes.

To see the pen strokes Emily made, to witness the story unfolding before her in a new way . . . It was more than Sophia could bear. She pored over the story she knew so well—but her heart pounded in her chest when she finished.

Because there was more to the story.

A single loose page, written in the same handwriting as the rest, had been stuck in the back of the journal. The tearing along the left side indicated it had been part of the journal once, but had come loose—or been ripped out.

Sophia leaned closer to make out the fading words:

I have always believed that everyone has a story to tell. Story is sprouting up all around us, if only we have eyes to see it. Story forms the fiber of our being, and story is what will remain when we are gone.

It is possible that no one will ever read my story—my real story. I plan to hide it away in the dusty attic of the parsonage, where boxes of unmarked memories have been left by former reverends and their families.

But stories do not need to be read by others to have power. We simply have to believe in their importance and trust that the One who wrote them had a reason for doing so.

We must embrace that story and remember that who we are is not defined by the ups and downs of our lives—the failures OR the successes. Nay, we are instead defined by Whose we are.

Upon writing this, I have left my position of governess and moved back to the uninhabited parsonage, which Edward's family graciously allowed. Four of my manuscripts are published and I am working on another. Because of my promise to my former employers, I did not give my name as Emily Fairfax.

Instead, I built a new identity: Robert, after my father, and Appleton, my mother's maiden name.

Today, I choose not to leave Emily Fairfax behind but to take her with me as I forge on through life, allowing my experiences and the Light within to shine ever *brighter. For I am not the sum total of my experiences. I am much, much more because the Light has claimed me.*

I started writing because I thought it would save me, but ultimately it is not our deeds that have such power. For we can never do enough with only our own strength or even the borrowed strength of other people. It is to another strength we must look, to first build and then to sustain us.

No. Way.

This couldn't be real. Robert Appleton—the author who had meant so much to Sophia—was not only a woman as she'd grown to suspect, but was in fact Emily Fairfax, the woman whose personal story had taken up space in Sophia's heart for so many months.

So many things coming together. Her life. Emily's. Even Ginny's—for there was something in this letter for her too. Sophia somehow knew it.

What had Kathryn written? Ah, there. Yes. This was the missing piece to her puzzle. Like Abigail, William's professor friend, had said: *"The picture on the puzzle might not even make sense until the last piece is popped into place. Then it will form a beautiful picture."*

All of this . . . It didn't mean anything on its own. But the cumulative effect was something wondrous to behold, and it all added up to one thing: Moving forward and healing didn't come from marching through life alone, determined to succeed with no help. And it didn't come from wallowing in her shame. It didn't even come from standing in her own strength.

It meant taking the hand of a Savior and letting him lead her, wherever that might be.

44

GINNY

The times she'd run before, at least Ginny had been moving toward something.

Now? She'd just spent an hour in the car, driving to meet Sophia after a night of fitful sleep. When she had slept, she'd dreamed of her parents standing on a platform over her head, looking down and laughing. Garrett and Samantha stood on another, ignoring her completely. And Steven was nowhere to be found.

Ginny pulled into the driveway of the B&B where Sophia was staying. Her friend had asked her to come, said she had something important to show her—and of course Ginny had agreed. Not only did she want to be there for Sophia, but she'd do just about anything right now to distract herself from the mess that was her life.

But as her car rolled down the bumpy drive lined with rhododendrons and trees, her breath caught at the sense of serenity that suddenly overcame her. It was as if she'd left the world behind when she'd turned from the main road onto this side one—entering an inner sanctum of calm like she'd never known before.

Finally, she reached the house. It looked like most other B&Bs

she'd seen in the English countryside—a restored longhouse with a
slanted black roof, stone outer walls, and charming white windows.
The surrounding gardens and a bit of farmland stretched behind it.
As she climbed from her car, clucking greeted her from the chicken
coop off to the right.

"Ginny!"

She looked up to see Sophia emerging from the front door. Something about her seemed . . . lighter. She fairly bounced as she strode
toward her.

When she reached Ginny, Sophia wrapped her in a long hug. "I'm
glad you're here. I have so much to tell you."

Ginny let herself receive the embrace. "I have so much to tell you
too." She tried to find her normally sunny disposition, but right now
it seemed lost forever.

Sophia cocked her head. "How about we stay overnight? Would
William be able to man the store for you tomorrow?"

Ginny shoved her hands in the back pockets of her jeans. "I don't
know. I should really get back . . ." But why? What was the point, if
Garrett was only going to take everything from her?

Man, she needed to snap out of this gloom and doom.

"Actually, sure." She pasted on a smile. "I'm guessing he won't
mind. I don't think he has class till the afternoon."

"Great." Sophia looped her arm through Ginny's and led her
inside, up the stairs, and into her room.

The adorable surroundings distracted Ginny momentarily, as did
the task of texting William to find out his availability for tomorrow.
She slid onto the bench seat under the window and stared out at the
fields behind the house.

In the far distance, she could make out the horizon above the
ocean. If she had a superhero's vision, maybe she'd be able to see across
the sea to her parents' estate—the place of her birth, her first home.
How much had that influenced who she was? How had being George

and Mariah Bentley's daughter driven the course of her life, landed her here? Was she supposed to return? Should she never have left?

Ginny let her forehead sink against the cold window.

"Hey."

She looked up to find Sophia clutching something to her chest—a book of some sort. "Is that it? The journal?"

"It is." Her friend sat at the opposite end of the bench. "But before we talk about it, what's going on with you?"

"Garrett wants me to sell." The story tumbled out, every agonizing detail. Ginny didn't try to put a positive spin on it. She just let it out in all its messy detail. By the time she finished, her nose was stuffy and her eyes ached from spilling tears. "I thought I knew what I was supposed to do, who I was supposed to be. But turns out maybe I was wrong. Maybe I'm just a Bentley no matter how far I run. I mean, my first instinct was to battle and destroy Garrett. Then my next was to run away. How can I want both of those things? Will I ever know who I am? Will I ever have a place in this world that's really mine?" Ugh, she was so sick of herself and all her questions. She wouldn't blame her friend if she was too.

"I'm sorry about Garrett. You're a wonderful person and friend who doesn't deserve anything she's going through." Sophia was quiet a long moment. "But I'm starting to believe there's a reason for everything that happens. Others might call it fate or karma. But I think it's God. He's been directing our steps this whole time, Ginny. Even when we didn't believe."

Ginny pulled her knees into her chest and rested her chin on top. "I wouldn't say I don't believe in God. I guess I just never thought of him as being much more than some guy in the sky with the power to crush us if he wanted to."

"I know what you mean. My mom raised me in church, but my own faith has wavered in the past few years. I thought I had to do everything on my own, but it turns out I don't. I've slowly opened myself back up to that childlike faith I had once upon a time. And in doing that, I've figured out why Emily's story inspires me so much, why I felt this burning need to know if she was real or not."

Where was Sophia going with this? How would talking about any of this really help? "Why?"

"Because the woman I read about spent her life finding a huge chunk of her purpose, her everything, in Edward, the man she loved. But ultimately, when she couldn't have him, Emily turned to God. And she was much happier for it."

Her dad had always called religion a crutch, something weak people leaned on for support. But maybe it would give Ginny some perspective. "I'd like to read that story sometime."

"Actually . . ." Sophia held up the book in her lap. "You should." She handed her the journal.

Ginny took it in her hands, ran her fingertips over the leather board cover, fragile around the edges but surprisingly well preserved. "I feel like a bad friend. I should have read this before now, when you first found the notebook. I guess I just thought it was your thing and I didn't want to interfere—plus I've just been so busy—but I should have read it to support you."

"Don't worry about that. I think you're reading it exactly when you're supposed to. There's one entry in particular . . . I think it was meant for both of us." Sophia stood. "I'm going to leave you for a bit, but I'm here if you need me."

"Okay."

As Sophia left the room, Ginny inhaled deeply and dove into Emily's story. Though she wasn't one for reading, she was sucked in immediately, sympathizing with Emily, drawing from her strength, crying with her over the way Edward rejected her—how well she knew that feeling—and wanting to slap Rosamond.

And then she reached the last page. She could barely breathe as she read the words written so long ago . . . but words that applied to her today.

We must embrace that story and remember that who we are is not defined by the ups and downs of our lives—the failures OR the successes. Nay, we are instead defined by Whose we are.

And then:

Today, I choose not to leave Emily Fairfax behind but to take her with me as I forge on through life, allowing my experiences and the Light within to shine ever brighter. For I am not the sum total of my experiences. I am much, much more because the Light has claimed me.

If this was true, then it didn't matter that Ginny was a Bentley or a Rose or a failed daughter or a betrayed wife. She was all of those things and yet none of them—not at her core. She may not belong in Boston or even in her own bookstore, which she'd helped build from the ground up and had rescued when her husband abandoned it.

But God . . . if he'd really led her here, to this place of peace, and he'd really been with her through all of it, then maybe he saw her as more than the labels she'd given herself.

And maybe he was claiming her, like Emily said. Could it be she finally had found her place to belong?

Ginny placed her hand on the window and stared out toward the ocean once more. It was strong, powerful, overwhelming, immense. She'd always seen it as what divided her: the person she'd been on one side, and the person she wanted to be on the other.

Now, she saw. In a way, it was the thing that had brought her together.

45

⁂

SOPHIA

What a difference three months could make.

Sophia leaned against the strong trunk of the Story Tree at Elliott Manor, remembering the first time she'd read about this place in the lines of Emily's story.

Then, she'd been paralyzed by her past, unsure of her future. Now, the past no longer had a hold on her. God did.

And as for her future, it was still unsure. But she was learning to be okay with that.

Well, most of the time. She still couldn't help the nerves that tingled as she waited for William to show up. She and Ginny had stayed a couple of extra days with Kathryn and returned late last night, so she and William hadn't spoken in four days. Not since he'd left her at Tintagel Cliffs—things tenuous and uncertain between them.

This morning, she'd texted him to see if he'd be willing to meet her. He'd said he would head over after his early morning class.

Clouds dotted the sky, but the sun peeked through occasionally. In the distance, seagulls cawed and circled above the waves. The wind rustled the pages of the story in her hand.

At last, his tall figure appeared. William looked more handsome than ever in his slacks, button-up shirt, and sweater vest. He'd gotten a haircut too—the curly locks that had grown in during the summer months had been trimmed, giving him a more professorial, casual air.

He stole her breath.

"Hi." The word was full of so much hope and equal parts defeat. Poor man. How her silence must have tortured him after he'd poured out his heart to her at the cliffs.

"William." She longed to throw herself into his arms. "Thanks for coming."

His jaw flexed and he nodded.

"I was wondering if you could do me a favor."

"I thought we were going to talk about—"

"Please." She held up the papers gripped in her hand. "After you left . . . I finally did it. I wrote my story. And I was hoping—praying, really—that you might take the time to read it. So whatever happens after this, at least you'll understand me a little better."

He hesitated for a moment, then without a word, he took the papers from her and rounded the other side of the tree. He sat, his legs spread out before him.

What if, after all this, she lost him? What if her silence in the face of his "I love you" had ruined it all?

No. What was that verse Kathryn had shown her yesterday? She pulled out her phone, looking at the note she'd pinned: "Live in me. Make your home in me just as I do in you. In the same way that a branch can't bear grapes by itself but only by being joined to the vine, you can't bear fruit unless you are joined with me."

As long as she was being supported by the vine, she couldn't ruin anything. God was in charge. Not her.

Sophia stuffed the phone away again and waited, staring at the lighthouse in the distance.

Finally, William stood and approached her. His eyes shone with unshed tears. "Sophia. I had no idea what you suffered. You told me, but . . . I just didn't get it."

"I don't think I did either. Not fully. Not until I wrote it." Sophia paused. "But that is my past."

Then she dug into her purse for the tiny trowel she'd brought with her. When Kathryn had given it to her, she hadn't understood why. Not until last night, when it became very clear what she was supposed to do. "Will you help me?"

He looked so confused, she almost laughed. "Well, it's called the Story Tree, right? It's probably seen a lot of beginnings. Maybe some endings. I just figured it's a good place to bury my past. Maybe something good can grow from it."

William pursed his lips, shook his head. "You amaze me, Sophia Barrett." He still gripped the pages in his hand. "Of course I'll help you. But what will Claudia Vetters think?"

"I got permission from her assistant. He looked at me funny, but said as long as the ground didn't appear to be disturbed, he wouldn't tell." Sophia did laugh this time. Who knew she could be such a rebel? Emily had rubbed off on her over one hundred and fifty years later.

Together, they dug a small hole in the soft dirt around the tree's roots. Sophia placed the pages of her story in the earth and handed the trowel to William. Without a word, he softly covered it, leaving the last scoop of soil for her. She covered the final bit of white paper and patted the dirt down smooth.

She stood, brushing off the specks of brown from her jeans. William did the same.

Now for the last part of her plan. Sophia pulled a folded piece of paper from the left back pocket of her pants. "That was my past. *This* is my present—and, I hope, my future."

William pressed his lips together in that adorable focused way he sometimes did. He took the paper from her. On the front, she'd simply written, *"I'm staying."*

He stared at the paper for a while. "Really?"

"Really." She'd called Joy yesterday and explained the situation to her—that she no longer felt like social work was her calling, at least not like it had been. Her friend completely understood and confessed that Veronica had offered to buy LifeSong. Joy had just been waiting to see what Sophia decided before accepting.

That meant for now, Sophia was jobless once again. But for the first time, she was actually excited to see what came next—and where God might lead her.

"So." William finally moved his eyes back to hers, and in them she saw love like she'd never experienced before. "What does that mean? For us?"

"Turn the paper over." Her whispered words nearly got lost in her throat.

Time seemed stuck as he flipped the page and read the words she hadn't been able to say out loud that day at the cliffs: *"And I love you, too, William Rose."*

In an instant, he had her in his arms. Tears leaked down her cheeks—and William kissed every one of them away.

46

GINNY

Today was both an end and a beginning.

Ginny sprayed furniture polish on the bookstore's front desk and rubbed it in with a rag. How many times had she dusted this place? How much love and attention had she put into every nook and cranny?

Nearly the whole town—from Mr. Trengrouse to Mrs. Lincoln to Mary Patrick and her whole clan—had stopped by at some point today to wish her well wherever the road may take her next. Thankfully, her identity didn't come from a place. Or a person. Not anymore.

The new owner would be here in a few minutes. They'd signed the papers this morning, and Ginny had requested one last closing before turning over the keys for good.

It had all been much easier than she'd anticipated. In fact, until she'd given it up, she hadn't even known what a burden she'd been carrying. The freedom she felt before the ink was even dry had surprised her.

Of course, once she'd decided she was okay with selling, Garrett had backed off on his other divorce demands. Despite Mother's insistence that they could crush him due to his infidelity, Ginny wanted no part in that. They'd managed to settle things quickly and amicably, and now were merely waiting for the courts to do their thing.

Ginny's parents had expected her to come "home," but she'd finally gotten up the courage to tell them she was applying to culinary school. Her father had surprised her by telling her to work hard and make him proud. It would take time and patience, but maybe Mother would eventually accept that Ginny was her own person. It had taken Ginny herself long enough.

"Knock, knock." Sophia opened the front door, her messenger bag slung over one shoulder, a huge grin on her face. "You ready?"

"I think so." Ginny put the polish away and grabbed her keys from inside her purse. She slid the bookstore's key from the ring. With a slow turn, she took in every aspect of the bookstore.

Sophia approached and stood next to her. "Are you okay?"

"I am. I have a lot of great memories here, but it's time to make new ones."

"Oh." Sophia reached into her bag and pulled out a thick envelope. "Speaking of that . . ."

Ginny caught the name on the return label and let loose a quick gasp. "Is that . . . ?"

"It is. I saw it in the mailbox and couldn't resist bringing it inside." Sophia thrust it into her hands. "Hurry up and open it."

The envelope was heavy—that had to be a good sign, right? "I'll wait. This is your moment."

"Whatever. It's *our* moment. And right now, you need to open that envelope."

Almost as if someone else controlled her limbs, Ginny ripped it open and pulled the top page from inside. Her eyes scanned the words. "I got in."

"Of course you did!" Sophia squealed and threw her arms around Ginny, causing the envelope and paper to fall to the floor.

They both laughed.

Ginny stooped to pick up what she'd dropped. She read the paper again, this time out loud. "The London Culinary Institute is proud to offer you acceptance into our Pastry and Confectionery program. Our courses are eight weeks long, and the next available start date is October 14."

"I thought you'd applied for January."

"I did. It says there was a last-minute opening for this term."

"Are you going to take it?"

"Would that be nuts? I mean, that's only like three or four weeks away and there's a lot to do to get ready."

"It's not nuts if that's what you want to do. I'll help you get ready, and I'm sure we could draft others into helping out too."

Ginny grinned. "I can't believe it."

"I can. I'm so proud of you. You're doing it. Pursuing your dream, wherever it takes you." Sophia brushed a tear from her cheek. "Though I'm going to miss you something crazy."

"Man, I hadn't really thought much about that part—moving away from everyone I know, to a new city." Sophia and William were like the sister and brother she never had—since she'd never related much to her own—and then there was Steven, the one who'd encouraged her to dream bigger in the first place.

After their encounter the day Garrett had shown up, Ginny had apologized, and of course Steven had shrugged it off and forgiven her. But things had been awkward, and that was her fault. She just couldn't get past the feelings he stirred up in her, and she didn't feel right pursuing something until her divorce was finalized. Even then, she needed time to heal before jumping into something new.

Ginny shook away her thoughts. "Okay, your turn." Wait, where was the key? She'd had it in her hand when Sophia had given her the envelope. Ah, there it was, peeking out from underneath the desk. She must have dropped it in her excitement. Ginny snatched it, then turned to face Sophia once again. "You have become my best friend,

Soph. I don't know how I would have made it through these last months without you."

"Don't make me cry again." But the words came with a few tears anyway.

"It's just . . . God knew I needed you."

"He knew I needed you too."

Ginny stepped forward and pressed the key into Sophia's palm. "You are going to make this bookstore into something even better than it is now."

"I have quite a legacy to live up to."

A few days after Ginny announced she was going to put the bookstore on the market, Sophia had come to her and made an offer. Ginny couldn't believe she hadn't thought of it before. Of course Sophia should have it. She loved books and believed reading was therapy—she would use this place not only as a business, but as a way to reach hurting people too. The townspeople already loved her, and surely it wouldn't be long before William asked her to marry him.

What a beautiful thing to happen to such a kind and caring person.

"Well, I'll leave you to your new place of business. Of course, it's not like you haven't been living here for nearly four months." Turning over the key had been a mere formality. "Guess I'd better get home and start packing." Sophia had purchased both buildings from Aldwin and Julia, but she'd told Ginny she could stay as long as she liked.

Now, though, Ginny had somewhere new to go. With only a short time before classes started, she would need every spare moment to prepare. But there was somewhere she needed to stop first.

With another quick hug, Ginny left and walked the cobblestone street until she reached a place she'd been avoiding. At her knock, Steven opened his door. Between the five o'clock shadow and rumpled red hair, Ginny must have caught him in the middle of a nap or a long evening of work.

"Hi." She shuffled her feet on the porch.

"Hi." He moved aside. "Come in."

"Okay."

He closed the door behind her and they both stood there in silence. Where was the easy camaraderie? Had she destroyed it forever?

She reached into her bag and pulled out the packet from the culinary school. "I wanted you to be one of the first to know."

He raised an eyebrow. "Know what?"

"I'm going to culinary school."

He held out his hand, searching her eyes with his own, asking permission.

She handed over the envelope.

Pulling out the paper, his eyes scanned it. A slow smile spread across his face. "I knew you'd get in."

She folded her arms across her chest. "Thanks for believing in me when I didn't."

"So . . . you're leaving." For a moment, the smile disappeared.

"Yeah."

"Okay." He returned the envelope to her hand. "Hang on. I'll be right back." He exited the room and headed down the hallway toward what she assumed was his bedroom. A moment later, he came back with a small box in his hands.

A ring box.

Had she given him the wrong signals? How could he possibly think . . . ? "Steven, what are you—"

"Calm down." He laughed. "I'm not proposing to you."

"Oh. Right. Of course. I didn't think that." Ahem. "So what's that?"

"Here." He took one of her hands and placed the small box in her palm. "I hated seeing you lose it."

It couldn't be. But as she opened the box, she couldn't help the gasp that flew from her mouth. Nestled inside the satin lay her grandmother's ring.

"But I sold it. How did you . . ." She paused. "You saw me right after I'd left the antique store." Then he'd taken off on some errand.

"I bought it back, to give to you someday." He held up his hands. "Not like that." His fingers pulling through his hair made it even more mussed. "I thought you should have your ring back because it was your grandmother's, not because it represents your first marriage. I hope I didn't screw that up."

"Um, no." Ginny stepped up to him, rose on her tiptoes, and kissed him on the cheek, lingering to whisper in his ear. "This is the nicest thing anyone has ever done for me. It's perfect." She stepped slightly back to face him again. "But it must have cost you thousands. I can't repay you."

"Are you joking? This moment is payment enough."

They stood like that, a breath apart, for what seemed like minutes when it was really only seconds.

Finally, Ginny moved away. She slid the ring from the box and placed it on her right hand's ring finger.

This man was something special. And while she wasn't ready for a romantic relationship right now, her heart knew that she wasn't going to need healing forever.

"You know, I'll be awfully lonely up in London. I'd love for you to come visit sometime. Once I'm settled in. Maybe after the holidays?"

He stepped forward and grabbed her hand, rubbing his thumb over the ring—and her fingers. "You couldn't keep me away. And that's a promise."

47

✦✦✦✦✦✦

SOPHIA

Stories always had endings. Sophia knew that. But she hated to see this one reach its conclusion.

Ginny was leaving for London tomorrow. Before she left, they had one thing they wanted to do.

They stashed a basket of goodies—Ginny's cupcakes and a few rare books from Sophia's bookstore—into the trunk of William's car and got inside, where William and Steven waited.

Sophia squeezed William's arm. "Let's do this."

He winked at her and pulled onto the street. "I look forward to meeting this woman who made such an impact on you ladies."

"Hopefully she's home." She could have called, but Sophia wanted to surprise Kathryn.

They drove the winding path toward the B&B where everything had changed six weeks ago. So much had happened since then, including making up with William, changing professions, hiring a moving company to pack up her house and put her things in storage until she was able to get back to sort it all, selling her house in Phoenix—it had gone for top dollar after one day on the market—and spending every spare moment she could with the man she loved.

Her mom had made plans to come visit next month, and Joy hoped to come out around Christmas as long as her parents were doing okay. They planned to travel up to London so Joy and Ginny could meet—and William had mentioned maybe coming along and trying to hang out with Garrett. Things were far from perfect between them, but if Sophia and William *did* end up getting married, she knew William would want his brother at the wedding. The fact he was trying spoke volumes about who he was.

Yes, her story was working out better than she had ever imagined it—or could have written it herself.

"There." Sophia pointed to the mile marker on the side of the road. "It should be just up here on the left."

Ginny and Steven stopped chatting in the back seat as they drew nearer.

Here the trees bent closer together, creating a canopy over them, obscuring the sun except in a few places where it filtered through the branches. The leaves had begun to turn a variety of colors—from brilliant reds to cheery yellows and burnt oranges.

William turned down the drive toward the B&B and pulled into the small parking lot. All of them climbed from the car, and Ginny grabbed the basket from the trunk. Sophia took in a deep breath, and crisp air filled her lungs. A bird chirped somewhere above, and a few fallen leaves skittered past her feet as they walked up the front steps and through the door.

Alice stood behind the front desk again. "Why, hello! You're back. And I see you brought friends."

Sophia and Ginny greeted Alice with a hug.

"We did." Sophia grabbed William's hand. "This is my boyfriend William and our friend Steven."

Alice smiled at them both. "Welcome to the Rambling B&B. Were you all wanting to stay the night? You're in luck, if so. A big party just canceled and we have several rooms available."

"I wish we could, but we just stopped in to see your mother. Is she here?"

"Oh no. She's actually on holiday visiting my sister in Edinburgh. She won't be back for another week. I'm sorry." Alice snapped her fingers together. "But you know what. She did leave something for you. She had a feeling you'd be back soon."

Ginny raised an eyebrow. "How did she know that?"

As she headed behind the registration desk again, Alice waved her hands in the air. "Mum has a sixth sense about people, it seems. Try growing up with that. I couldn't get away with anything."

They all chuckled as Alice rummaged behind the desk and finally popped up holding the archival box that Kathryn had placed in Sophia's room on her last visit. She handed it over to Sophia.

There was another note on top:

For Sophia and Ginny, two amazing women,

I hope by now you have both found your peace and realized that the God of the universe loves you and is capable of anything. Please do me one last favor and return this journal to its rightful owner. I have a feeling that Hugh Bryant is finally ready to see this again, and that you should be the ones to return it. You will bless him greatly by giving it back. Help him remember who he once was.

All my love,
Kathryn

Sophia lifted the lid of the box and found Emily's journal inside.

Ginny took the note and read it. "I'm still a little confused why this belongs to Hugh in the first place. He was related to Edward, not Emily, right?"

"Yeah." Sophia shrugged. "It was discovered on his family's land. As far as I know, it's the only piece of evidence that reveals Robert Appleton's true identity. That makes it pretty valuable."

"I guess. It seems like all this should be about more than money, though."

"I agree." Sophia bit her lip. "All I know is, we've been given one last task. Shall we?"

"Absolutely." After they thanked and hugged Alice—who was eagerly eyeing the cupcakes they'd given her and Kathryn—they headed back to the car.

An hour later, they all stood on Hugh Bryant's doorstep.

When Hugh opened the door and saw Sophia and William, he actually smiled. "I was hoping you'd return."

"You were?" Sophia couldn't keep the surprise from her voice.

He opened the door wider and pointed to the box in her hands. "Did you find it?"

She grinned. "We did. And we are here to return it to you."

With a nod, he waved them in. They all came inside and headed toward his living room. Once they were all seated, Hugh finally spoke. "Was it at the B&B?"

"Yes. Evelyn's friend Kathryn had it, just like you thought she would. She asked us to return it to you." Sophia stood and handed the box to Hugh. "She thought maybe you were ready to have it back."

This close to him, she could make out the lines around his eyes, his mouth, the creases in his forehead—all the same as the last time she'd seen him. But something about him had changed. Ah, there was now a light in his eyes.

"She was right." He opened the box, pulled out the journal, and began leafing through it.

Sophia returned to her spot on the couch, where William slipped his hand into hers and planted a kiss on the side of her forehead. She leaned into him.

Her eyes met Ginny's. Her friend smiled, something fresh and warm burning in her own gaze.

Finally, Hugh cleared his throat and looked up at them all. "Thank you. I can't believe you've returned what was lost so long ago."

Sophia hadn't meant to become the spokesperson for the group, but it felt right. "We're simply the messengers." How amazing it was that William and Ginny and Kathryn—and Emily—had been put in her life, and now she was being put in Hugh's to continue the circle of love and light.

"I wish I could repay you somehow."

"Believe me, having the chance to read Emily's journal was enough." Sophia sighed. "I only wish she had gotten her own happy ending. I mean, she did, in a way. I know it looked different from what she'd wanted, but I can't help but be a bit sad that she and Edward never got to enjoy a life together."

A wide smile spread across Hugh's face. "You don't know." He flipped to the last page of the journal. "Hmm. It's not written in the journal."

Sophia sat up a little straighter. "Know what?"

"Makes sense, I suppose. Not all British marriage records have been digitized, and parish registers tend to be restricted . . ." Hugh waved his hand. "Let me explain. Your visit sparked something in me—a desire to know more about my family's legacy, which I had staunchly ignored because of a few events in my past that convinced me it wasn't worth knowing. But your zest, your zeal for a story that wasn't even part of your heritage, made me ashamed that I didn't have that same passion for my own. So I recently reconnected with some distant cousins. And they told me a wonderful tale."

Delight curled through Sophia's whole being as she relaxed against William and listened to the beautiful story woven into history, one that had brought everyone in this room together.

EPILOGUE

⬅︎⬅︎⬅︎⬅︎

EMILY

1866

I heard the laughter first.

It floated on the breeze, across the top of the water, twisting through the garden as I walked toward the tree. I hadn't visited this place in years—not since I'd learned Edward had become a father.

And I had no intention of visiting it that day. But the laughter drew me, as if from a ghost.

Because it sounded just like him, twenty years before, when we were children playing together. Before all the strain, before life pulled us in different directions.

And I knew it was madness—maybe my spinster life of writing at the parsonage, alone most of the time, had finally driven me to the edge—but I had to see for myself.

As I rounded the corner and caught sight of the fading sun on the horizon, I saw the shadow of a young boy swinging from the tree. Drawing nearer, I watched him jump from the lowest branch and tuck into a ball as he rolled away from it. Had he no sense of the danger in playing so close to the bluff's edge?

Intent on warning him, I quickened my pace. But when I got near enough to see him clearly, I could not contain my gasp.

He looked at me, brown hair flopping into his bright eyes—eyes I'd memorized and knew better than my own.

It was Edward, or, at least, a younger version of the man I'd grown up with.

And yet, it was not him, for his stature was slighter than Edward's had ever been.

He stopped and stared at me. By the look of him, he must have been five or six years of age. "Hello."

"Hi." It was all I could manage at the moment.

His perky little smile could melt the coldest heart, I was sure. "I'm James."

So this was Edward and Rosamond's son.

That meant they were here.

Edward's mother always sent me a warning when they would be coming, so I could make myself scarce. I think she did it as much for her family's sake as for my own, but it didn't matter.

She hadn't sent word this time.

I managed somehow to find my voice. "I'm Emily. Lovely to meet you."

"You as well." He looked around me. "Papa!"

My heart felt as though a thousand horses stampeded across it. The air stood still as I slowly turned on my heel.

There stood Edward, his jaw hanging slightly askew as our eyes locked. How could he still have this effect on me, years later? Time and distance should have diminished his pull—and yet, they had not.

He strode toward me and stopped mere inches away. What was he thinking? I longed to know, but could not ask. I didn't have a right to hear his thoughts anymore.

"Papa, this is Emily. We just met."

The little voice broke our daze. Edward smiled, his eyes still on me. "I know, son. We're old friends." Then he finally took his gaze from mine. "Cook just made cake, and you may have a slice if you hurry."

With that, the little boy scampered away.

Edward and I were alone by our tree, as we'd been so many times before.

"I didn't know you were back."

"Mother has been feeling poorly, so we surprised her with a visit."

"Is she all right?"

He shoved his hands into his pockets. "Just some chronic fatigue. The doctor believes she will recover with some extra rest. But she loves her parties, you know, so getting her to abstain from a few is no easy task."

I turned to face the ocean. "Yes."

For a moment, we didn't speak. I had no idea what to say. Just as I'd determined to stick to a safe topic like the weather, Edward spoke. "I didn't know you still lived nearby. Mother said you quit being a governess for the children years ago."

"I live in the parsonage. I have for five years now."

"Our parsonage? How could I have not known this?" A pause. "But I suppose Mother didn't want me to know. I even asked her once . . ."

"Asked her what?" I lifted my eyebrows in his direction.

He studied me for a moment. "Do you live there alone?"

"Of course I live there alone."

"So you never married?"

"No." I lifted my chin away from him, toward the sea, but I couldn't stop the tremor that overtook it. Didn't he remember what I'd told him?

"Emily. Look at me."

But I could not.

Not until he was beside me, gently turning me to face him. I took a step back and found myself against the tree, letting it hold me up. I'm sure my own legs would not have been capable in this moment.

"There's something you should know. Maybe you already do. It's the sort of thing people love to gossip about."

"I'm not exactly in the habit of conversing with many people. I spend most of my time alone, writing. I've had several books published already." Why was I rambling?

A slow smile spread over his lips. "Of course you have." Then he tenderly took my hands in his. "Last year, Rosamond died. She contracted a disease thanks to her . . . exploits." His eyes bloomed with pain.

"Oh, I'm so sorry." I threaded my fingers between his. Poor Edward. Poor James.

"I did love Rosamond, in a way. After all, she gave me James. And in the end, she realized what she'd done and how her actions had affected us all. The last six months of her life were the best we had together."

My heart swirled with emotions, my head with tangled thoughts. "What you must have been through. I can't imagine."

"Emily." His grip on my hands tightened. "After that night in the library, when we . . . I was faithful to my wife. I never strayed. I put all thoughts of you and me out of my heart forever. But right now, I can't help but wonder . . ." He took a step closer and lowered his face to mine, not stopping until our noses nearly touched.

All I could hear was the ocean below, the rattle of the leaves above, and the breath between us.

A tear leaked from the corner of my eye and trailed down my cheek. Was I really standing here, with him, hearing what his heart was trying to tell me? Was I brave enough to speak the words for us both? "What are you wondering, Edward? If maybe there's another chapter to our story? One we didn't see coming?"

"That's exactly what I'm wondering."

And then he kissed me, and it lit a flame that burned with an eternal oil. When at last he pulled away, he whispered the words I'd longed to hear since I was a girl.

"I love you, Emily Fairfax. Will you marry me?"

I couldn't help myself. "On one condition."

He laughed. "I should have known this would come with conditions. Well?"

I pushed my hands through his hair and tugged him toward me once more. "That you will always give me plenty of inspiration for my stories."

His grin turned wicked. "I promise to give you many, many pages' worth of inspiration."

"Good. Then I accept. Now be quiet and kiss me, you oaf."

"With pleasure."

As the man I loved drew me closer, I lifted my eyes toward heaven and surrendered my future once more.

A NOTE FROM THE AUTHOR

Lately, I am learning more and more about the power of our words. I've become more conscious of the words I speak over myself as well as what I say to other people. It's more than "positive thinking"—the words we say ultimately contribute to the stories we weave, and I want my story to be as positive and hope-filled as possible, regardless of my circumstances.

I've also become much more aware of the lies that I tell myself—"You are not worthy." "You are not enough." "You will never achieve what you want to achieve."—and the need to replace those lies with the truths that God says about me. I have listened to Lauren Daigle's song "You Say" on repeat lately, and it has become a theme not just of this story you hold in your hands, but one in the story of my very life.

Yes, the power of our words is monumental, and while words have the power to heal, they also have the capacity to hurt. According to The National Domestic Violence Hotline, "Domestic violence (also called intimate partner violence [IPV], domestic abuse, or relationship abuse) is a pattern of behaviors used by one partner to maintain power and control over another partner in an intimate relationship."

However, abuse is not just limited to physical violence, though that is what many of us think of when we hear the word. It also includes emotional abuse—the words spoken by one partner to another.

If you, like Sophia, have experienced abuse of any sort, my heart aches for you. I pray in reading her story you have felt hope where perhaps there was none before, and I urge you to reach out and get help. Free 24/7 assistance can be reached at 1-800-799-7233 or https://www.thehotline.org.

We each have a story worthy of telling, and I pray that you, dear reader, find the strength to shout yours from the rooftops so it cannot be ignored.

ACKNOWLEDGMENTS

As I sit down to write this thank-you card of sorts, I am first most thankful that I get the chance to do it again. It amazes me when I think of that six-year-old girl who had a dream in her heart and the fact that it came true! I am so incredibly grateful that I get to do what I love.

To my fabulous readers, thank you for spending time not only to read the stories that once only existed in my mind, but also for every review you have left, every note you have sent to me, and every person you have told about my books. You have inspired and encouraged me beyond measure.

To my husband, Mike: Your constant belief in me and the way you have supported me in so many practical ways has meant so much. I couldn't have asked for a better partner in this writing endeavor—or in life.

To my boys, Elliott and Theodore: You make my world so much brighter and more entertaining. You have become woven so tightly into my life that you've changed my story for the better. Never forget how much you are loved.

To my stepmom, Kristin, and mother-in-law, Nancy: Once again I must thank you so much for the time and energy you sacrifice weekly to give me extra time to write. I know the boys love spending time with you, and they are so blessed to have such amazing grandmas.

To my agent, Rachelle Gardner: God really smiled on me when he sent you my way. You were the agent that I didn't dare dream of having! Thank you for your constant encouragement and all the ways you work hard for my benefit.

To my editor, Kimberly Carlton: Girl, it's been a blast working with you! I've loved every moment. Your insights were so spot-on with this story, and thanks to you, it's better and stronger. I am so grateful for your enthusiasm and reassurances whenever I feel uneasy about this whole writing gig.

To Karli Jackson: You rock this editing thing, and I'm so glad we got to work together again! So proud of you for pursuing your dreams on the work front and mommy front. You inspire me!

To my wonderful team at Thomas Nelson (specifically Becky Monds, Amanda Bostic, Paul Fisher, Allison Carter, Laura Wheeler, Kristen Ingebretson, and anyone else who touched this book): Working with you has been a dream. Thank you so much for helping this story become a reality, and for doing such an amazing job in supporting your authors. I am so incredibly honored and blessed that I get to publish with you.

To my amazing writer friends, especially Gabrielle Meyer, Melissa Tagg, and Alena Tauriainen: No matter how far apart we are, I know you ladies will be there to pray for me and give me exactly the advice and encouragement I need to keep going. Thank you for walking this writing journey with me forever and always.

And finally, God: Thank you for stepping into this story, for writing it with me, and for reminding me time and time again that my story matters because you say it does.

DISCUSSION QUESTIONS

1. Sophia has always wanted to learn how to surf because it's a way to connect with her absentee father. What's something you've always wanted to do and why?
2. Whose storyline (Sophia's, Ginny's, or Emily's) was most compelling to you and why?
3. Maya Angelou said, "There is no greater agony than bearing an untold story inside you." What do you think of this quote, especially as it relates to Sophia, Ginny, and Emily?
4. Ginny has struggled her entire life with doing what was expected of her versus following her own dreams. What advice would you have given after she failed to convince her parents to let her attend culinary school?
5. Sophia finds it difficult to accept help from others, believing she needs to be strong like her mother. Can you relate to her reticence?
6. Which relationship (romantic or otherwise) was your favorite in the story and why?
7. Joy tells Sophia that it's not enough to simply recognize the lies we believe about ourselves and our circumstances—we have to replace that lie with truth. What do you think about this? How have you seen the battle between truth and lies

play out in your own life or in the lives of those closest to you?

8. For much of the book, Sophia blames herself for David's abuse, even though she'd never blame another victim. Ginny believes in other people's dreams but can't see her own working out. Do you think it's much easier to be kinder to other people than to yourself? Why or why not?

9. Kathryn tells Sophia, "Take these flowers, for example. I can't just sit around waiting for them to decide if they want to bloom or die. Growth won't happen without a little intervention. They were designed to bloom, yes, but circumstances and a harsh environment sometimes make it impossible for them to flower on their own. They can't prune themselves. And you can't prune yourself, dear." Do you agree or disagree?

10. In your opinion, what was the sweetest or most romantic gesture in the book?

Read more from Lindsay Harrel!

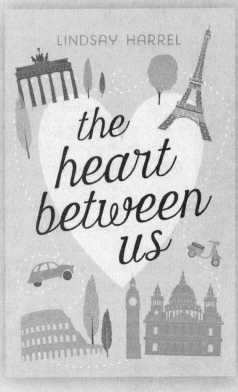

Two Sisters, One Heart
Transplant, and a Bucket List

ABOUT THE AUTHOR

Lindsay Harrel is a lifelong book nerd who lives in Arizona with her young family and two golden retrievers in serious need of training. She's held a variety of writing and editing jobs over the years and now juggles stay-at-home mommyhood with writing novels. When she's not writing or chasing after her children, Lindsay enjoys making a fool of herself at Zumba, curling up with anything by Jane Austen, and savoring sour candy one piece at a time.

Connect with her at LindsayHarrel.com